Praise for THE GODMOTHER

"Get to know Leigh Esposito, who brings us a tale brimming with a verve and verisimilitude lacking in the work of many of today's writers. Esposito's eternal Sicily is a very real place; the reader can almost hear the noisy streets of Palermo and taste the food in its open-air markets. But mostly, this is the story of powerful women in an eccentric context where one doesn't usually expect to find them. In that respect, it is the rarest of excursions, breaking new ground in a crowded genre. Here the very term "godmother" is redefined forever. This is feminist fiction at its finest, challenging us to think far outside the box into the movement's next wave. Be prepared to see your preconceptions revised."

— LOUIS MENDOLA, AUTHOR, *THE KINGDOM OF SICILY 1130-1860*

"Join powerhouse Raffi Truvarizzi—the Godmother—on her journey of self-discovery through a Sicily so vivid, you'll choke on the ash of Mount Etna, taste the sharp bite of prawn carpaccio by the Ionian Sea, and immerse yourself in culture and cannoli. As Raffi's troubles find her through her trek, threats, both newborn and ancient, reveal themselves. Forced to decode her complex family tree, she persists in seeking the truth of her bloodline—all with the F.B.I. all in hot pursuit.

"With Esposito's prose so detailed and visual, you'll feel the women who infuse the story with their divine-feminine, witchy powers, and—after the melancholy descends on you from putting down this book that has expanded your horizons in the real world— you'll wonder whether *The Godmother* is a story more aptly shelved in non-fiction.

"In the end, you'll find yourself wishing you had a Godmother of your own: a solver of all problems, a seer of all truths, finding her counsel aside a plate of soul-nourishing pasta—the coolest of the cool."

— SALVADOR PASKOWITZ, SCREENWRITER, *THE AGE OF ADALINE*

"With vivid language and palpable passion, Leigh Esposito writes about women, their particular struggles, and the mystical side of living."

— DOLORES ALFIERI TARANTO, AUTHOR & HOST, *THE BELLA FIGURA* PODCAST AND *THE ITALIAN AMERICAN* PODCAST

"*The Godmother*, an astounding debut from novelist Leigh Esposito, is a sweeping tale woven from magic, myth, and the mob. Inspiring, poetic, and culturally rich across disciplines and oceans, *The Godmother* will leave you feeling connected to the Divine Mother in her countless forms. It reminds us of the power we hold inside, whether we believe it or not."

— ASHLEIGH RENARD, AUTHOR, *SWING*

THE
GODMOTHER

A NOVEL

LEIGH ESPOSITO

SELVATICA
BOOKS

Palm Beach Gardens, Florida

For information about this title or to order books and/or electronic media, contact the publisher:

Selvatica Books
P.O. Box 32841
Palm Beach Gardens, FL 33420

Cover and interior design by The Book Cover Whisperer:
OpenBookDesign.biz

979-8-9875613-5-5 Paperback
979-8-9875613-0-0 Hardcover
979-8-9875613-3-1 eBook

Printed in the United States of America

FIRST EDITION

SELVATICA
BOOKS

For Patrick and Delores Vassallo. Sempre.

For Declan Brando, my most wonderful.

Nowhere has truth so short a life as in Sicily.
— GIUSEPPE DI LAMPEDUSA

1

People always stared at Marina Ramón. By now she was used to it, though she did not understand it any more than a plantain grasps its sweetness, or a dahlia knows its hue. She might have guessed the obvious culprits: her cool almond skin, those scallop-shell lips, the meandering body that curled like a seahorse. Then there was her fame, the immensity of it, which she bore with head bowed and gaze averted; that also played a part. But there was a hidden force beneath these things, a power that drew all eyes to her like hummingbird to nectar, and this Marina could not see. People stared at Marina Ramón because she made them remember.

They remembered the year Marina first appeared on *Las Encantadoras*. Her character, Luz, burst through the door of an abandoned casita on a rainy night in the fictional town of Brazos de Cristo, soaking wet, in a cheesecloth-thin dress that could end marriages (if men watched telenovelas). They remembered the jobs to which they'd called in sick on the day Luz revealed herself to be a twin, sister to Blanca—also played by Marina—who was evil and always wore red. And they remembered the ominous homilies that echoed throughout Mexico on the Sunday after Luz and Blanca first practiced witchcraft.

Yet, somewhere along the way, it was Marina who had forgotten. Bad choices, naïveté, even willful blindness had landed her on a cold stone bench outside a Miami skyrise. And though the mid-morning passersby still stared, her ten-year absence from the world of telenovelas made their memories hazy. She was familiar, yes, exquisite, always, but their curious looks also took in a woman undone—discarded by her husband, screwed over by sinister procedures with names like *injunction*, which sounded medical, and *ex parte*, a Latin word for when a judge takes your children away while your back is turned.

Mired in these thoughts, Marina did not notice at first that a woman had come to stand in front of her, coughing discreetly— then less discreetly—to get her attention. Probably an autograph request. Marina forced herself to look up. The woman's face was pleasant, familiar, and flushed as if she'd just run a great distance. Sunlight struck a gold pin on her lapel: a spoked wheel, an insignia Marina could not place.

In one swift, furtive move, the woman tucked a small white card into Marina's hand. The card bore no words save an address scribbled in bold black strokes: *2020 Northwest Fourth Street.*

"It's been three weeks," the woman said. "Your children need you. Go now, before things get worse."

"Go?" Marina's brows shot up. "*No entiendo.*"

The woman grabbed Marina's arm, the grip so forceful she gasped. Before Marina could cry out, the woman raised a finger to her lips. "*Necesitas ver a la Madrina*," she hissed. You need to see the Godmother.

DIONE SPINOTTI LIKED TO say her first breath came on the downbeat—a D-flat arpeggio, *subito*—agile and ascending, like Dione herself. Her father, Dino, owned Dino's Place, the on-deck of jazz infamy. Dino's gift was to figure out what made a guy great, cultivate it, and then get the hell out of the way. In fact, it was onstage at Dino's Place that bebop behemoth Jimmy Algiers wrote his biggest hit, "Killing Time."

For the virtuoso of variation, Dino's favorite lesson was one-note, and it went a little something like this: *You just gotta play your own tunes.* The future jazz demigods all took this advice, though they weren't the only ones listening. Dino's daughter listened too.

Dione wrote her first song when she was eight years old: "Didi's Blues," recorded on cassette in 1987 in her Morningside Heights bedroom. She recorded it again twelve years later—in a studio—with her first pro trio, Didi and the Spins.

Now, Dino was a pianist at heart: Harlem stride was in his soul. The piano is a beautiful instrument for women, he often said—more like begged—watching in horror as Dione did the graphic things saxophonists had to do, like empty her spit valve on her bedside table and clean the bell of her horn with what looked like a toilet brush. He would have *thrilled* at his daughter's long, pretty fingers dancing octaves over ivory. But Dione on sax? That gave him *agita*.

"I could say I picked the tenor because it's the best sax for solos, because I wanted to be like Algiers. The truth is, I picked it because it was the biggest sax I could carry—and because my father said no."

This was in *Bass/Clef Magazine*, 2004, when Dione appeared on the cover, naked, all five feet and one inch of her wrapped around a Selmer Paris Series III.

Her career sped by like an acid trip. She went up, she went down, but she *always* kept it about the music. Which is part of what had gotten her into this bind. In an ominous shift, for the first time ever, her label hated the new—admittedly experimental—album. And they would not back down.

"You need to *collaborate*," her manager said with the adrenal twang of someone about to lose money. "The sax isn't a stand-alone instrument anymore. You're not Hawk Mackey."

"And you're not a musician."

"Trust me, Dione. They're going to bury it if you're not careful."

She never trusted her manager.

A handler from her label came around next. "How's this for a compromise?" he asked in a sunny tone, as if she was a toddler with a plastic horn and not a ten-time Grammy winner. "We'll sex up the cover shot. Let's face it. Your looks sell your albums. No one cares about the saxophone."

She proposed a different compromise involving her sax and his flat ass.

"They're done with you, Dione," said her agent, the third and final horseman. "The album's dead. They've got some hot young violinist on the up-and-come." His breezy tone told her he was repping the hot violinist too. "They can't promote you *both*."

Which was nonsense. Jazz fans don't care what's between your legs, so long as you've got the chops.

Someone else in her position might have slunk off to Switzerland, bought a chalet. Dione Spinotti, however, was not so easily dispatched. She had no desire for children, but that did not mean she lacked the human impulse for legacies. This was her baby.

Only one person had the influence needed to free her album from Corkscrew Records and release it to the world, where it belonged. That person was an old friend from college with whom she'd lost touch: Raffaella Truvarizzi. Otherwise known as the Godmother.

NEOPHYTE PSYCHIC ISABEL IBARRA was destined to follow in the footsteps of her aunt Mary Fortune, the famed Cuban American astrologer who'd predicted fifty-three international elections and helped the luminaries of Miami navigate their lives by the stars. Mary Fortune was a colorful woman, known as much for her prescience as for her collection of boldly pigmented, shockingly expensive, handwoven Italian sweaters, which her late third husband had referred to, with affection, as horse blankets.

Now all Isabel had left of her aunt were memories. Mary had died one month before, taken by a brain aneurysm while cruising the harbor on her late second husband's boat. No suffering, no mess...and no deathbed—just as she would have wanted. Mary hated goodbyes. Her bereft family, on the other hand, was desperate for one final look at their fiery matriarch. Unfortunately, their impassioned requests for an open casket were denied. According to the coroner and undertaker—both loyal Mary Fortune clients—the body had been corrupted from exposure to the elements. Not threat nor plea nor bribe would change the outcome. Casket closed.

Mary died a wealthy woman, leaving four grown daughters, whom she had loved dutifully, as a mother should. But the child most precious to Mary was her niece, Isabel, the only daughter of Mary's much-younger sister, who died under tragic circumstances when Isabel was four. *Vibrio vulnificus*—sepsis, Isabel was told, from a raw oyster pried off the rocks along the Rickenbacker. Isabel's mother used to stop there on her way home from cleaning mansions on Key Biscayne, shucking bivalves straight into her mouth, tasting Cuba in the brackish sea pooling under her tongue.

After that tragedy, two things happened: no one could wear a string of pearls without sobbing, and Isabel went to live with her Aunt Mary. Before long, Isabel began to demonstrate the Gift. None of the daughters had it; they were destined for careers as office administrators, doctors, and lawyers. Mary could not hide her disappointment.

Her attention slipped from her daughters to her young niece. "You're like me," she told the girl. "And you'll take my place when I am gone." It was no surprise Mary's daughters despised their cousin (and oysters, for forcing her upon them), and did their best to make her feel unwelcome. Isabel felt like an intruder in her own childhood.

Mary knew this, and she consoled her niece with a solemn promise: When Isabel was ready, her aunt would make her the next Mary Fortune. Isabel would have a house, a laptop full of Mary's top-secret charts and notes, and Aunt Mary to guide her.

Mary's death put an end to that fantasy. The daughters, decimated by the loss of their mother, took consolation in banishing their cousin. Isabel found herself in a motel room in Hialeah eating beans out of a can.

In a dream, one week before Mary's will was to be read, Isabel saw the faces of Mary and her daughters floating, disembodied, over a cobalt sea. She saw a giant gavel crash down onto sparkling asphalt, cracking the pavement into three pieces, each shaped like a horse-blanket sweater. And she heard a name spoken in her aunt's voice—a name she recognized from the annals of her aunt's most treasured clients.

Raffi Truvarizzi, intoned Mary from beyond. At this, Isabel shot up in bed, her sheets soaked with sweat. If only she'd heard a different name! Any name but Truvarizzi. She was petrified to seek out the woman everyone, even her ancient aunt, referred to as "the Godmother."

2

The house sprawled across four oversized lots like a languid panther with a bougainvillea pelt in an iron cage. It was not only impenetrable, but unknowable, its tangle of vines a living veil, the contours concealed by mangrove trunks and date palms. Nose to the gate, the stone limbs of centuries-old statues were barely visible if the hedge parted to reveal a cracked elbow here, a starred crown there, a bird perched on a muscled marble shoulder. But this was not a good day to go peeking through the gate.

On this hazy June Saturday in Miami, the massive grounds of 2020 Northwest Fourth Street were guarded—heavily, conspicuously—by women. Some were large and covered with tattoos, their sturdy thighs stuffed into cargo pants like sausage links. Others were light-footed and limber in tight leggings, their glossy hair tucked into camo caps, the telltale bulges at their ankles whispering *gun*. Upon closer inspection, some were not women at all, but girls: teenage girls, large as the sausage-legged women, lacrosse sticks lodged at their sides like bayonets. Looking otherwise nothing alike, all stood with the uniform dignity of the Queen's Guard.

The street was packed with cars in every direction: Maseratis;

hatchbacks; giant armored SUVs; a ridiculous Hummer limo, the kind high schoolers take to prom. The Miami police should have shown up and started writing tickets, barking orders through megaphones, shutting this down. And they would have done just that, were this another residence. Instead, a handful of officers paced the perimeter like schoolyard monitors, inconspicuous despite their uniforms, if only because they were so much less interesting than the women with the cargo pants and lacrosse sticks and ankle heat.

A few shrill chirps from deep within the grounds suggested music, but the hedges had done their job, and no further sound slipped through. To know what was happening inside today, you needed an invitation.

✦

MARINA WANTED TO TURN back and forget about this. Sitting in an old, borrowed sedan that smelled of sunscreen and cigarettes made her feel, not just anxious, but ashamed. What an *idiota* to have come here: to the home of a stranger on the advice of a stranger, something her life in Mexico had trained her never to do. The only reason she did not hit the gas and leave this *enredo* of cars and cops behind was the women. Maybe it was false comfort, like how her son, Victor, could not fall asleep without the bathroom light on, but, with those women here, she felt protected. Plus, it seemed unlikely she would be murdered at what appeared to be a giant party—though, of course, it had been done.

At last, she got up the courage to extract herself from the geriatric car, approach the gate—higher than the beanstalk in Graciela's favorite book—and press the round black button on the call box. A crackle sounded on the line, but no reply. She pressed the button again. Another crackle...silence. She was considering whether to press the button a third time when the speaker crackled on its own, and an angry voice shouted, "What?!"

Marina's pulse set off at a sprint. Angry people—her first director, her soon-to-be ex-husband, whoever was on the other end of this box—made her so anxious, she thought she might collapse from the adrenaline. She should have taken that new pill before she came here.

With a deep breath, she turned her thoughts to Victor and Graciela, for whom she would brave all the angry crackling voices in the world. "I'm Marina?" Marina said into the box. "I was sent here by..." She searched for the words. "...by a woman with a pinwheel?"

Not a pinwheel, she chided herself, a pin *shaped* like a wheel. But it was too late for corrections. If this voice misunderstood and sent her away, she would almost be relieved. No one could help her, anyway. She was as doomed as the people of Brazos de Cristo whenever evil-twin Blanca got mad.

The angry voice sighed. The box crackled off.

Marina was ready to flee when she noticed, a couple yards down on her left, a cargo-pants woman. She had a long black braid and brown pitted skin, and her eyes stared straight ahead, except when they flicked to Marina to make sure Marina didn't do anything crazy, maybe, like whip out a handgun or vault the fence. On Marina's other side stood a youngish woman in a silver bodysuit and futuristic sunglasses, which was a little much, Marina thought. But who was she to judge, after a decade on telenovelas?

She felt a jolt of strength. If these women were tough, Marina could be tougher. They might have guns, but she was a *mother*. Before she could plan her next move, a spark of color moved through the hedges like a bright purple flare, morphing at last into a sullen-faced *Boricua* who cracked open the pedestrian gate.

"You have the wheel pin?" snapped the Boricua.

Marina shook her head, *no*, and held out the small white card. This seemed to both satisfy and infuriate the Boricua, who threw the gate wide, spun on her heel, and disappeared back into the grounds so quickly Marina wasn't sure she was meant to follow.

Marina shot a quick glance at Cargo Pants and Silver Jumpsuit. Neither flinched. Before the gate door slammed closed behind the Boricua, Marina darted in and hastened after her, struggling to keep pace down the limestone path. The Boricua walked with an angry gait, arms swinging as she marched, and Marina followed her as if under a spell, until they reached the entrance to the house.

The first thing she noticed was the door knocker: a gold, spoked wheel, just like the pin on the woman who'd sent her here. Above the door, an incomprehensible Latin motto marked the lintel. The knocker, the motto, the rambling Spanish mansion. She was reminded of an episode of *Las Encantadoras*. "*Oscuridad*," it was called. Darkness. She crossed herself.

Marina stepped inside, her battered designer slides silent on the waxed concrete. The room was vast—Marina had never seen anything like it—the walls painted a blue so dark, they were almost black; original paintings hung everywhere. On the opposite end of the room, a wall of tinted windows revealed a party in the back: a four-piece band, at least a hundred people dancing, some with their arms around each other and obviously drunk, others in sharp suits and huddled in trios and quartets, talking business. The interior, however, was silent, save when the glass door opened to admit a server or a stray guest, and fragments of jazz and conversation burst in, extinguished moments later when the door slid shut.

Standing there, gaping like a fool, Marina realized the Boricua was motioning for her to keep moving. "*Vamos, vamos,* Jesus Christ, give me a break," the Boricua muttered.

Marina hesitated. "*Perdón.* Are you the—"

The Boricua tapped her foot.

"—*Madrina?*"

"Uh *no.*" The Boricua rolled her eyes as if Marina had just asked whether two times two made twelve. "The *Madrina* is...."

And, at that moment, the Boricua seemed to realize she was talking to *Marina Ramón.*

A series of expressions flashed across the Boricua's face. She was incredibly expressive, Marina thought. With training, the Boricua could act. Right now the Boricua was trying to smile, and it was frightening. Marina preferred her angry.

"Will you please come with me?" the Boricua said with a clipped, formal tone. This attempt at politesse was almost as disturbing as the smile.

Marina followed the Boricua toward the wall of windows, but before they reached it, the Boricua cut left down a hallway, rounded a corner to the right, and arrived at a closed door. She rapped a quick merengue pulse on the wood, then flung it open, flashing her teeth at Marina like a child saying, "*Cheese!*"

"The Godmother," said the Boricua, pointing inside.

✦

MAKING HER WAY BACK to the party from the bathroom, Isabel Ibarra watched, wide-eyed, as Marina Ramón stumbled into the house. Isabel tried not to stare. She went straight to the glass accordion door, heaved it open, and stepped into the backyard, avoiding eye contact with anyone.

She had lost count of the celebrities at this party. Hoping no one noticed how she was dressed, she sank into a plush white chair and willed herself invisible. Not that it mattered, or anyone cared, but she wished she'd worn something nicer than a pastel romper and flip-flops; seated, the romper fabric barely covered her thighs. And she should have blown out her hair instead of letting it crinkle into pin curls. The blond color made it look extra frizzy. Aunt Mary would not have approved.

Isabel's heart was doing the same gallop she experienced five years before when she called General Custer "General Custard" in history class. Marina *Ramón*. Mary's favorite. Isabel and her aunt used to watch *Las Encantadoras* together whenever Isabel stayed home sick from school.

While Marina Ramón had never come to see Mary, many of the Godmother's guests had been Mary's clients, which meant Isabel knew their secrets. The secrets she could remember, anyway. Her eyes had glazed over when her aunt pulled up the charts on her laptop and started throwing around phrases like "Chiron in Libra." Although Isabel had the Gift, she didn't much care for astrology. The psychic arts that interested her were not to Mary's liking.

Isabel spotted Congressman Ramsburg by the bar talking to

a tall woman in a black blazer whom Isabel recognized as Rhona Corrado of the *Miami Times*, the only reporter, famed for her cherry-red lipstick, to whom the Godmother gave interviews. Rhona used to come see Mary for "works," which were expensive rituals involving things like graveyard dirt and bird bones, but which were *not* black magic, not magic at all, Mary had insisted, they just got you what you wanted and didn't hurt anyone, so why not? In Rhona Corrado's case, what she wanted was a bigger byline.

That poor congressman, though—his wife went crazy a few years back, and Mary sent him to the Godmother, whose mother had also gone crazy, and in much the same way. Mrs. Ramsburg now lived at *Apollonia Truvarizzi House*, a converted estate in the Gables founded by the Godmother for women who'd lost their minds. Mary said the Godmother had built the home in honor of her mother—the mother who would never have a home again.

And there was Misa Riù, another of Mary's clients, dancing with a teenager Isabel presumed to be Misa's son. Misa ran Hablavision, the Spanish-speaking network that gave the world *Las Encantadoras*, of which Misa was the creator. Mary always said, with characteristic non-humility, that the show had been born on Mary's own green velour couch.

Isabel scanned the yard for more celebrities, but the faces all started to blur together, probably because she'd let the bartender make her a margarita and she hadn't eaten all day—except the stack of pancakes and the bacon and the *papas*, but that was hours earlier, and the banana and the almonds, which didn't count because they were healthy, and the Frappuccino, which didn't count because it was liquid.

The party was bigger than most weddings she'd attended, both in size and in opulence. A constellation of hi-boy tables was scattered around a Spanish-tile "patio" the size of an entire lot. Overhead, café lights cut back and forth, skimmed by flower and balloon arches and banners offering congratulations in Italian to someone named Brando, who must be the Godmother's son. She deduced he had won a lacrosse championship *and* been accepted to Penn.

Maybe that was him up there with the jazz band, wailing away on the drums like a human whirlwind. Handsome, slender, and gangly, with black eyebrows that overlined his dark eyes, he was grinning up at the saxophone player, a tiny woman whose instrument was about two-thirds her size and whose smoky eyes were closed in a merry upside-down *u*. A flippy brown bob crashed into her cheeks with every toss of her head. Isabel peered closer.

The young drummer was the envy of the first row of spectators, teenage boys who all but drooled at the lady saxophonist. Some of the boys, like the women guarding the house, carried lacrosse sticks, but with gold-plated handles. These must be Brando's fellow lacrosse champions. There was something about the sax player; Isabel recognized her from somewhere. Pilates in the Grove? Vogue Salon?

Oh, right. *Dione Spinotti.* The air felt thin, or was it that Isabel was unaccustomed to this altitude? She began a respirational incantation she'd devised, a quick and efficient one. *Out calm, in clear. Out calm, in clear.* To a casual observer, it would look like nothing more than a few deep breaths, and this was the point. The Ibarra women had learned to cloak their powers in the commonplace.

In a moment she felt better. Mary did not like when Isabel practiced spells—*Our family has paid enough for that business,* she used to say, unconcerned by the irony of her position—but Mary wasn't here now. If she were, Isabel thought, Mary would have already introduced Isabel to half the attendees.

Her eyes drifted down to the chair, nicer than any in her Aunt Mary's fancy house, even though it was an "outside chair." The dark wood and cloud of white cushions reminded Isabel of Morocco, her dream destination, where she planned to travel someday for her solar return. She raised her phone in front of her face for a selfie that was meant to capture the chair, but accidentally snapped a photo of the big white banner strung between two giant mango trees that read, *Auguri, Brando!*

Brando Truvarizzi. His mother, Raffaella: The Godmother. Isabel was struggling to keep it together. If only she had her aunt's laptop, she would know everything about these people, and knowledge was the great equalizer. She wished she had paid closer attention to Mary's gossip all these years, but she'd never allowed herself to consider the reality that someday Mary would not be here. The burden (or opportunity?) of taking on Mary's clients had seemed remote. But the laptop would have absolved Isabel of every reverie, every time she'd been too absorbed in her empanada or pastelito, too busy *looking* attentive, when she should have been attentive for real. This was what happened, Mary said, when things came too easily to you.

The laptop. It held every note and every chart on every client since Mary Ibarra became Mary Fortune. But that slim silver rectangle was lost to Isabel now too. She'd searched for it after her aunt's death, but it was nowhere: a place Isabel had come to know quite well.

3

Marina's eyes struggled to adjust. The room was dark and elegant, lit by stained-glass lamps and a dim torchiere; the window, which must look out on the backyard, allowed no light through heavy curtains. In front of the window, an antique pheasantwood desk, polished to a shine, took up most of the space. Over this desk hung the room's focal point: a portrait of a breathtaking young bride, her heart-shaped face framed by a widow's peak and a spray of tulle, black eyes slanted up at the corners. The bride wore an enigmatic smile behind which could be any kind of woman. *La belleza es una mascara*, Marina's mother always said. Beauty is a mask.

Below the portrait sat a woman about Marina's age: mid-forties, dressed all in white silk, bare feet propped atop the oiled wood. The woman's face was smooth and unadorned, with black brows slashed like bold brushstrokes over large eyes that seemed to take in everything about Marina at once. It was a beautiful face when, as now, it was peaceful—but Marina imagined it could also be quite ugly, if you caught the sharp nose at the wrong angle and it appeared hooked, like a *bruja*.

Streaming over the back of the leather chair, the woman's hair was long and wild, coiled in dark Medusa waves. One shapely arm hung at her side where a bull mastiff in a jeweled collar lay beside two pristine white sandals. The woman's fingers grazed the dog's enormous head. Its yellow eyes squinted with pleasure.

This woman in white looked neither old nor young; made not from the sparest parts, she was of lavish construction. Marina's body would look much the same if she allowed it to, but Marina had been fighting her body since she was ten years old.

She took a deep breath. "Godmother?"

The smooth face slid into a smile. "Come," said the Godmother, not unpleasantly, a riptide of power beneath the word.

Marina wasn't sure how close to come. Were they supposed to embrace? Kiss on both cheeks? But, no, she saw now she was meant to sit in the small wooden chair in front of the desk, which placed her, despite their similar heights, about a head shorter than her hostess.

"You were sent here to see me?"

Marina shifted in her chair. It was hard. "*Si, Madrina*. By a lady wearing a pin like a wheel. She said I needed to come here before it was too late. She knew my children were taken from me by—" Marina stopped. The Boricua handed her a tissue. "—by my husband. I'm not sure how this woman knew my situation. Maybe there was an article online? I used to be an actress."

The Boricua snorted. "Mama," she said to the Godmother, pointing at Marina, "she star in my favorite telenovela, Mama, ever. *Sabes, Las Encantadoras?*"

The Godmother shook her head, *no*.

The Boricua sniffed. "Well, anyway, give me a break."

Marina pulled her chair closer to the Godmother. At the mention of the telenovela—the career—she had given up, a hot pressure formed in her chest.

"Godmother, I don't know you. I know *of* you, of course—" her face reddened, "—but our paths have never crossed. What I do know is my husband wants to ruin me."

"Ruin you how?"

"He has a new *amante*. I caught him on the nanny cam with her, and, when he got home that night, I met him at the door like a fiend. I pushed him, I stomped on his feet." She gazed off, then whispered, impressed by her own moxie: "I slapped his face."

"Hah!" cried the Boricua.

"I didn't hurt him, though," Marina continued. "I promise I didn't." She paused. "I did hurt his car."

The Godmother nodded, her face composed, her hands tented on the desk. The dog, sensing the loss of her attention, opened its eyes as if it, too, were listening. She waved her hand, *continue.*

"My husband pretended he was sorry. Then he went and did something called *ex parte* and took my children away. He told the judge he was afraid for his life, just because I keyed a few lines into his special car. His favorite car." She thought of all their fights over that car. *Don't slam the door, Marina. Take off those jeans, the grommets scratch the leather. You left fingerprints near the handle. No, you cannot drive it.* "He loved his car more than our family."

As Marina stifled more tears, the Godmother gestured to the Boricua, who left.

"Do you have a lawyer, Marina?"

"*Ay*. No. I went to see everyone in town. They say they're "conflicted out." Or *I'm* conflicted out? I don't understand, but I think it means—"

"I know what it means, Marina." The Godmother let her hand rest on the mastiff's head again. The dog practically purred. "I was a lawyer once."

"You...?"

The Godmother shrugged, stroking the mastiff's head. "I didn't listen to my mother." She turned to look up at the portrait for a long minute. "'There are more honest ways to make money, Raffaella.' That's what she used to say, and she was right. But sometimes we don't listen. And we pay for it."

Marina shuddered at what she recognized as a veiled warning. It was how Marina would have played "intimidating."

"Anyway," the Godmother said with a sad smile, "I gave it up."

Marina guessed the Godmother's mother was dead, and that the pathos in the Godmother's smile was about the bride, not the defunct vocation. Marina was touched that a woman this powerful would reveal her vulnerability. It made Marina like her more, though she had the good sense not to fear her any less.

"So, this *conflicted out*—"

The Godmother flapped her hand. "That won't be a problem."

Marina was confused. To hear the lawyers tell it, this was both a problem and an insurmountable one. "It won't?"

"No. What else?"

Just like that, the Godmother could solve everything? If this was true, Marina would have to go find the lady with the wheel pin and give her an autograph. Assuming she'd want one.

"There is one more thing." Marina coughed. This part, she was almost too mortified to vocalize. "My husband, he's old-fashioned." She toyed with the hem of her dress. "He helped me manage my money so I wouldn't waste it. I used to buy a lot of frivolous things. Handbags, jewelry. He bought those things for me with his money and put mine away."

"I assume you don't mean under the mattress."

"Ah, no," Marina whispered. "He invested it all in some *special real estate fund* that can't be touched."

"The money can't be touched by whom?"

"Well." Marina paused. "It can't be touched by me."

The Godmother nodded. "What about the money you share? As husband and wife?"

Marina felt her face flush. The tears were rising again, and she knew they would be the ugly kind. She had spent years training herself to cry pretty in public, which meant she could only allow feelings when she was alone. What was happening to her now, with this woman in white—dangerous in some way, but also a friend, or at least a protector, like the women guarding the gate outside—hadn't happened since her childhood in Guadalajara when she'd cried to her own mother. Once Marina became an actress, she trained herself not to cry that way. It made her look like a bulldog.

There was a silence, during which the Godmother continued to stroke the dog's head, tutting and shushing until the dog fell asleep. Marina was wondering if the meeting was over when the Godmother swung her legs down from the desk and stood. She regarded Marina with a direct, appraising gaze that reminded Marina of her audition for *Las Encantadoras*. That awful director. At last, the Godmother smiled. "It's done. You don't need to worry anymore. You have a Godmother now."

Before Marina could react, the Boricua returned, followed by a waiter carrying a tray with three glasses of red wine and a large plate of thumbprint-shaped pasta tossed with sausage and broccolini.

"When was the last time you ate a proper meal?" asked the Godmother.

The Boricua placed a glass of wine each in front of Marina and the Godmother, keeping one for herself. She set the pasta next to Marina's glass.

Marina shook her head. No time for proper meals. Her body was coursing with cortisol. Her stomach had been empty for days. She needed her children back, then she would eat. She returned to the subject at hand, for the first time impatient.

"But how do I *not* need to worry about money or this 'conflicted out?' I can't accept...."

The Godmother took a long, slow sip of wine, her eyes dropping to her fearsome dog. When those eyes returned to Marina, the former telenovela star was conscious of the bareness of her arms.

Now the Boricua sidled up to Marina—did she take a quick whiff, or did Marina imagine it? —and pushed the pasta plate closer. Marina was about to push it back when the Godmother's leveling look said Marina must at least try to eat. She picked up her fork and made a show of it, pushing food around until, by some strange alchemy, pretend became reality, and she was devouring the food like an animal. Minutes later, only a crime scene of olive oil and broccolini buds remained.

Marina looked up and found the Godmother nodding with approval. Enunciating every word, the Godmother asked, "What's your husband's name, Marina?"

"Ian McBride," said Marina. She said it like an epithet.

"You mentioned your husband had a favorite car. What kind of car would that be?" The Godmother gave Marina a deliberate look. "I'm very interested in cars."

Marina felt hope start to percolate. "It's a ten-million-dollar LaFerrari. One of a kind."

"Good," said the Godmother. "Very good." She looked to the Boricua, who was already tapping something into her phone.

"Give me a break," came the response.

When the Boricua was done, the Godmother turned back to Marina.

"Someday, and that day may never come, I will call you for a favor," the Godmother said, her deep voice dropping so low that Marina had to lean in to hear. "But today, accept this gift on the day of my son's graduation." She made a gesture to the Boricua, *we're done here*, and waved Marina away with the affection of a longtime friend. "Now, go. Enjoy yourself. The next time I see you at this house, you'll bring Victor and Graciela."

Marina's vision went wavy. *Victor and Graciela.* Her hand slid forward, fingers outstretched, and the Godmother's hand left the mastiff to grasp Marina's own until the hands joined palm-to-palm. The Godmother gave one brief squeeze, then withdrew.

"Thank you," said Marina, standing. "From my heart."

As the Boricua led her from the room, Marina turned back to wave goodbye, but the woman in white had faded into the soupy darkness. The last thing Marina saw before the Boricua closed the door was the bride's face, smiling down from the wall like a benevolent goddess.

As Marina retraced her steps, the glass door leading to the party opened again, and she caught the first fumbling notes of the jazz band learning a folk song. The guests clapped and catcalled, but Marina had one thing on her mind. *Victor and Graciela.* She couldn't wait to get her babies back. As she stepped outside the house and emerged into the backyard, she realized she hadn't told the Godmother her children's names.

RAFFI AND THE BORICUA remained alone in the room together. They were going over the list of women who still waited to be seen. The Boricua was Trinidad "Trini" Bianchi, the Godmother's half-Puerto Rican, half-Calabrese aide-de-camp. Her wiry purple hair, a sort of hirsute mood ring, showed she was happy today to celebrate Brando, who was like a son to her too. The day before, her hair had been orange. Not good.

"Who's next?" asked Raffi, lifting her hair off the back of her neck, head to the side, stretching. These audiences tired her, but she only let fatigue show in front of Trini, who had seen everything. She had known Raffi since before it all began.

Trini clicked her tongue as she scrolled the phone—whispering names, crossing out some and scoffing at others. She was the gatekeeper.

"Mami? Most of these is no important today. I tell Lina she can thank you next week."

Lina was a single mother whose landlord refused to call an exterminator for an infestation of rats so bold, poor Lina had caught one hanging from the light fixture by its tail. The landlord's refusal ended when Raffi sent Trini to pay him a visit, a file folder with his sex-offender rap sheet in hand, her hair dragon green.

"Good. That's good." Raffi's eyes closed for a moment. She pulled out her own phone, pressed a button, put the phone to her ear. It rang for a minute, then she toggled it closed and sighed. There would never be an answer, she knew. But knowing and accepting are not the same. "Who else?'

"Judge Paz send a case of that tequila you like, the *añejo*. Is from her family's farm in Mexico." At the word *Mexico*, Trini's lip curled. She cleared her throat. "The judge say she's sorry she can't be here, but she have church."

Raffi raised an eyebrow. Celia Paz had some nerve. "On a Saturday?"

Trini sipped from her wine and shook her head in disgust. "She get reelected and she get cocky, Mami. Ho!" Trini cha-cha'd across the floor. "Maybe she don't get reelected next time."

"I'd hate to see that happen."

"Hah! I wouldn't." Trini took another sip. "She's a *Mexicana*."

"Did Misa make it?"

Trini nodded. "She's here. I make sure she get enough wine,

then I ask her about *Las Brujas de Bal Harbour*." Trini brandished her glass and took another robust sip.

"That's the new telenovela?" Raffi patted the mastiff's head. She could never keep Trini's shows straight.

"The only telenovela right now, Mama. Better than *Las Encantadoras*, except no Marina Ramón. *Con* Marina Ramón, *Las Brujas* would be *perfecto*."

Raffi grinned at Trini. "*Very* good," she said. Trini was a font of brilliance. "That's an excellent idea."

Trini downed the rest of her wine. "What is?"

"*Las Brujas de Bal Harbour* and Marina Ramón."

Trini leapt up. "Can be?"

"Anything can be," said Raffi. "If you have the right friends."

"Sound like Marina Ramón have the right friends now." Trini resumed scrolling through her phone. "Okay!" She frowned, but she was always frowning—when she wasn't dancing—so it would be more accurate to say her frown *deepened*. "Dione want to see you after she finish playing."

It was obvious Trini did not like Dione, though Raffi suspected the Boricua could not have articulated why. Probably because Trini's default position on famous people was that they were useless unless their fame came from telenovelas. "And *Isabel Ibarra*"—Trini pronounced this name in an American accent, her worst form of mockery—"wanna see you too."

Raffi blinked. Had Isabel Ibarra even been invited? "Mary's niece. Why?"

Trini shrugged. "Can be to say sorry for not inviting you to the funeral."

"I'm not sure there was a funeral," said Raffi. But a death without a funeral did not feel like a death at all. The Godmother lived this truth.

"Mary Fortune was no your mother, Mama."

Raffi was silent, then said, "I know."

"Good. Keep knowing."

"Send in Isabel Ibarra." Raffi rubbed the back of her neck, then paused. "What happened to the music?"

The house was mostly soundproof, but, even so, it was clear the music had stopped. There was only the cacophony of people who had spent the last hour shouting over the speakers and had not yet adjusted to the quiet.

The door flew open, and Dione Spinotti walked in.

✦

"DIONE," SAID THE GODMOTHER. "What am I going to do with you?"

Dione Spinotti, who set off sparks onstage, looked now like a hot air balloon with the flame turned off. "I don't know, Godmother. I don't know."

"Why did you let it go this far?"

Dione shook her head. "I fucked up." Her left leg began shaking, *presto*. "Nervous leg," her father Dino called it. Helpful for keeping time. Not helpful for keeping cool.

The Godmother began to pace, the loyal mastiff's eyes following her movements back and forth. "How could you put yourself in this position?" She sounded like the good cop in an interrogation.

Dione threaded her hands through her short hair and pulled hard. "I signed a bad deal."

"That's an understatement."

"I didn't want to bother you."

"Asking before the situation deteriorates does not bother me. *This* does."

Dione's leg stopped shaking. "I tried to handle it myself."

"And?" The Godmother stopped pacing and made as if to stroke her chin. "Did you handle it?"

Dione hung her head. When she lifted it again, her eyes were heavy with tears. Dione had not cried but twice in her life. The first time was when the reed broke in the middle of a competition solo. The second was when her father died.

"Tsk," the Godmother said, rubbing one finger with another like she was peeling a carrot. She began to move again. "Well, I'm not going to let this happen to you, Didi. Whatever you did, whatever you ever do, so long as you're loyal to me, I will always support you."

So long as you're loyal to me. Dione registered the caveat. Her right leg took up the rhythm, *prestissimo*, double-time.

The Godmother stopped in front of Dione's chair. She slid between her old friend and the desk, perching on top in one smooth, elegant motion. The mastiff whimpered. "How's your mother?" said the Godmother, as if they'd just now sat down for coffee.

Her mother? "Good," she said, trying to sound casual. She didn't ask about Polly, whose twenty-one-year-old self beamed down at Dione from the bridal portrait. What a gorgeous ghost.

"Did you get something to eat?"

Dione blanked. Where was this going?

"Trini, make sure Dione gets something to eat."

"Okay, give me a break," Trini grumbled.

The Godmother put her hands on Dione's shoulders and squeezed. "You're better than this, Didi. You're better than all these people. You have something most of us don't have, that I always wished I had. *Genius*."

Dione knew jazz had been her old friend's passion too. She'd just never had what it took.

"You're going to stop wasting your gift," the Godmother continued, squeezing Dione's shoulders even harder, "and you're going to stop it *now*."

Dione's face jerked as if she'd been slapped. She couldn't think what to say back to this. She wanted to run.

Just as quickly, the Godmother's expression went calm again, almost sedate, like she'd just had a massage, a long nap, and a cocktail. "That's enough. I'll get you your record. But first you have to make me two promises."

Dione fell hard to her knees with a sob. "I'll do anything, Godmother! If you told me to cut off my ear, I'd say, 'Right or left?'"

The Godmother frowned. "Save the drama for the stage. And you don't cut off nothing for no one."

"Whatever, then. Just tell me, Godmother."

The Godmother gestured, *get up*. "Keep writing," she said, her face so close to Dione's that Dione could smell the familiar perfume of honey and spice.

Dione was overwhelmed with relief. She had no doubt: she was free. The Godmother always won. "Easy. Done."

Trini rose and opened the door. Dione's time was almost up.

"The second promise is that you won't wait until you're in

trouble to come see me." The Godmother regarded Dione from the hook-nosed side of her face. "*Ever again.*"

A cold *glissando* went up Dione's spine. How her friend had changed since they'd first met at Columbia. Back then, the only thing frightening about Raffi Truvarizzi was her last name.

4

A woman with purple hair was trudging toward Isabel, giving her the distinct feeling she was about to get a spanking. This must be Trini. Isabel knew all about *her*. Mary and Trini didn't like each other; both wanted to occupy the top position in the Godmother's life and resented the other for the perceived encroachment.

As Trini approached, Isabel realized from Trini's expression that sitting on this white outdoor chair had been a bad idea. And when Trini got even closer, Isabel realized she not only shouldn't be sitting on the chair but certainly shouldn't be eating on it.

Trini stalked up to where the girl was sitting, then stopped, glared at the plate in Isabel's hand, and jerked her head toward the house. "*Vamonos*. Let's go."

Isabel lifted her fork full of cannoli and tried for a grin. "*Momentito?*"

"No. *Ahora. Andale.* Now."

"Can I bring this with me?" Isabel asked, nodding toward the plastic plate crammed with food.

Trini seized the plate and handed it to a passing waiter. Isabel watched it go like a departing lover.

With a sigh, Isabel followed Trini into the house, past the kitchen, down a small hallway, and to a closed door. Trini flung the door open with a grunt.

"Isabel." The woman behind the desk rose. Isabel recognized her as the Godmother, Raffi Truvarizzi. She had her son's same dramatic brow, a longer version of his inky hair. Isabel had seen her face in the papers, in magazines, in the old Rhona Corrado article Mary had framed in her parlor, which Isabel made a mental note to revisit.

"You're pretty," Isabel said, before she could stop herself. Isabel had a habit of not stopping herself.

The Godmother's mouth twisted at the compliment. She gave a brisk click of her tongue and Isabel jumped when a dog the size of a small horse emerged from behind the desk and trotted out of the room. Trini closed the door just behind its tail.

The Godmother walked to the window and parted the curtain. Outside, Isabel could see Dione back on stage, a kick-line of lacrosse players behind her.

"I was so sorry to hear about your aunt," the Godmother said, her back still turned. "She meant a lot to me. I know she meant a lot to you too."

"Thank you, Godmother. That's nice of you to say." Isabel's eyes strayed to the portrait above the desk. This must be the Godmother's mother, Apollonia. *Polly*. The one who lost her mind.

The Godmother turned around and caught Isabel looking

at the portrait. "Was there a funeral?" she asked. "I didn't see a service listed in the paper."

Isabel was being tested.

"There was no service," Isabel said, relieved this was true.

"Wouldn't Mary have wanted one?"

"Well," Isabel said, looking away. "There was a problem with... Mary's condition. The funeral would not have been ... right."

The Godmother looked unconvinced. "But still."

Isabel held up her hands. She had not been privy to the discussions and arrangements. Mary's daughters had closed ranks, happy to send their cousin out of the house and off to the sidelines. Isabel was only the niece.

Remembering the purpose of her visit, Isabel mustered her nerve.

"Listen, I don't want to take up your time, you want to get outside to your party, it's just that Mary sent me here, in a dream, she whispered your name, so I had to see you," Isabel said, all in one breath. She sucked in another. "Also, the lawyers—in real life, not my dream—said you're supposed to come to the reading of Mary's will. She wanted you there."

Isabel exhaled, grateful her task was done. She rummaged through her big silver tote with the name of a makeup line embossed on the side and handed the Godmother a crumpled tube of papers.

The Godmother accepted the papers without looking at them, then pointed a finger at Isabel and rotated it counterclockwise, *rewind*. "You say she *sent* you to me?"

"In a dream," Isabel repeated, undeterred by the Godmother's skeptical expression. The Ibarra women dreamed of the dead. The phenomenon was as natural to Isabel as speaking to the living. "I was scared to come here, but I forced myself, for Mary's sake. I figured I can't avoid you forever." She paused and considered the veracity of her statements. Yes, she nodded, this was all accurate. Then her heart ached as it hit her, again, that Mary was gone. In a wistful voice, she asked, "Did my aunt ever mention me?" This question—the tenor of it, the vulnerability and pain—broke the Godmother's stare.

"All the time." The Godmother sank back into her chair and put her feet up. "But why am I needed at Mary's will reading? I doubt she would have made me executor. She would have told me."

Isabel's demeanor shifted. She put a hand to her temple and closed her eyes. Raffi and Trini exchanged glances.

"She left you a gift," said the girl in an odd, vacant tone, as if she were not speaking but being spoken through. "Something she did not want to discuss with you in life." She looked up and caught the look that passed between Raffi and Trini. "Sorry," she said with a grin. "Aunt Mary hated when I did that."

"Tell me about your dream," said the Godmother.

Isabel reviewed the details. Mary and her daughters' faces floating over the cobalt sea. The giant gavel hammering asphalt. *Raffaella Truvarizzi* in Mary's voice. The Godmother sat in silence for so long, Isabel wondered if her aunt's client was one of those people who sleep with their eyes open.

"So," said the Godmother at last. "I'm the gavel."

"You're the gavel," Isabel said, happy she did not have to launch into a long explanation. This lady was sharp.

"And when do they read the will?"

"Three days from now. On Tuesday."

"Where?"

"The Tower Theater on Calle Ocho."

The Godmother laughed. "Only Mary Fortune could make an exit like this."

+

WHEN ISABEL HAD GONE, Raffi rose. She bent at the waist, let the top of her body hang down, and grasped her opposite elbows, black hair falling over her head like a mantle. "Are we done?" she asked when at last she stood up.

Trini, who had been waiting impatiently, held up her hand. "Who you want to go to Corkscrew Records for the *problema* with Dione? Moll Portage? Philly Baldessari?"

Raffi thought for a minute. "I'll do this one myself."

Trini made a note on her phone.

Raffi motioned for Trini to come closer. When Trini was in front of her, Raffi took Trini's hand in both of hers. Trini softened. Raffi knew she was more than a boss to Trini. She was the daughter Trini never had.

"I want you to go see Judge Paz. Tell her she was missed at the party and thank her for the *añejo*. Then I want you to ask her to help Marina Ramón."

"Yep!" Trini chirped. When it came to the Godmother, Trini did not tolerate ingratitude. Celia Paz needed to pay up. "I call her tonight, Mami. I meet her for coffee this week. Hah!" Trini rhumbaed in place with a wicked grin. "She gonna be sorry if she don't listen."

"Good. That's good." Raffi looked into Trini's eyes and brought their clasped hands to her heart. "What would I do without you?"

Trini flushed the color of her hair.

"Now," Raffi said, dropping Trini's hand, "if that's all, I want to go to my son's party."

"*Claro*," said Trini, leading Raffi down the hall and sliding open the heavy glass doors with a huff.

When Raffi emerged from the house, the guests went mad. She laughed and waved, kissed her fingers, waved again, then pointed up at her son as if to say, "Not me, *him*." The crowd fell quiet as Dione called Raffi up to the stage and, at first, she demurred, though it was obvious she had every intention of obliging. Her guests erupted when, at last, she climbed the steps.

She took the microphone off its stand and backed up to where Brando still sat behind the drum kit. "Thank you for being here to celebrate my baby boy, Brando." The crowd applauded and, from the front row, the lacrosse team whooped. She turned to look for her son and saw Brando gazing back at her, flushed but loving it. "Since he was little, my Brando has been special. I know everyone says this. Everyone's kid is student of the month. Everyone's kid is gifted." Titters of recognition rippled through the partygoers. "But, in this case, I'm right. I am godmother to you all, and that is my honor. But I am mother to one. I could not be prouder of my son."

She gestured for a glass of champagne from the nearest waiter, as a fleet of others distributed glasses to the guests. "Let's toast to my Brando." She raised her glass. "Bravissimo, Brando!"

"Bravissimo, Brando!" Echoed the crowd.

"And now—" Raffi gestured toward the food, the bar, Dione and her band "—*mangia bene, e grazie tutti!*"

Brando jumped up from the drums and threw his arms around his mother to more cheers. He grabbed the mic from her hands.

"I think I've disappointed my mother once in my life. By choosing Penn over Columbia!"

Another round of laughter.

When they were off the stage, Brando hugged his mother again, lifting her off the ground as she laughed and swatted him. He leaned in and whispered, "You're too much with all the Italian stuff, Mom. You weren't born in Italy. Can't you just speak English?"

Raffi cuffed him on the chin and whispered back: "The Italian stuff is my job, *figghiu miu*. Don't ever forget it."

5

Corkscrew Records was proud to be different from other labels. Corkscrew hired women and persons of color, fought for artists' freedom of expression, and treated their people like family. For these reasons, Corkscrew attracted the finest jazz and blues musicians in the American canon. With a healthy balance sheet, a strong artist roster, and an unmatched reputation, it was inevitable that Corkscrew would draw the attention of an apex predator like HRH.

HRH, like its fellow behemoths in the alphabet league, owned so many labels, its French CEO remarked, "It would be more expeditious to list the labels we do *not* own." HRH was also litigious. Speaking on the condition of anonymity, an attorney in their in-house legal group told the *Times* it was a common internal joke to refer to HRH as a "law firm that also sells music."

The company's headquarters was in Santa Monica, California, a full city block of stucco and glass on a sunny stretch of PCH. Inside, trendy cubicles on the bottom floors gave way to lavish penthouses on the upper. The publishing stronghold was on the top.

Publishing was the quiet menace behind HRH's dominance,

though there was nothing ominous about the reception area, with its faux gold-leaf walls, or the Andy Summers original Fender Monochrome mounted over the couch, or the coffee tables topped with crushed compact discs that glittered like crystals. The air smelled of patchouli. The vibe was mellow. You should be impressed.

Two days after Brando's party, Raffi sat in this reception area in a white cashmere track suit waiting for Juju Taylor, the chair of HRH's music-publishing division. She'd researched him and deduced Juju's power derived from pulling off the single most valuable music grab in the history of song-selling: the Ringers catalogue. Nomadic since the sixties, the catalogue had become a lucrative snowball, padding with millions every time it changed hands as a realization swept the music industry: the best songs had already been written. Now the thing to do was take pieces of these original songs and build new ones, like folding leftovers into an omelet and calling it breakfast. Armed with the Ringers catalogue, HRH could do things the way they wanted: own everyone, answer to none.

"Missus Truh . . .?" the receptionist called, abandoning the pronunciation with a grateful smile as Raffi rose. She followed the young woman, whose ripped jeans and vintage band tee seemed a kind of uniform, spying, as they walked, Masai bead paintings, Māori helmets, Damascus-steel samurai swords, Inuit totem poles, and, of course, hand-hammered Tibetan singing bowls, all displayed without irony in the offices they passed.

On the windowless right were the conference rooms, each named for a different hit song owned by HRH and identified by the receptionist. "This is 'My Two Pink Shoes,'" she said, pointing to a room dominated by a pink glass chandelier built around even pinker stilettos. "'Mystery Mama,'" she said, a Ringers tribute room: the wallpaper made of faded Agatha Christie pages, sinuous female silhouettes painted over the typeface in yellow.

At the end of the hall, just before Juju's office, was a conference room dedicated to the keystone of the HRH catalogue: Jimmy Algiers' 1967 hit, "Killing Time." All four walls were painted black, with a sculpture on one wall shaped like a giant revolver cocked at an oversized gold clock on the facing wall—shattered, in the middle, by an LED bullet, acrylic blood streaming from the wound. Raffi's face went blank as they passed this one, though Trini would have noticed something shift in her demeanor. "Killing Time" was the backbone and heartbeat of "Ring Shawt," the chart-decimating hit of HRH's most prized current artist, Witch Daddy. "Ring Shawt," built on the foundation of "Killing Time," was the most lucrative track of all.

"Killing Time" was at the root of Raffi's plan.

They reached Juju's office, twice the size of the others, and chock full of things that belonged in a museum. Juju himself— generically handsome, not tall enough to be imposing nor short enough for ridicule—sat on his desk, tapping away on his cell phone, looking busy in a casual way and far too young to be responsible for pillaging hundreds of millions of publishing bounty.

The receptionist knocked on the open door to get his attention. As Raffi and the receptionist waited—the receptionist antsy and uncomfortable, Raffi at ease—Juju continued typing, waving the phone-free hand without looking up as if to say, *just a sec*. When he was finished, he looked up and offered a grin intended to be boyish.

"Hey there, welcome, welcome," he said, striding forward, offering his hand. "Juju Taylor." His triumphant tone suggested the announcement of a lead actor nomination for the Academy Award. "Raffi Truvarizzi?" His pronunciation was perfect; he even rolled the *r*. "Please, sit," he said, gesturing toward a chair finished in buttery cigar-colored leather. I recognize you from your photographs. I must say, you're very striking in person."

Raffi raised both eyebrows. She could not be less interested in flattery. She knew she was striking. She owed that to her mother. But one need not comment that the sun is yellow.

"I know Philly set us up with this little meeting today, but I have no idea what it's about," Juju confessed, as if charmed and intrigued by the twists and turns his amazing life gave him. "I just know Philly said we had to sit down and kibbitz, so here we are."

Raffi had gone through Philly Baldessari for a purpose. Philly was one of her oldest friends, a Skaneateles chum. Philly's grandfather had founded the Salt City Gang, Syracuse's erstwhile entry into the world of organized crime, which dried up with the Erie Canal. Before they disbanded, however, the Salt City Gang invested well, and the Baldessaris now held voting shares in all the major entertainment firms—including HRH.

Philly was also best friends with Witch Daddy, born Albert Shawn Marbles, whom she'd met at Cornell University in the 1990s. Now they were both in their forties, Philly the representative of her family's holdings, Witch Daddy at the height of his power as a recording artist. All Philly had to do was pick up the phone, and she and Witch would be sharing hash browns at the IHOP on Martin Luther King. Juju Taylor could not ignore Philly.

"I'm trying to help a friend with a contract issue. An artist with one of your jazz labels. Corkscrew," said Raffi in a low, even tone.

At the mention of Corkscrew, Juju made a show of smiling fondly, as if contemplating a favorite child. "Corkscrew, right— Vanessa Liao," he said, naming the ingenue who'd displaced Dione. Raffi noticed a telltale glint in his eye when he said the violinist's name. He was having an affair with her. Raffi knew the mien of a philanderer.

"I don't care about Vanessa. I'm here about Dione."

Raffi could tell Juju recognized Dione's name, though he thought he could hide it with a furrowed brow. "That name sounds familiar." He snapped his fingers. "Sax player?"

Raffi nodded. As if telling on some naughty children, she said, "Your record executives told my friend Dione that her album can't be released. They said they only have the resources to promote Vanessa Liao. But we both know that's not true." Raffi gestured around the room at the thirteenth-century Egyptian papyrus and the five-foot amethyst tower and the *ofrenda* containing what appeared to be a solid-gold dreadlock. "It's hard to believe any HRH label would be short on cash."

"Well, they all have to maintain their balance sheets. We can't prop anybody up." He awakened his phone screen as if checking to ensure everyone was still working away in their respective divisions, pulling their weight.

"Of course not. But let's be honest. My friend Dione can be tough. I've known her a long time." Raffi stroked the soft leather and shrugged. "She's difficult."

Juju avoided the bait.

"They all are," he said, waving his hand. "We had Porsche Malloy in the '80s," he said, invoking the hair band that trashed every hotel room during their legendary Feral Snake tour. "We know difficult."

Raffi inclined her head. "Perhaps we should just leave aside a discussion of why, then, and focus on how to solve my friend's problem. She's an exceptional talent, and she's sold a lot of records for you. I would think you'd love for her to sell more." She winked. "We both know a sax player won't cannibalize a synth-rock violinist. They're different categories." She smiled. "I would consider it a personal favor if you reversed course."

Juju raised an eyebrow. His blithe demeanor was fading.

"I'm sure we *can't* reverse course, Ms. Truvarizzi. There's nothing I can do. Though...." He laughed and shook his head, the boyish grin hardening. "That's not true. I could do something. I just don't *want* to." There was no mirth at all in his eyes now, just emptiness above the bright veneers. "I don't interfere with that side of things." He shrugged, breaking the tension. "I'm only Publishing."

"Only Publishing" comprised seventy-nine percent of HRH's revenue. You didn't need a law degree to read an SEC filing.

"The issue is more complicated than you realize," Raffi said with narrowed eyes, looking, she suspected, much like her mother. "Have you heard of Dino Spinotti?" The question had a light touch, like a feather on a hi-hat.

Juju scrunched up his face. Nope, he sure hadn't.

"Maybe you should do some research. He could have quite an influence here. Granted, he's dead. But the people who might be loyal to him…and what that might mean for you.…" She tutted like he was no more than a wayward child. "I'm sure, for example, you've heard of Karintha Kesi."

"Karintha Kesi. 'I named my own damn self.' Of course, I know her, she's one of ours. Jimmy's daughter, and a damn good jazz musician. Boy is she a handful. Wants to buy her masters back. But a deal's a deal." He shrugged. "You know," he said, cupping a hand over the side of his mouth as if letting her in on a secret, "she didn't change her name in real life. We write all the royalty checks to Marcella Algiers."

Raffi feigned surprise. She knew everything about Juju Taylor, Karintha Kesi, and HRH before she walked through the door. "You know," she said, hand cupped to mouth, mimicking him, "Karintha's father Jimmy was a student of Dino Spinotti's. Dino is Dione's father. Karintha and Dino were close in the old days, up in Harlem. Karintha could make things messy for you."

Raffi watched Juju catch a whiff of muscle. He was about to lose control. "Karintha knows where her bread is buttered. There's *nothing* you can do to change my mind." After a beat, he added, "Tell Dione I'm sorry, but the album stays in the morgue. It's a business decision. As they say, it's not personal."

Raffi made a face that said, *touché*. Then she spoke again. "As you wish. But once I go into action, I'm not one to stop."

"So what? I'll wake up tomorrow with a horse head in my bed?" he said with a sneer, then reddened. This was not the time to hurl stereotypes. If anyone had heard him, he'd have to repeat sensitivity training. Again.

Raffi was delighted by his misstep. He was unraveling. She

would enjoy this. "You watch too many movies, Juju. I'm just a straightforward gal. I don't bluff."

"Neither do I, Ms. Truvarizzi," he said. "You were a lawyer. I assume you know what a contract is? So let me be blunt: I *own* Karintha Kesi."

"Do you?" asked Raffi. "Are you sure?"

"*Silvia!*" he called. The receptionist appeared. She must have been right outside the door. "Ms. Truvarizzi is leaving."

"Thanks for your time, Juju. I won't be in touch," Raffi said.

She followed the receptionist down the hall. They had taken a few steps when, behind her, in Juju's office, she heard the distinct sound of a Tibetan crystal bowl emitting a long, low hum.

Climbing into the back of the big black SUV outside, she called Trini.

"Get me Karintha Kesi. Let's see if she'd like to own her music again. Her dad's too. And call our West Coast PI, what's her name, the underwear model?"

"Berry."

"Call Berry and have her educate Mrs. Taylor on her husband's extracurricular activities. *Capisci?*"

Raffi could hear Trini dancing over the phone. "*Capisco*, Mama. Juju Taylor is done."

6

Mary Fortune's was not a typical will reading. By her instruction, the family rented the old Tower Theater on Calle Ocho, near where her first husband's restaurant still stood. Everyone present, including the lawyers, was served a Cuban sandwich, three *croquetas*, and an ice-cold *limonada*. The sounds of chewing and finger-licking belied the solemnity of the occasion.

Wearing an architectural white dress, her coarse hair untamed, Raffi sat in the last occupied row next to Isabel, who huffed down the Cuban and two *croquetas* within minutes of sitting down, crumbs littering her mint green skirt. Raffi had chosen the seat next to the girl. She was drawn to protect those who needed it, and Isabel Ibarra was manifestly in need of protection.

The lawyers read some prefatory remarks, then the lights dimmed, and a movie appeared on the screen. More accurately, it was a compendium of family movies: the girls playing in the yard, puppet shows and Christmas plays, a montage of Mary's shih tzus in the arms of various daughters at various ages, a tiny Isabel sitting behind a fan of tarot cards looking serious. The daughters and their husbands, occupying the two rows in front of Raffi and

Isabel, cried throughout. Next to Raffi, the girl did not cry, but her hands gripped the armrests and her face looked wan.

The home movies stopped, and Mary overtook the screen— the Mary of recent times, wearing a cream-colored horse blanket with delicate gold fringe and a hideous grimace. Murmurs emanated from the front rows. Even in death, Mary made her daughters nervous.

"I played these movies for you so you would remember the good times, before I tell you the news that will make you curse my name," Screen Mary said into the camera, a real natural.

"*Mamà!*" One of the daughters cried, reaching out her hand, as if to say, *Never!*

"Every penny I have, I leave in a trust to be administered by La Madrina, Raffaella Truvarizzi!" Screen Mary announced, like a magician revealing her final trick.

At this, as Mary grinned at the camera, there was a horrible sound of gasping, of thick Cuban hair slapping against the crushed velvet seatbacks and high heels scuffling against the floor, as each of the daughters turned to stare at Raffi. Isabel went even more rigid, clenching the ruffles of her skirt, her face almost gray. Raffi did not flinch. The more surprising the revelation, the less visible the reaction—that was her code. It was a lesson the girl next to her could stand to learn. Inside, however, Raffi was floored. Why would Mary do this?

"This money is to be used for the good of *all* women," Screen Mary continued, her eyes glinting. "I am told these terms are too vague to be enforceable, and that I am basically giving all my money to Raffaella Truvarizzi. Good!" She sneered, presumably at

THE GODMOTHER | 49

the counsel of her attorneys, who were, at that moment, nodding, *yes*, that is exactly what she had done.

Mary shrugged and went on. "*La Madrina* will know what to do with the money. As you all know what to do with yourselves. You girls have been blessed. Others? Not so much. This money is for them."

As her eyelids fluttered, the daughters bowed their heads and the lawyers studied the floor.

"Let anyone who interferes with my will be three times punished!" Mary boomed.

Raffi looked to Isabel at her side. The girl's eyes were closed, eyelids moving just like her aunts, rapidly, as in sleep.

"I hope they don't all start speaking in tongues," said one of the lawyers, a bit too loudly. The video concluded with Mary looking peaceful.

"You will each receive a copy of my trust instructions. My jewelry and effects, my house and cars, go to my daughters. To my niece, Isabel Ibarra, I leave my horse blankets in the storage unit in midtown."

Isabel's eyes flew open. A ripple of snickers spread like a toxic cloud from the front rows: the daughters enjoying the disappointment of their rival.

The lights came on and everyone but Raffi stood up, the daughters squabbling amongst themselves, already debating which pieces of jewelry they each wanted, as they edged out of their seats. They took turns hugging their cousin, but their hugs were more condescension than consolation.

The daughters also hugged Raffi, who had not yet moved

to get up, so they had to bend all the way down to embrace her, bottoms in the air. Raffi disliked the daughters; she sensed they'd closed ranks against Isabel, and Raffi had no tolerance for when the strong and many align against the lone and vulnerable. Raffi accepted their embraces but did not reciprocate.

As if they had just received Communion, the daughters filed down the aisle with heads bowed, but with a gleeful energy that said they couldn't wait to celebrate today's terrible surprise for Isabel, which almost made up for not getting the money themselves. The lawyers came after, one of whom, a slender man with a yarmulke-shaped bald spot, stopped at Raffi and Isabel's row. He offered Raffi a small blue envelope.

Raffi looked down at the envelope. She could feel Isabel's intent gaze over her shoulder. The envelope was addressed to both Raffi and Isabel in Mary's distinctive hand, the letters all jiggly like they'd been spit out by an EKG. Raffi looked up, first at Isabel, then at the lawyer.

"Thank you," she said to the lawyer, but it sounded like *leave*, so he did.

Inside the envelope was the address of the storage unit and a four-digit code. Nothing else.

"Huh," said Isabel.

Raffi turned the slip of paper over in her hands.

"Why would she give it to both of us?" asked Raffi.

Isabel's hand went to her temple.

"She wants us to go together," Isabel said after a minute.

"You have a radio antenna in there?" Raffi asked, pointing

at Isabel's head. She did not buy the girl's clairvoyant act one bit, but she could tell the girl believed it herself.

Isabel smiled. "Something like that." She paused and asked, unsure, "Should we go now?"

"I have a meeting in an hour," Raffi said. Which was a lie. What she had was a headache.

"Tomorrow?"

"Can't," said Raffi.

"Don't you want to know what's in there?" protested Isabel. "It can't just be sweaters."

"Can't it?" Raffi asked, thinking Mary could make the bestowal of a breath mint into something momentous.

Isabel put a hand to her temple again. No signal.

She's not exactly Mary Fortune, thought Raffi. But it was to the girl's credit that she had not thought to dispute her aunt's will, given how it had turned out for her. Somewhat less to her credit, neither did she think to wonder why Mary's horse blankets were in a midtown storage unit and not hanging in her closet where they had always been.

7

Isabel huddled under the scratchy coverlet on her saggy mo-
tel-room bed, *Las Brujas de Bal Harbour* playing on the battered
television, laptop balanced on her knees. Isabel's twenty-fourth
birthday was coming up in ten days, and she was trying to plan a
trip for her solar return. Usually, her Aunt Mary did this for her.
It was a Mary Fortune trademark, after all.

The solar return—the position of the sun at the precise anni-
versary of one's birth—was a special chart predictive of the coming year. But Mary was the first astrologer to peer into the skies
and deduce that where you were on your solar return could shift
your fate. *Change your location, change your fate.* This type of
discovery was what made Mary the best, as she often pointed out.

For some reason, remaining in Miami was usually out of the
question. Year after year, Mary told her clients, "Miami is not
good. You might die, or worse: become poor."

Mary seemed oblivious to the hassle—not to mention ex-
pense—of leaving town every birthday. But Isabel had another
theory: these solar return trips might be a quest for quest's sake,
a "fool's errand." Yet another Mary Fortune gambit.

Now Isabel was under the gun. Distracted by the brouhaha surrounding Mary's will, she had delayed planning this solar return. She willed herself to focus on the charts, but her mind kept drifting to the horse blankets. The stars were far less intriguing than that midtown storage unit.

She took a deep breath, opened her electronic chart, and keyed in the coordinates for Morocco: her dream destination. This year, Morocco would bring isolation and family troubles, and she'd had enough of those of late. It was a relief, though; Morocco would take up all the money Mary had transferred into Isabel's account—Isabel's yearly stipend for the express purpose of funding her solar return—and, if Isabel could find a more budget-friendly location, she might have enough left over to ditch this motel for somewhere cockroach-free. It was tempting, even, to scrap the solar return trip altogether, but it was unwise to deviate from Mary Fortune's protocols.

She checked the Caribbean—cheap, but with a material risk of disappearing in the water and never resurfacing, so that was out too. She ventured across the Atlantic. The northern countries were abysmal. Iceland? Terrible food, she'd lose weight there for sure, but it came with awful surprises and indecisiveness. She didn't need more of these, either.

Her fingers smashed away at the laptop, keying in locations across the world. For a good solar return, she would travel anywhere.

On a hunch, she keyed in *Sicily*. She had been thinking of the Mediterranean island ever since she'd met the Godmother, fragments of whispers now made conscious. *Strange*. The chart said Italy—Sicily—would be ideal. Sicily was "opportunities and beginnings, a chance at love." If the universe could not hold up a physical banner, this was the closest it could come.

Deep in her belly, an overwhelming hunger surfaced like a kraken, which happened when she had to make a decision. She ordered a sausage-and-pepper pizza from Nachio's—Cuban chefs; the thing was a *croqueta* in disguise—and, minutes after its arrival, stood over the particle-board desk and ate the whole thing right out of the box, her heart clattering as if it were the barrel of a gun and not a giant fried pizza she'd just crammed down her gullet.

Before returning to her laptop, Isabel grabbed the tarot cards from her silver tote and pulled a card from the middle. The High Priestess: intuition. She was right about Sicily. The cards don't lie.

Then came the whispers, louder now. *Raffaella Truvarizzi.* The whispers said it too.

There had to be a reason for the dream, the storage unit, and now the perfect solar return in Sicily. *The Godmother must come.* She knew it like the redheaded nun on *Las Brujas de Bal Harbour* knew the moment she fell for the priest. Just as the cards don't lie, neither do the whispers. This wasn't her mind moving the planchette. This was the claircognizance that was her birthright. She did not need to touch her temple. *The Godmother* must *come.*

Isabel would have to announce this revelation tomorrow, when she and the Godmother would visit the storage unit at last. Isabel was scared, yes, but who wouldn't be scared to demand of the Godmother's time, more valuable even than her favor? *I'll channel Aunt Mary,* she resolved. *I won't take no for an answer.*

✦

THE GODMOTHER AND ISABEL rode the elevator upward, a cheerful electronic female voice calling the number of each passing floor. Whereas Isabel kept glancing at her phone and scrolling through her social media feed, the Godmother stood silent, both hands hanging at her side, at rest in her surroundings. It was 10:00 a.m., and Isabel had already downed a mango smoothie, two cafecitos, and a double cheeseburger. Nerves made her even hungrier than decisions.

Isabel had arrived at 2020 Northwest Fourth Street an hour earlier, just as Marina Ramón left carrying something that looked like a check and smiling to herself. The two women crossed in front of the gate like two paramours trading places in the same lover's bed. Once admitted to the grounds, Trini made Isabel wait outside. Isabel suspected this was punishment for being the niece of Trini's arch-rival.

When the Godmother came out dressed in simple white jeans and a tee, she looked at Isabel with different eyes than the day they'd met. Isabel imagined her own mother would look at her with a similar expression were she alive: a mixture of tenderness, concern, and irritation. In that moment, Isabel understood why so many women (and a few lucky men) were keen to call Raffi Truvarizzi "Godmother."

IT HAD BEEN MANY years since Raffi had driven the streets of Miami with a chatterbox in the backseat. The ride with Isabel reminded Raffi of that time—but Isabel sat next to her in the front, and was, therefore, much harder to ignore. The girl made Brando seem like a mute.

Trini had been slated to drive them, as was her usual practice, but she'd had to back out at the last minute when other matters intervened. In short: Trini had to go scare someone.

"You do such a great job of not looking at your phone," Isabel gushed from the passenger seat. She had taken the bus from Hialeah so they could ride together. It was Isabel's suggestion, and Raffi did not recall agreeing, but the girl had shown up at her door.

The line of conversation did not end upon their arrival. As they exited the storage-facility elevator at the top floor, Isabel prattled on. "I can't put my phone down. Ever." Either the girl had a tireless capacity to discuss her addiction to technology, or she couldn't think of anything else to say.

Raffi was distracted, assaulted by a memory: the bright fluorescent lights, and their brighter reflection in the white linoleum floors, reminded her of the hospital where she'd first taken her mother. "Don't do this," Polly had pleaded. "I would rather not live."

Mary's storage unit was one of the two largest in the building. It took up half the entire floor. The entrance, a metal pull-down door, faced south. Isabel glanced at the unit's mirror image on the north side. Then, lock in hand, she fumbled in her pocket for the slip of paper with the code. Raffi rotated the watch on her wrist and thought of the horse blankets.

Made in Italy, the horse blankets were handwoven from the softest thread in hues with names redolent of poetry—colors like Aztec Emerald, Desdemona Pink, Beluga Black. The brand name, Pado, Esperanto for *path*, signified the designers' notion of the sweaters as movable art. These garments were meant to accompany one on life's journey. Each had its own lyrical name and convoluted origin story. For an exorbitant sum, you could even have one customized.

Mary must have amassed hundreds of them. She had bought at least one per month for over twenty years and accepted even more from her clients, providing her size in advance, in case they were looking for gift ideas. Raffi expected to find a veritable stable of horse blankets on the other side of this metal door.

The lock gave with a strident shriek. Looking up from her crouch at the base of the door, Isabel grinned. She grasped the handle and yanked upward, the door groaning in its ungreased tracks as it rumbled open. Isabel stepped in first. Following close behind, Raffi allowed herself a private smile. This whole thing was so "Mary."

THE STORAGE UNIT WAS larger than Raffi had expected and darker too. Perhaps retaining childhood fears, Isabel backed up, the apogee of her rear end headed straight for Raffi, who darted out of the way.

Raffi waited for Isabel to forge on, but the backside did not budge. Moving around the girl, she strode into the unit, which she secretly found eerie too. Tentative footfall like the clatter of tap shoes said Isabel was close behind her.

One thing became clear: there was no stable of horse blankets here. The space was almost empty. Only one hulking shadow lurked at the back.

Raffi fumbled around for a light switch. What were you supposed to do, wear a miner's helmet? She exhaled in frustration when a light popped on from behind. Isabel, looking triumphant, had engaged the flashlight function on her cell phone. At least there was one constructive use for it.

As they approached the back wall, the hulking object took form as a rack holding three horse blankets wrapped in clear plastic. Sliding her cell phone from her back pocket and flicking on her own flashlight, Raffi approached the rack.

"Some inheritance," Isabel said, then laughed—then sniffled. Raffi might cry, too, if she were in the girl's position.

Raffi removed one sweater from the rack. She tore off the plastic. Vivid colors leapt out at her. She was aware of Isabel by her side, and the crackle of the girl tearing off the plastic on the other horse blankets. Raffi's fingers stroked one soft sleeve, her finger pads sensing the Italian women soaking the yarn in dye; the Indian women crushing indigo, saffron, and madder root to make the dye; the Zhongwei goat high on its desert steppe, horned like a warrior, provider of the yarn itself.

This horse blanket was unlike any Raffi had seen. The front was an idyllic, if portentous, tableau: a dark-haired woman picnicking in a valley under a pale sky, the ruins of a fountain at her side. Behind her, a brooding volcano loomed shrouded in mist. Raffi flipped the sweater around and her breath caught. The back was consumed by flames of thread in every shade of red and orange, shot through with rivulets of gold. It was the volcano mid-eruption. Through a clever trick, the tongues of flame migrated from the back and out the side, threatening to devour the woman's peace. It was so realistic, Raffi felt sweat beading on her neck, despite the air conditioning.

Raffi turned the sweater over again and shone the flashlight on the yarn-woman who sat, unaware of her fate. The woman's hair was wild. Even rendered in thread, Raffi made out a prominent nose. The woman was *her.*

"Did it happen to you too?" Isabel called. The girl shuffled over and poked her head around the side of Raffi's arm to survey the sweater. "Yep," she said matter-of-factly. "Same."

Raffi looked at her.

"Look," said Isabel, brandishing the horse blanket in her hands.

The sweater depicted a small white cottage on the beach, just before sunrise. White thread danced light on the water's surface, and three figures—two old women and one plump blond child between—strolled through the spray hand in hand.

"This," Isabel said, pointing at the cottage, "was my house in Cuba. My *family's* house in Cuba. Castro gave it to our servants in the 1960s, so I've never been there. And this—" her finger trailed to the round cherub, "—is me."

Raffi leaned in. The cherub had the same halo of curls and pleasing plumpness as the adult Isabel. It was an undeniable likeness.

"What's she trying to tell us?" Raffi mused. Theories unlocked, whirled, locked, and rotated. The wheel was moving. She called this type of thinking her "Godmother mind."

Isabel grabbed Raffi's arm. "Put yours on! Maybe something will happen."

Raffi's looked down at her arm and the girl's hand retreated. Raffi's skin prickled. She had the silly thought that, if this were a movie, she would slide into the horse blanket and become invisible.

Easing the volcano sweater from its hanger, Raffi tossed it around her back and shrugged it on. No, she was not invisible, but a visceral charge coursed through her. She felt like the center orb shooting off electricity in one of those round glass balls. If she believed in magic, this sweater would be it.

"Now mine!" cried Isabel. She whipped on her own horse blanket and tilted her head as if expecting the thread to start singing. Clearly disappointed when nothing happened, she said, "If this sweater is me and that sweater is you, who's the other one?"

A smart question. Raffi grabbed the third sweater, scanned the front, and frowned. Turquoise and red shapes leapt out against a navy background on the front. On the back, a pale hawk crested a red-rock ridge against an evening sky. In the foreground, a silver-haired woman in a feathered headdress sat cross-legged on rust-colored clay, eyes closed, a stand of teepees glowing behind her.

"Does this mean anything to you?" Raffi asked.

"I was just going to ask you the same thing."

Raffi ran her fingers over this horse blanket, searching for answers. She imagined bloodroot and prickly pear, onionskin and sagebrush, a hint of Navajo tea. "It looks like the American West. Navajo iconography, maybe? The colors are non-traditional."

"How could you know that?" the girl asked, grabbing the sweater and appearing to search for other clues.

"College."

Isabel went silent for so long, Raffi wished she'd timed the girl; this could be a record.

"These are not normal Pado sweaters," Isabel said at last.

"There's nothing normal about this," Raffi amended. She shoved her hands in the horse blanket's pockets, where they

THE GODMOTHER | 61

disappeared into the lapping flames—then paused, reached deeper into the right pocket, and removed a small beige envelope.

"This keeps getting better!" cried Isabel, and Raffi had a glimpse of what it would be like to spend Christmas morning with her. "What does it say?"

Raffi opened the envelope and read in Italianate Spanish, "*Destino.*" She hesitated. "Destiny?"

"Destination," Isabel corrected. Her hand slipped into the pocket of her own sweater, emerging with an identical envelope which she opened.

"*Primeros Pasos,*" she said. "First Steps."

Raffi rifled through the pockets of the third sweater and extracted another envelope. "*Misterios.* Mysteries?"

"Secrets," Isabel stage-whispered, her eyes like platters. "You know what I think this is?"

"Not in the least."

"I think this is a fool's errand!"

"*What* is a fool's errand?" It was hard to keep up with the Ibarras.

"A fool's errand is a quest for quest's sake," Isabel explained.

"So, the *sweater* is a quest?"

Isabel shook her head. "I think she *gave* us the sweaters so we'd *go* on a quest."

"Right," said Raffi, as if Isabel had just declared the world flat.

"I *am* right! She wants you to come with me to Sicily next week," Isabel insisted. "For my solar return."

Raffi started. "Sicily?" Her eyes narrowed and her nose turned to the hook.

Now *that's* interesting, she thought.

✢

"WHY ARE YOU DRIVING so fast?" Isabel said, clenching the grab handle.

"I'm not driving fast," said the Godmother over the din of the engine. "I'm accelerating."

Isabel touched the Godmother's arm, concerned, but the Godmother recoiled, and Isabel dropped her hand. "Are you mad at me?"

"Why would I be mad at you?" The Godmother changed lanes, cutting off a neon green sportscar.

"Do you believe me about Sicily?"

They merged onto the highway at eighty miles an hour in a sixty-five. "I believe *you* believe you about Sicily."

Isabel had expected resistance. But lately it felt like she was always climbing uphill. Maybe she should retreat to her motel room and leave it alone.

This is important. Don't back down.

"I won't," Isabel muttered out loud. She grabbed the steering wheel and yanked it hard to the right. The SUV careened sideways.

The Godmother slammed to a stop in the shoulder amid a chorus of honks. Throwing the car in park, she whirled on the passenger seat.

"Are you insane?"

"You just...you have to come!"

The Godmother's stare was cold.

"Look at your horse blanket, Godmother. Sicily! And the card in the pocket: destination! If anything, you're the one who's supposed to go, not me." Isabel sighed. "That's not true," she admitted. "I'm supposed to go too."

"I understand you feel you are receiving clues and messages—"

"I *am* receiving clues and messages."

"I'm sure you are. Your clues and messages are noted."

The Godmother eased the car back on the road, exited the highway, and stopped at a red light. A squat, stylish, old woman tottered into the crosswalk. She was about Aunt Mary's height, with the same frosty highlights and penciled-in brows. Come to think of it, her blouse resembled a satin horse blanket. As the old woman passed the SUV, she looked right at Isabel and glowered.

You're going to let her intimidate you? Don't forget, I helped make her!

The light turned green. Even Dead Mary was so heavy-handed. Isabel mustered all the authority she could, which is to say, she imitated her aunt.

"You're making a big mistake if you don't come. Aunt Mary spoke to you through me, and she said, 'Go.' Isabel rummaged for words until something came through for her. "'Go find out where you come from.'"

The Godmother looked at Isabel with a strange expression.

"I come from Skaneateles, New York."

"That's where you were born, not where you're from." Isabel paused. "You've had questions for a long time."

The Godmother's dramatic brows twitched. What could she be thinking?

Jesus Christ, Isabel thought. *It's just a trip to Sicily.*

✦

THAT EVENING, IN HER dingy motel room, Isabel's face was so close to the laptop screen that the tip of her nose left a grease mark, the quick clatter of her fingers on the keyboard like a muffled hailstorm. She had thrown herself down a rabbit hole of research on the Godmother, whose reaction to the proposed trip to Sicily had nagged at Isabel the remainder of their silent car ride back from the storage unit.

Then, on the bus to Hialeah, the whispers had grown louder. Isabel had struck a nerve. She needed to figure out why.

Hours into her reading, however, she cursed her own determination.

It seemed, when the Godmother didn't get what she wanted, the consequences could be anywhere from humiliating to lethal—usually the former, thank God, though more than once someone in Raffi Truvarizzi's orbit had turned up dead. Yet she'd never been prosecuted for a crime. Any evidence was circumstantial. Usually, there was no evidence at all.

Isabel fantasized about withdrawing her invitation for the Godmother to join her in Sicily, but the thought of reneging on Raffi Truvarizzi made her more anxious, not less. For ten minutes, she considered whether to walk to the liquor store on the corner for a bottle of cheap wine. Wine: a great silencer of whispers. Also, a natural companion for dark chocolate. The liquor store would have chocolate, too.

Enough. Everything—whispers and fears, wine and chocolate, Raffi Truvarizzi—went silent. She fumbled around in her room gathering items for a calming spell: lavender and howlite, a candle dipped in rue, *you are here, you are here,* a long exhale, her pale eyelids clenched closed until the light behind them burned blue.

No more nerves. Instead of fear, curiosity. Her eyes blinked open.

Something didn't add up. The electronic paper trail on the Godmother ended ten years before, with the article Isabel remembered from Aunt Mary's wall, a framed newspaper cutting that hung there among the paintings of saints for so long, the plaster underneath was ten shades lighter. It was an interview with Rhona Corrado: the first of many, and the first attribution of the moniker "Godmother" to Raffi Truvarizzi.

The photo accompanying the article showed Raffi clad all in her trademark white, lounging in her palatial backyard, flanked by two bull mastiffs, possible parents of the mighty Piccolo.

All those years, Isabel had ignored the article, dismissing it as irrelevant. Now that Isabel had finally read it, the article confused her, starting with the headline: *"Raffi Truvarizzi: 'I'm Not The Godmother.'"*

Huh.

Skimming down, Isabel noted the article was more a list of denials than an interview. In no uncertain terms, Raffaella Truvarizzi told Corrado she wanted to make several things clear:

She was not associated in any way with the Mafia—Sicilian, American, or otherwise.

She was not affiliated with the notorious mobster Sally Truvarizzi and denounced his many crimes.

She was an Ivy League-educated philanthropist whose sole

concern was raising her son and helping other women.

She was not now, and had never been, known by anyone, other than by family in the Catholic sense, as The Godmother.

Isabel sat back on the bed cushions, which smelled of Cheerios and a deep, musky odor she did not care to contemplate. She considered the words of ten-years-ago Raffi Truvarizzi, who had gone to such lengths to deny she was the Godmother—an unnecessary denial at the time, as it was a name by which she had never been known. Interesting, thought Isabel. Her only question now was whether Raffi Truvarizzi's denials were a sincere attempt to deny she was a Mafiosa...or a clever ploy to conceal that she wasn't.

8

Juju Taylor would not stop calling. At the Godmother's instruction, Dione ignored him and sent his voice mails—three per day and three minutes each—to Trini without listening. That is, until the afternoon Juju called from a blocked ID when Dione was sitting around critiquing old Dione and the Spins tracks. Distracted by the off-tempo bass line and cursing herself for hiring that bassist in the first place, she answered.

"Dione!" bellowed a voice.

At first, she thought it was a telemarketer and was about to hang up, but the voice was familiar.

"Who is this?" she asked. She often received calls from obsessed fans. She'd changed her number four times in four months.

"It's Juju Taylor!" His voice had gone up a register. He sounded unstable.

Dione's ears perked up. Had he just hit a high C? She decided to torture him.

"Dudu?"

"*Juju from HRH!*"

At Dione's silence, he cleared his throat. This was the part, Dione thought, where Juju Taylor groveled.

"So! I had a nice visit from your *friend* Raffi, and I just thought—hey, we've had a relationship for so long now, there's no reason we need any *middleman* to figure this out."

"You need to call Raffi Truvarizzi," Dione said, almost, but not quite, pitying him. "You and I don't have anything left to discuss."

Juju feigned surprise, as if he had no idea why she would be upset with him for trying to bury her record and ruin her career.

"We're in a tight spot here, Dione, and what do they say? It's not *personal*, right?" He laughed as if he'd made the wittiest joke. "You and your *friend* should understand *that*."

She was offended at the insinuation—"Italian Americans conduct their lives by cinematic versions of Mafia rules"—when the buzz of the empty line sent Juju's desperation back around like a boomerang. And then it began. Dione rocked back in her chair. Sometimes it was just a snippet of a phrase that wafted off like a little lick of smoke and dissipated. But, moment by moment, the snippets multiplied. Snippets became skeins, skeins became braids.

Hearing things. She was hearing things.

She'd been uninspired since Brando's party. Even though she knew she was supposed to be writing—she had promised the Godmother—all she could think about was her hostage album. Her imprisoned art. As an alternative to perseveration, she had listened to old tunes and picked apart the performances—not her own, but her band's. No one could keep up with her, which is why she was always so keen to solo. Otherwise, she watched a lot of TV, smoked excellent pot, and ate everything in the kitchen.

She had a little mantra that excused this behavior: *You can't force jazz.* You just can't. You're the vessel. The source is unknown. Now, on this phone call—sweeping in, bubbling up, oh *man*, she was hearing things—the rhythm came from Juju's breath. His prosody was syncopated. It had an actual form. It went:

Scah-da-da-daaa...dat, dum dat—

Scah-da-da-daaa...dat, dum dat—

The meter, five-four, not her usual time signature, but there wasn't time to think, there was barely time to grab the nearest grease pencil and look around for laminated paper. There was none, so she put the phone on speaker, left it on the chair, and threw her body in the direction of the glass side table. In big, sloppy, bold red grease-wax, she scribbled across the glass, getting down the beat before the vamp led her in: bluesy, rocked back on its heels, a few bright notes trilling *altissimo* above the line—she scribbled those too—and then breaking back into the main theme, *glissando* on the blue, then—

Scah-da-da-daaa...dat, dum dat—

Juju Taylor's drivel was *music.*

"Look, I'm going to level with you, Dione," Juju said, almost rushing the beat now, but not quite. "This Vanessa Liao thing puts us in a bind. We have a hot, hot property—like Dione-Spinotti-in-the-early-aughts hot—and she's violin-rock, which there isn't even a market for, so we need to *spin* it—ha, *spin it*, get it? Like Dione and the Spins? —as a sort of *fusion....*"

The Godmother was right, Dione thought. He *is* fucking Vanessa Liao. "Mmm hmm," Dione said, emphasizing the first syllable and liking the cadence. The mmm-hmm came in on the sixth measure, pitting the pleading scat line against the parried mmm-hmm. It was call-and-response. The soul of jazz.

"...and I mean, the *confusion* it might cause for two, you know, *attractive* female instrumentalists to release albums at the same time...."

"Mmm hmm," Dione purred, her excitement mounting. She'd got it now. Having covered the side table with red grease, she stumbled toward the music room, grabbing the phone and cradling it against her shoulder as she went, saying "mmm hmm" at responsive intervals. God, it was magical, he never slid out of that—

Scah-da-da-daaa...dat, dum dat—

She got on her hands and knees with the grease pencil and wrote on the hardwood floor. Her housekeeper was going to kill her. All the pent-up resentment and boredom and defeat flooded onto that floor. The phone fell from her shoulder. She had all she needed from Juju Taylor.

She wrote and wrote. The light outside faded. She pushed back the Tabriz rug and wrote more. Voices came in on the bridge, measure by measure, beat by beat, she pushed the rug back even farther until it was flipped all the way in half, the center medallion its fulcrum, her body heaving over the intricate double weft, sweat on her upper lip and under her arms and on the floor, her hair matted, spilling, all of it streaming out of her, oh *man*, she was hearing things.

When it was over, she found the phone kicked off to the side. She lifted it to her ear: nothing. Juju Taylor was gone. But he would call again the next day, and this time she would not answer. She did not need permission from Juju to do *this*.

Dione stood up, the energy shooting up through the soles of her feet, into her spine, and out the top of her head. She was not Dione Spinotti the mortal now. She would never be mortal again. It was as good as done, and she knew it like you know when someone is watching you from behind or the doorbell is about to ring or you're going to turn over that ace and win the pot.

She strode over to where the horn hung on the wall. It was waiting for her like a stallion stomping in its stall. Her first and only love: the saxophone.

Neck strap first, always. Then a fresh reed. She lined up the embouchure, double lip, just like Jimmy Algiers, meant to preserve her teeth at first but now it was the only way she knew.

She closed her eyes and lifted her chin. *It's all in my head*, she thought, a little joke she had with herself. *I'm just hearing things.* The accusation leveled against women throughout history. Except she now knew it was not flaw but fuel. *Hear this*, she thought.

Dione drew up her shoulders and neck, fretted her fingers over the plates. She cracked it open with a growl, then skipping stones on water, now *glissando*, it was right there on the glass table and the floor, but she didn't need notations now. She didn't need anything. It was all in her head.

Drawing deep from the bottom of her lungs, spurred by neurons exploding like fireworks, fingers, mouth, tongue, teeth, the essence of Dione, all sixty-one inches of her, detonated, caught fire, dispersed. You could call it what you wanted, no euphemism could capture the blast that shook the earth when Dione Spinotti began to blow.

9

Judge Celia Paz had the top spot on the long list of people Trini didn't like. For starters, Paz was not only a *Mexicana*, but a Spanish *Mexicana*—descendant of the *conquistadores*—and she spoke with a quasi-Italian cadence that sounded like a taunt. Trini had complained that morning about being sent to meet with the judge, had begged the Godmother to send her attorney, Moll Portage, instead, but the Godmother would not let her off the hook. In elaborating on the task at hand, the Godmother had remarked that Paz's court decisions often contained some variation on the phrase "On my grandfather's *hacienda* in Spain...." Trini knew the Godmother had said this to rile her up. It had worked.

Arms crossed over a red tee that said in bold letters *I'd Rather Have No Friends Than Fake Ones*, Trini now faced off with the *Mexicana* at a bustling, Argentinian-run, French café, the two women with identical double espressos and twin hairstyles, only Paz's hair was dyed black, and Trini's was still purple. Trini sneered across the table at the judge, who had just finished talking about the importance of avoiding even the appearance of impropriety in the law. This was Paz's way of saying she wouldn't help.

"Mama." Trini lowered her head as she leaned her elbows on the table and glared up at Paz like *come on.* "The Godmother know your colleague Judge Lunken love the Children's League. The Godmother want to support the Children's League too. All she ask you to do is tell your friend Lunken to accept the Godmother's gift." Trini gave Paz a meaningful look. *You know what I'm talking about.*

Judge Lunken was Marina Ramón's judge.

Paz tossed her head and Trini snickered, recognizing from experience the phantom hair-flip of a woman who has forgotten she just lopped it all off.

"I can't speak with Judge Lunken about that, Trini." Paz shook her head again, the insincerity of her regret setting Trini further ablaze. "I can't be a part of anything that would suggest undue influence on a fellow member of the court. I'd do anything for the Godmother but that."

Trini pursed her lips. She was almost excited by the judge's disobedience. Somewhere down the line, it meant Trini could punish this *fulana.* "Mama, the Godmother not gonna like this."

"I'm sure she *isn't,*" said the judge.

Correcting Trini's grammar! She could not believe it. The *Mexicana* better not mention that *hacienda* in Spain.

"Unfortunately," Paz continued, "I simply can't do anything to tarnish the reputation of my courtroom. A woman of the Godmother's stature should understand. It's hard enough for us to climb the ladder; we can't afford to make mistakes."

"Listen, Mamita, you climb the ladder because the Godmother put the ladder there for you. Before the Godmother, you chase an ambulance. You need some respect."

As if looking for the waitress, the judge turned in her chair to survey the other patrons. Trini followed her gaze. A man at a table near the window seemed a little too alert. "Eh, Papi?" Trini hissed at the man, who looked up from his newspaper with a cool gaze. "Keep your eyes out the window."

The man looked back down at his newspaper.

The judge leaned forward and said to Trini through gritted teeth, "Look. I will always appreciate what the Godmother did for me. But I'm a sworn officer of the court now. I take that very seriously. The appearance of impropriety, Trini. I just can't do it."

This lady had some *cojones.*

"*Pero* you don't care about impropriety when you take the Godmother's money." Trini moved so she was eyelash to eyelash with the judge. A man at another table by the espresso machine looked over, and Trini swiveled her head in his direction. He looked away. Trini turned back to the judge. "The Godmother's godchildren don't say no, Mama. *Mira*—look: she no gonna like this."

"Perhaps *not*," said the judge.

Trini opened her mouth to respond but decided against it. She'd have her response in time. Instead, she drained the dregs of her espresso and kicked back her chair. It clattered to the floor, again drawing eyes.

"*Basta*, Mami—enough. I go straight to the Godmother with bad news. Good luck with *the appearance of impropriety*," Trini said in a flawless American accent.

"Good luck to you, too, Trini. Please give the Godmother my regards," Paz said.

"I make sure *not* to," said Trini before stomping out the door.

RAFFI WAS IN THE sculpture garden picking herbs from the base of her favorite statue, Athena Glaukopis—Athena with the owl, a millennia-old piece—when Detective Abby Gambol came by. The detective walked right through the gate; she ran extra security for Raffi when it was needed, and she was one of the few people Raffi trusted with the code. Abby was not a small woman, and that had been used against her in the past. Her thighs were like pylons. Her long dark braid snaked over her shoulders like a cobra. Her eyes were sharp and wise. Today, they were also amused.

The detective strode up to where Raffi knelt near a wicker basket heaped with rosemary and sage. Raffi held up a sprig of rosemary, and the detective brought it to her nose and inhaled.

"Is this a social visit?" Raffi asked.

"A call came in today from someone called Ian McBride," Gambol said without prelude, and with just the hint of a smirk. "Seems he went out to his five-car garage this morning looking for his LaFerrari and found it...undesirably altered."

Raffi made a show of concern. "Altered how?"

The detective's lips twisted. "It was crushed into the size of a suitcase."

Raffi was pleased. She had hoped to compress it to the size of a child's lunchbox, but she allowed there are limits to demolition. "Was Mr. McBride upset about this?"

"He was crying like a toddler."

Raffi reached out and placed a hand on the taller woman's shoulder. "That is a shame." She felt inside her basket for a bunch of sage. "Take this home and infuse it into your butter. It's called compound butter. Once you try this, you'll never go back."

Detective Gambol took the sage and stuck it in the front pocket of her tight cargo pants. "Thank you, Godmother."

"You're so welcome, old friend." Raffi regarded Gambol with genuine concern. "Any more problems with your department?"

Two years back, a sting op went wrong, and the Miami PD had been looking for a scapegoat to pin it on. After the Godmother's intervention, they'd been forced to look elsewhere than Abby Gambol.

"No problems at all. I have a new partner now. She's so much less of a dick."

Raffi nodded. "Good. Very good." She motioned toward the house. "Will you come in? I was just about to make lunch."

The detective shook her head. "I'm on the clock," she said with obvious regret. Raffi knew her cooking was legendary.

Raffi gestured Gambol in for a hug, and the women embraced. "I hope Mr. McBride gets the justice he deserves," Raffi said as they drew apart.

The detective raised an eyebrow and tossed her braid like a whip. "I'm pretty sure he just did."

BEFORE SHE WENT BACK into the house, Raffi stood under the lintel and its motto, *flocci non facio*, trying to slow her breathing. She'd once heard it said, *Revenge is a dish best served cold.* The saying had consoled her when she was weak—before she became the Godmother. It was not that she had let herself get walked on, she told herself, she was just waiting for her anger to *cool.* But, by the time it had, she ended up doing nothing. The revenge saying was a deterrent in disguise; the subversive message was, revenge was a dish best served not at all.

Now she couldn't get enough of it. And when women like Marina Ramón came seeking retribution, it thrilled Raffi to listen to the harms done them—because it meant a great big revenge binge was nigh.

She was not proud of this. She was not ashamed of it, either. Her old therapist had called her an "exploding doormat" and said, when Raffi eventually blew, there would be a mile-high mushroom cloud. Her old therapist had been right, except the mushroom cloud had no upper limit.

Her breathing controlled, she pushed through the front door, closed it behind her, and exhaled so long she felt shorter afterward. Pulling her phone from her back pocket, she dialed the person she had called every day for the past decade: her mother. The phone rang five times. Voicemail. A couple years back, the greeting had changed from her mother's strong pre-illness alto to a prim, canned message, *The party you are trying to reach is unable to take your call.* Sometimes the phone rang three times instead of five or the voicemail kicked in right away. There was no meaning in any of it.

She shucked off her slides, left the herbs in the kitchen for Trini to handle, and headed down the hallway to her office. The room was only slightly less dark when she'd turned on the stained-glass lamps and the torchiere, so she lit some candles and sat in the wooden chair facing the bridal portrait. She needed Polly.

Raffi cleared her throat, ran one hand through her hair, and leaned toward the portrait. "Ma," she said.

The bride smiled with encouragement.

"Staiu ennu 'n Sicilia."

Speak English, Raffaella. You know I hate that language.

Raffi sighed. "I'm going to Sicily."

The portrait considered this with far more patience than would the actual Polly, who had conducted most conversations on her hands and knees while cleaning between the vents with Q-tips or from the top of a ladder polishing the brass chandelier. "Get to the point, Raffaella." That's what her real mother would say.

Why would you want to go there?

Raffi stood and paced; Piccolo, hearing her movements, came running, claws clattering on the hardwood floor, and sat at attention.

Is it because you want to find out just how phony you are?

Polly had always despised phonies. She had also hated politicians, teachers, money, salespeople, institutions generally, the Catholic church specifically, and, above all, anything to do with Sicily.

Raffi chuckled. Her mother's sharp tongue was as reliable as the seasons. It was the absence of Polly that hurt, not her vitriol. Vitriol was the seam beneath Polly's affection. Worse than her opprobrium was her silence, which meant she did not care. As long as the bride lashed out, she still loved.

"I don't need to go anywhere to figure out I'm a phony," said Raffi.

The bride was one of the few people in the world who knew Raffi's secret: that the Godmother was an invention. Raffi and Mary Fortune had dreamed up the whole persona on Mary's green velour couch one Tuesday afternoon.

"They think I'm a criminal, Mary," Raffi had lamented that fateful day, her head on Mary's lap, messy curls spilling over Mary's bejeweled hands and the well-worn cushions. Polly had long since disappeared, and Mary had fast become the closest Raffi had—besides Trini—to a mother. "You should see the way people look at me. The mothers at Brando's school accept our playdates because they're afraid I'll put a hit on them if they don't. All because my name is Truvarizzi!"

"So, your last name is Truvarizzi," had come Mary's reply. "Plenty of people share a surname. Do you know how many Ibarras there are? What does it even prove?"

Raffi had run through the explanation. Hers was one of a handful of family names the Italian government had assigned to orphans before the nineteenth century. Truvarizzi came from the Sicilian variation of the Italian verb *trovare*, to find. In essence, the name meant "foundling." In Southern Italy, land of passion and poverty—and popes—orphans had proliferated like recipes for sauce, their devout Catholic parents reluctant to claim them. There had once been many Truvarizzis.

Then, Raffi told Mary, at the turn of the twentieth century, along came Salvatore Truvarizzi, Senior: *Il Erudito*, "the Scholar," a Mafioso so clever, he was responsible for more deaths than any Don in history despite never personally killing a soul. This *Il Erudito* had a son: Sally Truvarizzi, Junior. "Sally T."

It was a cheerful name for a man who stuffed his nemesis into a commercial blender and used the product to fertilize his garden. Sally T was no scholar, but his organization was the stuff of genius. He ran a sophisticated criminal empire that spanned Europe and America for decades, and the authorities never came close to finding him. Dead or alive, he was history's most virulent ghost.

The Truvarizzis disappeared. The family name had always signified a chain broken, a child discarded, so perhaps its holders did not find it difficult to abandon the name in turn. The only Truvarizzis Raffi had tracked down were one Gilda Truvarizzi, a crone ensconced atop the chaparral outside Corleone, and Tonio Truvarizzi of Calabria, a widowed shoemaker. There were no Truvarizzis in America. As far as Raffi knew, she and her parents rounded out the tally of Truvarizzis in the world—unless Sally T was alive, a thought she preferred not to consider.

Mary had absorbed all this information in silence, eyelids closed and fluttering, a shit tzu at her feet sighing with the tempo of its owner's breath, up and down, until Mary's eyes opened. She had transformed into Mary of the Schemes: the most potent Mary of all.

"And you don't know your true connection to this Sally T?" Raffi had shaken her head. "I gave up asking."

"But fear, even unjustified fear, can be useful," Mary had said, stroking her chin as if just now formulating a plan, though everything Mary Fortune did was premeditated. "Fear has built empires, Little Girl! You can use it to build yours." Her eyes were like those of the saints cluttering her walls: febrile, aflame. "Fear and money, that is—and you've got both."

The divorce from Brando's father had been the initial source of Raffi's wealth. According to Mary, however, the *true* source was the astrological strategy Mary devised and Raffi followed: no settlement communications during Mercury retrograde; all motions filed with Mars ascendant; *nothing* on the full moon, just disappear into a hole if you can, and wait at least two days to resurface.

In the end, Raffi had emerged with enough money to buy a stake in the Baldessari investment group run by her old friend Philly, until Raffi learned she had a knack for reading the markets herself. Her net worth would exceed even that of her robber-baron ex-husband. This satisfied her.

But money, while useful and even pleasurable, did not *mean* anything to Raffi. Other than her son and her portfolio, she felt she had nothing significant to show for her life—until she was given a second gift from Mary Fortune, who had found a use for it all: the money, the dreaded surname, the lost woman to whom they belonged.

The Corrado interview had been the Godmother's grand entrance. Rhona was one of Mary's clients; a prod from Mary, and the interview was set, no questions asked. *You've heard of Raffaella Truvarizzi?* Mary had asked the then-fledgling reporter. *No? Well, everyone's about to. And* you'll *be the one to tell them.*

"I need a break," Raffi said to the portrait. "I've always been curious about Sicily. I know you think it's a cesspool, Ma, but it's in our veins."

The portrait looked unconvinced.

Raffi sighed. "It could also be interesting to see if any...relatives present themselves."

You're not on about him *again, are you?*

"I'm interested to know who shares my blood," Raffi said, defiant. It was frustrating to always be on the defense with your mother, even when she was just a picture. "Dad either doesn't know the truth or won't tell me. And, of course, *you* never cared." She shook her head. "You can't understand. You're an Angelini. Even your name sounds innocent."

In truth, Raffi had never understood why her parents kept the name Truvarizzi. One day, in her fragrant backyard in Skaneateles, New York, twelve-year-old Raffi had cornered her father Nino and demanded he tell her *why*. Why not change it? Why leave them with this *mark*? All he had said in response, her usually calm and gentle father, in an odd tone, high and tight, neither calm nor gentle, his Sicilian stilted, was, "*This* is our name, Raffaella. We have no choice."

But why would you go to Sicily with this girl? It would make more sense to take Trini.

Raffi blinked away her memories. "I need Trini to keep things running at home."

Brando, then.

"He has lacrosse camp. You know how he is about that."

Go by yourself.

Raffi tried to quell her exasperation. "I think I owe this, at least, to Mary. Isabel is her niece. She seems passionate about this. I can oblige her and serve my own interests as well. And it would please me to travel as a tourist for a change."

Portrait Polly looked bored.

You don't have time for pleasure trips. You're the Godmother.

Raffi got the sense the portrait bride would prefer that Raffi became the Mafiosa she had been pretending to be this past decade. Joining the Mafia, however, was the last thing Raffi would ever do. She was tired of Sicilian criminals. All her life, she'd been accused of being one.

Raffi wasn't alone in being suspected, either. Hers was an extreme case, but you didn't have to be named Truvarizzi to be accused of Mafia connections in America. You only had to be Sicilian American.

No, Raffi had not wanted to feed the American Mafia machine, which was insatiable. Quite the opposite. She had adopted the veneer because *The Godmother* allowed her to protect women who were otherwise undefended—as she was once and would never be again.

But she was lying to herself. She'd had selfish reasons, too. It felt good to wield power. As time went on, she had grown to enjoy it more and more, had expanded into these names—both the Godmother and Truvarizzi—until the barbed armor she hid behind fit. She was not weak anymore.

So, what about him?

Raffi pulled her chair closer to the desk and examined the bride's face.

"He might not be alive."

And if he is?

Raffi did not answer.

You might as well find him, Raffaella. Look in caves and crags. Where the insects hide.

"And then?"

And then ask him who the hell he is to you.

Raffi pushed back the chair and dismissed the portrait with a wave.

"You suggest I show up in Sicily with a twenty-year-old psychic, sniff out Sally Truvarizzi, the deadliest mobster in memory, who, assuming he's alive, hasn't been seen in years, and say, 'Sorry I've been pretending to be related to you, but, hey, incidentally: am I?'"

Other than the psychic and the apology? That's what I would do.

⨁

RAFFI LAY ON HER bed with a cool cloth over her forehead, the Georgian blue walls soothing the dull ache that had begun after her talk with the bride. She had set up a chess board on the shagreen bedside table and was halfway through a game against herself. She liked to play both sides.

After a while, she heard Trini come home, and the tenor of the door-slam told Raffi the meeting with Paz had not gone well. A slam itself did not harbinger bad news; the only way Trini closed a door was to slam it. *This* slam was punctuated by Trini's shoes firing like missiles into the wall. Raffi hoped they hadn't hit a painting.

"Trini!" she called, but her purple-haired general was already in the doorway, Trini's tanned face flushed and her eyes livid.

"What's that in your hand?" asked Raffi.

Trini peered down at the plastic bag clutched tight in her palm. "Red hair dye."

Raffi pressed on her temples where a migraine was forming. "Uh-oh."

"Good match," said Trini, jerking her head toward the chess board. She sprang to the bedside table, clicked her tongue, and killed the black rook with a white knight. Raffi groaned.

"So, Judge Paz won't play nice?" asked Raffi.

Trini did a salsa sideways. "Ho! She got a problem, Mama. She thinks she a *reina*, like she don't owe nobody nothing." Trini threw back her shoulders and tossed her head in an exaggerated imitation of the judge. "Now she's an *officer of the court*. She can't do *undue influence on a colleague*." Trini's was a chosen patois. When she wanted to, she could put the Queen's English to the test. As usual, her American accent was as contemptuous as it was flawless.

Raffi closed her eyes. Normally, she would be all over this, savoring it, working with Trini on the payback. But the conversation with her mother's portrait had drained her. Her eyes opened.

"I'll want to think on this one, Trini. I'm going to Sicily in a few days—"

Trini put up her hand. "*Sicily?*"

"With Isabel Ibarra."

Trini looked worried. "She's blackmailing you?"

Raffi laughed. "She asked me to go with her. Mary would want me to. And...I need a break."

Trini stared at her.

"A vacation," Raffi said.

"Huh," said Trini, furrowing her brow, as if Raffi had introduced a new concept. "Well, *mira*: you don't ask no questions. You just look around, relax." She shaded her eyes with one hand and scanned the room like a spectator checking the crowd at a baseball game. "Watch and listen, Mama. Don't get crazy." She was trying to sound blasé, but Raffi heard her alarm. Raffi had not expected such an acute reaction, but Trini was a woman of extremes—a feature of her Calabrese side.

"Don't worry. I'm not on some genealogical mission," Raffi said, rejecting the notion raised by the portrait. "You know I haven't taken time off in ten years?"

Trini nodded. She knew.

Raffi cleared her throat. "So. The judge?"

"She need to be *corrected*. You don't wanna send the message Celia Paz can get away with this."

Raffi slid her hands around to her thick brows and pressed the heels of her palms to the brow ridge. The headache was migrating. "What do you have in mind?"

Trini made a wicked face. "She love that agave farm in Mexico, Mama."

"As tempted as I am to commit my first act of agricultural terrorism: no. Destroying the farm would hurt her family, too. This one's just for her."

Trini looked disappointed. "Think, then, Mama. You know Celia Paz."

Despite the pounding in her head, Raffi willed the ideas to come. Rotate, click, rotate, click. The Godmother brain never failed her.

"Paz didn't recuse herself from that rape case where the defense lawyer was her secret ex-lover," Raffi said. Her hands slid down from her brow to form a seat for her chin, her headache forgotten. "Paz let the trial go all the way to verdict and then suspended the sentence without disclosing that relationship."

Trini nodded. Her eyes had a nuclear glow. "Is *perfecto*, Mama. If there's one thing the judge don't like, it's *the appearance of impropriety*."

10

No one at Miami International Airport could miss Isabel Ibarra. The girl wore French fuchsia sweats and a hopeful expression that was almost heartbreaking, shiny yellow spinner suitcases at each flank. The unmarked plastic shone with the brand-new gleam of an unseasoned traveler.

"She look like a neon ham sandwich," said Trini, slamming to a stop at the curb. She hopped out and hauled Raffi's bags out of the trunk. "Enjoy your trip, Mama." She embraced her boss. "I'll be busy while you're gone."

"U.M.?"

Trini moonlighted as a translator for the University of Miami.

"*Si*, Mama. A book called *The 1960s*." She wrinkled her nose. "Bad years for me. My mother give me a mop top."

From the look on Trini's face, Raffi opted not to ask what a "mop top" was. "Keep me informed. Look out for Brando," said Raffi.

"*Di certo*, Mamma. Of course." Trini's father had taught her Italian. When the mood struck her, she traded Puerto Rico for the boot. "Well. Have fun," she said with a wicked grin. She jumped into the SUV and pulled into traffic, offering a middle finger in the general direction of her fellow drivers.

"Good morning, Godmother!" Isabel shouted between cupped hands.

The girl was the opposite of discreet.

Behind her sunglasses, Raffi made her habitual scan for feds and journalists. A little boy watched her over the top of his hand-held video-game device; otherwise, no one seemed to pay them any mind. It was a matter of time.

Isabel pulled out her ticket and motioned toward a porter. "Should we?"

Raffi gave a brisk shake of her head and pushed away Isabel's ticket. "You have a new ticket."

The girl looked as amazed as if Raffi had just announced they were traveling by Zeppelin. "I *do?*"

"I took over the flight arrangements."

Isabel had insisted on planning the trip, and Raffi had allowed it. But the Godmother drew the line at flying coach.

Raffi waved over the porter, and the man took her ID but could not tear his eyes from Raffi's face to look down at it. After a few long moments, he took Isabel's ID, too, and rushed off to check them in.

"Here you go, Ms. Ibarra, Ms. *Truvarizzi,*" he said when he returned with a cart for their luggage. "I hope you enjoy your flight to Sicily."

Raffi gave the man a twenty and set off, Isabel rushing after. Over her shoulder, Isabel shouted, "*We will!*"

Entering the airport, Raffi made straight for the priority line.

"Why don't we have to wait in the long one?" asked Isabel.

"Because of our new tickets," said Raffi.

"Like," Isabel lowered her voice, "VIP?"

This was going to be a long day-and-a-half.

"Why do we get to sit in this lounge?" the girl asked after they had presented their passports—*My first passport! The pages are still hot!* —cleared security—*Hands up or hands out? Hands up? How high?* —and entered the premium lounge.

"Our tickets," Raffi said without looking up from a travel magazine she'd found on a rack by the entrance. She signaled a passing waiter for a glass of champagne. Raffi was an anxious flier. Champagne calmed her nerves.

Isabel nodded, eyes wide, and skipped off to the complimentary buffet. She spent ten full minutes discussing the food with the long-suffering woman behind the counter, returning with a smorgasbord of incongruous food: spicy Korean beef, two sliders, an array of brie and crackers, a waffle, and a chocolate chip cookie. "This is totally—" she gave Raffi a meaningful look, "—VIP."

If Isabel's mind was not blown already, it hit the stratosphere at the gate when Raffi and she sailed past the long line of grumbling passengers to board with Group One. "We get to *cut*?"

Raffi thought of Mary and prayed for patience. "Yes."

"Oh, *right*—"

"Don't say it," said Raffi.

The plane was a wide-body aircraft with a strong safety record; Raffi had checked. But as they inched forward in the long "VIP" line—everyone was in Group One these days—Raffi's heartrate accelerated with each step.

When Mary was alive, Raffi had gone to her for pre-flight amulets of graveyard dirt and herbs to keep the pilots sharp and the airwaves smooth. With Mary's death, this was Raffi's first time flying "unprotected" in ten years.

She was three passengers from the front, overcome by a grim fantasy of the hungry Atlantic devouring the plane like an angry sea god, when she realized there was a hold-up in the line. The hubbub was coming from a table set up before the jet bridge, where two women in TSA uniforms were conducting searches of carry-on bags selected at random. From what Raffi could observe, these bag checks involved raking long nails through the selected passengers' belongings: crumpling folded clothes, exposing private things like disposable butt wipes and vibrators, and booting up laptops. As Raffi and Isabel reached the front, one such chosen passenger, a handsome silver-haired man with designer everything, was pitching a fit about his exorbitant roller bag.

"Your fingers are nicking the leather!" he yelled in a panicked voice, as if he'd just woken up from surgery and found the wrong leg amputated.

While the man carried on about all the confidential information on his laptop—you don't have actual confidential information on your laptop if you're screaming about it in an airport, thought Raffi—a different man stepped out from the side and placed a hand on her arm. He was dressed in a hideous olive-green de-signer-knockoff suit, and his sandy hair was clipped into a failed Julius Caesar.

"If you'll come with us, ma'am," he said with a southern accent. Behind the man, two uniformed officers stood with arms folded.

Here we go. "Of course." Isabel clutched at Raffi's arm, but Raffi shrugged her off. "This is normal," she said, as if every international flight was kicked off by a random man pulling her out of line—which, oftentimes, it was.

Isabel seemed unconvinced. "It is?"

"Absolutely," said Raffi. "Just part of the VIP experience," she said, and winked. She did not want the girl to worry any more than her temperament already dictated.

"I'll see you on the plane?"

The girl looked so desperate.

"You will," said Raffi.

Isabel grimaced and stepped toward the TSA ladies and their eager talons, as the man in the green suit led Raffi away, followed by the two officers. "Do you want to search my bag?" Raffi heard Isabel ask one of the TSA ladies, and, despite the tense circumstances, Raffi couldn't help but chuckle at the girl's audible disappointment when they told her no.

"I'M SITTING *HERE*?" ISABEL squealed when the flight attendant directed her, not right toward Coach, but left toward First. The shock of her good fortune distracted her from Raffi's abrupt disappearance. That, and the smell of warm nuts roasting in the galley oven.

The flight attendant smiled. "First row, 1D, left center. It's all yours," she said in a type of friendly voice Isabel had never heard before—the kind you hear when you've spent a *lot* of money.

When she reached the first row, Isabel was staggered to find that her seat was more like a miniature room, complete with television, table, blanket, and what looked like a makeup bag placed on her seat. She whistled and placed her new yellow carry-on in the overhead compartment, looking around to see if anyone was noticing how *VIP* she was.

Nope. The other passengers seemed unimpressed. One row behind her, the silver-haired man with the precious leather roller bag and confidential information was already asleep.

Tossing her silver tote into the space below the monitor, she grabbed the makeup bag and dropped into her seat to explore further. In a small cubby to her right, she found a pair of *headphones*. She wondered if she could take them with her later, but she didn't want to do anything out of order, so she pressed the button with the outline of the flight attendant on it and a bell chimed.

"Yes?" said the same flight attendant, returning with the same obsequious smile.

Isabel lowered her voice and gave the woman a meaningful glance. "Can we take these with us?" she asked, tilting her head at the headphones.

The woman smiled a different smile now, the kind you give a small child who has drawn a rudimentary house with four stick figures in front. "No, unfortunately. Those have to stay on the plane."

"Oh," said Isabel.

"You can keep this, though."

The flight attendant reached across Isabel, releasing a strong scent of vanilla from her perfume or deodorant or body soap, and plucked up the makeup bag. Unzipping it, the woman held the bag open for Isabel to observe its contents.

"Toothbrush, toothpaste, sleep mask, body lotion, soap, socks. I'n't that *nice?*"

Isabel looked up at her, assessing the accent. "Tennessee?"

The flight attendant flushed. "Nashville."

"When's your birthday?"

"November 27," she said. "Sagittarius."

"Hmm...," Isabel said. "You love freedom."

"That's why I'm a flight attendant."

Isabel nodded. "So let me ask you something."

"Sure."

"Can I get, like, a burger on this thing?"

The flight attendant laughed. "You'll get dinner."

Isabel fell into an awed silence. The flight attendant glanced behind her at the silver-haired man, who had woken up and was making the universal bring-me-a-drink signal with his right hand.

"I'll be back, hon. May I bring you a glass of champagne?"

Isabel leaned in.

"May you bring me two?"

"So, you're going to Sicily," said the man in the green suit.

"How'd you figure it out?" said Raffi.

After a long, silent walk down a warren of corridors, they sat, in a small interview room with dirty gray walls and fluorescent lights, around a metal table that looked straight out of a morgue. Raffi sat on one side of the table, the green-suit—presumably an FBI agent, thirty-something years old, with pockmarked skin—on the other. The uniforms stood by the door.

The agent fixed her with an intense stare that lasted so long, she made a show of checking her watch.

"You're pretty glib for a woman whose *friend* just died," he drawled.

Raffi restrained her reaction, which was sharp and visceral. *What friend?*

"What friend?" She echoed aloud. Did he mean Mary?

"Judge Paz. It's just breaking on the news." He studied Raffi's face. "It was a *lupara bianca.*"

Raffi sat back hard in her chair. She was shocked, and she let it show.

"She's *dead?*" Raffi said, struggling to believe it. *Dead?* The judge must have been mixed up with some bad characters. "She was supposed to come to my son's graduation party last Saturday, but she was stuck in church." Raffi pressed her hands together and raised them to her mouth. Now that the news had settled in, she had to feign further dismay. In the immediate aftermath of learning someone has died, one tends to feel bad. It takes a beat to remember what an asshole that dead person was. "I'm just horrified. She was a wonderful woman."

The agent sneered. "I'm sure you loved her very much."

He pushed his chair back, the legs screeching against the floor. His walk, as he approached Raffi, swung hip-to-hip, like a cowboy. The green-suit was a Texan, she guessed. Planting one fist just to the left of where she sat, he leaned down to look her in the eye. Now she *knew* he was a Texan.

"You didn't ask about the *lupara bianca.*"

Raffi waved her hand in front of her face with a delicate expression.

"Did someone have onions at lunch?"

"I'm serious, Truvarizzi. You still have time to turn it around. Tell us what you know." Beneath his horrible haircut, the Texan's ears twitched. "Give him up!"

"I don't know who *'him'* is, but I hope the FBI will reimburse me for my flight if I miss it. I paid full price." She leaned over. "I need the frequent flier miles."

"I'll ask you again. What do you know?"

"Nothing." She changed tacks. "How did she die? If you don't mind my asking."

"We think someone ran her car off the road. It was found abandoned off Dixie Highway near her house in the Gables—right around the corner from a *construction site*."

Raffi's brows knit together in exaggerated confusion, below which: a well of relief. The Texan had nothing.

"I thought you said she was dead?"

"She's obviously dead." He pulled up his fist and shifted on his feet. "We just haven't found the body."

"Bless you heart!" Raffi said, laughing as she stole the South's favorite put-down. "Don't you know about *corpus delicti*?"

He stalled, running a quick mental search. "That near San Antonio?"

"Not exactly," said Raffi. "*Corpus delicti* means you need proof of a crime to prosecute one. A body is always helpful. You could also do well with blood, or scratches on the interior door, or a scrape of paint from the car you *think* ran her off Dixie. Come across anything like that?"

The Texan was silent.

"Have you *heard* of evidence?"

"I know you know something."

They fell silent, the Texan staring at Raffi as she studied a hangnail on her pinkie. "I'm sorry. Are you waiting on me?" she said at last.

"I'm warning you."

"Warn me all you want," she said, turning the full power of her amber eyes on him. "But from what you've said, Judge Paz may have been kidnapped by construction workers. There's no *lupara bianca*. This isn't a movie."

The Texan slammed his hand down on the table. "God damn it!"

"I'd prefer you not speak that way in my presence," Raffi said, crossing herself. To the uniforms by the door, she said, with a sweet mile, "I was raised Catholic."

They smiled back.

The Texan stalked into the corner, hands in his horrible hair.

"Are you going to Sicily to meet with your boss, Sally Truvarizzi?" He said to the wall. "Otherwise known as Sally T?" He turned back around.

"No, I have to swing by the North Pole and pay a visit to Santa Claus. Otherwise known as Saint Nick." She hesitated, pretending to think. "Did you get clearance from the agent in charge of my file to question me today?"

All three men looked in different directions.

"Right. I'm free to leave, then. I do hope you catch whoever disappeared Judge Paz from her car. I suggest you start with the cartels: Mexican, Colombian. Then maybe the Russians? Just brainstorming."

"Get her out of here," said the Texan.

"What's a *lupara bianca*?" said one of the officers as he escorted her out.

"It's a Sicilian way of killing where the body's never found," Raffi said before the door closed behind her, though her breezy demeanor evaporated as she hurried back to the gate.

What on Earth had happened to Celia Paz?

"You're here!" squealed Isabel as Raffi came up the opposite aisle. Their tickets were for two adjoining seats with a retractable divider in between. "I thought you wouldn't make it!" She lowered her voice. "What did that weird guy want?"

"Stock tips," said Raffi. She threw her bag in the overhead bin, slammed it shut, and slid into her seat. The interaction had left her sapped.

At that moment, there was one person in the world Raffi wanted to talk to, and that was Trini. Trini was her pillar. Trini was the only one Raffi could trust. Trini was, at that same moment, probably hard at work translating a passage about the poetry of Bob Dylan.

Judge Paz *dead*? Raffi was even more worried for Trini than herself; Trini had recently fought with the woman in public, a café full of diners looking on.

But Raffi could not call Trini now. It wasn't safe. What mattered now was not what she had done—which was nothing—but what law enforcement *thought* she had done, and how she acted now she knew she was a suspect.

"Is there a flight attendant around?" Raffi said.

"We have an *awesome* flight attendant," said Isabel. "Her name is Shawna. She's from Tennessee. She's a *Sagittarius,* like you—"

"Hold on." Raffi rubbed her forehead. "I need a minute."

Isabel touched her own forehead in the same place. "Someone was hurt. That man thinks you did it."

This was like spending time around Mary Fortune.

Again, Raffi thought with dismay. *Again,* someone in her way had come to harm, and as troglodyte-dumb as the Texan was, he was not off base in thinking Paz's disappearance sounded like a *lupara bianca.*

The synchronicity—Paz's refusal to help, her subsequent disappearance—was one Raffi had experienced before. The film producer who harassed one of Raffi's girls, threatening to ruin her career if she refused to *please* him? His car was found at the bottom of Mulholland Drive: empty. The Miami drug dealer who kicked his wife and kids every time he sampled his wares? He got off easy. No disappearance, he just woke up one morning with no feet. The Senator who tried to form a committee to investigate her criminal connections? Fell off a boat in the Caribbean; when they found his body, the toxicology report showed enough heroin to kill a horse.

It was the stuff of murder ballads. Mary, when she was alive, attributed these well-timed accidents to the mysterious plans of the Universe. The mysterious plans of the Universe were Mary's default explanation for anything she had not seen in the stars.

Right now, Raffi wanted Trini, but if she couldn't have Trini, she would have a drink.

"Excuse me," said Raffi, holding out her arm as the flight attendant passed.

The woman stopped at their aisle and turned off the call button. "Oh, wonderful!" she said. She smiled at Isabel. "Your mom finally made it."

It took Raffi a moment to realize she was the mom. "May I have a glass of champagne?"

"Oh, I'm sorry," the flight attendant said. "Unfortunately, we can't serve drinks now until we're airborne. The captain is getting ready to push back from the gate."

"I understand," said Raffi. She held the woman's eyes. "Bring me a glass of champagne."

The flight attendant looked startled. Then she seemed to remember the name of the passenger in seat 1D and her fair skin flushed. "Of course, Ms. Truvarizzi. Right away."

THEY HAD BEEN IN the air for an hour and Raffi was on her third melatonin. She needed sleep to keep sharp, but sleep was hard to accomplish with Isabel Ibarra seated next to her.

First, Isabel had engaged in an exploration of the retractable seat divider, raising it all the way, lowering it and propping her chin on the plastic, then drawing it all the way down and reaching a hand over to slap Raffi playfully on the arm. She was drunk. Raffi blamed *Shawna*.

Then the girl pulled a travel-sized game of Trivial Pursuit out of her silver makeup tote bag—a gift with purchase, Raffi felt a twinge of pity—and started setting it up. Raffi assumed the girl was going to play against herself, as Raffi did with chess, when the girl asked, "Do you want to be pink or green?"

"Neither."

Isabel shrugged and turned over a card, reading aloud: "Which Greek philosopher taught his pupils by posing a series of questions?" She paused. "*Ay*, I don't know. Rumi?"

Raffi took another melatonin.

And then Isabel pulled out her last trick. She reached into the silver tote and extracted a tarot deck. As Raffi looked on with growing dread, Isabel fanned out the cards and looked at Raffi as if expecting a reaction. Behind an arc of tarot cards, the girl looked more poised than Raffi had yet seen her.

"This will help you relax," said Isabel.

Raffi raised an eyebrow. "I'm already relaxed."

Isabel nodded, undeterred.

"I want you to think of today," said the girl, "and the journey we're about to take."

Raffi thought instead of the word *rompiscatole*: Sicilian for 'pain in the ass.' "I thought your Aunt Mary didn't approve of tarot."

Isabel looked dismayed to be reminded of this unhappy fact. "She didn't. She said tarot is witchcraft and astrology is science."

"That's a bit hypocritical. What was all that graveyard dirt and crow's blood, if not witchcraft? Or was that science too?"

Isabel shifted in her seat as if weighing whether to reveal something. After a brief struggle, she spoke.

"My *Bisabuela* Isabel was accused of witchcraft back in Cuba."

Now the girl had Raffi's attention. Mary had never said anything about problems with witchcraft in Cuba. Come to think of it, when it came to her personal life, Mary Fortune had revealed little.

"I love tarot," Isabel continued. "It speaks to me. And reading *caracoles*—seashells—I'm good at that too. I also get those radio signals," she smiled, touching her head, "and sometimes my dreams come true—like, literally. But Mary didn't like those things after a while. When I was younger, she thought they were adorable, but as I got older, she almost seemed scared of what I could do. She pushed me toward astrology."

"You should do what you want," said Raffi. "Your Aunt Mary would want you to be happy."

The girl shook her head. "Not if it meant doing witchcraft." She began gathering up the cards.

Raffi put one hand over Isabel's. "Don't." She fanned the cards back out and was pleased when the girl's expression brightened. Raffi plucked the card on top, and Isabel turned it over. The Eight of Cups.

"I'll choose another one. The number cards bore me," said Raffi. With Isabel's disapproving frown, she almost resembled Mary.

"The Eight of Cups," Isabel said, ignoring the comment. She regarded the card for a long moment, then raised her eyes to Raffi with a gaze clear and direct. "What are you ready to leave behind?"

Raffi shook her head. She realized then that she'd been hopeful the cards would tell her something. God, she missed Mary. Mary traded in answers, not questions. "That won't work on me, Isabel."

The girl cocked her head; her lips began moving as if she were counting figures. Raffi watched, amused. Appearing to complete her internal calculation, the girl said: "What are you afraid of?"

Isabel Ibarra did not give up easily.

"Fear is an indulgence," said Raffi. She had learned to keep it out at all costs—otherwise, like a deadly traveling salesman, it would extract its own price.

The girl appeared to consider this. "But you do feel fear," she ventured.

Raffi felt she had been polite enough. "Are we done now?" The first-wave melatonin was kicking in.

"No," said Isabel. "You need to pull two more cards. Then you can sleep."

Again, Raffi sensed Isabel imitating her aunt. Mary was bossy. Her clients might have held the purse strings, but she had always made it clear: she was in charge.

Raffi thumbed two consecutive cards and tossed them onto Isabel's tray. "There."

The Wheel and the World. Raffi was pleased. She liked the picture cards.

"The World means complete integration," said the girl with relief. "Something you have long worked for—or hoped for—will come to fruition. It's literally an *amazing* card." She paused. "Does this make sense?"

"No," said Raffi. It did not make sense because it was a card pulled at random from a deck.

Isabel seemed to consider posing a follow-up question, then shrugged and turned to the other card. "Now, the Wheel is easy. That signifies *you*. It's your symbol." At Raffi's blank stare, Isabel added: "It's confirmation that the reading is for you. Though it can also indicate a reversal of fortune, so maybe, like, prepare for the unexpected."

Raffi removed the eye mask from her toiletries kit and slipped it over her forehead like silk ski goggles, not removing her fingers from the strap so she could be quick to pull it down. "Anything else?"

"No. You can sleep. Your future looks fine." Then Isabel looked down at the three cards and pushed at one, a frown crossing her face like a shadow.

Raffi caught the girl's expression and wondered, briefly, what the girl had seen. But she fell asleep before she could give it thought.

✦

RAFFI WOKE TO THE flight attendant's voice, saying, "We have now begun our initial descent into Palermo's Falcone Borsellino Airport. *Benvenuti in Sicilia.*"

She felt her stomach lurch. She had awakened, as she always did, in the body of Raffi Truvarizzi, and even after all these years, it took a moment to remember this was not who she was anymore. With conscious effort, she stoked the fire in her core: righteous anger. Then the sluice lifted, and in came the ice that traversed her veins: numbness and impenetrability. She coursed with contradictions until she burned with power. By sheer force of will, every day of her life, Raffi became the Godmother.

Now, under the oddest of circumstances, she had arrived in Sicily, though strange happenings had become commonplace since Raffi entered the world of Mary Fortune. She brought her chair upright and stared out the window at the rolling fields and terracotta rooftops of her ancestral island.

Her thoughts drifted back to Judge Paz, from Paz to Marina Ramòn, from Marina to all the women waiting for her to effect their rescue, but she pushed all this from her mind now. The Godmother's long list of obligations would be waiting when she returned. For this one week, Raffi Truvarizzi would take time for herself. If the mysteries of her heritage were hidden in this land, then perhaps she would encounter those, too. But, for the first time in a decade, she had no agenda. With every sense she had, she would feast on Sicily.

Sprawled out below her, closer by the minute, loomed this land that was and was not her home.

11

Before she opened her eyes, before the ritual of remembering herself, Raffi knew she wasn't in America. She could smell it in the brine of the air, feel it in the swish of the starched cotton sheets. Even the morning light was a different shade.

They had arrived the previous evening, fighting their luggage along the Via Castello Maniace, no porters in sight. Although the southeastern town of Ortygia was a lovely choice for their first destination, Isabel could not have charted a more arduous route. They should have flown into Catania, not Palermo. Instead, they spent nearly as much time on a series of regional buses as they had on the plane ride from Miami. At least, that's how it felt. The breaking point was the forty-five minutes they spent searching for their hotel on foot, Isabel's bags eloping down the uneven streets.

When at last they found it, the Hotel Ortygia was less opulent than what Raffi would have chosen. Underneath all the gilded accents and colorful ceramics, the lobby was close and quotidian. Among the many extravagances Raffi allowed herself, one was to lay her head on a pillow no less comfortable than her own, and to wake up in a space no less luxe than her bedroom. The Hotel Ortygia failed these tests.

And yet Raffi was taken with the small hotel, with its modest handful of rooms and nineteenth-century finishes: the geometric patterns of Arabic tiling on the cozy seven-foot ceiling, the russet sponge-paint covering the walls. The rooms were aesthetically appealing; someone had decided to make this an "art hotel." Behind the bed hung vibrant portraits of two women: one blonde, one brunette. Raffi imagined Isabel paging through traveler photos on Internet booking sites and selecting the Hotel Ortygia based on this apt detail.

Raffi's favorite part of the room was the balcony: tiny but charming—Was that not the realtors' euphemism for small? "Charming?"—with an unobstructed view of the opaque pre-dawn sea across the street. Stumbling outside with the first gleam of sunrise, Raffi sat on the wrought-iron chair, the cushion damp with early dew, metal cold against her legs. The Ionian Sea sparkled as if covered with a child's exuberant toss of glitter; its pungent scent puckered her nostrils. *I should have come to Sicily a long time ago,* Raffi mused. The closest she'd come was Positano on the Amalfi Coast. She could feel it in her bones: there was no parity between Sicily and anywhere else in the world.

Raffi's thoughts traveled a century back to her ancestors two hundred kilometers west in the hillside village of Lercara Friddi, none of whom would have set eyes on the bruised blue of this morning sea. Most would not have left Lercara their entire lives. Being here felt like a vindication for them.

With thoughts of family, her mind turned again—this time

to her father Nino, who had been weird when she'd called to ask for introductions to any Sicilian relatives. Of course, he reminded her, there were no Truvarizzis, and the Angelinis were all dead (including Polly, he did not say but implied). Only after she pressed him did he cough up two Sicilian cousins who might serve as hosts. One, Pasquale, was in Nino's maternal line, and the other, Donatella, was in Polly's. Raffi was surprised her Sicilian family was so sparse but, having always ignored Nino's musings about the Old Country, she had to take him at his word. The necessary calls were made. Raffi had not yet told Isabel about these familial detours. She made it a point to reveal information when necessary.

She watched a sleek gray yacht pass in the distance as two fishermen launched a battered skiff in the foreground. The juxtaposition seemed symbolic of an island caught between worlds.

She thought of Isabel, the girl slipping into her reverie like an intrusive thought. As a travel partner, the girl had proven both maddening and enchanting, with her ill-conceived plans and unnerving revelations. It was refreshing, though, to spend time with someone new. For the past decade, it had been the same major players every day; only the supplicants—her godchildren—rotated.

When Raffi could tear herself away from this view, she would dress in her usual white and join the girl for breakfast. At some point, when she felt like it, she would call Trini and check in about Celia Paz, whom she had reassured herself was of little concern. Raffi was innocent, and had the best attorney in Florida, Moll Portage, on her payroll. For now, she would dive into the pleasures of Sicily and leave the Godmother at home.

+

ONE ROOM DOWN, DAMP from the shower and preparing to dress, Isabel was remembering the Godmother's tarot reading on the plane the night before. Stuck to the bottom of The World had been a fourth card drawn accidentally, though there are no accidents in divination. It was a card of endless interpretation. It could mean danger, endings, shedding what no longer serves you. In many circumstances, its augury was positive—a scythe clearing the weeds to make space for new growth. Regardless, Mary had always been adamant: if you can avoid it, never tell them what you see when you pull this card.

Telling them invites it!

If only, Isabel posited, because most laypersons cannot see beyond fear to meaning.

The black rider, the pale horse, the eternal city.

Death.

✦

JUDGING BY THE FLAKY pastry debris on the tablecloth, Isabel was well into breakfast when Raffi reached the dining room. The girl had taken the chair facing the wall, leaving the red-velvet-up-holstered outward-facing banquette empty. It was a gesture of deference that was not lost on Raffi, who felt a surge of warmth at the sight of Isabel's back hunched over her plate, the girl's lilac eyelet blouse straining at the seams.

Raffi never sat with her back to the room.

The girl was doing battle with a cream-filled *bombolone* as Raffi approached.

"Good morning, Godmother," Isabel said, her voice muffled by the Italian doughnut, a hand shielding her mouth.

"Good morning," said Raffi. She pointed at the breakfast spread and continued past before the girl could swallow.

If the Hotel Ortygia was not extravagant, its breakfast was. Three tables smiled into the room like an upside-down rainbow. Upon this altar stood lemon-glazed pastries with cherry dots and loaves of bread shedding crust at the joints where slices were severed. Platters of cured meats dappled in all shades of red mixed with hard cheeses cut into triangles gathering beads of sweat and soft cheeses dolloped into dainty stainless-steel cups.

Presiding over this bounty was a woman in black pants and white button-down shirt, her hair the color of children's cough syrup.

"You like honey?" the woman called out like a carnival barker. Without waiting for a response, she lifted a jar with a honeycomb pattern etched into the glass. "This is the *millefiori* honey, the honey of a thousand flower." She took the grooved dipper from the jar and let the gold, silky fluid drip out, smiling, to Raffi's mind, suggestively. "We make nearby, in Val di Noto. You try."

Raffi held out her plate, and, in the time it would take to butter a slice of toast, the woman had filled it with cheeses, salami, and pastries. With surgical precision, she drizzled honey over the cheeses and salami—not the pastries—and left a lavish pool of *millefiori* in the center.

"For dipping," the woman said, curving and hooking her finger.

"*Grazie*," said Raffi, retreating to her banquette seat, thinking this would be the end of the interaction.

It was not.

"I am Agata," said the woman, pulling a chair to the table,

crossing her legs, and sitting back with arms folded behind her head. "You have been to Sicily before?"

Raffi picked up her utensils and made a show of cutting a wedge of perspiring cheese. "No," she said.

"First time going anywhere," said Isabel, pointing at her own head before slipping a honeyed fig filled with ricotta into her mouth.

Agata nodded, the picture of wisdom. "First time is the time you fall in love. You visit which town?"

Raffi looked at Isabel, the plan-maker, who held up her finger as she finished chewing.

"After Ortygia we move on to Taormina." Isabel spoke the name of each town in a Spanish accent and a loud voice, as if Agata were not Sicilian but deaf. "Lercara Friddi next, and, last, Palermo."

Raffi, in the middle of dipping a coin of blood-red sausage in the honey, paused with fork en route to mouth. She had not discussed Lercara Friddi with Isabel. She didn't know the girl even knew the name of the town. Raffi caught Isabel's eye and the girl smiled.

Agata, stroking her chin like an old man between cigar puffs, flicked Isabel on the shoulder.

"Eat the honey with the meat, like your friend," she commanded, then cocked her head as if deep in thought. "It's okay," she concluded, back to the topic of their travel plans. "You choose good places. Only—Lercara Friddi?" She made a rotten-egg face. "I choose for you Cefalù instead. You go there, not Lercara. If you must leave Ortygia at all."

Raffi speared another bite of sausage. "*Lercarese sugnu.*"

This statement—in Sicilian, not Italian—changed Agata's mien.

"Ah, you are *Lercarese*," said Agata. She sounded like she'd just discovered Raffi was armed. "And your name?"

Raffi was silent. Agata's voice sounded too casual, the question more than friendly.

"*Ma nannu era Lercarese*," said Agata, at Raffi's reticence. "We may be cousins."

Raffi was certain Agata's *nannu*—grandfather—was *not* from Lercara Friddi, and even more certain they were not cousins.

"Raffaella Truvarizzi," she said. She expected Agata's face to go grey at the name, but the woman did not react. "And this is Isabel Ibarra."

At the next table, a man in a fedora jumped up, knocking Isabel's chair leg, and rushed off without a backward glance. Raffi noted his average build and shabby shoes, scrambling for details the way one grasps at the license plate numbers on a stolen car. She had not seen the man sitting there. Usually, she saw everything.

"Eh, *viecchiu*! Ever heard of '*Mi scusassi?*'" Agata hollered after him in Sicilian. "Old men. So rude." She winked at Raffi. "*Allura. Ciau*, ladies, enjoy the honey."

She retreated to the kitchen.

"So," Raffi said, shaking off the encounter and turning to Isabel. "Lercara Friddi? Did the Ouija board tell you that?"

Isabel laughed. "I researched you online."

"And the Internet told you I arranged for us to visit my cousins?"

Head bowed—part-modest, part-mischievous—the girl said, "I might have used a *little* magic."

"I don't believe in magic," said Raffi. "I believe in instinct."

Isabel looked unconvinced. "You went to see my Aunt Mary for years. You must have believed in something."

Raffi paused to consider the girl's words. "I suppose I believed in your Aunt Mary."

Isabel rested chin on fist and regarded Raffi with what Raffi's *nonna* used to call "googly eyes"—the foolish facial expression of someone falling in love. "You're so reasonable," Isabel said.

Raffi did not feel reasonable. She felt lax for chatting the morning away with the girl and the red-haired waitress, oblivious to her surroundings. "Why do you say that?"

Isabel counted on her fingers. "You wear all white but don't worry about getting dirty, you never overreact, you think about what you say before you say it, which has never been a personal strength..."

"Wearing all white is my least reasonable quality," Raffi interjected.

"I'm not reasonable," continued Isabel, without regret. "Never was."

Raffi had an urge to hug the girl, with her cream-stained blouse and endearing humility. "I'll let you in on a secret," she said, forgetting Agata and the man, the banquette squeaking as she leaned forward. "I wasn't always this way." She was about to tell the girl that being reasonable was a choice, and to explain how she had pulled off this part of her transformation, but she stopped herself. That she had trusted Mary Fortune did not mean she should trust Mary's niece. She changed the subject to their plans for the day. "We should make sure to run them by Agata, too, for her approval," she said at full volume.

Across the room, the red-haired waitress, out of the kitchen and reading their lips, scowled.

Isabel giggled. "I'm just going to pop back to the buffet before we go," she said, rising. "I've never had honey like this before. I can't resist."

"Why should you resist?" Raffi raised her tanned arms, bare in the sleeveless sundress, and shook them. The soft skin that hung beneath the muscle jiggled. "I admire a woman of substance."

As the girl skipped off to the buffet, Raffi's playful demeanor evaporated. She turned to make eye contact with Agata. The woman held her gaze for a long beat before skulking back into the kitchen for good.

Let the message be clear: Raffi Truvarizzi did not get intimidated. It was the other way around.

12

"*O*rtygia, bedda Ortygia!*"

The captain, a swarthy young man named Enzo, gestured at the city with pride as his little red boat with matching red awning withdrew from the marina, slipping under an old stone bridge and tottering out to sea in the afternoon sun.

"*Talè quantu è bedda a città vecchia!*" called Enzo, thrusting his square chin at the Old City of Ortygia.

"What did he say?" Isabel whispered to Raffi. "Is that even Italian?"

"Sicilian," Raffi said with amusement as the girl, frantic, paged to the glossary at the back of her guidebook. "A strong dialect of Sicilian." Raffi put her hand over Isabel's; the frantic page-turning stopped. "You won't find Sicilian in here." Raffi pointed toward Enzo, then swept her hand to indicate the jagged Ortygia coastline and the whole of Sicily beyond. "You'll find it out there."

Isabel looked worried. "But what did he say?"

"He said, 'How beautiful is the Old City.'"

The girl brightened and turned to Enzo. "It is *so* beautiful!" Holding up her guidebook, she read, "'Ortygia has been the historical center of Syracuse since antiquity. From above, the island takes the shape of a hatchet, forming a line longer than it is wide, slicing into the Ionian.'" She lowered the guidebook. "Wow," she said to Enzo, whose smug nod implied he had built the city himself.

Raffi scanned the harbor, searching for threats. The only danger here was that of the froth-lapped rocks outside the city walls—rocks that had torn holes in the foreign armadas of antiquity.

This boat trip came courtesy of an emergency act of triage. The original plan, made by Isabel, was a group boat ride, the kind advertised in kiosks filled with pamphlets and attended by throngs of tourists, mostly Americans from the tri-state area.

"Not happening," Raffi had said, then laughed at Isabel's crestfallen face. Contrite, Raffi organized this private boat tour with Enzo, for which Isabel now shot Raffi grateful glances when his face was turned.

"The island of Ortygia," said Enzo, usurping Isabel's guidebook, "was create-a when the goddess Asteria change into a quail and throw herself into the water."

Steering the boat with one hand, he acted out this mythical creation story with the other: flapping one wing as Asteria-the-quail, making as if to fling his body leeward, vamping like an island-shaped woman, and looking, to a casual observer, like someone having a stroke.

"What an amazing story!" Isabel raved. "Miami, where we're from? Definitely not created by a goddess." She paused. "We had a female founder, though. Julia Tuttle. She was badass, if you like old White women."

Enzo shrugged. Raffi suspected he understood a quarter of

what the girl was saying. "We are lucky in Ortygia. We live in the place-a where the gods touch the land."

Isabel, stunned silent by the beauty of both harbor and guide, sat back, her blue eyes clear as Sicilian seawater.

The city behind them, Enzo steered the boat north up the coast toward a famous rock formation Isabel had found in her guidebook: one giant rock, one smaller, the two separated by a narrow isthmus.

"Is this the Two Brothers? The *Scoglio due Fratelli?*" Isabel asked, pointing ahead at two enormous rocks in the starboard distance. She opened her guidebook to Enzo's visible chagrin. Raffi imagined he did not appreciate having his monologue usurped. "'The larger, the mastodon, stands twelve meters high; the smaller rises to five.'"

Enzo sprang over and, with one hand on the wheel, pawed the guidebook closed.

"In Sicilian, we say, '*I Ru' Frati.*' No '*scoglio,*' no '*fratelli.*'" His standard-Italian pronunciation sounded as contemptuous as Trini's American accent.

Isabel looked dismayed. "I'm sorry, Enzo." She raised the guidebook. "They don't give us the Sicilian dialect in this."

"No dialect!" barked Enzo. "Is the Sicilian *language.*" Enzo's handsome brow, genial mere moments before, had dropped into a glower. The boiling point for Sicilian tempers was measured in seconds.

Enzo was right, Raffi explained, *sotto voce.* Sicilian was the oldest Italic language and the closest to Old Latin. Once a language of poets and kings, Sicilian in the modern era was often dismissed as a dialect. "It's not," said Raffi. "it's a language of itself, *within which* there are many dialects. Like Enzo's," Raffi said with a wink. The girl sniffled and smiled.

The young boat captain opened his mouth, poised to continue railing at the girl, when Raffi cut him off. Sicilian outrage aside, Raffi would not allow any incursion on Isabel.

"*Futtatini*," she said. *Take it easy.*

Enzo snapped to attention. *Futtatini* is not a word that shows up in guidebooks. "Ah, *sei Siciliana*," he said, his tone a shade less haughty. A Sicilian discovering another Sicilian was the ethnic equivalent of two soldiers revealing their swords.

"As I say," Enzo said, "in the Sicilian *language*," he shot Isabel a look, "we call-a the Two Brothers Rock '*I Ru' Frati*,' which mean the same thing. The rocks were formed from the legend all Syracusan know: two brothers sit in the ocean and talk forever across the sea."

They arrived at the rocks. The little red boat traced the long flank of the larger, seeking a rift in the bottom that concealed a secret cave. Or not so secret—as they approached, another boat emerged, their own boat's twin in blue, teeming with tourists who, from the sound of it, hailed from the exotic shores of Chicago.

"*Ciao*, Rodolfo!" Enzo yelled to the blue boat.

"*Ciao*, Enzo!" Rodolfo shouted back.

"That was supposed to be our tour," Isabel whispered to Raffi, eyebrows raised.

The little red boat slipped through the cleft and into the rock. As Enzo answered Isabel's questions and found excuses to touch her arm, the potent bouquet of the sea struck Raffi with the suggestion of life beneath. Raffi pictured a profusion of marine creatures: red crabs wielding asymmetrical claws; blinking starfish opening and closing like fists; stingrays and moray eels gliding among the Neptune grass.

"We have many octopus here," Enzo said, noticing the direction of Raffi's gaze as the boat reemerged from the rock into open water. "Yesterday, we find octopus with nine-a *tentacoli!*" He said, as if stating a fact: "This is a miracle."

Raffi remembered something Mary used to say. *Pay attention to numbers divisible by three.*

The little skiff cruised in silence and Raffi wondered if the girl was thinking of Mary's words too—until Isabel, who had leaned over to trail a hand through the water, cried out as Enzo wrenched her backward.

"*Pelagia noctiluca!*" He pointed at a translucent, iridescent, purple creature bobbing along on the surface.

Raffi peered. "Jellyfish?"

"*Si*," Enzo said, crossing himself, probably less for the dangerousness of the creature than for the litigiousness of American tourists. "In Sicily, we say: be careful the thing you see, and more careful the thing you don't."

If Raffi believed in messages from the Universe, this would have been a conspicuous one. Her commitment to reason over mysticism did not prevent her from feeling a chill. She was already wary of Sicilian shadows. She had been dodging one her entire life.

"*Allura*," Enzo trilled, breaking the spell. "As we come back to *la Città Vecchia*, I will tell the ancient battle with Giorgio of Carthage."

Isabel threw down her guidebook and went to stand next to Enzo, fingering his shirtsleeve and exclaiming as they cruised on. The flirtation was mutual.

Tilting her face to the sun, Raffi thought of Brando when he was a tiny boy just happy to receive his mother's love. Now her son was college-bound—not abandoning her but taking flight—and this was what any good parent wanted. But here came Isabel, who, despite her recent appearance in Raffi's life, seemed as happy to share Raffi's time as once had her son. It felt good to be wanted as a person, not as the Godmother.

Raffi remembered, too, her dynamic with Polly, whom Raffi had followed around like a little duckling. She still yearned for that maternal comfort, and in this yearning was the wheelworks that propelled her forward, the tickle beneath the itch that made her dial her mother's number every day and whisper to the bridal portrait when she felt lost.

Mary had understood it better than anyone: no matter how old a woman grew, how much power she amassed or wisdom she accumulated, how many rings on her trunk or lines in her face, she would never stop seeking her mother.

13

After the boat ride, Raffi and Isabel trolled the streets of Ortygia in search of Caffe Archimede, a *pasticceria* where the baker had invented a pastry that Captain Enzo described, pantomiming his own crucifixion, as divine.

Finding the bakery proved difficult. Isabel's mapping program lagged behind the twists of the labyrinthine streets. It seemed every time they followed one path the map re-routed them, sending them back to where they'd begun. Perhaps this was because Ortygia was an island within an island: all directions were correct. There was no wrong way, only different—and longer.

The townspeople seemed to understand this. Either that, or they just gave terrible directions.

"Caffe Archimede?" said a tiny old woman with a three-haired goatee, grasping their arms and squinting up at them as if she'd never heard of such a place. "Ah, *si!*" she cried. "*Prego.* Turn where the white shirt hangs from the clothesline, then go up two street to the Caffe Rosetti—but not the Ristorante Lampedusa, or you go too far—"

Isabel looked up from typing on her phone. "Turn right or left at the white shirt?"

The old woman smiled.

"You see the old man with the black dog?" said a silver-haired man who spoke English with an Irish accent. "Where the street bends like a broken elbow? Follow the elbow to Caffe Gioia, with the yellow umbrella. Go inside and ask for the owner, Angelo. He'll tell you where to go."

"Ah, Caffe Archimede," sniffed said Angelo. "Good pastry, but is *pasticceria—dolci*, no food. I bring you sandwich with the black pig prosciutto and some *vino bianco*. Then my daughter take you to Archimede for sweet."

Mollified by their patronage, Angelo assumed a grandfatherly air, installing himself at their table as Agata had in Ortygia. The black boar, he explained as they ate, came from his brother's farm outside the city.

"Taste, *signurini*, the acorn the black pig eats. My brother, he feed by hand from the little piglet until strong and big. Big, not fat—not like the American pig filled with hormone. *Risgrazia*," he said, flicking four fingers out from under his chin, an expressive Sicilian curse.

"He said 'disgrace,'" Raffi whispered to Isabel.

"That one I got," Isabel whispered back.

"The pig at my brother's farm," continued Angelo, "live in the countryside, sleep under shady trees. He hear the bird sing, feel the sun on his skin. You eat the happiness of the Sicilian pig." He pointed at the paper-thin sheets of cured pork and sat back with his hands on his belly, satisfied he'd conveyed how lucky Raffi and Isabel were to be eating this sandwich.

The prosciutto was a universe away from any Raffi had tasted. The flavors were more complex, the salt sumptuous but not overwhelming on the palate, the residue lush. Maybe it was Angelo's rhapsodic description, but Raffi could feel the pigs' sun-drenched days grunting and huffing acorns, their lazy naps in the shade, their entire joyful communion ripe on her tongue.

When they'd finished, Angelo's daughter walked them to Caffe Archimede, which, it turned out, was only two turns away on another quaint, cobblestoned alley. Displayed in the bakery window was an arrangement of golden, spiral-shaped cookies coated in chopped almonds.

"These are the specialty of the *pasticceria*," said Angelo's daughter, pointing at the cookies and pushing open the door. "*Ciao*, Roberto," she called to the tall man behind the counter. "These ladies were looking for you." She waved and left.

Isabel wasted no time. "We want your spiral cookies."

At Roberto's furrowed brow, Raffi repeated the statement in Italian.

"*Si*, the Archimedes Spiral!" He retrieved a tray from under the glass case and beckoned Raffi and Isabel to come nearer. Up close, the cookies shone with a delicate glaze. "You try."

He picked up a cookie, broke it in half, and handed one piece to each, in a gesture reminiscent of Holy Communion.

Isabel's eyes closed at the first bite—an ecstatic expression Raffi would come to call Isabel's Pastry Face—and when Raffi bit into her own half, she understood why.

It was a flavor rocket. Within the almond essence danced a *tarantella* of orange: the deep, heady tang of Tarocco blood-orange twirling with candied orange peel, just bitter enough to temper the sweetness. Not *millefiori* but orange-blossom honey completed the citrus triumvirate.

Raffi thought she had been exposed to every Italian dessert in her childhood, but there was nothing like this in upstate New York. The Ortygians must have been too prosperous to immigrate to America and bring with them this delicacy.

"Archimedes was the mathematician of Siracusa," said Roberto the baker as they ate. "I name this cookie for him because he discover the spiral. We Syracusans are very proud of Archimedes."

Unfortunately, Roberto recounted, Archimedes had come to a terrible end. Absorbed in drawing a theorem in the sand, he had been stabbed by a Roman soldier.

"'Scientists posit that if Archimedes had not died, we might have landed on the moon in 1069 instead of 1969,'" Isabel read from her guidebook as they strolled away from the café. Her non-guidebook hand grasped an oversized bakery bag filled with biscotti dipped in pistachio and walnuts, miniature tarts filled with fig paste and hazelnut cream, petite *almondini*, and, of course, Archimedes Spirals. Roberto had gone to get a bigger bag mid-order.

It was late afternoon and shadows engulfed the narrow streets. Cruise ships had relieved the town of most tourists; besides a few stray locals and those visitors fortunate enough to find lodgings in the Città Vecchia, the streets were quiet. But through the calm air snaked a ripple of anticipation. The sleepy city was dreaming of a lively night.

Above the terminus of the alley to their right, the sun hung low over strung-up laundry and yellow-and-red Sicilian flags, sending down crimson rays like a ripe tarocco burning in the sky.

"What time did I say dinner was again?" said Isabel.

"You didn't. You said you wanted us to be spontaneous."

"That doesn't sound like me," said Isabel.

They walked on, preferring small paths to main streets. Raffi turned around twice with the feeling of eyes upon her—a feeling to which she was well accustomed. Sicilians were always on the lookout for outsiders, too. Nino used to say a Sicilian could spot a foreigner from behind a closed door.

Near sunset, they came to an oasis in the heart of the city: a freshwater spring, the water dark and viridescent, papyrus bursting from the center where water would spout from a man-made fountain.

"Look!" Isabel jabbed a finger toward a family of white ducks splashing beneath the papyrus. The ducks' feathers glowed incandescent in the fading light, the scene as if conjured by a Dutch master: ghostly luminosity against the dark.

"'The Fountain of Arethusa,'" Raffi read from a bronze placard on the stone wall bordering the fountain. They found a bench and sat, the warm evening air folding around them like an envelope. Isabel tore up an Archimedes Spiral and tossed pieces into the water. The ducks darted and fluttered, competing for scraps.

It was here, at Arethusa, that the bird-goddess threw herself into the sea and birthed the island of Ortygia. In the (rare) silence while Isabel checked her phone, Raffi considered that the Arethusa legend contained an ancient truth: the line between birth and sacrifice does not exist. The two words converge into motherhood. Maybe Raffi's own mother Polly had been sacrificed so Raffi could become the Godmother. Without Polly's illness and the fissure it left in her life, Raffi would have been too nurtured to feel weak. Weakness had been her path to strength.

The flesh tingled on her arms. She was being watched again—and not as a foreigner. She turned, keeping her features expressionless.

Across the fountain, a petite blonde woman held up a cell phone as if taking a selfie.

"She's on you," said Isabel, dropping her phone to grasp Raffi's wrist, her eyes hazy.

Raffi looked to the girl, confused, and then back to the blonde, who had lowered her phone to stare, unflinching, at Raffi. Raffi felt as she had when she first saw Brando's father one spring evening in Manhattan. He was struggling with a handful of groceries on the opposite sidewalk, a stranger until he looked up from the plastic bags and caught her watching him. In that look contained the promise that she would know the contours of his body beneath his thin grey tee shirt, the feel of his lips on her neck. What does not happen in a year, the Italian saying goes, can happen in an instant. A similar shock rocked her now. She wondered what the woman's eyes looked like behind her sunglasses. She wondered why she wondered.

"There is an exchange of energy," said Isabel in the same vacant tone.

Raffi removed her sunglasses and met the woman's stare. Neither moved, and the girl was right—something passed between them, no less real because invisible. A higher force pressed the pause button. Nothing existed but this woman—not Isabel, not Sicily, not the chthonic goddess and her font of sorrow.

Raffi slipped the sunglasses back on. "Let's go, Isabel," she said.

The woman walked away without a backward glance, and Raffi watched the blonde's retreat before guiding Isabel in the opposite direction.

As they walked in silence toward the hotel, Raffi could not shake the woman from her mind. Even behind dark lenses, Raffi had felt those eyes bore into her skin. This loss of control would be terrifying if she allowed it. She began the practiced work of expunging her discomfort when she glanced sideways at Isabel and found the girl gazing at her with a knowing expression. There was no privacy around an Ibarra.

Halfway between Arethusa and the Hotel Ortygia, Isabel pulled Raffi into a quaint restaurant famous, according to her guidebook, for its *spaghetti allo scoglio*. Wine glasses in hand, they traded Mary Fortune anecdotes until they laughed themselves to tears. Then dinner came, and the spectacular seafood pasta was presented in a large ceramic bowl with coiled tentacles for handles. They oohed and aah to their server's delight.

A growing pile of seafood shells on their shared discard plate, Raffi let the blonde fade from her thoughts as the girl told her, although Raffi already knew, that Isabel's mother had died when she was a child. ("Are there oysters in this?" the girl had asked anxiously, of the pasta.)

Raffi, in turn, chose to share that her mother was gone, too, though she did not elaborate. The stiffness that separated strangers was starting to melt, but Raffi had learned not to trust. And yet, to her surprise, Raffi felt herself trusting.

They left the restaurant, the waxing moon lighting their path back to the hotel—their *circuitous* path, as Isabel insisted she knew a shortcut and got them lost again—when they were startled by a howl at the intersection of two darkened streets, the streetlights out in both directions. Emerging from the shadows came the source of the howl: large, white, more wolf than dog. It looked wild and out of place—not the sort of canine an Ortygian would keep for a pet.

"Look," Isabel whispered, pointing to a statue beside the dog: a three-sided female figure. One figure held a torch, one a ring of keys, and the third a coiled serpent. A goddess in triplicate. *Pay attention to threes*, Mary whispered.

"Here, sweetie," Raffi called to the dog. She missed Piccolo.

The dog's eyes met hers then flicked away. Raffi moved closer and held out her hand.

"Careful," Isabel hissed. "You could put a saddle on that thing."

Raffi crept closer, palm up and open. The dog watched her, unconvinced.

"Hey!" Isabel shouted.

Raffi had been concentrating so hard on the dog that she hadn't noticed a figure emerge from the shadows in the stretch of road at her back. She turned and faced the outline of a man. The face was obscured, but she made out the shape of a hat. She stared into the darkness. By the statue, the girl stood silent.

Raffi stepped out, anchored her legs wide, and crossed her arms. "Come into the light," she said in calm Italian. "Or leave."

The silence magnified. The white dog, observing from the sidelines, looked bored and skulked away. The man was still.

Raffi took a step forward. The man did not move. She took another step, and another, until at last came the swish of shoes swiveling on stone.

He was gone.

Raffi turned to the girl and found her sweet face contorted in fear. Raffi shook her head, *don't worry.*

"It's okay?" asked Isabel. Her face was white as the dog.

"You would know if it wasn't," said Raffi. Another B-movie attempt at intimidation, she thought, trying to make light of it. But she did not feel light.

"Come," said Raffi.

They resumed walking, the dark junction behind them, the triple-sided statue watching their steps up the silent Sicilian street. By unspoken agreement, they did not discuss the incident. And while Raffi was rattled, the gift and girdle of fame had made her accustomed to being followed for reasons usually more tiresome than concerning. As the minutes passed, she was more irritated at the intrusion on her precious leisure than unsettled.

Despite her practiced calm, though, her subconscious took her to a strange dreamworld that night: one of white wolves and tentacles and a man in a fedora with only blank flesh where a face should be.

14

At breakfast on their last morning in Ortygia, Agata came to the table to ensure they were eating enough honey, and to tell them about Etna.

"*La Mamma* is active," Agata said, pulling up her chair, eyes and nostrils flaring.

"La Mamma?" said Raffi.

"Mamma Etna."

"Active?" said Isabel, her eyes flitting between Raffi and the waitress.

"Yes, but do not worry. She is always active," said Agata.

"We're going to Taormina today. Isn't that near…La Mamma?" said Isabel. "Maybe we should cancel Taormina. What do you think? Noto instead?" She grabbed her guidebook.

"Her lava would not reach Taormina," said Agata. "From Taormina, La Mamma will be beautiful. You will see the ashes of her tears." Agata waggled her fingers above her head, miming volcanic flurries.

Isabel nodded, uncertain. She resumed eating, which seemed to calm her. After the girl had dipped her last slice of prosciutto into the *millefiori*, Raffi proposed a final pass through the streets of Ortygia. The girl's *yes* was immediate. No doubt she was thinking of pastries.

Overhead, the sky was plated silver. They walked with the awkward intimacy of a first date, Isabel grabbing Raffi's arm as they headed for Caffe Archimedes. When, armed with a box of spirals "for the bus ride to Taormina," they arrived at the fountain, they found it swarming with visitors, the peace of dusk destroyed by guides shouting in German, French, and English.

Isabel drifted toward an English-speaking group, presided over by a Briton who spoke with Shakespearean flourish to a dozen tourists too polite to be American. *Canadians*, thought Raffi, following the girl.

"This fountain," pronounced the Briton, "was born when the chaste nymph Arethusa, running from the *amorous* advances—" he smirked, "—of the river god Alpheus, rose from her undersea home and transformed into a natural spring."

His audience murmured as he nodded, as if pleased with his own sagacity.

"Any questions?" he asked, though his manner discouraged it.

Isabel raised her hand.

"Yes?" he said, looking to the spot where a tour lanyard should have hung around her neck and frowning.

"I thought Asteria was the one who threw herself down and made the fountain!" Isabel shouted through her funneled guidebook. "I thought she turned into a quail!"

The guide cleared his throat. "That *is* another legend, yes, but the *predominant*—"

"What is it with women throwing themselves onto the ground here?" Isabel interrupted.

The man's expression curdled. "Serious questions only, please."

While Isabel raised her hand again, Raffi skimmed the crowd. Everyone had their phones out. Absent was the woman from the day before, and Raffi realized she was disappointed. She also realized she had chosen her white eyelet blouse and linen pants in anticipation of seeing the woman again.

The girl was watching her, so she pushed the thoughts from her mind. Even an Ibarra can't read a thought that isn't there.

"Ready to head back?" said Raffi.

Isabel appeared to think for a moment. "I think I'm done torturing him, yes."

Tracing the previous night's route, they came to the quiet intersection and the three-sided statue. The midday sun revealed the variegated-marble composition of the figures, dark veins cutting through putty-colored flesh. The objects in the statue's hands, however, were hewn from black basalt.

"Ah, the Hekataion," said a voice behind them.

They turned to find a genial middle-aged woman with curly brown hair, an overstuffed paper bag balanced on her hip like a toddler, vegetable tendrils and a long loaf of bread poking out from the top like movie props.

"The Hekataion?" said Raffi.

"This is a Hekataion: the statue with the three faces of the goddess Hecate."

Isabel stroked the basalt flame in the nearest figure's hand. "I know Hecate. She's the goddess of witchcraft."

The girl looked sad. She was probably thinking of her great-grandmother in Cuba.

"Hecate is *la dea liminale*: the liminal goddess," the woman continued. "She cannot be defined. In that, is she not like all women?"

"History professor?" said Raffi.

The woman smiled. "Antiquities." She stepped closer to the statue. "You see the objects she holds? Hecate is a guardian. It is she who decides whether to light the way or obscure it, lock the gate or open it."

Isabel, who had been rifling through her guidebook, looked up in confusion. "Whose statue is this?" she asked.

"I don't understand," said the woman.

Raffi did not understand either, but she was used to it by now.

"I mean, who put it here?" said Isabel. "Does it belong to a shop?"

"I never considered that question," the woman said. "I do not know."

"Wasn't it erected by the town?" said Raffi.

"No," said the woman, circling the statue. "The municipal statues have a brass plate on the plinth that bears the title and benefactor. This one is unmarked. And the plinth is unanchored. If we were strong enough, we could lift it up and take it with us."

A silence descended until Isabel asked: "Has the statue always been here?"

The woman shook her head. "In Sicily, only La Mamma has always been here. Everything else was stolen."

✦

THEY FOUND AGATA LINGERING by the bell stand. She offered to walk them to the bus stop for the Etna Trasporti, making the euros Raffi pressed into her hand disappear so fast, Raffi wondered if the waitress moonlighted as a magician.

"Don't be afraid of La Mamma," Agata said, pulling Isabel's large yellow suitcases toward the bus stop like a nanny dragging children by the wrist. "In Sicilian, we call Her *Mungibeddu*: beautiful mountain. You will see. She burns, but She is just. And She hears our prayers."

With a whoosh of airbrakes, the Etna Trasporti came to a jaunty stop in front of them. Animated voices shouted in a cacophony of Sicilian, Italian, German, and English. Arriving luggage was thrown down from the rack on the roof, and new bags tossed up.

Once in their seats, Raffi and Isabel looked out the window as Agata helped a British family negotiate five purple suitcases. Raffi wondered if the family would occupy the same rooms she and Isabel had slept in.

"*Ciao*, Ortygia," Isabel whispered, then fell asleep so quickly Raffi thought the girl was faking—her head flopped back on the seat, pastry bag clutched in orange-stained hands.

As the bus pulled away, Raffi kept her eyes on Agata, wondering if the waitress gave her honey spiel to every guest at Hotel Ortygia. She leaned forward to grab a magazine from the seat pocket when she saw a man wearing the flat Sicilian cap called a *coppola*, head down, brush past Agata and slip something into her pocket. Agata nodded toward the bus and spoke in his ear before they parted.

Raffi forgot the magazine. Her body iced over. A transaction had occurred. Raffi was sure of it. She raised her phone to her ear and called the number of someone who always picked up.

"Mama," answered Trini on the first ring.

"Trinidad. It's the middle of the night in Miami," said Raffi, relieved.

"I do the translation until late last night, Mama. This *1960* give me agita. And then…I take a break."

This meant she had been up watching telenovelas.

"Any news?"

"Ho! Juju Taylor have a problem."

Raffi pressed the phone tighter to her ear and turned away from the other passengers, toward sleeping Isabel. "What kind of problem?"

Trini's voice went giddy. "The kind when your *Investigadora Privada* Berry find a lot of bad things, Mami."

"Like?"

"Like he sleep with that violin lady Vanessa Liao."

Raffi felt smug. She might not be a psychic like the Ibarras, but she was an expert at reading people. "And?"

"And he complain to his wife about Karintha Kesi *y* Witch Daddy. He say ugly words, Mama, ugly things we don't tolerate no more. One might say," she added in her exaggerated American accent, "he cast aspersions upon them."

Raffi could hear her dancing over the phone.

"I fly to California, Mama. I go to Juju's *house*. Ha! I ask him if he want me to play the recording of him talking ugly about Karintha Kesi and Witch Daddy. He say, 'What recording? There's no recording!'" I say, 'The recording your ex-wife make, Papi.' He say, 'I don't have an ex-wife.' I say: '*You do now, Papito!*'"

Raffi laughed. "*Perfetto, Mamma.*" She paused. "And the other matter?" She meant Judge Paz.

"*Nada*, Mami. We don't know nothing. *Pero...*"

"*Pero* what?"

"*Pero* if I am you? I stay longer in Sicily."

Raffi weighed how much to say in response. "How much longer?"

"You find a nice place, spend a week or two more, relax."

Good advice, as usual. "Fine. We'll check out an olive festival. Go to the beach."

Through the line came the sound of Trini snapping her fingers, the sway of cha-cha hips. "Mama? *Si.*"

"Other suggestions?"

Trini cleared her throat. "Don't call me again the rest of the trip," she said, then hung up without explanation.

Raffi held the phone with her thumb and middle finger, spinning it, thinking. Trini would have been in touch with their sources at the Bureau. Raffi was still a person of interest, that was clear, and in the most high-profile disappearance with which she'd ever been associated. Celia Paz was a state judge now, but rumor had it she would soon be appointed to the federal bench—or would have been.

Maybe the answers are here in Sicily?

Raff was not a fool. Her last name was Truvarizzi, and her worst opponents tended to get punished not only through her deft form of justice, but also by an unsubtle hand. Sally T could be behind these violent retributions, whether to punish her for using his name by making her a target for law enforcement, to maintain the surname's association with Mafia power, or even—she hated this thought—to help her. Confounding her analysis, Raffi's worst enemies shared a characteristic that allowed other plausible causes for their respective ends: they had all gone bad.

She decided to distract herself with some good news. Unlocking her phone, she texted Dione: *You are free, Didi.*

Without waiting for a response—it was barely dawn in New York—she called Misa Riù. Unlike Trini, Misa did not answer on the first ring. "Godmother," the Hablavision producer said, her voice groggy. "What a nice surprise."

"How are you, Misa?"

Misa was silent, and Raffi heard the rustle of a bathrobe and the sound of Misa tiptoeing from the room so as not to wake her latest boyfriend.

"We're great, Godmother. Manny loves Pinetree. He thanks you every day. Everyone seems invested in his success."

"I'm glad to hear it."

Misa had come to Raffi three years before, when her son Manny was a fourteen-year-old applicant to Pinetree Academy, the best college-prep school in Miami. Middle-school Manny had gotten a little lost during his parents' divorce, made some mistakes with hallucinogens. There'd been an incident; he was caught in a supermarket parking lot, resisted the police, snorted "Oink!" in their faces. He'd gotten off easy—probation and community service—but Pinetree had refused him.

"Except that he's brilliant," Raffi had told the headmaster, a mountain of a man, outwardly benevolent, but with a frightening edge uncontained by a hale façade. Students and staff were terrified of him. Raffi saw him for the bully he was. "Manny is the kind of kid who wins international fellowships and cures diseases. He belongs at Pinetree."

"Manny committed a drug-related *crime*," said the headmaster. "Would it be fair to the other parents to put someone like Manny among their children?"

"Is that a question your prep school considered when your father made that statutory rape charge disappear in the '80s?"

Now Misa was one of Raffi's most loyal godchildren.

"I'm calling about Marina Ramón," said Raffi without prelude. "I want you to bring her back."

Misa was silent, then said, "Tell me more."

"She belongs on that new show of yours. *Las Brujas de Bal Harbour.*"

"That's not a bad idea," said Misa.

It was not an idea. It was a command.

"I'd consider it a personal favor," said Raffi. "Though it's more a favor to *you*. Anyway, I can't take credit for the idea. This one came from Trini. No one like your biggest fan to tell you how to run your show."

Misa chuckled and Raffi was about to turn the conversation back to social matters when the view outside the window stopped her short. She made Misa promise to move fast, and hung up.

She turned back to the window. Etna—La Mamma—had begun to smolder. White clouds billowed from the concave mouth at Her peak; from a smaller cone, a stream of charcoal shot through the white. This dichotomous cloud traversed the sky, blighting the coastal landscape to the east, where Taormina lay.

Isabel snorted hard in her sleep and snapped awake. In seconds, she went from groggy—*stunad*, as Raffi's *nonna* would say—to hyper-alert, clutching the armrests and looking around with wild eyes.

Prying one hand off the armrest, she grabbed Raffi's. "Is it okay?"

Raffi did not withdraw her hand. She held Isabel's in her own and said, "We're safe."

The girl's eyes went unfocused. "Yes," she said in her strange, blank tone, receiving—or purporting to receive—messages from the ether. "But that doesn't make me feel better," she said in a normal voice. She edged so close to Raffi that her tousled blond hair fell across Raffi's shoulder.

"Look." Raffi gestured toward the multicultural bus passengers, who regarded the volcano with interest but not concern. "Do they seem worried?"

Isabel pursed her lips. "Maybe they don't know better. Maybe they're psychopaths who don't feel things the way we do. Like those people who climb mountains without ropes."

"A whole bus of psychopaths?"

Isabel turned and surveyed the passengers. A fair-skinned couple behind them was conversing in German as they watched the mountain.

"Mary had a German client," the girl hissed. "*Berthe*. Do you have any idea what it takes to upset a German?"

Raffi squeezed the girl's hand. "There are a lot of Italians on this bus. Are Italians known to be calm?"

"No," the girl admitted.

"The bus driver—does he seem like he's driving us toward oblivion?"

"No," Isabel mumbled, fingering her guidebook. "He could be a psychopath, too."

"Ah, yes. The old bus-full-of-psychopaths theory."

"We should go somewhere else," the girl said. "It's not too late. They thought Pompeii would be okay, too, and look what happened there." She twisted away from Raffi to stare at Etna.

"Look at me, Isabel." Raffi reached out to touch the girl's chin, moving Isabel's face back around until their eyes met. "You can handle this."

"No, I can't," said Isabel. "I *know* we're going to be okay and I still can't handle it."

"You don't give in to fear," said Raffi, telling the girl and reminding herself. "You use it as information."

Isabel seemed to forget the volcano. "What kind of information?"

"About what kind of person you are. The strong are as scared as the weak. They just don't let fear win."

✦

ETNA SIMMERED AS THE bus pulled into the terminal at Via Pirandello, volcanic output waiting at the edge of town as if too well-mannered to enter without asking.

A hillside town on Sicily's eastern coast, Taormina's terracotta structures were tucked into rugged terrain softened by an explosion of flora both cultivated and wild: poppies pushing through cracks between stone paths; colorful *Strelizia*, the bird of paradise, poking up like curious cranes; the waxy, passion-pink petals of *aloe vera*. Presiding over all was the kingly cactus in its myriad forms, from *ficu r'igna* of the green needles and watermelon flesh, to ungainly *Opuntia ficus-indica*, prickly pear cactus, resembling either a hodgepodge of uneven bricks or a collection of knuckled hands sprouting yellow flowers.

The summer sun, magnified by a layer of insulation from the smoke, was hot on their backs as they climbed the driveway to the Hotel La Francisa—another last-minute pivot by Raffi and treat for Isabel. A restored relic of the Grand Tour era—*francisa*, meaning "French woman," was a nineteenth-century euphemism for "foreigner"—the Hotel La Francisa was still the best hotel in Sicily.

The hotel's famed balconies, wrapped around the Mediterranean façade like tiers on a cruise ship, had once teemed with writers and aesthetes: the cultured European elite who lingered on their two-year jaunts to inhale culture and spices, exhale literature and art. Where once these artists and heirs brandished snifters and puffed cigars, now hedge-fund millionaires and tech billionaires aired drenched workout clothes as oligarchs entertained actresses and CEOs chatted with media moguls. Soon enough, Raffi thought with satisfaction, all these would be joined by purported Mafia maven Raffi Truvarizzi, who had pulled, not strings, but iron cables to secure two neighboring rooms overlooking the volcano.

Isabel looked anxious as she rolled her suitcases up the meandering path to the hotel entrance, though Raffi couldn't tell if it was the daunting majesty of the La Francisa, the approaching fumes, or something else—a psychic vision? —that troubled the girl. Whatever her concerns, the girl soothed them in the only way—besides eating and divination—she knew how: by talking.

"Did you know the first inhabitants of this area were the Siculi?" Isabel struggled for breath. "And the Siculi were among the earliest settlers of Sicily? They came here after the Sicani, who lived in central Sicily, near Lercara Friddi, your family town. Later, the Siculi were conquered by the Greeks!"

Raffi grunted. She was tiring of facts-about-Sicily. She wanted to feel the place, not learn it.

Above the lush greenery that formed a tunnel to the hotel, the encroaching smoke, urged on by a mounting northwesterly wind, invaded the town at last, its manners all run out. Isabel dashed ahead, burying her face in her shoulder as if escaping a house fire. Raffi entered the La Francisa and found the girl gawping at the lobby.

The interior was stunning but standard for a hotel of this ilk: soft white color palate with deep eggplant accents; yellow Murano chandelier; gilt-edged accent tables; the scent of freesia. From the girl's reaction, Isabel had never set foot in a five-star hotel.

Raffi walked to the front desk and got in line behind an older man in a fedora. The hat made her think of the rude man from the breakfast room in Ortygia, who had left the room in a hurry after hearing the name of her hometown. Her eyes trailed down to this man's shoes: battered, brown, unremarkable.

She had an urge to see his face. Under the pretense of reaching for a brochure listing the hotel's activities, she leaned forward, but he turned away to slide the room key into the opposite pocket. He was gone moments later, his back receding as he moved toward the elevators.

This was ridiculous. Thousands of old men wore fedoras—especially in Italy.

"I apologize," said the check-in clerk, who could not conceal a shudder when Raffi gave her name. "We cannot offer the rooms you reserved. All our west-facing guests are being moved east."

"What's wrong with the west-facing rooms?" She turned her nose to the hook.

"The ash," said the clerk.

Isabel, returning from an unsubtle photo shoot in the lobby, caught the last word. "What about the ash?"

"Do not worry, *signurina*," said the clerk. "It is more nuisance than danger. Your clothes would be ruined, nothing more. Still, we cannot allow you to take a westward room. This means—" the clerk flinched, avoiding Raffi's eyes, "—you must take a room together."

Raffi squinted at the woman, waiting until she flushed the color of a tarocco before saying, "That's fine."

The clerk exhaled with relief. Outside the lobby windows, the volcano brooded.

"It's beautiful," Raffi observed. "I would love to see more of it."

Polly entered her mind, and, for a moment, Raffi was taken back to the night her mother turned up in a burn unit and everything changed.

Then the clerk smiled, revealing uneven teeth jailed by shiny gold braces, the odd detail bringing Raffi back to the present.

"Do not worry, *signura*," said the clerk. "La Mamma will follow you everywhere. It is not possible to ignore *Mungibeddu*."

THE ROOM WAS A suite—everything upholstered in the same white, eggplant, and gold as the lobby, each flourish so luxurious, Isabel was afraid to touch so much as a light switch. There was even a *parlor* between the two bedrooms. The scent of now-familiar *millefiori* honey permeated throughout, and not a hint of smoke until the Godmother came back from tipping the porter and opened the sliding-glass doors. Below the hotel's maze of topiaries and sculptured follies, the sea swirled toward the neighboring beach of Giardini Naxos, where rocks strewn about the brilliant blue water looked like coins in a wishing-pool.

Isabel found her room, collapsed on a bed of marshmallow, and sighed. Her languor lasted exactly one minute until she was on the phone with the concierge. She had made a cardinal error: there was no dinner reservation for that night.

"If you *really* want the local cuisine," said the concierge with suspicion, no doubt accustomed to tourists who want not the local cuisine, but what they *think* to be the local cuisine, "then you must visit Ristorante Gelsomina. But know that Chef Gelsomina is very particular. You will eat as she decides."

This sounded fine to Isabel, save two questions.

"Is Gelsomina's near the volcano?"

"Everything is near the volcano."

Isabel grimaced. "Does she give you a lot of food?"

"This is Sicily, *signurina*."

Touché.

"They will send a shuttle for you. Eight o'clock."

"*Grazie*," said Isabel. She was about to hang up when she heard the concierge calling out through the line. Lifting the phone back to her ear, she said, "Yes?"

"*Signurina*," he said, his voice uneasy. "There is one more thing I must tell you about Ristorante Gelsomina."

Isabel frowned. "They don't take credit cards?"

"It is not that—though they do prefer cash." He paused. "But no, *signurina*, it is just—Gelsomina? They say she is a witch."

"Then I'll be right at home," said Isabel.

15

Ristorante Gelsomina was in Castelmoro, a town two miles up the mountain from Taormina, and the so-called shuttle to the restaurant was nothing more than a beat-up Peugeot piloted by a handsome maniac. Careening around blind corners on the wrong side, ignoring traffic signs and signals, and cursing in Sicilian, he left them at what looked to be a private residence and drove away in a hail of gravel before Raffi could confirm they were in the right place.

There was nothing to indicate this was anything but a family home: a sprawling, hilltop home with panoramic sea views to the east, ominous Etna to the west. The house was surrounded by fields of grape vines and olive trees, the air redolent of lavender. Raffi and Isabel stood on the perimeter, unsure whether to retreat down the hill or venture inside, when a dented Fiat screeched up behind them, scattering stones and depositing an elderly couple who strode toward the eastern end of the structure before disappearing around the side.

They followed the couple around to the back, where a rustic, vine-wound pergola sheltered candlelit tables overlooking the water. Happy multilingual chatter filled the air.

"You come from La Francisa!" a boisterous middle-aged waiter shouted, rushing up to greet them. He introduced himself as Paolo, led them to the only open table, and pulled out both chairs. "Please."

Once they were settled, Paolo—one of Gelsomina's many brothers, it turned out—got down to business.

"You like the food of the sea, or the land?" Paolo asked, pen poised over a small notepad as if a foundational theory of the universe would be revealed in the answer.

"Both," Raffi said in English, and thus kicked off an intricate culinary dance with the phantom Gelsomina as choreographer.

First arrived a large platter bearing four splashes of translucent, pale-pink, quivering flesh, each gelatinous blob dotted with an apostrophe of yellow. "Prawn carpaccio!" Paolo announced before disappearing.

The soft prawn flesh, lacking the tangy brine Americans call "fishy," finished sweet on their tongues.

"Holy Jesus," Isabel said.

"*Bedda Matri*," Paolo corrected, materializing. "Sicilian for *beautiful mother*. As the American says," he assumed a caricature of an American accent, "Ho, my God."

"*Bedda Matri*," echoed Isabel.

With a different wine came anchovies fried in olive oil with chili flakes and mint. "*Masculini con la mente*," said Paolo.

"*Bedda Matri*," said Raffi.

Lightly fried prickly pear cactus: "*Bucce di fichi d'India a cotoletta.*"

"*Santa Maria!*" cried Isabel.

"*Amin*," Paolo said, crossing himself.

When he returned with the fried rice balls for which Sicily is famous, he dropped the plate like a rapper drops a mic. "*Arancini con tonno e melanzane.*"

"Enough, enough," they laughed, as he announced Gelsomina's witty final act: *patate fritte all'aqua di mare*, potatoes fried in seawater.

"This dish makes me feel emotional," said Isabel.

"That's funny. Me, too," Raffi said with a sad smile. "It reminds me of my son when he was a baby. I used to swim with him in the ocean. I don't know where that little boy went." She could still feel the squishy sand between her toes, the warmth of Brando's chubby body in her arms. She cleared her throat. "What does it remind you of?"

"My mother," Isabel said. Her mother and the beach house in Cuba that Isabel had never gotten to see. Also, those raw oysters off the Rickenbacker that made her an orphan.

Raffi realized with surprise that she had not called Polly since they arrived in Sicily. It was the first time since her mother disappeared that Raffi had even a day pass without trying. She rose and excused herself, as the girl put down her fork and touched a hand to her temple.

In Gelsomina's starlit courtyard, Raffi pressed her mother's contact on the phone and listened to the ring. Her heart raced.

She prayed her mother would answer and knew she wouldn't. She believed anything was possible and knew it wasn't.

The automated message came on after three rings.

Raffi hung up. "Ma," she said into the darkness.

She pulled a wrinkled photograph of the bridal portrait from her pocket.

"Why did you hate it here so much?" she asked the bride. She inhaled the air rich with orange blossom, rosemary, and a ribbon of garlic from Gelsomina's kitchen. How could anyone hate Sicily?

You're not doing anything worthwhile, said the bride, ignoring Raffi's question. *Just eating and flapping your jaw with that girl.*

It stung. "*Tu sei mai contenta*, Ma." You're never satisfied.

Raffi slipped the photo into her pocket and went back inside.

At the table, Raffi found Isabel absorbed by the sight of Gelsomina's sweet encore: two cannoli filled with artichoke-and-pistachio cream.

"You waited for me?" said Raffi. She placed her hand over her heart, then swiped it across her forehead in a mock-faint. "I never thought I'd see the day when Isabel Ibarra showed restraint around a pastry."

"I'm not an animal," said Isabel.

"What's this?" Raffi asked, pulling the dessert plate closer. The plate was charcoal gray, almost black, the perfect camouflage for a fine black dust sprinkled all over. Raffi swept her index finger across the plate and brought it to her lips. The powder tasted like the burnt remnants of a ceremonial fire.

Paolo dashed up to the table, both arms full of plates such that he could only gesture with his head. "*Cannoli con crema di carciofi e polvera di montagnu,*" he recited, clicking his heels as he marched off to distribute the plates.

"*Polvera di montagnu,*" Raffi said with admiration, mulling over the words. "I wonder how she gets it."

"Gets what?" Isabel asked around a ghoulish mouthful of green ricotta cream.

"The *polvera di montagnu.*"

"Please translate."

"The dust of the mountain." Raffi leaned back in the wooden chair. "That's volcanic ash on your dessert."

Isabel held up the last piece of her cannoli. Shrugging, she tossed the morsel into her mouth.

"My mother thought she was burning," Raffi said before she could stop herself. "She showed up in a hospital, screaming she'd been set on fire."

Isabel stopped chewing.

"We had to put her in a special home after that. Mount Olympus. Right on Skaneateles Lake. The nicest place I could find. After we left her there, my mother never spoke again. All she wanted was to sit in the garden."

Raffi remembered red and pink *impatiens*, long pine shadows, a stone bench colonized by lichen.

"The staff got used to her sitting out there and stopped paying attention. She was so peaceful. She seemed...extinguished. This calm woman in the garden was nothing like my mother, though, even before the delusions. She had always been fiery." Raffi forced a chuckle that caught in her throat. "One day, she went out into the Mount Olympus garden and never returned."

Isabel, pretending not to know the answer, asked, "She died?"

"Disappeared. They should have been watching her, and I blamed them at first, but I had to let that go. If anyone could slip her chains, it was my mother."

Isabel reached out to touch Raffi's arm. Raffi did not resist. "How awful for you—and for your father, too." Isabel shook her head. "To lose your partner? It's totally devastating for older people."

Raffi's parents had not been partners, though. More like allies in a strange détente Raffi never understood. They had not been old, either, when Polly disappeared: Polly sixty, Nino seventy. For long-lived Sicilians, they were just getting started. "My father seems to have managed well enough," she said.

They sat in silence until Paolo came back with the check.

A half hour later, as another handsome lunatic drove them back to the hotel in his so-called shuttle, Raffi peered into the darkness outside the window and wondered what Mary would have made of Gelsomina.

"You know what?" Isabel said, interrupting Raffi's thoughts. "I'm not afraid of La Mamma anymore."

"No?"

"Nope."

"Why's that?"

"Because of Gelsomina."

"*Because of Gelsomina*," Raffi parroted. "That makes no sense."

"It *totally* makes sense. Serving me the crumbs of the thing I dread most? Godmother," Isabel said, her blue eyes pale in the inky night, "you fight fear your own way, but this? It's the oldest witch trick in the book."

16

All night, She burned. *Mungibeddu*, Queen of Fire.

The porcupines and martens felt Her first, their pads light on the ground, tiny ears pricked, listening. The porcupine knew Her mounting fury; rolling his flesh and flexing his needles, he froze, offering himself. But She did not require his sacrifice. He waddled eastward, his quills like tuning forks, finding shelter in Her pockets.

The marten stretched her nails to clutch the darkness of the Mother's flesh, probing the loose volcanic surface for stable ground below. Not finding purchase, she climbed trunks and clung to branches, awaiting word. The trees that held her grew at the Mother's grace. Their roots were born in Her ashes.

As midnight arrived, Her simmer intensified into Strombolian eruptions: explosive bursts of sprayed sparks, lava bombs vaulting Her flanks, lapilli cascading like a shower of hot spittle. Tephra glowed red as they broke free from Her vents, hardening to obsidian as they cooled. Her lava interrupted, she writhed.

Jabal-al-burkān, Arabic: Mountain of Fire. *Mons Gibel*, Old

Latin: Mountain-Mountain. *Mungibeddu*, Sicilian: Mountain Beautiful. *Etna*, Latin: I burn.

How many times had they changed Her name before they found one that fit? Mamma Etna: Burning Mother. It was the only one that captured her full power: to create and destroy, to begin and end. There was, too, a deeper name no human could speak, written in a language Her mouth alone could form. Hers was the tongue of flame. She spoke it now.

At dawn, she broke open, erupting in the seconds before sunrise. Molten reams escaped Her mouths, cooling into bocce-sized pyroclasts and tephra like bowling balls. She roared. Her children—the fauna tucked into Her flesh, the people that woke to watch as She lit the dark—had all eaten Her harvest and cooled in Her breeze. She had showered them with favor. Now, they shared Her suffering.

Raffaella Truvarizzi and Isabel Ibarra, asleep in a suite facing the sea, dreaming in tandem, did not see Her explode. Soon after they woke, though, they would know it. Through the door to the hallway would drift the excited hum of staff murmuring as they passed with carts and trays and newspaper deliveries. Raffi and Isabel would hear newscasters shouting through the walls of neighboring guestrooms, saying:

At 6:25 this morning, eruptions occurred at three of Mount Etna's craters, with spectacular fireworks at the Voragine summit crater and subsidiary eruptions at the New Southeast and Bocca Nuova craters. Wildlife and villages in the surrounding areas are moderately threatened.

The news, as usual, getting the tiniest shard of it right.

✦

HAVING DREAMED OF POLLY, Raffi woke disoriented, heart thumping.

Polly was trying to tell her something in a language Raffi didn't understand. It was an ancient language, and the words streamed from Polly's mouth like linguistic static. Above her lips, Polly's eyes pleaded.

If only Raffi could decipher Polly's words, her mother would be free.

Now they were in a car, Polly in the passenger seat, the tempo of her speech increasing.

Raffi sobbed. They were going too fast.

Polly repeated the words, her eyelids fluttering. Her voice had become a monotone. There was no Polly inside.

"Ma!" Raffi screamed.

Her eyes opened. She brushed a hand over her face. Her cheeks were wet.

The bedside clock read 7:00 a.m. She grabbed her phone, fingers dialing as she stumbled from the bedroom.

The voicemail picked up on the first ring.

She exhaled hard and sat on the couch. The dream was already slipping from her mind like cobwebs in the wind. Reaching for the remote, she clicked on the television, releasing a jumble of voices. A live image shot of the volcano beneath an umbrella of dark smoke consumed the screen.

Isabel emerged from her bedroom, blond ringlets askew.

"Etna erupted this morning," said Raffi. "Big time."

Isabel rubbed her eyes. "Really?" She sounded neither upset nor surprised.

Raffi glanced up at her. "Radio signals?" she said, pointing to her temple.

"Tarot," said the girl. "Last night, I pulled La Torre," she said. "The Tower." At Raffi's confused face, she added, "Chaos and destruction. What comes before rebirth. Taken together with my dream, I knew."

"What dream?" asked Raffi, then remarked, "Gelsomina's cannoli crumbs really did the job, then. No fear at all?"

"Seems like," said Isabel.

"If only airplanes were edible," Raffi joked.

✦

ISABEL WAS GLAD THE Godmother had dropped the subject of her dream. Mary had taught Isabel not to share her dreams with anyone. Although Isabel supposed this advice was rooted in fear of persecution, she followed it anyway, even though the danger of persecution was over.

Last night's dream had involved a conversation with a bipedal donkey named Kevin, who told her to "look into the mouth of the Mother."

"My mother? Laelia Ibarra?" Dream-Isabel was confused.

"No," said Kevin the Donkey, sounding annoyed. "Not your *mother. The* Mother. *Mamma Etna. The one that brought you here."*

"There's too much smoke. I can't go now."

The donkey's sensuous lips puckered. "This is your chance. Don't be a mule."

"*But what if it erupts?*"

"*She erupts as we speak. Tomorrow will be the best time to see Her.*"

"Look, Kevin," said Dream Isabel, *her irritation matching the donkey's.* "I refuse *to ride you into that volcano. I'd rather drink wine at the beach.*"

"Excuse me." Kevin sniffed. "*What makes you think I'd let you ride me?*"

"*I just assumed.*"

The donkey brayed. "*I may be the donkey, but you're the one acting like an ass.*"

Reviewing the dream, Isabel decided two things. First, her self-confidence needed a boost if she was getting put down by a dream animal. Second: before the day was over, she was going to ride a donkey to the top of Mount Etna.

17

Raffi descended the Corso Umberto and passed under the Porta Messina, her soft white tee whipping like a sail in the wind. The air smelled like charred sugar. Along the roadside, yellow-fisted cacti waved fragile fingers as two notions of the day jousted in the dome above: a cerulean sky and brilliant sun to the east and bruised clouds to the west. Etna, almost entirely obscured by charcoal plumes, seemed calmer now, reminding Raffi of Miami after a hurricane.

She thought of Isabel, who'd trooped down to the hotel store after breakfast and returned with long sleeves and a windbreaker, announcing that, instead of sipping almond wine with Raffi at a café, she'd be taking a private tour of Mount Etna on the back of a donkey. Raffi, whose policy when confronted with absurdity was not to react, nodded. She was grateful Isabel hadn't invited her along.

On her left as she moved down the hill, the crumbling remnants of an ancient Roman wall sprang up and followed her the length of a football field before terminating abruptly. From there, the town began, starting with a gelato shop, a line of tourists out the door. Local teenagers, distinguishable by their tawny good looks and the facility with which they managed their *brioche con gelato*, sprawled out on the curb, kissing between bites and trading quips in Sicilian. At the end of a long row of youths, a young man sitting apart from the others lifted his head as Raffi passed.

Pieces of him jumped out at her, as in a montage. He was too much to absorb all at once. Forge-scorched eyes, the brows thick and black; lips pink at the center like a slice of ripe fruit; the broad shoulders and narrow waist implying hours in the water, his tanned form a dark blade slicing Sicilian sea. Like Raffi, he wore head-to-toe white, a perfect complement for his extravagant darkness.

She moved through his baking gaze, felt his eyes touch her body as would the rough palm of his hand. It had been years since a man caught her attention. With the practiced detachment that had become her hallmark, she wondered where these stirrings might lead.

But after the initial heat, her thoughts, to her surprise, went to the blonde from Arethusa. Raffi imagined the color of the woman's eyes behind those mirrored lenses. Were they black, like this man's? Perhaps they were violet. She experienced a fleeting temptation to ask Isabel: *Who is that woman?* The girl probably knew already.

Rounding the corner to the Piazza Duomo, the old Norman part of town, Raffi felt a need to sit and collect herself. Luckily, sitting is what one is meant to do in a Sicilian *piazza*. That, and eating.

She looked around and chose Caffe Sirenetta, a charming restaurant nestled into a corner of the square. Normally she wasn't hungry so soon after breakfast. Time around the girl must be increasing her appetite. Or maybe it was Sicily working its secret alchemy, stoking all sorts of cravings.

After negotiating with the charismatic host, she was parked at a small table under an umbrella, observing the antics in the square. Two fair-skinned children, not locals from the way they'd let hazelnut gelato melt all over their hands—Sicilian children are gelato-fluent—were running from their parents in a way that was amusing to everyone but the parents themselves, who looked on the verge of unraveling in a stream of expletives. Raffi remembered well those years of parenting when dignity is subjugated to survival. One of the fair-haired children, a boy in pink leggings, had just climbed atop the first tier of the *piazza* fountain when Raffi was startled by a quiet voice nearby.

"Bad manners, the Americans."

In the shade of the same umbrella, but one table over, sat an old man wearing a tan fedora. Again, she had failed to notice a *vecchio* in a hat. What was it with her lately? She gave a polite nod and looked down at the paper menu, noticing, with disgust, grease-stained fingerprints along the edges. She did not like to think about other people touching her menu.

"I blame the parents," the old man continued. He spoke in accent-less English but was clearly Sicilian. He looked to be around eighty, though he had the pulled-tight look of too much plastic surgery and the hair poking out from his fedora was dyed an uncanny brassy blond that clashed with both the hat and his sallow skin. Perhaps even Sicilians were not immune to the modern obsession with youth at all costs.

"Mmm," said Raffi, not looking up from the menu. If he did not stop soon, she would ask to be moved.

The waiter arrived wearing jeans and a casual expression that said he could take her order or leave it. Raffi asked for an espresso granita and a small plate of *pignolati*, a local treat of fried, sugared dough. While she waited, she scrolled through her phone pretending to be absorbed in reading. Then the waiter brought her order and she forgot everything but the sweet *pignolati* and the ice-cold granita.

After a few minutes, she became conscious of Sicilian jazz playing over the restaurant's tinny speaker system. She thought of Dione and frowned. Dione had not responded to Raffi's good-news message. Checking the time, she dialed her friend.

"Godmother!" Dione answered, out of breath. She sounded high.

"You haven't reacted to your liberation," said Raffi.

"You won't believe what I did."

For a second, Raffi's stomach lurched. "What?"

"I wrote the biggest hit of my life, your life, Jimmy Algiers' life, I mean the biggest hit *ever*."

Raffi exhaled. She'd half expected her friend to have done something nutty, like fly to Corkscrew and kick Juju in the teeth.

"You wanna hear it, Godmother?"

Yes, Raffi wanted to hear it; she could almost hear it now. It was brewing in the bebop rhythm of Dione's speech.

"Play it for me, Didi." She pressed the phone against her ear and looked around for the waiter. She wanted the check so she could leave when her drink was finished. Although he sat in the shadows and had not spoken to her again, the old man made her uncomfortable.

She heard Dione scrambling around—chairs creaking and whining, a rug flapping back against the floor. Raffi caught the familiar sound of the sax strap going around Dione's neck, the groans and shifts of her compact frame assuming the weight of the large brass tube.

"Ready?" said Dione.

Raffi closed her eyes as the first bright notes unfurled into a jazz masterpiece. The song would be among the most played jazz instrumentals in the history of the idiom, and, Jimmy Algiers be damned, Dione was right. This was, without a doubt, *The* Song. Raffi fought a brief pang of jealousy. She had always loved jazz, had wanted to blow like Dione. The trumpet was her instrument, but lessons in her teens left her with fragments of reveille and the realization that she would never be a musician. But she would cast no *malocchio* on her friend. She was the Godmother, envious of no one.

Dione stopped playing in a flutter of half-notes and came back on the line. "Well?"

"Phenomenal," said Raffi. And it was.

Dione yelped. From the sound of it, she was jumping up and down on her Persian rug. Raffi grinned, then stiffened. The old man was listening to her conversation.

"I'm going to buy you the biggest drink the next time you're in the city," Dione squealed, still jumping.

"All I want is your loyalty," said Raffi. "Someday, and that day may never come...."

She could hear Dione smiling. "I know, I know."

They hung up and Raffi looked around again for the waiter, who was standing in the penumbra of a flower-choked trellis. She watched as, talking to one of his colleagues, he formed the outline of a woman's body with both hands and finished in an uncouth motion with his fist.

"Do you come from Taormina originally?" the old man said, as if continuing a conversation. His spoke with quiet authority in a voice between a whisper and a growl.

"No," said Raffi. "My family comes from Provincia di Palermo. Lercara Friddi." She paused. "How did you know I was Sicilian?"

"You look like a girl from my village," he said. "Something of the Greek in the eyes, Roman in the nose." He sipped from his espresso. She noticed that only his thumb and first two fingers grasped the handle; the ring and pinky fingers jutted out at a harsh angle, forming a gnarled, effete fan.

"And your village?" she asked, surprised to find she was curious.

"You wouldn't know it."

"Try me," she said, and he spoke the name of a village she'd never heard before. Although he enunciated clearly, the name seemed to leave her mind the moment he spoke it. She was disappointed. For some reason, she had thought he might say Lercara.

"You know the name of this café, *Sirenetta*?" He removed his sunglasses, revealing preternaturally blue eyes. "The figure on top of the fountain," he said, squinting towards the square. "You know what it is?"

She made out the shape of a small statue with a human head and animal tail.

"This is what the locals call *La Sirenetta*. The mermaid."

He put his sunglasses back on. The line along his nasolabial fold suggested an unremitting low-grade displeasure that might have been charming, even seductive, in younger days. It was a line one wanted to remove by pleasing him.

"If you look closely," he continued, "you will see the Taorminesi have misnamed her. She is not a mermaid. She is a queen with scepter and crown."

Raffi gazed across the square. The disobedient children had been replaced by a tour group taking photos in front of the fountain.

"You know—" he drained the rest of his espresso, "—the crowned woman is much newer. Her torso replaces the Minotaur: the half-man, half-bull of legend. The Minotaur is part of the symbology of Taormina."

Symbology. How odd this old man was, with his teacup manners and six-figure words. She loved stories like this—the real history of the place, something Isabel would never find in her guidebook.

"Look at the figure on your way up to the Madonna," the old man said, tossing a few thick coins on the table and rising effortlessly despite his age. "You'll see what I mean." He grasped the back of his chair, and she noticed his hand was unable to flatten, the two hooked fingers tented. A deformity.

"Up to the Madonna?" She was confused. For the second time, he spoke as if continuing a conversation.

With flagging patience, he said: "The Madonna della Rocca, the sanctuary above the village. You must go there next. It is a small church carved into the rocks. Very beautiful. You will see everything from up there, even your mother." He turned to walk away.

"My *mother*?"

He wore the trace of a smirk. "*The* Mother, *signura*. Mamma Etna, the volcano. What did you think I said?"

She was certain she'd heard him right the first time.

"Follow the road up from town and take a right turn where the sign reads 'Via Crucis'. The path goes all the way to the sanctuary." He pointed in the near distance, where the road spiraled upward. "You must see *La Sirenetta* first, though. I think she will interest you."

What would this stranger know of her interests?

He doffed his hat before strolling off with his hands in his pockets. Despite the sparse crowds in the square, he seemed to disappear.

Raffi stared off in his direction. What a strange encounter. Perhaps, she thought with a chill, the old man was a seasoned undercover agent sent to spy on her. If he was spying, though, should he not have stayed silent? She would not have noticed him at the nearby table had he not spoken up. He had the gift of invisibility—she had read that somewhere; she could not remember about whom.

Taking a cue from her anonymous friend, she placed a handful of coins by the pepper grinder and slid back her chair. The waiter was now making a gesture with his tongue and two fingers that made her want to smack him as she passed.

She emerged from the shade of the café and strolled toward the fountain, pausing so a family of five wearing matching green shirts could take a photograph. Finally, she stood beneath *La*

Sirenetta. From twelve feet below, Raffi stared up at the figure of the crowned woman curving out from the top of the fountain in an L-shape, like a spigot pointing up. Sure enough, the pale stone bust was soldered atop a bull's body hewn from older, red stone. This was not, however, the only indignity done to the ancient bull: its hooves had been chiseled off, the mutilated remains of his body now mistaken for the "mermaid's" tail.

I think she will interest you.

He was right. The crowned female astride the male godhead was an unsubtle redistribution of power; had the vanquished Minotaur been removed entirely, there would be no sign of the mermaid-queen's coup. Raffi tried to glimpse *La Sirenetta*'s eyes, but the figure sat too high. How *La Sirenetta* felt about her triumph was, from Raffi's vantage, a mystery.

As if a volume dial had been turned by an invisible hand, Raffi picked out a tune playing in the back of her head: Dione's new song. Keeping time with the beat, Raffi took the curving road through town until she arrived at the sign that said 'Via Crucis'. She would find this mysterious sanctuary with its view of The Mother.

THE MOUNTAIN STEPS WERE jammed with people. Twice Raffi considered turning back, but the old man had piqued her curiosity. Around 500 feet, the crowds thinned and a box hedge on the low stone bordering wall gave way to klatches of humanoid cacti, whispering and pointing and waving her on. Up here, the steps seemed carved by the gods who sculpted the hillside itself. Maybe they had been.

Halfway up, she spotted a sculpture in the shade of a dying

lemon tree. It portrayed three figures in oxidizing metal: one prostrate, another struggling beneath a large cross, and a third figure, who, standing behind the cross-bearer, bore the weight. Raffi felt a heaviness as she passed the sculpture. It was Simon of Cyrene helping Christ to his end.

A couple hundred feet higher the vista opened wide. To the east, the beach at Giardini Naxos sparkled against a line of gawking prickly pears. To the west stood Mamma Etna, where, at the same moment, Isabel was riding a donkey into swirls of volcanic denouement.

That morning, concerned for the girl, Raffi had stopped at the concierge desk to inquire whether touring Etna post-eruption was as dangerous as it sounded.

"Ah no, signura," the concierge said. "There are many ways to approach Her. Usually, they go to Her from the east, where She fall."

"Where She...fell?"

"*Si*. When the Trifoglietto of Etna collapsed and sank into the ground, She form a valley that can never erupt again. Taormina is near to that valley, on Her peaceful side. The Taorminesi never worry about La Mamma for this reason."

"And when did this collapse happen?"

He looked at his watch. "Twelve thousand years ago?"

18

Isabel hopped off the bus at Piano Provenanza, the tiny outpost from which all Etna tours depart, feeling like she'd landed on the moon. The path into the volcano was graveled with petrified lava; there were no trees or flowers. It looked barren and uninviting. After the locals' raving about the fecundity of La Mamma, Isabel wondered if she'd been the target of an elaborate prank by the whole island of Sicily. What could grow in *this*?

The only people around were a man sitting on the fender of a battered Jeep and the androgynous teenager who ran the snack bar by the chair lift. The former called to her and announced he'd be taking her to the place where the tour started. She was relieved. She did not want to start the tour *here*.

"Quiet today, no?" she asked him.

He shrugged. "Most people cancel the day after the eruption."

She wondered if she had been too bold in coming here. "Is it safe?"

"*Cento per cento*," one hundred percent, he said with such confidence Isabel felt uneasy.

They climbed into the Jeep for a short, bouncy ride over

barren terrain, until a shock of conifers sprang up out of nowhere and the tiny faces of forest animals peeked out from their shade. They had reached Etna's northern flank. At the ride's end, Isabel was handed off to her next guide, a fellow blonde named Cristina, who dressed like an Eagle Scout and chewed tobacco like an old man.

"I am sorry for this," Cristina said, releasing a dark stream of tobacco juice by Isabel's sneaker. "I learned this bad habit from a Canadian baseball player."

Isabel was impressed. "You know a Canadian baseball player?"

"No," said Cristina. "I dressed up as one at a costume party last year. I chewed the tobacco only to appear *autentica*. This is how I become addicted."

"Right," said Isabel. It was not often she encountered someone more eccentric than herself.

"Please, our friends await," said Cristina, gesturing at two donkeys who stood blinking nearby. One was brown with giant teeth, the other fawn-colored and gentle-faced.

Isabel approached the darker one. "You must be Kevin."

Cristina laughed, revealing teeth almost as dark as the donkey.

"Not Kevin! They are both she-donkeys. You will ride Lingua," she said, indicating the brown one, "and I will ride Glossa." She mounted the fawn-colored donkey and observed Isabel's hesitation with amusement. "You are afraid?"

"No, no," Isabel said, dismayed. "They're both female? You're sure?"

"You would like to see for yourself?"

Isabel frowned. "Is there a way to exchange mine? I was looking for one called...Kevin."

"Signurina, please. All our tour donkeys are female. You don't want to ride a male up the *Mungibeddu*," she said ominously.

Isabel was disappointed, but she had no choice. If she was going to ride a donkey up the mountain today, it would have to be Lingua. Dream-Kevin had seemed none too keen to be ridden, anyway. She grabbed the reins, thrust a foot in the stirrup, and hauled herself onto Lingua's back with determination. Tapping her heels, she set off after Cristina.

With no other tourists around and an easterly wind, the air was clear. The only sign that Etna had erupted was a muted smell of smoke that dissipated as they entered the Ragabo Pine Forest. Isabel felt a deep peace settle over her like a weighted blanket.

"*Guarda!*" Cristina shouted from time to time, urging Isabel's gaze toward a porcupine hiding in a crag or a hare darting between trunks. She pointed out landmarks like the Grotto Corruccio, which she avowed would be packed again by tomorrow and would smell like "underarm."

They continued in and out of dense forest for another hour, at one point passing under a forty-foot-long, ten-foot-high ridged cavern formed by lava flow. Flanked by pines and cloaked in silence, it was hard to imagine it on fire.

"It is like a womb," Cristina observed of the cavern. She stopped short of saying what was on Isabel's mind: that the cavern resembled a giant vagina.

Twenty minutes beyond the cavern, they reached the Craters

of Bottoniera: seven black hills with depressions at each peak, surrounded by birches and riven by trails carved into the scree. The sun overhead lit the pale birch barks, gilding everything in white gold.

"The Betula Aetnensis Woods," Cristina whispered as if they'd stepped into a church. "The last birches in Sicily. They can only survive in volcanic soil. Betula Aetnensis are like the John the Baptist of trees. They prepare the ground for new life."

The slender arms of the birch branches extended in blessing. The only sounds were the breeze rifling through the leaves and the intermittent spitting of Cristina and her donkey.

"Now we come to the Pitarrone Barracks where the donkeys rest, and you enjoy a snack."

They had reached a glade where Cristina motioned for them to dismount. For the first time that day, they were not alone. A woman in her fifties wearing a thick sweater knelt on a plaid blanket, her face buried between the legs of a telescope. At their approach, the woman withdrew from the eyepiece and regarded them with the same one-eyed squint she probably used to watch the stars.

"Humph," the woman grumbled, and Isabel imagined the woman assessing the taxonomy of these newly introduced specimens: *homo sapiens* and *equus africanus asinus*, neither celestial nor wild. The woman went back up into the undercarriage of the telescope and began to fiddle as Cristina tied up the donkeys and spread out her own blanket, a neon yellow flannel with the words *Andiamo Etna* printed in black along the border.

Cristina began setting out a picnic on the blanket, extracting food from her rucksack: grapes, cheese, *cornetti*, and a pointer-finger of salami. Isabel watched her, troubled. This was not enough.

"I used to have a Takahashi," said the woman with the telescope, tossing the comment at Isabel like a pop fly. Her hair was jet black and cut to the chin, a giant streak of white down the middle suggesting something cataclysmic had happened inside her skull. The woman's accent was unfamiliar to Isabel's ears. It fell somewhere between Scottish and Caribbean. "Then I got my Ritchey-Chrétien f/9."

That the woman wore a thick, knit cardigan sweater suggested she'd descended from a higher elevation; that the sweater was inside-out showed peculiarity. The sweater bothered Isabel. It was familiar. Meanwhile, Cristina, obviously not encountering this person for the first time, averted her eyes as Isabel sat cross-legged on the blanket.

"Apochromatic refractor, one-thousand-forty millimeters at focal-length eight," the telescope woman mused.

Isabel bit into the small, stale cornetto and grimaced. She would rather go hungry.

"High-quality instrument. *Garbage* with galaxies," the woman continued in her deadpan voice, her eyes narrowing at Isabel. "I'm Jan," she said. "My family lives on islands. I don't really get humans, so I spend my time with stars. She's afraid of me." Jan pointed at Cristina, who hummed to herself and pretended not to hear.

"What do you call yourself?" said Jan.

A sharp lightning of pain went off in Isabel's temple. It was a radio signal. "Isabel," she said.

Jan frowned. "You're not hungry?" She surveyed the unfin-
ished food.

"Not for this," Isabel said.

Jan nodded with approval. "Better nothing than junk."

Isabel studied the woman, trying to place her accent again.
Once more, Jan seemed to hear her thoughts.

"The accent you are hearing is Bajan, which means I'm from
Barbados. I moved here ten years ago. The stargazing in Barbados
isn't bad, but the people are boring. And nothing ever erupts." She
looked disgusted. "People usually think I'm *Welsh*."

Jan must be psychic too, thought Isabel. She wondered how
it was for the woman; every psychic was different. For Isabel, a
force took over her mind like autopilot on a car. She became not
speaker but mouthpiece.

"I'm setting up for a celestial event in five days," Jan went on.
"Not sure what it's going to be. Meteor shower, maybe. I dreamed
about it. And this is the angle in the sky where it was." She made
a triangle with her hands and framed a slice of sky.

They will come to you, Mary used to say. *The prophets and
oracles. The insane.*

"So, you think I'm crazy," said Jan.

Isabel realized then what was so familiar about the woman's
inside-out sweater.

It was a horse blanket.

"Your sweater!" she blurted.

Jan looked down as if surprised to find she was wearing a
sweater at all. "This? It's from a shop in Milan. Got it when I picked
this gal up from the importer." She patted the telescope again.

"Did you know the frame of a telescope is even more important than the lens? Shoddy frame, shoddy photos." She babbled on in telescope-speak, at first oblivious that she had lost her audience. She stopped. "Are you still on about the sweater?" She rolled her eyes. "The brand is called Pado. Here. Look."

Jan removed the sweater and turned it right side out. Isabel's breath caught. Mary had the same one. It was called Zodiac: silver stars on a navy background, the constellations joined by neon yellow thread. Isabel thought of all the times Mary had held the sweater open so Isabel could burrow in closer and listen to her aunt's stories.

The sweater was like seeing a ghost.

"I usually don't spend this much, even though I'm very rich. But I liked this one because, you know, the stars." Jan peered at Isabel. "Hey!" She snapped toward the edge of the dell where Cristina stood chattering into her cell phone. "You got a tissue?"

Mary. Isabel had not stopped to mourn her aunt's death. She had been too distracted by the mystery of the horse blankets, the trip to Sicily, and her nascent friendship with the most powerful woman she had ever known. It hit her now like a sucker punch.

Cristina, who had dared to enter Jan's orbit with a pack of tissues, touched Isabel's arm. "I'm sorry you are sad, *signurina*, but we must go."

Isabel nodded, turning aside to blow her nose. When she was calm, she looked to Jan and saw the woman had lost interest. Her focus had returned to the telescope and her preparations for the unknown celestial event.

Isabel had mounted her donkey and was urging the beast

forward when Jan appeared next to her, a firm hand on the bridle, peering up.

"You know, the best place to stargaze is on a hill," said Jan. "Preferably a big one, taller than anything else around. The word for hill in Italian is *colle*. Try to find one in seven nights. Wherever you are."

19

Raffi brushed a rivulet of sweat from her temple. At the next overlook, she came to another sculpture, this one placed between two pumpkin-shaped cacti known as *cuscino di suocera*, the mother-in-law's pillow. Raffi recognized this sculpture as Saint Veronica offering her shawl to Christ. The shawl was known as Veronica's Veil.

A pair of southern gatekeepers fluttered down to perch on Saint Veronica's shoulders, the black "eyes" on the butterflies' orange wings watching Raffi as she contemplated the sculpture. Veronica's tender, melting expression mirrored the Virgin's own sorrow. Raffi was filled with an angry pride. Women have a miraculous capacity to bear suffering, she thought. When others turn away, women hold the veil.

A gruff female voice wafted up from below to break the silence. "*Ti piacia?*"

Raffi turned around. The voice belonged to the smallest person Raffi had ever seen: a tiny nun, no bigger than a grade-school child, in a pale blue habit that terminated in a pair of brown leather hiking boots covered in muck. She must have been at least seventy years old.

"*Si, mi piacia*," Raffi answered. She liked sad things. They made her feel less alone in her grief.

"Ah, you are American," said the sister, switching to English.

Raffi bristled at the implication her Italian was not up to snuff. The little nun noticed and grinned.

"You will come with me to the sanctuary. I will introduce you to Sister Agata," she announced as if this were the solution to everything. Holding out a child-sized hand topped with long, red nails, she said, "I am Sister Giuseppe Regina."

"I'm Raffaella," said Raffi, accepting the hand and shaking it.

"*Allura,* Raffaella. *Amunnini!*" She winked and translated: "We go."

They climbed in silence. Raffi was grateful the nun did not pause; momentum at this incline was crucial. Sister Giuseppe was strong. Beneath the blue habit, Raffi made out the muscles of the nun's backside shifting gears. When they reached the intermediate summit, Sister Giuseppe Regina stopped short.

"And now," Sister Giuseppe Regina said, sweeping her hand across the tiny mountaintop *piazza*, "the sanctuary."

The sanctuary was part-building, part-mountain: unremarkable from the outside, carved from Tauro taupe and crumbling in parts. The view, by contrast, was breathtaking. The Ionian coast, the Castello Saraceno, tawny hillsides strewn with goats and almond trees, murmuring cacti, all spread out below in a visual feast. To the west puffed Etna.

Sister Giuseppe Regina scowled at the volcano like She was a rival from another convent. "Come," said the nun, grabbing Raffi's arm and pulling her through the low sanctuary door.

It took a moment for Raffi's eyes to adjust to the dim light. The sanctuary was a hollowed-out space in the mountain, its lichen-thatched rock painted with a border of gilt flowers. A table at the front of the room held a sculpture of the Madonna of the Rock wrapped in twinkle lights, the Christ-child nuzzled next to her.

"This is how many Sicilians prefer to view the Lord," said Sister Giuseppe Regina, touching the Christ-child's cheek. "Not as carpenter, savior, or dying man, but as an infant, pure in his mother's arms."

Raffi admired the figures. "That's beautiful," she said.

"Beautiful?" The sister cocked her head. "Eh. It is what it is." She leaned forward. "You know, the true worship of the Sicilian is of the Mother. She, the one who loved the Lord so dearly, that He could love the world in turn."

The nun spoke with such authority that Raffi wondered whether this was an accurate description of Sicilian devotion or the theology of one Sister Giuseppe Regina. Before she could probe, another nun emerged from the wooden door of the sacristy. Unlike Sister Giuseppe Regina, the second nun was clad all in white, breathtaking, and even older. On her wimple, she wore a large gold medallion of the Virgin Mary.

"Welcome," she said in heavily accented English. "I am Sister Agata."

Sister Giuseppe Regina jerked her chin at Raffi. "*Si chiama Raffaella.*"

"*Piacere*, Raffaella." Sister Agata smiled. "Is Sister Giuseppe

Regina take good care of you?" She touched the shorter nun's sleeve, and Raffi was charmed to see Sister Giuseppe Regina blush. The little nun obviously held Sister Agata in high regard. Or perhaps, Raffi thought, there was more than sororal admiration here? Sister Giuseppe Regina would not look out of place at a bar in the Castro.

"I was telling Raffaella that Mary, Mother of Jesus, is the center of faith for the Sicilian Catholic," said Sister Giuseppe Regina in Sicilian. It seemed this was an ongoing conversation for the two women because the older nun nodded without pause.

"I believe my sister is right, but it is not only the Virgin we worship. We also revere the mother given to us by God. Your mamma," she said, pointing at Raffi's heart, "is the face of the Madonna for *you*."

Raffi felt like she had been slapped.

But you didn't worship your mother, nagged the voice in her head. *You left her behind. College. Miami. Even now. What are you, some kind of hero for calling her cell phone every day?*

"Raffaella?" said Sister Giuseppe Regina.

The nuns rushed to surround her, clucking in Sicilian.

"It's emotional," Sister Agata said, mistaking the source of her tears, "this realization that the mother we are given at birth is the mother we serve in God's name."

Raffi wiped her eyes and looked around to confirm no one else was there.

"But God gives us many mothers, Raffaella," said Sister Giuseppe Regina. "We can also offer our devotion to a grandmother or aunt. And, of course," she added, "there is always our *godmother*."

Raffi narrowed her eyes. Did she imagine it, or had Sister Giuseppe Regina's lip twitched?

"And you, Raffaella?" said Sister Agata. "Do you have a mother to bear the living face of the Madonna for you?"

Raffi thought first of Polly, then of Mary Fortune, who'd said, *I'm not your mother, Little Girl. But you can think of me as your Little Mother. Your Pequeña Madre. I will always be that for you.* Then she conjured Trini tossing her rainbow-colored hair and shouting "Ho!"

"I've had some wonderful women in my life," said Raffi and then gave in to an urge for honesty: "But my real mother, the one who brought me into the world, is—" she touched her forehead, "—sick."

Sister Giuseppe Regina pulled a handkerchief from the folds of her skirt and wiped at Raffi's eyes with the rough touch of a window cleaner buffing a streak. "The woman who seeks the Madonna della Rocca has a pain in the place where Mamma lives," she said, clapping hand to heart. "Here."

Raffi looked down, resolving not to look up again until she had stopped crying. When at last she did, Sister Agata was standing next to her, holding out a gold medallion necklace identical to the one the older nun wore. She motioned for Raffi to take it from her hand. Raffi stepped back, alarmed.

"Sister, I can't take your necklace!"

Sister Giuseppe Regina flapped her hand. "We have more of them in the back."

Raffi stared at the nuns for a long moment, then all three began to laugh.

Sister Agata fastened the necklace around Raffi's neck and placed a hand on her shoulder. "Take help when it is offered, child. Even as you are a mother, so you will always be a daughter too."

"Sick mom or not," piped Sister Giuseppe Regina.

Raffi fingered the medallion, the metal thick and heavy like real gold. She realized they were standing in an inverted Hekataion: three women facing in.

20

When Raffi suggested they extend their stay in Sicily, Isabel was quick to agree. The girl had nothing to rush back to in Miami. All that awaited her there, Raffi knew, was a dingy hotel room and a life suspended in action.

For this late addition to their itinerary, they chose the waitress Agata's recommendation of Cefalù, a breezy north-coast fishing town famous, per Isabel, for its delectable *frutti di mare* and even more delectable fishermen. Like many parts of Sicily, Syracuse included, it was also a former Greek colony and showcase of Norman architecture. Perhaps in Cefalù Raffi could have a respite from prying eyes; for the first time since they'd announced their plans to Agata, no one knew where she and Isabel were. Spontaneity and anonymity went hand in hand.

Another reason Raffi did not mind extending their trip: it delayed her arrival in Lercara Friddi. On the one hand, she was eager to see where her family had come from, the epicenter of Truvarizzi secrets. On the other, Nino's Cousin Pasquale had insisted they stay at his "penthouse" in the village. Raffi preferred hotels—always—but Lercara Friddi was short on tourist accommodations. She did not like this, either.

Their first day in Cefalù, Isabel had hoped to lure Raffi to the beach below the old town in search of something called *Sfoglio of Madonie*, a salty local cake. An unfortunate handheld *arancina* bought at a bus stop the night before, however, had Isabel in the toilet the entire morning. Raffi took to the streets alone.

Cefalù was glittery and pungent: the Tyrrhenian Sea the color of absinthe, the air thick with sardine. Unlike the elegant buildings that bordered Ortygia harbor like swanky cocktail-party guests, Cefalù's jumble of terracotta buildings were papier-mâché bricks packed together by an overzealous child. The sky billowed like a blue silk tarp. According to the hotel concierge, God did not allow clouds over Cefalù.

Raffi wandered down to the stretch of pavement that doubled as a dock, enjoying her solitude. She was comfortable alone. Mostly, she preferred it.

She bought a cheap straw hat and, on a whim, a ticket for a boat ride full of tourists from Long Island. The boat had a bright green awning and was piloted by a captain even handsomer than Enzo. ("But much less charming," she would tell the girl later at her crestfallen face.) Hat stuffed low over her unruly waves, Raffi watched the town from the water, following the captain's hairy finger to notable sights both high—the twin peaks of the Norman Cefalù Cathedral—and low—a quartet of old men paddleboarding in matching yellow bikini bottoms.

Cefalù's defining feature was the imposing Promontory of Hercules, a colossal rock that rose from the center of town like a reverse sinkhole, threatening to do whatever an enormous rock could do to the village below. Across the top, sacred icing on an earthen cake, was a temple to the goddess Diana. Isabel would be happy to learn that, unlike the nymph-made Fountain of Arethusa in Ortygia, neither Diana nor any other goddess had thrown herself on the ground to create this landmark.

After the boat ride, Raffi found an unassuming café on a quiet alley—Cefalù, like Ortygia, was a town of alleys—and ordered the local delicacy *pasta taianu*, a baked pasta with eggplant, meat, and raisins layered into a pan, followed by the anticipated *Sfoglio of Madonie*. This experience she vowed to withhold from Isabel altogether. There was only so much the girl could take.

Replete, Raffi strolled through the meandering village, thinking about telling Isabel enough about her day to tease the girl without devastating her. As she turned a corner on one of the many cobblestoned streets that swept through Cefalù in an endless curve, she spotted an urn in the shape of a Medusa in a pottery-shop window and stopped. The ceramic Medusa's black hair wound in muscular coils around the attenuated white body like a boa constrictor choking its prey. Raffi continued walking past the shop, then sighed at the next bend in the road. She had realized, in the way women do, that she was going to turn around and buy the urn.

Pivoting on her heel to retrace her steps, Raffi was considering where to put the urn in her house when she saw Polly. And the world stopped.

Polly.

It couldn't be Polly. But it *was* Polly, even though it could not be, and wasn't.

Polly-not-Polly wore a mid-length red shift. More than red: blistering, boiling, four-alarm red. Among the rush of thoughts that hit her, Raffi considered how poor a sartorial choice red was for a woman who was supposed to be crazy, hiding, or dead.

The woman in red who was and was not Polly lingered in the doorway of a leather shop four doors down from the potter, her back to Raffi, holding a brown saddlebag aloft to consider it in daylight. The woman put the handbag down with a shrug and Raffi had a clear shot of Polly-not-Polly scratching her head and checking under her nails in classic Polly fashion. Even the cilia in Raffi's ears stood up.

Raffi ducked into a doorway. Not-Polly turned as if considering where to go next. Now Raffi could see her profile. The gentle arc of the nose, the soft sweep of half a widow's peak. This could be her mother.

As if hearing Raffi's internal monologue, the woman's shoulders went rigid. She walked away from Raffi, her pace brisk but measured—rushing without wanting to seem rushed. Raffi's heart leapt and crashed. She followed the woman.

Not-Polly's steps quickened. Raffi sped up.

A dog darted across Raffi's path. Not a white wolf this time, but a scraggly little thing that yelped when Raffi nipped its tail in her haste. Not-Polly made a quick left down a smaller alley.

Raffi began to run. She whipped the left and caught a red blur at the short bend, this time turning right into an alley so narrow, Raffi's shoulders barely passed. There were no shops or cafés, only terraced houses painted in pastel shades mottled by the years and blended like friends who resemble each other over time. Tied to the miniature second-floor balconies, laundry crisscrossed overhead, so much the sky was blotted out, the bendy footpath dusk-dark despite the early afternoon hour. Dodging a noisy Vespa that pop-popped down the gentle incline, Raffi hurried along the parabola until she came to a crossroads. An alley left, an alley right, straight ahead. *Sinistra, destra, dritto.* She chose *dritto*: straight.

There! She saw red ahead.

Raffi raced, arms pumping. Polly would be 70 by now. Could she be running this fast? Considering Nino ran 10Ks at 80, and Sister Giuseppe Regina was up there climbing Mount Tauro, the answer was yes. Sicilians were sprightly.

Not-Polly glanced over her shoulder and Raffi felt a burst of joy. After all these years—in Sicily, of all places!

The alley dissolved into a main street and Raffi again made a choice. *Destra:* right. A ribbon of sea visible at the end of the street; a sharper blast of sardine. Tourists strolling, holding hands.

"*Signura!*" A man jumped out to grab her arm. "Please!" He pointed to a greasy marquee covered in photos of plastic food. "Join us."

She slapped his arm away and he gave a cry not unlike the dog's.

The crowd thickened. She sprinted and dodged. American voices. She burst through clasped hands like a marathon runner breaking tape, a trail of protests behind her. The woman in red had slowed to hesitate at another crossroads. *Sinistra, destra, dritto.* Which way would she choose?

There were too many people. It was harder now to run. Tourists drifted and shuffled, blocking, unblocking, blocking, unblocking her view. It was one long instant before Raffi had a clear line again.

Alla destra. The woman turned right. She was close enough that Raffi could have seen her face if the woman's hair had not fallen forward to hide it.

Raffi cupped her hands to her mouth and screamed: *"Ma!"*

The crowd stopped. The street went silent. Every woman turned around.

Concerned eyes, sympathetic eyes, eyes like arms pulling close a child, saying *there, there.* Shocked, Raffi scanned each face, forgetting, for one crucial moment, the woman in red.

Too late, she realized her mistake. The women on the street looked back to their companions. The voices resumed. The crowd flowed onward.

When Raffi reached the crossroads, the woman who might but could not be Polly was gone. Lungs bursting, sweat dripping, heart sinking, Raffi felt—as she did each time she hung up the phone with no answer, or cried to the portrait bride, or saw Polly's dark brow frame her son's sweet face, except far worse this time—that she'd lost her mother all over again.

21

"*Ciao, Cuscina!*"

A septuagenarian in crisp grey pants and pressed white shirt stood waving at the bus as it pulled into Lercara Friddi's tiny terminal. A good head taller than everyone else, cap in hand and bald pate gleaming, he had planted himself so close to the stairs down from the bus, the driver had to shout at him to move so the other passengers could exit. At last, the Godmother and Isabel stood before him.

"I am Raffaella's cousin, Pasquale," he said with one hand on his chest, speaking in the slow, clear English of a child reciting a nursery rhyme. "I recognize you from the family photograph your papa send." He embraced the Godmother. "You have not aged a day."

"How kind," said the Godmother, without interest.

Isabel imagined Cousin Pasquale also recognized the Godmother from her constant presence in the American press, though that didn't account for how intensely he was staring at her. The Godmother *was* a singular woman.

When he'd torn his eyes from his cousin, Pasquale looked

stricken at the sight of Isabel beside her. Like a steak under the broiler—God, she was hungry—his face bloomed through all shades of crimson. His eyes darted back to the Godmother, but, after performing the silent genetic calculation run by all Sicilians— Cubans, too—he settled his eyes on Isabel in a way that could mean one thing. Cousin Pasquale had a crush. He rushed forward to kiss Isabel two times on each cheek, demanding her name then exclaiming over its and her beauty.

Turning back to the Godmother, he launched into a series of questions about her father's well-being, lapsing into a long soliloquy about upstate New York winters and how Nino should stop being a macho and move back to Sicily immediately. The questions were, practically speaking, rhetorical. Cousin Pasquale did not pause long enough to receive a response.

"I am cardiologist," he said, apropos of nothing, as he reached for his guests' bags and attempted to drag all three down the ramp at once. Isabel noticed women half Pasquale's age swooning at him out the windows of passing cars. In the microcosm of Lercara Friddi, it seemed Cousin Pasquale was the most eligible bachelor in town.

Pasquale ignored the gawkers. His eyes were locked on Isabel. His mooning glances made her want to both laugh hysterically and hide her body behind a shield. All these concerns faded into the background, however, when the trio came face to face with a practicality that had not occurred to Cousin Pasquale earlier that morning: where to put their luggage.

"Ah," said Cousin Pasquale, shaking his finger and frowning at the trunk of his vintage ivory convertible. "Ah," he repeated, closing his eyes as if presented with the most troublesome aortic valve.

Isabel tried to catch the Godmother's eye, but she was scanning the crowd, her eyes almost sleepy, telegraphing boredom. Isabel knew it was a front. She could feel the Godmother's excitement.

"Ah!" Pasquale shouted, finger upthrust. "I take Isabel *alone*"—his eyes popped— "in the Fiat, and my *cuscina* will ride in a taxi with the luggage."

"No, cousin," said the Godmother. "That's not what we'll do."

She summoned a ruddy-faced taxi driver who greeted Cousin Pasquale by name and introduced himself as Stefano.

"Is no room," said Stefano, frowning down at the convertible.

"Is plenty room," countered Cousin Pasquale.

At last, Cousin Pasquale conceded: Stefano would follow the two cousins and Isabel to Pasquale's house on Via F. Aprile with the luggage. Pasquale's plan to get Isabel alone was foiled.

"Are you sure they won't get stolen?" Isabel whispered as Stefano loaded their suitcases into the backseat of his sedan.

Cousin Pasquale overheard. "You are in Lercara," he said. "I would worry if this were Naples. Those people are animals."

Isabel studied his face. "When's your birthday?" she said.

As he prattled on about birthdays and name days and feast days, Isabel slid into the glove box-sized back seat, leaving the front to the Godmother. Their chat required Isabel to lean forward, an elbow slung onto Cousin Pasquale's seat. She turned to catch the Godmother's eye, but found the woman lost in thought.

Ten minutes in, Isabel realized Cousin Pasquale had steered them toward the outskirts of town, cruising at an excruciating pace behind an old man with a cart and horse.

"You're going the wrong way," said the Godmother.

Cousin Pasquale shrugged. "I am so excited to see my cousin and her friend, I forget how to find my own home!"

The old man and his cart veered off onto a narrow dirt road and Cousin Pasquale continued down the winding two-lane highway stretching out into the golden haze. The light was softer here than the sharp, bold blues of eastern Sicily. Lercara was a photograph in sepia.

"Turn around," said the Godmother.

"*Certo, certo*," said Cousin Pasquale, craning his head from side to side as if searching for a turnaround and throwing his hands up as if to say, *What can I do?*

They were approaching a large, unsightly hill that rose above the smooth countryside like a boil.

The Godmother pointed. "What's that?"

"What's what?" Cousin Pasquale sounded worried, probably hoping his cousin had not found a place to turn so he could keep driving. "Ah," he said with relief, following the line of her finger. "That is Colle Madore."

"Colle Madore," Isabel repeated. *Colle!* "What does 'colle' mean?" she asked, though of course she knew.

"*Colle* means 'hill,'" said Cousin Pasquale.

And Jan had told her to find one in seven days to witness this "celestial event." Pretending to brush aside a curl, Isabel's fingers grazed her forehead. No information about the celestial event; the psychic-astronomer Jan had a better beat than her on this one. All Isabel could pick up on was a tension stewing in the Godmother over something that had happened in Cefalù, which, Isabel knew from her radio signals, had to do with the Godmother's mother.

"I am the president of an association for car enthusiasts in Lercara," said Cousin Pasquale in another non sequitur. "I have many fine vehicles. I will show you."

Eyes fixed on the hill, Isabel said, "I hope we have time, but it's my birthday tomorrow. We might have plans."

"Your birthday!" Cousin Pasquale said with delight. "But this is marvelous! We must celebrate together."

"Cousin," said the Godmother. "You will turn this car around. *Now.*"

Pasquale sighed. He applied the brakes, and the car rolled to a stop a few feet short of the hill, where a sign marked the entrance. Arrows pointed up a loose stone path to the top.

Isabel tried to see up the path, but the back seat gave her a bad angle. She picked up a faint signal: the soft sound of crying coming from inside the mound. There had been great pain here once. Pain that lingered in the land, more echo than ghost. Blood-pain.

"It's just a hill," said Cousin Pasquale, noticing Isabel's interest. He commenced the world's slowest five-point turn. "I must ensure the lane is clear," he said, motioning to the other side of the highway.

There was not a car in sight.

Back in town, Cousin Pasquale drove past two churches and four piazzas before the Godmother pointed out that they had thrice passed the sign for Pasquale's street. At last, their caravan pulled up to the building on Via F. Aprile, a one-mile journey that had taken an hour. Isabel was grateful for the detour. She had found her hill.

Cousin Pasquale led them up the marble stairs to his penthouse, Stefano following with the bags. It turned out being a cardiologist in Lercara Friddi afforded Cousin Pasquale plush digs—although, nice as it was, Pasquale's building on Via F. Aprile was just one in a row of subdivided houses smashed together. He explained that, during Lercara's sulfur-mining era, the town had high hopes for expansion. Builders constructed with the notion that space should be allocated sparingly. Lercara was squeezed into a tight grid despite acres of wide-open countryside around it.

"The penthouse," Cousin Pasquale announced when they reached the front door, then added, rakishly, "like the magazine."

Pasquale owned the two top floors of the building, and, if the walls of his apartment were any indication, his favorite things besides classic cars were swords, paintings of half-naked women, and crucifixes. Above the faded yellow living-room couch was a painting of a naked woman flanked by a katana blade and a giant cross, and a version of this tableau appeared throughout the penthouse, including in the guest room where a pair of entwined sylphs hung over the spot where Isabel unpacked. In her *bruja* gut, she knew she would spend her solar return with Raffi Truvarizzi on Colle Madore.

ISABEL CAME OUT OF the guest room and announced she was famished. An audit of Cousin Pasquale's pantry revealed two cans of olives, a sack of almonds, a box of biscuits, and a jug of local wine; his refrigerator was filled with Coca Cola bottles. When Cousin Pasquale was hungry, he went out.

"We go," he said, arm extended toward the door.

Raffi declined. She wanted to think without Cousin Pasquale and Isabel around to bother her. The incident in Cefalù with the woman in red had brought up not only a sliver of hope that her mother was alive, but a familiar fear that Raffi herself, like Polly, might be delusional. She needed to put that day behind her. A nap might clear her energy.

Christ, she sounded like Isabel.

"No, no, absolutely not," said Pasquale when Raffi announced her intention to stay back. Isabel, too, wrung her hands and looked disappointed. Raffi gave in.

As they walked, Raffi absorbed the peculiar charm of Lercara Friddi. The town seemed to straddle time. Teenage girls took selfies on the steps of the scalloped white Chiesa Madre and denim-clad youths nibbled *gelato* by the Piazza Duomo. Nuns drifting down the streets wore grey habits and righteous frowns. Old men on benches threw hand gestures back and forth in a game whose name Raffi had forgotten. Boys jousted on bicycles, ping-ponging insults as they raced past apron-clad *nonnas* who shouted after them.

So, this was the town that had made her. She sensed it was a place of hidden things, where demonstrative public life concealed a beehive of whispers. *Omertà* was the Sicilian code, and it meant silence—not only for the Mafia, but for everyone from the grocer to the toddler in the park. And Sicilians were not only discreet; they were difficult. As Nino told it, these were people who would argue with you for an hour about whether the sun always rose in the east.

"Ah!" Cousin Pasquale stopped by a storefront with a marquee that read *Bar Mario* in neon letters. "We are here." He motioned them inside, but Raffi lingered by a large poster affixed to the adjoining building. The poster depicted 1970s-style multi-exposures of a nun praying by the Chiesa Madre; in the center, superimposed over the nun, was the name *Michele Andolini*, plus tomorrow's date and a time, 2:30 p.m.

Her heartbeat quickened. Michele Andolini was the most famous Mafioso out of Italy besides Sally T. Unlike Sally T, though, he had never been in hiding. It was rumored that he had once been an FBI collaborator, though he had a habit of killing those who spread that rumor.

"What's this?" Raffi asked, pointing at the poster.

"Funeral," Cousin Pasquale said. "For our friend."

"Michele Andolini is your friend?"

Cousin Pasquale said, with forced cheer, "Everyone in Lercara is my friend."

"They put up posters for a funeral?" said Isabel.

"Funerals are big deal in Lercara Friddi," said Stefano.

Cousin Pasquale gestured toward Bar Mario. "Enough funerals, today is celebration. My American cousin and her friend are here at last. *Amunnini*, let's go."

Cousin Pasquale opened the door and ushered Isabel inside, calling for his cousin to follow.

Raffi turned from the poster, thinking. The Andolinis were rivals of Sally T. The truth of her lineage might be revealed in their reaction to her presence. She decided they would attend this funeral. It was also great public relations. *The Godmother Mourns Michele Andolini* made a great headline. To maintain her power, and her ability to help the women under her protection, it was imperative people believe she was what she purported to be.

Entering Bar Mario, Raffi found not a bar but a simple bakery:

the walls flat white, the counter lined with stainless steel, the overhead light a long fluorescent tube. But there was a warmth born of details. The floors shone. Not a fingerprint marred the display case. Franco, the baker-proprietor, came out from behind the counter to welcome them himself.

"*Ciau, Mricani!*" sang Franco the Baker, kissing his American guests on both cheeks and exclaiming over their beauty and charm.

"This is my cousin Raffaella and her friend Isabel from America," Cousin Pasquale announced. "Raffaella Truvarizzi," he said, emphasizing the name, eyebrows raised.

"*Si, si, certo,*" said Franco, as if she could be no one else.

"Come," Franco motioned to Isabel and Raffi, putting one arm around each of their shoulders. "We take a tour."

Franco led them back and forth on the outside of the counter, explaining each of his creations, from the *Cannolo Siciliano* to the spongy fried dough of the *Sfincia di San Giuseppe*, discussing the pastries with the solemnity of someone weighing which child to adopt.

"This," he said, coming to a tray in the middle of the glass case, "is the specialty of Lercara Friddi. You can only find it here. *Pantofola.*"

"Slippers?" Raffi translated. The pastries didn't look like slippers—more like children's fists powdered in sugar.

Franco ran around to the back of the counter and returned with the entire baking sheet. "*Pantofola* is a filled pastry. Some baker fill with lemon-flavored custard, or hazelnut, or *mandorla siciliana*—the Sicilian almond. Also ricotta, vanilla custard, fruit preserve—"

"You put all those things in one pastry?" Isabel asked with amazement.

Franco laughed. "No, *biddissima*. At Bar Franco, we put *mandorla siciliana*, *cioccolato*, and candied orange peel."

He set the tray down and broke one of the pastries open, spraying powdered sugar all over his hands and on the floor. "You see."

He watched as they bit into the soft *pasta*. The filling was a marriage of chocolate chip cookie and elegant cake. Candied orange peel conferred both bitter and sweet.

"*Bedda Matri*," said Isabel.

It seemed *pantofola* would be the next Archimedes Spiral.

Cousin Pasquale changed the subject to the next day's funeral, the apparent social event of the season. Franco had been asked to supply *pantofola* for the gathering afterward.

"You're bringing these?" Isabel lowered her voice. "We can probably stop by," she mouthed to Franco.

"Of course, we will attend," said Raffi. "It would be rude not to." She heard her mother's voice in her head accusing her of doing nothing. *Am I doing nothing now?*

Cousin Pasquale worried his hands.

"Surely, it is not necessary you attend a funeral," he said. "You are visitors. No one would expect—"

Imitating her father Nino, Raffi gave a quick nod of her head and clicked her tongue. She found the Sicilian gesture pleasing in its brevity. "We're going."

She caught Isabel watching her. Let the girl peek inside her now, and see that Raffi was made of steel. She could not wait to enter that church and read the truth in Andolini eyes. If she was the kin of their rival, it would be clear from their reaction.

"Can anyone tell us," Isabel interjected, "about Colle Madore?"

Cousin Pasquale looked off into the distance. Stefano coughed.

There followed an uncomfortable silence before Pasquale said, "It is a *sita arcaeologica* from ancient Sicily. We discover it in the nineties."

As with *La Sirenetta*, Raffi's interest was piqued. She loved history. "I'd like to see it."

"Me too!" said Isabel.

Cousin Pasquale about pulled his hands off his wrists.

"Of course," he said without enthusiasm.

Another long silence ensued.

"A funeral, an archaeological site...I'm pleased we'll have such a diverse experience of Lercara, *Cuscinu*," said Raffi.

Cousin Pasquale did not look pleased.

Franco, having wrapped up a small bag of *pantofola* for Isabel, turned to Raffi with a courtly bow. "Now, what can I get for you—Godmother?"

22

"*uscini.*" Cousin Pasquale stood in the doorway of their guest bedroom wearing pinstriped silk pajamas, a sleep mask around his neck like a bow tie. "I must tell you of my very bad habit with the television news."

It transpired that he could not fall sleep without listening to the news at full volume and could only remain asleep if it stayed that way, a fact for which he apologized repeatedly. Unperturbed, Raffi and Isabel yawned and waved him off. Television news would not stand in the way of sleep.

"It will be fine, Cousin," Raffi said. "Don't worry."

Isabel smiled from the bed where she lay ensconced in pillows. "Seriously, Cousin Pasquale. We're chill."

Cousin Pasquale smiled uneasily. "If you are sure."

Two hours later, Raffi cursed Cousin Pasquale's family line, the saint he was named for, her father for suggesting she stay here, and herself for running out of melatonin tablets one night too early. Cousin Pasquale had neglected to mention the fifteen-thousand-dollar home theater system he'd installed, not merely in his bedroom—which would have been bad enough—but on the wall shared with the guestroom.

"What is wrong with him?" she muttered to herself, falling back onto the bed and tossing over yet again. Isabel, who had saved her earplugs from the first-class toiletries kit, had fallen asleep immediately, leaving Raffi to listen, fuming, to news of political purges in totalitarian states and bombs detonating in former-communist republics—the whole racket reported in a stentorian British accent at cinema volume.

The next morning, Raffi was sitting at Cousin Pasquale's kitchen table staring out the window at the land beyond the neighbors' strung-up laundry when Pasquale appeared at 6:20 a.m.—twenty minutes after the timer shut off his TV and woke him. He was already dressed for the funeral. She wanted to strangle him so he could have his own.

When he saw the look on her face, he froze like a dog caught on the kitchen table. "Was everything…alright last night, *Cuscina*?"

She stared at him.

"Perfect," she said, unsmiling. "I'll just have to find a pharmacy today, my dear cousin. Unless you keep sleeping pills in the house?"

"I have many sleeping pills. How strong is your preference?"

Raffi did not hesitate. "I want to be knocked out."

✦

ISABEL ENTERED THE KITCHEN three hours later in a cherry-print sundress, a broad *ta da* smile on her face. She had slept two hours past Raffi and spent the remaining hour in the shower singing old Cuban songs in a parody of an Italian accent and applying her makeup.

"Good morning, everyone!" she said. Noticing Raffi's stony demeanor, she asked, "Is everything alright?"

Cousin Pasquale looked to his cousin, then deep into his coffee as if wishing to hide there.

"I'm a bit tired this morning—" Raffi shot him a dirty look, "—but Cousin Pasquale has suggested the three of us tour the town before paying our respects to Michele Andolini."

Isabel drew in her chin and frowned. "Who is Michele Andolini?"

"The man who died."

Isabel blinked.

"The funeral?"

"Oh!" Isabel clapped her hand over her forehead and giggled, then looked worried. "What about Colle Madore?"

"We'll go tomorrow."

Isabel opened her mouth to protest, but Raffi's look silenced her.

"Let's not kill ourselves doing everything at once. Oh, and by the way—"

"*Happy birthday!*" she and Cousin Pasquale yelled.

Isabel clapped her hands. "You remembered!"

It wasn't much of an accomplishment to remember Isabel's birthday. The past two days alone, Isabel had mentioned it as they were packing to leave Cefalù ("I can't believe this is my last day as a 23-year-old,"), on the bus to Lercara Friddi ("Does 24 count as, like, mid-twenties?"), after the trip to Bar Mario ("Are birthday cakes a thing in Italy?"), at the beginning of dinner the night before ("We're not celebrating anything special *tonight*, but tomorrow..."), and at bedtime ("The next time I open my eyes, it will be my birthday!").

Raffi handed Isabel a small box wrapped in red paper. Red fights the *malocchio*—the evil eye—Polly used to say. *The red dress...* Isabel grabbed the box. "For *me?*"

She removed the wrapping paper in one crisp tear to reveal a white box, then shucked out the black velvet one inside and opened it with exaggerated slowness, the way women do in jewelry commercials aired at Christmas and Valentine's Day—the kind of commercials that end in proposals and sobs and knowing looks shot toward the camera as if to say, *thank you for helping me make her so happy.*

"*Isabel!*" shouted Raffi.

At the sight of what lay inside the box, the girl had stopped breathing.

Raffi went to the sink to get a wet cloth, and Cousin Pasquale disappeared into his bedroom, returning with a stethoscope.

"No, no," said Isabel, pushing aside the washcloth—and the stethoscope, to Cousin Pasquale's disappointment.

She extracted the contents of the box and held it up to the light. It was a gold pendant necklace from a famed Italian design house. Raffi had walked into the boutique after her emotional trip to the sanctuary in Taormina, having decided by crossing the boutique's threshold to spend five figures.

The focal point of the necklace was the pendant, a Trinacria:

a triskelion formed from three bent legs arranged in rotational symmetry, with the head of a red-eyed Medusa in the center against a background of wings and wheat sheaves.

"The Trinacria is the symbol of Sicily, the image on the center of our flag," the saleswoman had told Raffi. "The eyes of Medusa deter evil; the wings and wheat signify our fertility, and the power of the feminine."

Raffi, rarely impressed by anything anymore, had fallen in love with the necklace. She wanted it for herself, which was the hallmark of a great gift.

"The eyes are Sicilian cinnabar," Raffi told Isabel, who seemed unable to speak. "That's what makes them so special to this location."

"This is too expensive!" Isabel protested.

It *was* too expensive—except that the girl had been passed up in Mary's will, an omission Raffi would never understand. The more Raffi thought about it, the angrier she was at Mary. A promise was a promise. The girl had deserved better.

✦

COUSIN PASQUALE KNEW THE cost of this necklace. Ginevra Randazzo, one of the few women who had ever managed to ensnare him, had once forced him, in a moment of weakness and Sambuca, to buy her something from the same designer. The blonde had the equivalent of a sportscar wrapped around her rosy neck. He felt like he'd been passed by a motorcade of cars bearing an insignia recognized by everyone but him. Did women in America buy each other jewelry this extravagant? This was a gift for lovers.

He was struck with a thought, a tantalizing one, which built and magnified until he was almost sure it was true and he, Pasquale Bruscato, the luckiest man in the world.

Raffaella, with her fancy divorce, that astonishing money and power, yet never another man. It was unnatural, it had long flummoxed him—much more than the whole Godmother thing, which, like anything Mafia-related, the Lercarese had long learned to ignore.

It was as obvious now as the red stones on the blonde's new necklace: the two women were a couple. *Bedda Matri*, right here in his house, he couldn't believe it. He was like an old-time screen star, the dapper hero in a racy film with a coy title. He daydreamed the marquee: *Una Famiglia Complicata, L'Amante di Mia Cugina*. Now he couldn't wait for the Andolini funeral. He would be the envy of everyone—*everyone*—although, as he was blissfully aware, they all envied him anyway.

"I am sorry," he said now to Isabel, his heart going so fast that he wanted, out of professional curiosity more than alarm, to turn the stethoscope on himself. "I did not get you a present for your birthday, *biddissima*. Please, allow me to make it up to you. Is there anything—anything at all—that Cousin Pasquale can do to make your day more special?"

Isabel stopped staring at the necklace, faced Cousin Pasquale, and popped a hip. "Can you find me a telescope?"

THE TELESCOPE TURNED OUT to be an easy get. It would have been difficult, Cousin Pasquale explained, if he were any other Lercarese. A normal person couldn't just waltz down Via Napoli, tuck into a storefront, and emerge with a Celestron SkyProdigy 130.

Cousin Pasquale, however, was, by his account, one of the most prominent men in town—not just for his prestigious cardiology practice, which connected him, by extension, to almost everyone in the area, but even more so as president of the classic-car-enthusiast society, *Gruppo Amatori VEicoli Storici*, known as GAVES.

Cousin Pasquale's GAVES friends had the time and money for expensive, equipment-specific hobbies, like knife-making, car-collecting, downhill skiing—and stargazing. Cousin Pasquale called his pal Luigi, who brought, in addition to the telescope, a companion pair of binoculars. Of course, there was a price.

"What does Balilla mean?" Isabel whispered to the Godmother. It was the only word besides *binoculare* that she was able to tease out from the torrent of Sicilian passing between Pasquale and Luigi.

"Balilla is Pasquale's car. The 1932 Fiat," she whispered back. "Luigi's demanding to drive it if we break the telescope."

Another intercession was required when Cousin Pasquale discovered that neither woman had a black dress for the funeral.

"Not even at home in Miami?" Cousin Pasquale asked, fascinated.

"Definitely not at home," said Isabel with conviction. "Miami is all about color and white." *Never black!* Mary used to say. *You attract what you put out.*

"I don't understand." Cousin Pasquale bumped his forehead with the heel of his palm. "How then do you mourn?"

Isabel touched the Trinacria charm on her chest. "I mean, a) we don't. And b), if we do, we do it in color."

Cousin Pasquale looked aghast. "When my mamma died, I wore black for a year. This is the Sicilian tradition. Once, in

Palermo, I was mistaken for a priest!" he said with pride. "To not wear black at all...." He shook his head. "Please excuse me, but it is almost blasphemy."

"Okay," said Isabel, determined to fit in. "Where can we find something black this late?"

Cousin Pasquale grimaced. "I know someone."

Within thirty minutes, Ginevra Randazzo was at the house with a stack of dresses thrown over her arm.

"Pasquale and I, we date five years, you know," said Ginevra as Pasquale picked at his nails, sighing.

"Five years *ago*," Pasquale corrected her. "For seven months. Ginevra's English is not so good."

"His mamma love me," she continued, ignoring him. "She want us to get married, but...." She narrowed her eyes at Pasquale as he squirmed.

"Please, Ginevra. The dresses," said Pasquale. "We do not have time for reminiscing."

"I bring the eucharist to his mother, I am never divorce, I have no children, I make the *timballo* from his mamma recipe..."

Isabel had to admit these qualifications were impressive. She felt for Cousin Pasquale, though. Ginevra had a face like an honest-to-God horse.

"*Allura*. No black at all?" Ginevra mused.

"*Nudda*," said the Godmother. None.

Ginevra brandished her vinyl garment bag. "*Un fà nenti*. No matter. Ginevra has just what you need."

"I can't believe this is happening to us," Isabel hissed an hour later as they exited Cousin Pasquale's building onto Via F. Aprile, wearing the two least offensive of Ginevra's dresses. Isabel's was a black, tiered, ruffled confection of a frock that made her look like an oversized flower girl. "I feel like a cake topper for a wedding in hell."

The Godmother lifted the long bell sleeves of her floor-length dress. "If it makes you feel any better, I look like a disco vampire."

The town was quiet as they walked toward the restaurant Cousin Pasquale had chosen for lunch. Despite the near-empty streets, Isabel was getting considerable attention from the Lercarese men. Passing here and there in small groups, clothed in their well-worn black funeral garb, they lowered their sunglasses and stared.

"What are they looking at?" said Isabel.

"It's the hair," said the Godmother. "Italians love blondes."

"You're not kidding," Isabel said, as the waiter tripped over his shoelaces to seat her in the best chair. Whereas the others had their backs to the street, Isabel faced the stone building kitty-corner to the *ristorante*, its antique wall inset with statues and draped with another Michele Andolini funeral announcement, this one featuring a newly added yellow sticker slapped across the top, declaring, in Italian, "Today!"

"What shall we eat?" Ginevra asked, poking her fingers into Cousin Pasquale's sleeve.

He sighed and rolled his eyes heavenward.

"And what shall *we* eat?" Isabel asked, giggling as she touched the Godmother's sleeve in imitation of Ginevra, Cousin Pasquale brightening at the sight.

The waiter returned to take their order, his eyes on Isabel.

"*Panelle*," said Cousin Pasquale, referring to the classic Sicilian snack of fried chickpea fritters.

"*Solamente?*" The waiter asked with surprise.

"No," said Ginevra. "No, no, no. Not just the *panelle*. He will have the *involtini*, too, with eggplant. I will have the *pasta con le sarde*, and we will share all three."

Ginevra sat back in her chair, satisfied.

"*Pani cunsatu anticu e pani cunsatu mudernu*," the Godmother said, pointing first to Isabel and then to herself as she ordered two typical local sandwiches, one "old" and one "new."

"That's a mouthful," said Isabel. She scanned the menu for the English translation and frowned. "Wait—will two sandwiches be enough?"

"Is plenty," said the waiter. He looked with longing at Isabel and shuffled away.

"So, Cousin," said Pasquale with a newfound eagerness. "You are ready for your first funeral in Lercara?"

The Godmother, who had been watching two black birds peck at each other in the street, looked up. "I'm sorry, Cousin Pasquale. Excuse me."

Isabel watched the Godmother push back her chair and round the corner into the street. She had felt the Godmother's mood shift. The impending funeral was making the Godmother antsy, and she was still upset about her mother.

Pain sliced through her thoughts, a blade in each temple; her vision went black. She reeled, groaning. Muted, as if from afar, she heard Pasquale and Ginevra exclaim with concern.

The pain passed as swiftly as it had come. "No, no," she said, touching her head to find it tender. "It's alright. I'm fine, please."

Satisfied she was alright—Cousin Pasquale offered to examine her—they settled back into their seats and resumed talking.

With the knife in her brain came a vision. Isabel rose from the table, pointing toward the bathroom, but, instead, she snuck around to the street. She needed to find the Godmother and explain what she'd seen: the Andolini funeral was not a safe place for Raffi Truvarizzi.

✛

RAFFI WANDERED INTO THE street. The buildings looked like they'd been wetted down by a giant hose. The paint was marred by a century of decay. There was beauty, though, in the grittiness.

The pedestrian traffic was kicking up as the funeral approached. Almost all the passersby wore black and marched toward the Chiesa Madre. Raffi did not have much time.

She drew her phone from her purse, black sleeves hanging against her ear as she dialed Polly's number. No answer. She wanted to call Trini next, but she remembered Trini's veiled warning and thought better of it. The Paz situation remained unresolved. Raffi would face the Andolinis without succor.

She was about to remove the photo from her pocket when she felt someone behind her and turned. Isabel stood inches from Raffi's nose.

"I had a radio signal," said the girl.

Raffi sighed. "Go on."

Isabel stared through her. In a low monotone, she said, "You will be approached at the funeral by a woman of power."

Raffi racked her brain. The Andolini organization was comprised of Andolini and his sons, plus a supporting cast of hang-around cousins and associates. All men. She knew of no Andolini *woman* of power. Other than herself, Raffi had not heard of any Sicilian woman of power at all—at least, not outside the domestic sphere.

"There's more," said the girl, looking at once reticent and compelled to speak. "You'll find the truth, but not the whole truth. You'll find your family, but not your whole family."

It seemed she had even more to say, but the girl fell silent, picking at her fingernails as Raffi considered how much to reveal; any response to the girl's odd comments would be a disclosure, and Raffi did not disclose anything unless necessary. But she was curious, so she settled on a question. "What do you know about my interests in Sicily?"

The girl exhaled and smiled with what looked like relief, as if she had been expecting to hear something else and was thrilled to be asked this instead. "I know your family came from here. There is a question of your identity. You won't rest until you have the answer. At times, it has been an obsession. It has to do with your mother."

The girl had started off right but veered off course. While Raffi was certainly preoccupied with her mother, Apollonia was not a Truvarizzi, she was an Angelini. It was her father's family about which she had questions.

Despite the considerable gifts demonstrated by the girl, Raffi reverted to her baseline belief that there were no psychics, just people who guess well.

"Thank you, Isabel," said Raffi. "I will take all this into account."

Isabel seemed to sense Raffi's skepticism. "You can trust me, you know," said Isabel. "I can help."

Raffi turned toward the restaurant. "Your offer is appreciated," she said, her tone a dismissal.

Isabel Ibarra was fun to travel with and a nice enough girl, but Raffi would not let her in. The fewer people who knew the woman behind the Godmother, the better.

23

Cousin Pasquale sponsored a pew in the Chiesa Madre. By virtue of his patronage, he believed it unnecessary to arrive early to the church. He slowed them to a stroll, kicking up his feet like a character in a musical as they made for the funeral. Halfway on, they were joined by Franco the Baker, who was locking up Bar Mario as they passed.

"*Ciau, Dutture!*" Franco called.

"*Ciau, Franco!*" said Cousin Pasquale.

"Where's all the *pantofola*?" Isabel said, regarding his empty hands with alarm.

"I already leave at the house of Michele Andolini," Franco reassured her.

They entered the Chiesa Madre—Cousin Pasquale, Pew Custodian, leading the way—and it was obvious he had timed their arrival a hair beyond propriety because everyone in the church turned, expecting pallbearers and casket. So expectant, then angry, were the glances in his direction that Cousin Pasquale made a hands-up gesture of surrender and laughed, mollifying the crowd, who probably chalked it up to the ignorance of an unwomaned man.

The mourners in the back cast circumspect looks at Raffi as she passed. She pretended not to notice. Up front, the Andolini family sat erect, heads fixed forward, backs straight as if they wore neck braces. Their posture showed not pride but dominion. Raffi had adopted the same bearing when she became the Godmother.

She sat in the pew and felt the time-worn wood beneath her hands. Her ancestors may have touched this very spot. But who were her ancestors? She felt like a swimmer stepping up to the starting block. It was time.

A powerful rumble announced the arrival of the hearse. Six men entered to somber organ music. Their swarthy, scarred faces wore matching grimaces; even the shortest among them was large and menacing. Bullet-silver casket aloft, they walked the aisle a half-step at a time. As they passed, the people on the aisle rose to kiss their own hands and touch the casket.

I am at a Mafia funeral, thought Raffi. This is not a test.

"*I figghi ri Michele Andolini*," Cousin Pasquale whispered, pointing out the deceased's sons as they passed.

The sons placed the casket before the altar and bowed, the mourners bowing with them, heads lowered until the men rose and filed into the first two pews. One son slung an arm over the back of the pew and traced the church with a cold and vigilant stare. He looked ready, at a moment's notice, to defend an attack. His eye caught Raffi's, and he held it, unblinking, then nodded before turning back around.

It was an acknowledgement. A thrill seized her body. The air was heavy with incense.

What had the girl said? A woman of power would approach her. Raffi would find her family, but not her whole family. Doubt eroded her earlier skepticism. She glanced across and caught the girl admiring the Trinacria pendant with tenderness, as if it were a newborn.

A priest emerged from the rectory, exuding disapproval, and stood before the casket with folded hands. He signed the cross with a look of admonition and spoke the words with which every Mass begins: *"In nomine Patris, et Filii, et Spiritus Sancti, Amen."*

"I thought they got rid of Latin Mass," Raffi whispered to Cousin Pasquale.

"Michele Andolini made a special request," said Cousin Pasquale.

The same grim man who had stared at Raffi before swiveled in his pew and locked eyes with her again. His lip twitched like he was fighting a smile.

This was going well.

The Mass went on in Latin, which Raffi had taken in school, so she knew when to respond and stand, when to kneel and pray. Before she knew it, the usher was tapping their pew for Communion. She would be inches from the Andolinis in minutes. She kept her eyes on Cousin Pasquale's bald head and its ring of wispy silver hairs. To center herself, she counted them. She'd gotten to thirty-six when she reached the front.

The diminutive priest, standing on a riser, held the wafer aloft and looked down the long line of his nose. She felt Andolini eyes on her back. She touched the wafer to her tongue.

It was time to dive in. She was not afraid. She had been preparing for this for a decade.

An arpeggio of male heads turned as she passed. She looked at each in turn; their corresponding looks said *I know you.* The Andolini women came next. Beside the sons sat an aging beauty who Raffi assumed was the widow. She wore a black tweed skirt suit and pillbox hat, a demi veil stretched over her eyes. Even behind the demi veil, her gaze burned.

Raffi returned to her seat. Her heart was not pounding. She felt she had no pulse at all. She had taken the Body of Christ in her family's hometown church in Sicily. She had done this in the presence of the Andolini family—a family with a name almost as bad as her own. All this for a girl from Skaneateles, New York. How could the bride not applaud this feat? But the bride was silent. Raffi had to congratulate herself. Her performance was over.

The casket traveled back down the aisle on the sons' shoulders, followed by a parade of straight-backed Andolinis walking two by two. When it was their turn to exit, Cousin Pasquale led Raffi, Isabel, and Franco the baker toward the church doors held open by two teenage boys with serious brown eyes and dark widow's peaks—presumably younger Andolinis. Raffi braced herself for a receiving line. Instead, she stumbled outside to find the clouds had lifted, replaced by golden Sicilian sunlight. She was so entranced by the sky that she nearly collided with what seemed like a Mardi Gras parade.

"The funeral procession," said Cousin Pasquale.

The sons had relinquished the casket to a crowd of hands. The procession surged forward, led by a brass band. Forlorn horns warbled over the bright clap of cymbals and the deep thump of drums. Voices shouted in Sicilian to compete with the music: voices saying what's for dinner later, did you see how low her dress was cut, weren't his sons handsome; voices wondering did the family want *il conzu*, the offering of food, or had it been refused; still more voices asking did his widow seem too sorrowful, or was she not sad enough?

"This is very picturesque," said Isabel. "*Old fashioned.*"

"We usually use cars now for the processional," said Pasquale curtly. "We are modern. It is Andolini who wanted the procession in the old style, on foot. My funeral, *biddissimi*, will be all cars."

Cousin Pasquale's dreamy expression suggested he would be buried in a car, too, if only "they"—The Catholic church? The ghost of his mother? —would let him.

"I don't want a funeral," Raffi said. "It's a waste."

Pasquale and Franco crossed themselves.

Polly would have concurred. Polly's mother's casket, with its rose florets and copper fixtures, had cost more than Polly and Nino's wedding. Polly could not forgive the frivolity of her mother's choice. She thought her mother would rest as peacefully in a simple wooden coffin and never know the difference.

Raffi remembered her parents' fight the night of her grandmother's death.

"Her soul will know the difference!" Nino had cried. "The dead haunt those who don't respect their wishes."

"That's a Sicilian thing. I'm American. Americans don't believe in ghosts."

Raffi had thought many times about what her father said next.

"You're no American," Nino fired back. "You can't deny
what you are."

Her mother went silent, and, too late, Raffi realized Polly
was headed for the stairs where Raffi had hidden to eavesdrop.
When her mother caught her there, Raffi cringed, expecting a
punishment. But Polly just stopped and looked Raffi dead in
the eye, as if Raffi were a stranger, before she continued up to
her bedroom.

"Forgive me," Cousin Pasquale said. "What do you mean 'a
funeral is a *waste*?'"

Raffi shrugged. "I'd rather be cremated. My son can scatter
my ashes over the ocean or put them on his mantel or fertilize his
plants. I don't care. If anyone wants a thimble of me, they can take
one too," she said, grinning at Isabel, who also looked chagrined.

"*Fertilize?*" Cousin Pasquale shrieked. "*Thimble?*"

For perhaps the first time since Cefalù, Raffi laughed heartily,
so loud it rang out over the horns and cymbals and voices of nearby
mourners arguing over whether the Neapolitan *sfogliatelle* or the
Sicilian *cassata* was the better pastry, and if the tuba player was
having an affair with the woman on flute, and would the widow
try to throw herself into the casket. Raffi's laugh made her companions look relieved, as if her good mood took a weight off them.
Raffi Truvarizzi never had this power. It was the Godmother who
affected people this way.

Carried along like ants in a line, they wound up the hill to the top of Cousin Pasquale's street, the crowd headed for a nondescript white building that looked like it needed a fresh coat of paint.

"*A casa ri Michele Andolini*—Andolini's home," said Cousin Pasquale, translating for Isabel and pointing to the building.

"I'm confused," said Raffi. "Isn't the cemetery after the church?"

Cousin Pasquale could not look more uncomfortable. "Michele Andolini has made another special request." He pulled Raffi close. "He wants to be cremated too." At Raffi's confused expression, he added, "So the funeral procession must go to his house instead of the cemetery. We will not speak of this again."

"Why have the funeral procession at all?" Raffi persisted.

"Cousin. That's enough," said Pasquale, and Raffi had a glimpse of his authority with patients.

They entered the house. What was a plain white box on the outside was an opulent mansion within— "to fool the tax collector," Cousin Pasquale said. Beyond the three-story, marble-floored entryway, a direct line of sight to the parlor revealed the casket amid a jungle of orchids and lilies. Raffi's eyes went to an easel with a large black-and-white headshot of the deceased.

Raffi took in the image of Michele Andolini. He had been almost handsome, with a strong nose that, like Raffi's, was hooked on one side, straight on the other. This photo from his thirties— about forty years ago—was taken from the hooked side. His jet-black hair and charcoal eyes cast a glamour that made him even more attractive. What detracted from his good looks was his flat expression. Although his lips smiled in the photo, the eyes were as dead as they would look if one ripped out the undertaker's stitches and pried his eyelids open. The word *executioner* came to mind.

If she had less self-control, Raffi would have shivered. *This* was what she pretended to be. She had never before been forced to confront it. Feelings seized her from all directions, pulling at her like impatient children yanking at her dress. Overwhelm was the predominant one; also, shame. But beneath these, at her secret core, there was pride. She had claimed as much power as Michele Andolini, and she hadn't harmed a soul.

Well—almost as much power.

A line of mourners shuffled toward the casket, and Pasquale motioned for Raffi and Isabel to join. Raffi turned and smiled reassuringly at Isabel, but found the girl looked concerned for *her*. Raffi squeezed the girl's hand. *It's okay,* she thought, surmising the girl could hear her.

Cousin Pasquale turned, caught them holding hands, and nudged Franco.

Raffi drifted left for a closer look at the demonstrative respect for Andolini. She saw a woman in a black tea-length dress kiss both Andolini's cheeks, leaning in to speak to the corpse, and interlacing her fingers with the corpse's own. A white-haired man clapped Andolini's shoulder like a schoolfellow; like the woman before him, he chatted with the late Mafioso, chuckling and shaking his head as if charmed by the dead man's wit. When he turned around, Raffi saw his face was streaked with tears. A stout woman with gray hair falling out of a topknot stepped toward the casket and commenced bawling so shrilly, Raffi almost jumped. No one else blinked.

"A professional," Cousin Pasquale whispered, of the gray-haired woman.

Raffi stared at him. A prostitute?

He amended: "A professional *mourner*."

Franco leaned around Pasquale to add: "We had three mourners in Lercara, but the other two, they move to Palermo. Not enough business here." He shrugged, as if to say *what are you gonna do?*

Before Raffi could come up with a tart response—professional *mourners?* —the attractive ginger-haired woman in front of Cousin Pasquale threw down her designer handbag, a loud crack splitting the air as the gold padlock on the front zipper struck marble.

All talking ceased.

Everyone looked on as the woman leapt onto the riser, wrapped her arms around Andolini's shoulders, and squished her cheek against his chest, sobbing words even Raffi couldn't decipher. Only through an intervention from the Andolini sons was the woman separated from the body.

A female voice cried out from where the Andolini women sat. *The widow.* She had leapt from her chair and was pointing a lace-gloved finger at the casket-sobber.

"Tina!" She thundered as the woman dismounted the casket, grabbed her fallen handbag, and ran for the door. "*Sdisgrazia!*"

There followed an excruciating silence during which everyone stared at the widow, who, in turn, stared with such intense vitriol at the door through which "Tina" had exited that the Andolinis standing near it stepped away, as if the door itself were cursed. When, at last, the widow resumed her chair, the noise and commotion started up again. What a shame Trini could not be here. These people belonged on a telenovela.

Cousin Pasquale was up next, then Franco, then Ginevra,

until no one stood between Raffi and Andolini. She stepped on the riser. Again, she felt like an athlete at the starting block. She imagined the women she protected cheering for her. Their salvation depended on her ability to pull this off.

Raffi was distracted from these thoughts by the deceased's similarity to his photo. The jet-black hair and tense-set mouth were preserved, though his lips were arranged in a thin line instead of that cold smile. Raffi imagined the stitches sealing Andolini's mouth. That mouth had given a lot of orders before it closed for good.

She was stooped over the corpse when a bony hand gripped her arm. The hand belonged to Andolini's wife, who stood scowling at Raffi with magnificent cat eyes. The widow was around sixty, and no less striking for her age. A lick of dark hair had escaped her chignon and curved near her frosted lips, above which was dotted a mole so perfectly placed it could have been drawn on.

"Come," hissed the widow in perfect English.

Raffi flashed to Isabel's premonition as she followed the widow to the crook of the room, where they settled behind a giant wreath of carnations and a banner with the words *In pace per sempre* written in red. Another brief silence ensued, after which—as with the spectacle of the corpse-hugger—the normal din of conversation and complaints resumed.

Having led Raffi into the shadowy corner, the widow glowered from behind the veil. Also behind the veil: concentric rings of yellow and purple beside one almond-shaped eye. The widow had taken a knuckle to the face.

"You saw that?" The woman jerked her head toward Andolini. "That woman hugging my husband right in front of me?"

This was just another woman, Raffi told herself. She must stay calm. "I saw."

The widow moved closer. "Do you have any idea how difficult it was?" She spoke through clenched teeth. "Being married to a man like *him*?"

Raffi peered through the flowers at Michele Andolini. He provoked a strong response.

"And the life I have now is *because* of what he was, not despite it."

Raffi did not know how to respond to this. In such circumstances, she said as little as possible. She settled on "I'm sorry for your loss."

The widow appraised Raffi. "You're Raffaella Truvarizzi," she said, moving closer, blowing warm minty breath in Raffi's ear. "I'm Serafina Andolini. I like you."

Raffi's eyebrows shot up. She had hoped for insight into her lineage, but the last thing she expected was Andolini approval. "You know me well enough to like me?"

Serafina ignored the question. "It's time for a woman to run a family. More of us should *join* you."

One of the Andolini sons was making his way over with purpose. The widow eyed him. "We should be allies," she whispered.

"Mamma," barked the son, glancing at Raffi. "*Basta*." Enough.

Serafina Andolini looked at her son as if trying to place him. "Michele?" she said faintly.

Her son reached for her hand and patted it, leading her away. After he had helped her back into her front-row seat, the widow raised her veil, looked at Raffi, and winked.

So, Serafina Andolini, at least, bought into Raffi's ruse. But what did the widow mean about being allies? Had Raffi spurred a female Mafia uprising? The remote consequences of once-unrelated actions always surprised her. A decade back, she had befriended the Cuban psychic Mary Fortune, and now she stood in the house of a dead Mafioso being called to unity by his widow.

Raffi looked for Isabel and found the girl waiting on the sidelines.

"It was her," said Isabel.

"The widow Andolini."

"I know," said Isabel.

Raffi was back to believing in psychics. "I would appreciate these details in advance."

"It doesn't work that way." Isabel paused. "Did she know anything about…?"

"About what?"

"You know what."

This was the price of befriending an Ibarra.

"We did not discuss my family history," said Raffi.

The din in Casa Andolini was becoming a roar. Young men and women in white shirts and black pants—more Andolinis, or maybe everyone looked like an Andolini by now—were circulating glasses of red wine on porcelain trays. Raffi and Isabel each took a glass.

Behind them, a circle of men and women listened to a rosy-cheeked man in the center tell about the time Michele Andolini fought him in the churchyard after catechism. The air around him was filled with the scent of strong cologne.

"*Vinciu,*" the man shouted of Andolini. "*Vinciva sempri,*" he emphasized, shaking his head with admiration.

"He won," Raffi translated to Isabel. "He says Andolini always won the fight."

Another group discussed the shame of the woman, Tina, for making her position so obvious. *Sdisgrazia,* they hissed, repeating the widow's word. But although it meant "disgrace," they said it with enthusiasm. *Sdisgrazia* was the Sicilian Schadenfreude. What fun would there be in a life without *sdisgrazia?*

A string of teenagers in the back row traded lewd faces and mouthed taunts as Franco and a young helper grabbed the trays of *pantofola* from the table behind them and began to serve.

"Excuse me," Isabel said, heading in Franco's direction.

Cousin Pasquale, like a Southern belle at a cotillion, had amassed his own group—all men—around him, the collective gaze of which was directed at Raffi and Isabel.

Raffi yawned, then startled as her eyes fell on a familiar face. Beyond the gossipers and obscenity of flowers stood a woman with a widow's peak, a patrician nose, and a low knot of glossy black hair tucked under a mantilla.

The woman looked like, but was not, Polly.

Not-Polly?

Before Raffi could move, Isabel stepped in her path.

"Godmother?" Isabel had returned with a *pantofola* in hand. "Why are your cousin and his friends looking at us like that?"

Over Isabel's frilly shoulder, Raffi watched as the woman with the widow's peak put her arm around a squirming young girl and led her away, presumably to a bathroom. Raffi would have to mow Isabel down to stop the woman. But she could not make a scene. Not here.

When her vision came back into focus, she found Isabel staring at her.

"Godmother?"

Raffi tore her eyes from the place where the woman had been. "Did you say something?"

"I said, why are your cousin and his friends looking at us like that?"

The woman in red.

Isabel bit into her *pantofola*. "Is it because he thinks we're lesbians?"

Raffi focused on the girl. She would ruminate later. "Yes."

"Hasn't he ever seen a woman give jewelry to another woman before? Or do only men buy necklaces in Sicily?" Isabel chuckled. "Godmother?"

Not-Polly.

Raffi pushed her mother from her thoughts. In Cefalù she almost had, but Raffi decided she would not tell Isabel about Not-Polly, now or ever. Telling Isabel would make it harder to put out of her mind. People had an aggravating tendency to remind you of things you'd said.

We should be allies, the widow had whispered. Allies in what? Who was *we*?

24

To keep her cousin away from Isabel's birthday dinner, Raffi leveraged his force against him, which, as a fan of swordplay (or at least swords), Cousin Pasquale would have had to admire, had he known what she was up to. He did not, however, suspect artifice when she said, "Cousin, I'll take Isabel to dinner alone tonight." With a meaningful look, she added: "You understand."

This statement made him so breathless, he had to sit down at the kitchen table.

"Are you alright, Cousin?" Raffi said. "Should I get the stethoscope?"

"Ah, *Cuscina*, of course you must go alone," said Cousin Pasquale. "But please allow me to reserve the perfect restaurant for your... *friend's* birthday."

Raffi saw right through this offer. Pasquale wanted to know where they were eating so he could show up.

"Of course, Cousin," Raffi said, mimicking his courtly air. "It would be our pleasure to take your recommendation."

Isabel appeared in the doorway behind them.

"Colle Madore," she announced.

It took Raffi a minute to realize Isabel was talking about that hill outside of town. "What about it?"

"We're going to Colle Madore after dinner."

"Tomorrow, Isabel. It's been a long day."

"Tonight," said Isabel, looking like Mary.

Raffi opened her mouth, but this time it was Isabel who silenced *her.*

"It's my birthday," said the girl. "You have no choice."

FREED FROM RUFFLES AND sleeves and dressed in matching white, the Godmother and Isabel glided through the streets of Lercara Friddi like apparitions. They chose to walk to the restaurant, disappointing Cousin Pasquale again. Isabel thought she caught a tear in his eye when they'd refused his offer of a ride. His yearning was almost palpable as he watched them from the front balcony, waving until they turned onto Via Napoli and out of sight.

Above the close-pressed buildings of town, a slice of sky bled from sapphire to cobalt: the precise shade of the sea in the dream that brought Isabel and the Godmother together.

"This sky alone was worth the trip," Isabel said.

The largest stars, the early risers, shone like sequins in silk.

"I'm still not sure how you did it," said the Godmother.

"Did what?" said Isabel, knowing what she meant but wanting to hear her say it.

"Got me to Sicily. It's been long overdue. I just never thought I would come with a twenty-four-year-old psychic."

Isabel laughed. She felt a rush of pride. The way the Godmother said *psychic* suggested she believed in Isabel's powers—and in Isabel herself.

"It's strange," said Raffi, "to find you belong in a place you've never been before. Maybe that's what Cuba will be like for you."

"Yes," said Isabel, to both. "And you do seem to belong here."

They shared silence for the length of Via Napoli, the right turn onto Via Aiello, and the pivot onto Cortile Nicolosi. By the time they reached Ristorante da Friddi—recognizable from Cousin Pasquale's description by its yellow walls and green shutters—a happy peace had settled between them. Isabel hoped this feeling would extend beyond Sicily.

At the restaurant door, the Godmother faced Isabel. "That's why I put off coming here."

Isabel waited for the Godmother to elaborate, though again she took her meaning right away.

"You said I seem to belong here," continued the Godmother. "That's what always worried me." She paused, her strong brows furrowing almost imperceptibly. "I also worried I *wouldn't* belong."

Isabel reflected on these words, searching for empathy like loose change in a pocket. No, she realized, she did not understand. For her, there was no crisis of identity. She was a Cuban raised among Cubans, in Miami, which was more Cuban post-Castro than Cuba itself. There were no dark family secrets. Even the *bruja* thing, among the Ibarras at least, was out in the open.

But Isabel understood loss. The loss of the seaside house. The loss of her mother, leaving Isabel with snippets of memories, like her mother's knees from below, a toddler-eye view, and a time in the car when her mother had turned around to look at her from the driver's seat, touching Isabel's little foot where it stuck out from the car seat, and said, "*Yo no te quiero, pequeña niña—yo te amo.*" I don't love you shallow, little one. I love you deep.

"I'm glad you asked me here," said the Godmother. "It was time."

Time for the Godmother to uncover the truth of her blood.

Through the windowpane, Isabel spotted a table set for three and a sign that read, *Prenotato.* Reserved. She felt a rush of pity for the excluded Cousin Pasquale, then frowned. A table for *three?* Cousin Pasquale was planning to party-crash. That wily old fox.

The Godmother cleared her throat and grasped the doorknob. "Shall we?"

Isabel nodded, afraid to speak and break the spell.

RISTORANTE DA FRIDDI'S OWNER-PROPRIETOR, Peppe, was an honorary member of Cousin Pasquale's car club thanks to his popular restaurant—an ideal meeting place—and his mint-condition 1992 Fiat 126. Like the Godmother and Isabel, Peppe was clad all in white; unlike the Godmother and Isabel, the front of Peppe's apron was smeared with violent streaks of purple and brown: grisly remnants of slain sea creatures. Peppe was so excited to greet them, he almost knocked over a table sprinting to hold open the door. No doubt he heard the news from Cousin Pasquale; apparently, it was not often a Lercarese had the privilege of hosting beautiful suspected lesbians.

"*Binvinuti, tanti agurii!*" Peppe shouted, kissing Isabel on both cheeks and offering a more subdued handshake to the Godmother.

They followed him to the reserved table, where he removed the third place-setting with the officious air of one removing a smear of dirt from a mirror. Cousin Pasquale would not be pleased with this eviction.

"Now," he said, "please allow me to bring you the very best of *Ristorante da Friddi*."

"*Grazi, signore*," Isabel said. Despite her gains in the Italian- and Sicilian-language department, she still spoke with her rhotic Miami-Cuban twang. The cadence was most conspicuous when she was hungry and all reserve vanished.

"*Pregu, picciotta.* I understand you wish to visit Colle Madore next," he said, as if Isabel were a small child who'd announced her plan to run for president.

Isabel smiled. "Yep."

Peppe waited for an explanation, but both women were silent. "That should be...nice?"

Wringing his hands, Peppe went on to apologize for having no sea urchin available, a fact that seemed to fill him with, not only regret, but shame. Sea urchin was the restaurant's specialty, he said, but it was out of season in summer.

"She only like the cold, clear water," he said, as if his inability to circumvent sea-urchin migration patterns was the worst ignominy. "Perhaps you return in winter." He brightened. "We win award for the pasta with sea urchin: the *linguine con Riccio*."

"I think we'll manage," said Isabel, who had performed an Internet search for sea urchin and found them too close to oysters for her liking.

As the food arrived and another Sicilian meal unfolded, Isabel felt the Godmother drift away, and Isabel suspected she knew where to: that bridal portrait in Miami, or, perhaps even farther back, to childhood memories of her mother.

"Go," said Isabel, tearing off a hunk of olive bread and swiping it in oil.

The Godmother paused mid-bite. "Go?"

"Call her."

The Godmother's face flushed. From the shine in her eyes, Isabel knew she had said something *right*.

"Don't start dessert without me," said the Godmother.

"I can't promise anything," said Isabel.

Across the room, Isabel caught Peppe watching them with eyes wide. He was still staring as the Godmother brushed past him and walked out the door.

THE STREET WAS EMPTY. No breeze stirred the ubiquitous laundry overhead. Next to the restaurant was an old stone house, the windows black as Michele Andolini's eyes. The excitement of the funeral had sent the town to bed early. The night air was still and dry.

Lifting her phone, Raffi conjured Polly's voice saying, "Hello?"

She dialed. Three rings. Voicemail.

It was senseless to cry. This call was like every other. She focused on the cratered sidewalk and wondered what could have caused the rifts in the concrete. Maybe a fault ran beneath Lercara Friddi, the town chafing against itself even below the ground.

Raffi sat on the curb next to an upended tricycle with a crude

sign across the handlebars that read, in block letters, *MUNNIZZA*.
Garbage. That could well have been her name: Raffaella Munnizza,
queen of the discard pile. A thing once loved, now tossed out in
the street. Descended from orphans and possibly criminals, too.

But a self-made woman, she reminded herself. A woman of
tenacity and determination, who had reimagined Sicilian power
as feminine—perhaps too successfully.

She stared through the tricycle, thinking about the daughter
she once was. She could hear the pulse in her ears; the street was
that quiet. *Ma.* Somewhere, perhaps wearing red, in Sicily or
America, was there still a Polly at all?

Raffi jumped as the door of the old stone house opened, and
a gray-haired woman in a lemon-patterned housedress appeared.

"Mitzi! Mitzi! *Stronzo!*" she cursed. "Excuse me, *signura*,"
the woman said in gruff Sicilian. "I lost my cat."

"I'm sorry," said Raffi. She hated cats. "What does she
look like?"

The woman considered Raffi, hands on her wide hips. "Like
you. Dark and secretive."

Raffi, ruminations forgotten, laughed. "I'm an open book."

The woman snorted. "If you see that little black scrounge
Mitzi, send her home." She pointed up at the flat rooftop where
a weathervane was starting to turn. "I'll be up there, watching,
if you find her." An incongruous gust of wind flapped the clothes
hanging up and down the street.

Raffi shivered. "Watching?"

The woman pointed upward again. "*Le stelle.* The stars.
It is the night to watch them." She gave Raffi a pointed look.

"You should get off that curb. There's ash in the air. La Mamma is smoking."

She turned and closed the door behind her.

Raffi looked down at her white cotton sundress, indeed covered in a light film of soot. Coupled with the choice to always wear white was a decision to get dirty. She took a last look at the quiet street before opening the restaurant door.

"I was about to call the *carabinieri*," Isabel said. "Did you have a nice talk?"

"I did—with an old lady outside. If we see a black cat named Mitzi, she belongs on the next roof over."

Before Isabel could reply, the lights dimmed. Peppe appeared with a perfect *Cassata Siciliana*: ricotta-filled almond sponge cake smothered in creamy glaze and garnished with candied pears and candles.

"Happy birthday, Little Girl," said Raffi.

From every corner of the restaurant, voices raised in song: Raffi, the young couple who hadn't stopped holding hands since they sat down, the large family by the door, even two leering men at the bar, all clapping along to the rhythm of the Italian birthday song. *Tanti agurii.* Congratulations on another year. The girl's sweet face glowed orange in the candlelight, and Raffi felt something in her chest go off like a sparkler.

Peppe handed Isabel a knife and, as she cut into the soft sponge of the cake, she closed her eyes tight. Raffi wondered what the girl had wished for, so she could make it come true. Cousin Pasquale was not totally off base. She and the girl loved each other, just not in the way he imagined. Raffi and Isabel shared the most ancient form of love: that between mother and daughter. Where Mary had been Raffi's *Pequeña Madre*, Raffi would be Isabel's *Piccola Mamma*.

The door to the restaurant opened and Cousin Pasquale burst in looking sheepish.

"*Aiiiiiiii!*" Raffi and Isabel shouted with mouths full of orange cake.

"*Aiiiiii!!!*" Peppe cried, rushing to embrace the man who had shared, for one blessed evening, his precious American lesbians.

"*Aiiiiii!*" shouted the men at the bar, who, it turned out, were also members of GAVES, Pasquale's car club.

The girl was wearing her most rapturous Pastry Face. "*Cassata Siciliana*, oh my God, Godmother, this is everything."

COUSIN PASQUALE HAD GOTTEN the whole restaurant drunk. By the time they were joined by the two men at the bar, Peppe had moved on from limoncello and cracked open a different yellow liqueur: Strega. The Witch.

The Strega smelled sweet and astringent, its flavor an overpowering fennel-and-mint. After one sip, Isabel had an immediate regurgitative reaction. After two sips, she put the glass down, she claimed, permanently.

But she picked it back up again. And again. Until she saw not one bottle of Strega but three. The four men—who looked like eight men, now, to Isabel—took turns refilling the women's glasses as the men told the story of the liqueur's origins.

"It began in Benevento, where the witches met under a large walnut tree," said Cousin Pasquale. There was a brief argument between Peppe and Pasquale as to where the walnut tree was located, then Pasquale continued.

"They gathered for banquets and—" Pasquale averted his gaze "—orgies, rubbing ointment on their breasts."

"Ointment on their breasts?" said Isabel.

"They would steal newborn babies and cause pregnancies to terminate," added Peppe, crossing himself and ignoring Isabel's question.

"I assume they had brooms?" said the Godmother, clinking glasses with Isabel.

"Sorghum," said Cousin Pasquale. "The villagers left sorghum brooms outside for protection, and the witch was forced to stop and count the fibers."

"They count until dawn," said Peppe, "when the *streghe* must leave."

"To this day, if you're chased by a witch, you say, 'Come get it on Sunday,'" said Pasquale.

"Come get it on Sunday," echoed the shorter man from the bar.

"What the hell are they talking about?" Isabel slurred in the Godmother's ear.

"But if you mention a witch, the cure for the hex is to say, 'Today is Saturday,'" Cousin Pasquale said.

"*Oggi è Sabato*," mused the taller man from the bar.

"Today is Saturday," Isabel repeated.

"And what," said the Godmother, "do these stories have to do with *this* Strega?" She swished the liquid in her glass.

"Ah," said Cousin Pasquale.

"Ahhh," said Peppe.

"It's PR," said Isabel with a hiccup. "Benevento is witch-town; they named their liquor after the most famous export."

"*Non esportano streghe*," they don't export witches, said Cousin Pasquale, crossing himself.

"They export this kind," said the Godmother, touching the nearest empty bottle. "My parents kept Strega in the house. I stole some from the liquor cabinet once. Threw up for a week."

"You know," said Isabel, standing to give a toast. "In Cuba, they say the women in my family were all witches." She leaned over and placed her nose against Cousin Pasquale's. "Every one of them."

The Godmother raised her glass to Isabel and drained it. "Does that include you?"

Isabel tossed back a shot of Strega and said, "I'll meet you at the walnut tree." She turned to Cousin Pasquale. "Bring your sorghum."

"I'm serious," said the Godmother, the first s extra-sibilant.

Isabel tottered over on one leg. "What do you think? Am I a witch?"

"I think today is Saturday," said Cousin Pasquale, trading glances with Peppe.

"If we don't leave soon, we can forget Colle Madore," said the Godmother, eyes popped wide, trying to look at her watch. "It's either eleven-thirty or twelve-thirty." She brought the watch closer. "Or one-thirty."

Peppe looked at his wrist. "It is ten o'clock."

"Skip Colle Madore, *Cuscini*," said Cousin Pasquale. "We are having such fun."

Isabel snapped to attention. "No. Colle Madore, we *must*," she purred, grabbing Cousin Pasquale's sleeve. "Will you pretty please take us, dearest Cousin?"

Isabel looked at the Godmother who in turn looked at Pasquale.

"Cousin," said the Godmother, "get your keys. *Now*."

25

When the position of the sun conjoined Isabel's natal sun— her solar return on her twenty-fourth birthday—she was lying on a white tablecloth atop a misshapen hill in Lercara Friddi, Sicily, accompanied by a woman she'd recently feared but now pretty much loved.

"You're missing the stars," Isabel called. The Godmother was struggling to insert the diagonal mirror in the eyepiece of the telescope and failing at the task. Too bad Jan wasn't here.

A muted wailing wafted up from the ground below— the same subterranean dirge she'd heard on Pasquale's joyride their first day. Stroking the soft grass beneath her fingers, Isabel imagined grabbing Colle Madore by the blades and lifting the top off to reveal the mysteries beneath. She pressed her ear to the hill and the wails slid into sighs. The Sicilian soil wanted to spill its secrets.

Isabel looked up at the Godmother and wondered, with uncharacteristic ill humor, why the woman would not just sit down and listen to the cries of her own homeland. Perhaps the difference between Isabel and the Godmother was in where they directed their attentions—Isabel's toward the inner world, the Godmother's toward the tangible. In tarot-speak, Isabel was the High Priestess: keeper of the sacred, guardian of the subconscious, queen of psychic awareness. The Godmother was the Emperor: a powerful ruler—a rock for her loyal subjects—with feet planted in the material realm.

Isabel was about to open her mouth and call out to the Godmother again but forgot what she was going to say. She had never been this drunk.

Given their state when they left the restaurant, they should have gone home, but Isabel had insisted. "It's my birthday," she said again, and even Cousin Pasquale seemed sick of hearing it. The Godmother and Pasquale finally threw up their hands.

Of course, no one had been capable of driving, especially Cousin Pasquale, but he insisted on getting behind the wheel anyway. In the infinite wisdom of the intoxicated, they let him. At least he compensated by going twenty miles per hour down the long country road to Colle Madore.

"I do not feel right to leave you here," Cousin Pasquale said as they pulled up to the gravel footpath that led to the top of the hill. He cut the engine.

"I wait here," he said, tipping an imaginary hat forward on his face.

"No, no," the Godmother insisted. "Go home and sleep."

"But it is dark. You are two women alone, with no man in sight."

"Alone with no man in sight is the safest place a woman can be," said the Godmother.

✝

THE GENTLE BREEZE HAD matured into wind when Raffi gave up

on the Celestron SkyProdigy. She retreated to the tablecloth where Isabel was sprawled with her ear to the ground. Raffi did not ask what she was doing.

She lay back with her arms propped beneath her head. The Earth seemed to tilt on its axis with the weight of her body. Raffi imagined the old woman in the lemon-print housedress, the weathervane spinning as she watched the same sky.

"Let's talk more about witches," Isabel said.

"They dance around walnut trees and count broom hairs," said Raffi. "What more is there to say?"

"They rub ointment on their breasts and have orgies," said Isabel.

"I love a good orgy."

"Be serious." Isabel rolled on her side facing Raffi. "Do you believe in us?"

Raffi sensed the girl was about to make this heavy.

"I think men have little tolerance," said Raffi, "for women who worship anything that isn't *them*. They invented words like *witch* to undermine whatever threatens their dominance."

"You probably wrote a paper about witchcraft and feminism in college," Isabel said with a hint of bitterness. "I wasn't a scholar like you. Everything I learned came from Mary."

"I didn't write a paper about witches in college," Raffi said. "I wrote a paper about witches in *law school*. 'Witches: Ecumenical and Secular Prosecutorial Mechanisms in Early America.'"

"Hah!" cried Isabel. "*Scholar.*"

"I learned more about witches from Cousin Pasquale tonight."

"I didn't like how he kept crossing himself," said Isabel. "I'm a

Catholic, but the way he did it—the way they all did it—reminded me how dangerous religious people have been for witches. In Cuba, Catholics hunted the women in my family. *Hunted.*"

Raffi could not find a worthy response to this. She wanted to reassure Isabel no woman would ever again be hunted for who she was. But this was not a promise she could make.

She thought of her law-school paper. Witches were burned in the public squares of colonial America. It was gruesome, but fire, at least, was spectacular. The burned woman's enemies watched her ignite, then smolder, her ashes raining on the skin of ally and persecutor alike, a part of her becoming a part of them forever. History did not ignore the women who burned. It was the women who hid, and disappeared, and went mad, whom posterity forgot.

"Everyone loves witches until they don't need them anymore," Isabel said. "The witches in Benevento that made babies go away? The townspeople asked for those spells. They got what they wanted from the witches and turned on them afterward. *That's* what happened to my Cuban grandmother."

Raffi watched as Isabel's eyes caught the moonlight. The girl was beautiful, particularly as she became less girl and more woman.

"I'm sorry," Raffi said. She decided to make the promise anyway. "That could never happen now, Isabel."

"Couldn't it?" said Isabel.

Of course it could. "I will protect you, Isabel," Raffi said, determined to stick with the truth. "Also," Raffi paused, formulating a delicate way to say what came next, "people aren't afraid of witches anymore because everyone knows they're not really...*real.*"

Isabel's mouth fell open. "How can you say that? How many predictions do I have to make before you accept it?"

"I think you have some unique abilities, Isabel," said Raffi. "But even assuming witches exist, which they do not, you aren't one anyway. You're an astrologer."

Isabel flipped onto her back. "I'm not," she said. "That's not my thing at all. It was Mary's."

Raffi felt a rush of irritation. "If you're not an astrologer, why are we here for your solar return?"

"That's a logical question for a reasonable person to ask. Maybe you forgot what I said in Ortygia. I'm not reasonable."

Raffi could not dispute this.

"When Mary died," said Isabel, "I thought I had to follow in her footsteps. I was desperate to get her laptop, understand her clients—to become her, if I could. But I realize I don't have to be what she expects of me. I choose to be myself."

Raffi heard the bride's voice in her ear.

Listen to this girl. She's twenty-four years old and she knows more than you. Your whole identity is derivative. Oh, people always suspected you of being in the Mafia. You really showed them by—what? Pretending to be in the Mafia?

Raffi fantasized about tearing up the photo.

Don't even think of it. You can't do anything without me.

Raffi heard goats bleating in the distance, a soft counterpoint to the bride's harsh words. She went to retrieve the binoculars and stood at the edge of the hill. Laid out before her in the dark, the quiet valley between the Torto and Platani rivers slumbered, gold fields and riparian banks obscured in the scant moonlight.

Unless the livestock had flashlights, the valley would stay pitch-dark until sunrise.

She pointed the lenses up and, after several blinks and twists, focused her eyes and the binoculars both.

There was Ursa Major and Ursa Minor, the Big and Little Dipper—constellations of childhood, easy to identify. And Boötes, home of Arcturus: the red giant, fourth brightest star in the night sky. Its color resurrected a memory of her mother. One of the many good memories she had lost along the way.

Raffi was nine years old. The summer evening had cooled to dusk. She was sitting on the flat section of roof outside the master-bedroom window using Nino's binoculars, when Polly came up behind her. Raffi had just finished a book in which the heroines sneak onto the roof of an abandoned farmhouse and spot a shooting star.

"Raffaella. What are you doing?"

Raffi had turned to see Polly emerge from the shadows of her bedroom looking unimpressed.

"Mommy, you won't believe this. I found an alien ship!" She pointed to a small red light high in the sky that blinked intermittently. "Here." Raffi pushed the binoculars into her mother's hands. "I think it's coming closer."

Polly grunted. "I don't need the binoculars, Raffaella. That's the light on top of the quarry. Keeps the planes from hitting it at night."

Raffi must have looked defeated.

"Hey," her mother said softly.

Raffi would never forget the expression on Polly's face. An insight, she saw later, into the soul of Apollonia Truvarizzi—not the mother but the actual person who wasn't trying to teach or guide, but, rather, to understand life for herself.

"Don't stop," Polly whispered, an uncharacteristic urgency in the words.

Raffi had known an important conversation was happening at that moment, one she would hold in her heart forever. Now here it was, surfacing again after all these years. Raffi had sealed the memory with details: the timbre of her mother's voice; Polly's big fluffy bathrobe; fireflies blinking all around them, one so close it almost flew into Raffi's eye.

"Don't stop what, Mommy?"

"Being how you are."

"How am I?"

"The kind of person who looks up."

"Raffi," said Isabel.

"'Raffi?'"

"*Godmother.* Put those down!"

Raffi lowered the binoculars, annoyed. And then she saw it.

The tail, they would learn, spanned five degrees, making it ten times the size of the full moon and a fraction of the size of Hale-Bopp, though equal in radiance. It was oriented above the star Capella on the northwestern horizon, Venus to its east, tail streaming like a searchlight moving upward. A comet, materializing like magic.

The red quarry light, Polly's long-ago words, the old woman

on the rooftop watching the sky and waiting for her cat... There was no wind now. The weathervane on the old woman's roof would be still.

Only the stars were in motion.

"SHE WAS RIGHT!" SCREECHED Isabel.

"The woman with the cat?" said Raffi.

"What woman with the cat? I'm talking about Jan!"

"Who's Jan?" said Raffi.

"The weird lady I met on Mount Etna. Jan. She's from Barbados, but nothing erupts there, so she moved to Sicily where she watches the stars and wears horse blankets."

Raffi waited for a point to emerge. Isabel grabbed her arm.

"Seven days ago, Jan told me to make sure I was on a *hill* in seven nights!"

A black cat darted across the tablecloth and rubbed against Isabel's leg, swiveling its head to meet Raffi's gaze with frank yellow eyes.

"Mitzi?" guessed Raffi.

The cat bolted.

"I thought astronomers could predict these things," said Isabel. "Can't they, like, see comets from the space station?"

"What does seeing them from the space station have to do with predicting them?"

"If they can see them from the space station, they can warn us."

"That's warning, not predicting."

Isabel scowled. "As I said."

But Comet Sadik-Weisman, as it was already known, had

been around for over a month, since May. It had been designated a Common Comet: the unspectacular sort that looks blurry even through a telescope and is monitored with moderate interest. Its fortunes changed, however, during its closest passage to the sun—its perihelion—when Sadik-Weisman came blazing around the bend no longer a Common Comet, but a Great Comet, streaking across the sky like a racecar trailing sparks.

This was what Raffi and Isabel witnessed on Colle Madore the moment of Isabel's solar return: Comet Sadik-Weisman's emergence from the perihelion and ascent into greatness.

Isabel scrabbled around on the grass.

"What are you doing?" said Raffi.

"Looking for this." Isabel popped up with phone in hand. The screen contained a near-incomprehensible diagram of the sky.

"But what are you *doing?*"

"I'm seeing if Mary's stars succeeded where I failed."

Conversations powered by Strega took strange turns.

"Failed at what?"

"I didn't see this," said the girl, looking defeated.

"Isabel," Raffi said. "Some things can't be predicted."

The girl opened her mouth to disagree, then her shoulders slumped. "I *know.*" She slid back to the ground. "Someone told you to watch the sky tonight, too, didn't they?" She touched her temple. "The woman with the black cat?"

Raffi dropped down beside her. "Yes."

"I don't believe in chance, Godmother. Everything has meaning," said Isabel.

"It has meaning if you give it one," said Raffi, watching the comet's trajectory, its speed imperceptible from this distance as it hurtled millions of miles away at millions of miles per minute through space.

"It's not just meaning, it's *mystery*. You wouldn't understand. The only mystery in your world is you."

Raffi opened her mouth and closed it again. For a while, they said nothing, Raffi smarting at a comment she did not understand but took offense to nonetheless.

"I don't want this to end," Isabel said, tipped forward like she might be sick, palms to the Earth. "This trip. This night."

"It has to end," said Raffi. "The end makes room for a beginning."

✦

HOURS PASSED. ISABEL SHARED the few memories she had of her mother; Raffi spoke of Polly and Brando. They dozed. Raffi yanked the blanket up to cover them, smoothing the fabric over Isabel. It had been years since she'd loved someone new.

"It's not only my mother's disappearance that hurt me," said Raffi when they woke to the sound of an owl. "It's the choices I made in the aftermath. I never would have married Brando's father, had I felt whole."

Isabel lifted a hand to her head.

"No, he didn't hurt me physically. It was much worse."

She could feel the girl listening. The girl was an excellent listener.

"When my mother was well," Raffi continued, "I looked to her to define me. When I was a kid, she thought I was great. But she got sick, and I was 'the one who put her away.' I became the one she hated most. And I had learned to seek validation outside myself. This is what made me vulnerable to Brando's dad."

The girl stayed silent. Goats bleated in the distance. The *maa* of a sheep.

"I think Brando's father loved me, but he showed it by putting me down. This was how he tried to keep me. And he liked the suspicions that I was related to Sally T. It helped him get deals done. He did what I do now. He used it."

"It wasn't his to use," said Isabel.

"No. And he said the worst things in private. He said there was no way someone as weak as me could have Sally T's blood. He said I was fat, I needed a nose job. When he found out Truvarizzi was a name given to orphans, he said I wasn't just first-generation Italian—I was tenth-generation unwanted."

"So THAT'S PART OF this, too," mused Isabel.

"What's part of this?"

"You're avenging the yous of the past: the women who got screwed, like you did. And you're proving Brando's father wrong."

Raffi pondered the uncomfortable thought that Brando's father influenced her at all. "It's possible."

The worst memory surfaced—the one that had left marks inside her like brands; even the residual pain of remembering singed at the wound. This was the land mine.

"He tried to take my son away. He was ruthless: froze my accounts, locked me out of the house, tied up every decent lawyer in Miami. He almost got away with it...all because of the invisible system that gives men like him the freedom to abuse. For a while, it even looked like he would win." She paused. "Marina Ramòn? I *was* Marina Ramòn."

"But he didn't win," said Isabel. "You did."

"When it came to protecting Brando, it turned out I had some ruthlessness in me, too. That's when the Godmother was *really* born. When my son was at stake, and I learned what I'm capable of."

"And now you have this persona around you. This picture of strength. You're the super-strong woman. The angel of vengeance. Nothing can stop you."

"I don't know that I'm a 'super-strong woman,' and I'm no angel," said Raffi. "I'm just a real woman who acts strong."

Isabel seemed to ponder this.

"Have you ever considered not acting?" she said.

Raffi had not considered it.

"Strength doesn't have to look a certain way," said Isabel. "You could try lowering the armor. You can still get things done," she hurried to add. "You just don't have to wear all white and act terse and trust, like, three people."

Brando, Trini, and now Isabel. The girl had already counted herself in.

"I'm not terse," said Raffi. She reached over to pat the girl's head. "The radio signals are strong tonight. The comet must be an accelerator."

Isabel laughed. "This doesn't come from radio signals. This comes from reason."

"But you aren't reasonable. That's what you said."

"I'll revise. I can be reasonable. It's just not, like, a defining characteristic."

Raffi's eyes closed. Strega, coupled with the previous night's poor sleep, eroded at consciousness.

"You're stronger than Sally T," murmured Isabel.

The girl's words covered her like a blessing.

26

Raffi's eyes opened to Cousin Pasquale's wrinkled face staring down at her. At first, the halo around his head from the blocked sun made her wonder if she'd died and been met at the gates by a worried saint.

She looked around and saw Isabel yawning behind Pasquale, her hair wrecked. Behind Isabel and Pasquale, tourists wandered the hilltop, gazing out at the sun-drenched valley and sneaking glances in their direction.

"Good morning, *Cuscini*," Cousin Pasquale said, hands clasped in entreaty. "I am very sorry to disturb you, but—" He made a helpless face.

Raffi sat up and looked at her watch. 9:00 a.m. She hadn't slept this late since, well—ever.

"The archaeological site has opened for the day, so…"

"Of course," said Raffi, rising to her feet, her head throbbing from the dual indignities of Strega and a night on hard ground. Brushing off her dress, she cast cool eyes over the nosy tourists, picking each off like a huntress until they looked away.

"The binoculars?" said Cousin Pasquale, no doubt thinking of his Balilla.

Isabel retrieved the leather case from the ground and handed it to Pasquale.

"Oh, thank God," he said, fumbling open the case and kissing the lenses. "I don't want Luigi near my car."

Isabel staggered to Raffi, groaning. "What did we *do?*"

"We ruined ourselves," said Raffi. "This day is shot."

"We don't have time to lose days. We're in Sicily."

"Too much talking." Raffi rubbed her forehead. "Go to the car. Both of you. I'll be there in a minute, I just need it not to hurt when I breathe."

"I mean, I can wait for you," said Isabel.

"Why? Would you miss me?"

"I would," said the girl without irony.

Isabel walked over to Cousin Pasquale and whispered in his ear. Blushing, he followed her down the hill and out of sight.

Raffi made her way slowly—faster and she might vomit—toward the path Isabel and Pasquale had taken. The gravel forked midway down; the right side descended all the way to the entrance, and the left traced a lateral curve around the side of the hill, to where a stream of tourists passed in and out. *Sita Arcaeologica*, read a sign with an arrow pointing left. Raffi followed the arrow.

Tourists gathered around a room cut into the hill's southern slope. It didn't look like much—hard-packed dirt beneath their feet, no roof, crumbling walls—but as she drew closer, Raffi saw a placard that said *Temple of Aphrodite.*

An elbow nudged her from behind. "Excuse me," said an American voice.

"Excuse *me*," Raffi said, turning to find herself face to face with none other than Tex, the FBI agent from Miami with the bad suit and temper. This time, he was in a khaki fishing shirt and Detroit Lions baseball cap that almost concealed his awful Julius Caesar haircut. The wispy strands of a nascent mustache covered his upper lip, which, at that moment, was curled into a triumphant smirk.

"Oh, Jesus Christ," she said with irritation.

His face fell.

"Did your boss at least write you a permission slip this time?"

He leaned in and whispered hot garlic breath in her face. "This time, I'm here under the full authority of the Federal Bureau of Investigation."

She held a hand over her mouth and almost gagged. Residual Strega and the Texan were too much to take.

He jerked his chin toward the edge of the hill, and they walked with feigned companionability to a quiet spot between a trashcan and the precipice. Their backs to the crowd, Raffi pretended to point out a landmark.

"Well?" she said. "What do you and the Federal Bureau of Investigation want to talk about today?"

He faked a laugh and clapped her on the back. "You're in deep, Truvarizzi. I mean deep."

"You know, my mother gave me a first name. Be polite and use it."

"I'm gonna use every name you've got when I write you a one-way ticket to federal prison."

She laughed.

"Federal prison? Why—did you find the judge's fingerprints on a backhoe loader?" She paused. "You know, all Italians aren't in construction. We also do waste management. And pizza parlors."

"Judge Paz got two calls right before she died. You wanna guess who they were from?"

Raffi did not want to guess. She wanted to *know*. She was poised to slingshot back a retort when the Strega made itself an issue. Sprinting to the edge, she bent with hands on knees and threw up a long stream of neon liquid.

He appeared next to her. "Feel the heat now, don't cha, Truvarizzi?"

"Not particularly," she said. "I feel the effects of an Italian liqueur that would put some actual hair on your lip."

He reached up to touch his moustache.

"I'll give you a hint," he said. "One of the calls Paz received that day was from a burner phone."

She lurched again. This time nothing came out.

"I said *a burner phone.*"

She closed her eyes. Sweat dribbled down her temples.

"Consider yourself warned, Tex. If you don't move now, I will throw up on you."

He jumped back as she released more Strega and part of last night's dinner near his feet.

"One problem solved." She patted her stomach and wiped her

face with a dusty arm. "That just leaves you."

His moustache was twitching so fast, it looked like it might detach and fly away.

"The burner phone had an international number. Guess which country?"

She cupped her chin in hand. "Liechtenstein?"

"That's not a country," he said uncertainly.

"You're right," she said. "It's a principality."

"The burner was from Italy." He paused to await her reaction. She gave none. He continued: "We're waiting for the Italian cellular carrier to confirm which towers pinged when the call was placed. If it was in Sicily, I'm gonna bring you in."

Raffi windshield-wiped her finger at him.

"That proves the opposite conclusion. I wasn't in Sicily when Judge Paz disappeared." She paused. "Also, did you say you're waiting for the Italian cellular carrier to confirm the towers?"

"That's what I said."

She burst out laughing. "You're waiting for an *Italian* company to get back to you?"

He grimaced. "What about it?"

Raffi turned to wave at a few concerned tourists who had begun edging closer. She pantomimed winding an imaginary cuckoo clock on the side of her head and pointed to him. They laughed and drifted away. She turned back to the Texan.

"I'm surprised the FBI has someone so inexperienced on my case."

She was not surprised, though. They wanted her to underestimate them by association. Tex was a foil.

"You know what I think, Truvarizzi? I think you're all hat and no cattle."

"I think you're all hat and no head."

Raffi's skin prickled. Before she looked, she felt the weight of those eyes. The same charge that had ripped through her body at Arethusa tore through her again. It was the blonde. The woman stood behind Tex with phone in hand; raising it to shoulder height, she snapped a photo of them—not to take a picture, but to show she could.

Raffi's hand slid to the neckline of her dress. She wished she was clean. The woman wore a sharp, black suit. It was already a sweltering day, but the blonde seemed unaffected.

"Hey." Raffi nodded toward the blonde. "Call off your goons."

The Texan looked confused. "Goons?"

He eyed the blonde, who stared at them both.

Raffi walked up to the woman and faced off against her. It was one of the most challenging battles in chess: Queens in opposition.

"Are you with him?" said Raffi.

The blonde closed the distance. She slid an arm around Raffi's shoulder, stuck out the phone, and snapped another photo. Anyone watching would think they were two friends taking a selfie.

Without a word, the woman walked away. Raffi considered doing something to get the woman's attention, to bring her back to Raffi's side. This was a nonsensical instinct. Generally, when strangers in black suits stalk you, you want them as far away as possible.

The Texan sauntered over and hooked his hands into his pockets.

"She ain't mine, Truvarizzi. Maybe you're in trouble with your boss Sally T for talkin' to the F-B-I." He laughed, and a piece of gum fell out.

"I don't have a boss," said Raffi, as Isabel strode up and stood where the blonde in black had been moments before, blonde for blonde.

"We've been waiting ten minutes," the girl complained. "Franco's going to run out of *pantofola*." She noticed the Texan. "Oh, it's you."

The Texan opened his mouth, but Raffi spoke first. "We're leaving, Isabel."

"You shouldn't get mixed up with her," the Texan said to Isabel.

Raffi doffed an imaginary hat. "Tex." She grabbed Isabel's wrist. "Let's go."

When they had reached Cousin Pasquale's car, Isabel put her hand over the handle.

"Watch out for them," she whispered, her eyes cloudy.

"Watch out for who?"

"All of them," said Isabel.

27

"Welcome to civilization," yelled Cousin Donatella from the landing of her Palermo penthouse.

Everything about Cousin Donatella was round, from the gelatinous belly she wore with the same pride as her designer blouse, to the cloud of raven hair framing her ever-smiling face, to the penciled-in arches above her black button eyes. Her short, nonagenarian body hooked like a candy cane, her head hanging so far over her plump chest that she always peered upward like a bejeweled imp.

Donatella watched Pasquale struggle up the stairs with Isabel's big yellow suitcase, then turned to Raffi and Isabel. "Did he drive you nuts yet?"

Cousin Pasquale had driven them to Palermo despite their insistence on taking a car. (Raffi was done with buses.) "Nonsense," he'd said, he was going to Palermo anyway; it would be a shame to hire a driver when the best one in Sicily was right here.

Palermo, the capital, was a marvel. Horse-drawn carriages in velvet livery carried tourists instead of livestock, and a perpetual duet of honking cars and Sicilian curses replaced the quaint calls

258 | LEIGH ESPOSITO

of Pasquale and his friends. Palm trees waved in the breeze and the sky above the broad avenues was cloudless blue. In the center of an intersection sat a woman with a mandolin playing a dirge from a famous Mafia movie. Rats ran down sidewalks and disappeared in the hedges surrounding posh palazzos. The city was both grander and dirtier than anywhere Raffi had been, in Sicily or otherwise.

Pasquale's silver Mercedes—his "daily driver;" he would not "flog a lady like the Balilla" on the highway—zipped past impressive structures from Palermo's past glory, like Porta Nuova, the triumphal arch featuring four solemn twenty-foot telamones, arms crossed over their stone bodies, that guarded the entrance to the Cassaro.

"Once this was a city of kings," Cousin Pasquale had said as they turned onto Via Maqueda. "Now it is a city of contradictions."

It was obvious he was quoting from a book. Cousin Pasquale was not a wordsmith.

Cousin Donatella's apartment was in the elegant baroque square called Quattro Canti: the four songs, or four seasons, each corner devoted to both a season and a Palermitan patroness. Pointing at a statue perched above one of the square's four fountains, Cousin Pasquale explained that Cousin Donatella's side of the square was protected by Saint Christina of Bolsena. Raffi had never heard of Saint Christina—or Bolsena—but the statue was lovely.

Before he hauled the luggage upstairs, Cousin Pasquale took them aside with a strange request. "*Please* do not tell Donatella about the Ferrari."

"What Ferrari?" said Isabel.

"Exactly," said Cousin Pasquale with chagrin. "If she ask—"

"It's being repaired?" Raffi offered. "You're painting it red?"

"It *was* red," said Pasquale sadly.

As Donatella heckled him from the balcony, Cousin Pasquale dropped the last bag in front of the ornate front door and turned to go.

"You're not staying?" Raffi said, surprised.

"I cannot remain," he said, as if a primary rule of the universe precluded his setting foot in Cousin Donatella's home. "It has been my pleasure to be with you, *Cuscini*. I pray we meet again soon." He crossed himself and kissed his fingers as Cousin Donatella rolled her eyes.

"Ciao, Pasqù," she said, pulling Raffi and Isabel in by the wrists and shutting the door on both Cousin Pasquale and the luggage.

"Shouldn't we get those?" said Raffi of the bags.

Cousin Donatella scoffed. "I have servants for that." She funneled her bejeweled hands and shouted, "Veru! Lia! *Veni ca!*"

Two pretty women—one in her twenties and brunette, the other older and redheaded—skittered into the room, bowed, and threw open the front door, revealing a sorrowful Cousin Pasquale lifting his fist to knock. They looked at Donatella.

"Just the luggage," she said in Sicilian.

They heaved the suitcases across the threshold and closed the door on Cousin Pasquale for good.

"Now," Donatella said, watching with disapproval as the two servant girls wrestled with the bags, "which of you is my cousin?"

Raffi turned her nose to the hook.

"I joke!" Donatella crowed, pulling her cousin down and in, so Raffi's head was squished against her cousin's ample bosom.

"And you," she said, rounding on Isabel. "Come hug your new Cousin Donatella."

Isabel zipped into her arms like a wagging retriever.

"*Biddissima*," Donatella said, petting the girl. "I love a nice blonde."

"Why didn't Cousin Pasquale come in?" said Raffi. "I've never seen him refuse an opportunity to—" She pointed at Isabel.

"He's jealous." Donatella fluttered her fingers at the sitting room with its wall-length tapestries, bold ceramics, and Venetian glass chandelier. "My penthouse makes his look like an outhouse."

"It does, Cousin Donatella," Isabel said with enthusiasm. "You live like a queen."

"Yes, I do," said Cousin Donatella. "Surrounded by art and admirers. I hand-selected each piece!"

It was unclear whether she referred to the art or the admirers.

Centered over the cerulean silk couch, the focal point of the room was a large portrait of young Donatella: dark hair framing the unlined face, lips soft and carmine pink, those same glittering, canny eyes shining from under the original eyebrows now memorialized in kohl.

It was obvious the piece Cousin Donatella found most fantastic of all was herself.

"Please," said Donatella, noting the direction of their glances with approval. She motioned for her guests to sit beneath the portrait in the shade of a potted palm so large it grazed the ceiling.

"Look what I have built for myself," said Cousin Donatella, sashaying around the room.

"And inherited," Raffi whispered to Isabel.

"You both would be lucky to have a fraction of my collection."

"A *fraction*, my God, Cousin Donatella, you speak, like, *amazing* English!" Isabel gushed. "Where did you learn it?"

"Ask Raffaella," said Cousin Donatella.

Raffi knit her brows.

"You don't remember?"

Was this another delusional family member? "Remember...?"

"I stayed with your family in New York for a year! When you were a little girl."

"I'm sorry, Cousin. I don't remember." She paused. "The only cousin from Italy who stayed with us was Cousin Dolly."

Cousin Donatella arched her penciled brow.

"Of course you don't remember, you were four years old. Your father should have reminded you." She softened. "Your mother and I became very close that year. I hadn't seen her since she left Sicily. She was always a little crazy, though. She had that look in her eyes."

Raffi frowned. "I'm not sure—"

"Of course, I'm a little crazy too. Most Sicilians are. But Apollonia...," Cousin Donatella chuckled. "I couldn't figure out if she hated your father Nino down to his guts or loved him like a brother. Probably both! But *Bedda Matri*, she was over the moon about you."

Donatella must be the anti-Sicilian, thought Raffi. Not only did she tell you everything, but she did so rapid-fire. Then she thought: loved him like a *brother*?

"I understand she's gone now, Raffaella," said Donatella. "I'm sorry to hear it."

Raffi pretended to examine the nearest urn. She wanted to ask Donatella if she knew the two Not-Polly's—the woman in red, and the woman from the funeral. Maybe they were the same person. Maybe that person was her mother.

"Do you girls want pizza?" said Cousin Donatella. "I had a friend in from Milano last week. I took him and his wife to my favorite *pizzeria* near the Fontana Pretoria. *La idiota* says to me, 'Oh, no thank you, I don't care for pizza.' Don't care for *pizza*?" She clapped a hand to her forehead. "Who could trust a person like that?"

"I wouldn't mind checking out that pizza place myself," said Isabel. "Are you hungry now?"

"Of course, I'm hungry now!" Cousin Donatella boomed.

Something clicked in Raffi's mind. "Cousin Dolly!" She snapped her fingers and pointed at Donatella, who grinned like a sated cat. "You're Cousin Dolly!"

Cousin Donatella effected a miniature bow.

"I remember we walked through a forest," said Raffi, the smell of fruit blossoms and manure coming back to her now. "There were giant trees. It smelled like cows and flowers. I held your hand."

"It was an apple orchard."

"But...you're *Dolly?*"

"Addolorata is a terrible name. Who names a child s*orrowful?*" She sniffed. "It's bad judgment."

"So, you changed it."

"Of course, I changed it."

"What does "Donatella" mean?" asked Isabel.

Cousin Donatella floated one hand up like a ballerina.

"It means gift from God."

She moved away from the chair and, despite her hooked posture and advanced age, stretched out in all directions like a seasoned yogi. "Well?" she said. "Aren't you going to get up?"

Isabel jumped up first, then Raffi, who felt like a child again in her cousin's presence. They waited as Donatella called for her handbag— "Veru!"—and her keys— "Lia!"—and sailed out the door, not bothering to make sure Raffi and Isabel were behind her.

✦

It turned out Cousin Donatella was a power walker.

"Pizzeria Pretoria is the best in Palermo," she said, skipping the steps at an astonishing pace. Raffi was afraid Donatella might fall, but it was Isabel who stumbled and cursed.

Exiting the building, Donatella pointed out the historical flourishes of the Quattro Canti. Her southern corridor was the gateway to the Albergheria District, the neighborhood associated with spring.

"I could have taken a unit on any of these corners. I chose this one because its patroness, Christina of Bolsena, annoyed me the least."

"What's wrong with the other ones?" said Isabel.

"Yes, they're all...*saints*," Raffi said. Who has a beef with a saint?

"They were weak! Olivia di Palermo, I mean, please. She gave all her money to the poor and went to heaven as a dove." Donatella looked disgusted. "*Good little martyr.*"

"You might argue she was Christlike," said Raffi. Donatella was proving fun to rile up.

"Christ stood up for himself. He disobeyed," Cousin Donatella said with approval.

Isabel, like a student driver attempting to enter a freeway moving at breakneck speed, opened her mouth to join in the conversation and then seemed to think better of it.

"And we know nothing about Santa Ninfa," continued Donatella. "No bio at all. What kind of patroness is that?" Turning east, she hooked a thumb at Saint Agata with grudging respect. "She's alright."

Raffi perked up, thinking of cough-drop-haired Agata in Ortygia and the sweet nun atop Mount Tauro. "Why *are* there so many Agatas in Sicily?"

"Saint Agata saved Catania from a great eruption. The people carried her veil to the river of lava as it came toward the city, and the lava changed course. Many Sicilians show their respect by naming their daughters in her honor." She paused. "You'll notice there aren't too many Ninfas."

"And Christina of Bolsena?" said Isabel.

Donatella's gaze turned lofty. "She fought with her father. An angel of the Lord called her to a life in Christ, but her papa would not let her go. So, she broke all his idols and threw the pieces out the window. You can imagine what happened to her next." She made the sign of the cross. "*That* was a woman."

By now they were marching along Corso Vittorio Emanuele, Isabel and Raffi winded as Cousin Donatella gained speed. Memories of Donatella-as-Dolly filtered back to Raffi with each pump of her cousin's arms. Donatella moved no less quickly now than she had decades ago.

At Pizzeria Praetoria, they stopped to buy a margherita pizza. During the contentious, rapid-fire pizza transaction—Cousin Donatella loved to haggle—she recounted that, in addition to learning English during her year in America, she had studied it at the University of Palermo, where she received her degree in ancient civilizations. Pizza in hand, they found an empty step in the dingy piazza and ate their slices folded over by hand, a pile of oily napkins accumulating between them.

"You're the second antiquities expert we've met in Sicily," Raffi remarked, thinking of the professor by the Hekataion in Ortygia.

"What else would we study? There is no future here." Cousin Donatella gestured at the statues flanking the piazza's entrance and the boarded-up, graffiti-tagged building across the street. "Our only hope is for people like you to rematriate, bring money back into this economy." Cousin Donatella appraised Raffi. "You have almost as much money as me."

Isabel watched with concern as Cousin Donatella took a third slice.

"I think you mean re-*patriate*," said Raffi.

"No, I mean *rematriate*. It's *Mother* Sicilia. We speak the *mother* tongue. *Mamma* Etna. *Ubi est pater?*"

"*Pater est ubique*," said Raffi.

"*Est extraneum*," said Donatella.

Raffi chuckled. "Extraneous is a little harsh."

"So's reality. We only need a mother."

Isabel stopped chewing. "You both speak *Latin?*"

Cousin Donatella stood, a final slice clutched between two sheets of wax paper.

"Now, I will show you the most phenomenal sight in Palermo—better than the mosaic of Christ Pantocrator and the Ballarò Market combined. Ballarò is a filthy place," she said behind her hand. "They eat octopus there. Standing up. *Quali animali*—what animals."

✢

THE MOST PHENOMENAL SIGHT in Palermo, per Cousin Donatella, were the Catacombe dei Cappucini, the Capuchin Catacombs: home, Donatella informed them, to one thousand mummified corpses in eternal repose.

"Soon to be one thousand and one," she added, gliding past a long line of tourists and breezing through the entrance with a perfunctory wave at the security guards.

"Is it Tuesday, Signura Donatella?" the younger, handsomer one called.

"This visit is special," Donatella shot back. "I brought my *cuscini Miricani*."

The guards whistled, as Raffi smiled to herself. Here, American cousins were a status symbol.

Cousin Donatella lowered her voice as they rounded the corner into the catacombs.

"I'm here every week. I'm a regular." Her expression hardened. "I have a mission."

A musty smell like an abandoned library rushed at them upon entering, the heels of their shoes on the flagstone floor sending muffled echoes down the corridors lined with niches and shelves, each with its own corpse.

Cousin Donatella stopped by an upright skeleton holding a Latin-inscribed tablet.

"This is Brother Silvestro of Gubbio," she said, as if introducing an old friend. "He was the first one in."

They strolled on, Donatella pointing out more corpses of note.

"This is Brother Vincenzo of Calabria," she said of a skeleton laying on its side facing the hall like a teen in a bunk bed.

Isabel, her guidebook left behind, had her phone out to follow along. She frowned and raised her hand.

"That's not Brother Vincenzo, Cousin Donatella, that's Brother Patrizio of Catania."

Cousin Donatella whirled on the girl. "You would question a scholar of antiquities?"

Isabel cowered. "It's just, this website says—"

"Don't believe everything you read," said Donatella. "Believe everything *I say*."

A passing tour guide raised his eyebrows.

"And here," said Cousin Donatella, pausing at the doorway to an interior room and lowering her voice, "is the Chapel of Sorrows." She led them to a small glass coffin in the center of the room surrounded by tourists.

"Tch!" she admonished, shooing the tourists like pigeons.

A security guard appeared and ushered everyone out, murmuring apologies to Cousin Donatella, who watched the tourists go with grim satisfaction.

"I'm their biggest donor," Cousin Donatella confided. "I get all the time I want with Sleeping Beauty."

Sleeping Beauty was Rosalia Lombardo, the most famous mummy in the catacombs. She was interred after dying of the Spanish flu in 1918—the last corpse to be admitted. The little girl was ensconced in a doll-size glass coffin and covered with a blue silken blanket, her blond hair in pristine curls and eyelids half-open to reveal lilac irises.

"Scientists say her eyes are open because of changes in the chapel's temperature and humidity, but we Sicilians?" Donatella shook her head. "We do not believe that. We believe this is a miracle. Sicilians always choose miracles over science." Cousin Donatella stood with her head bowed. "By age, she could have been my sister."

"We should all be cremated," Raffi said, preparing for a sporting debate but stopping at the sight of Isabel's tear-streaked face. The girl was thinking of her mother. Raffi recognized it; she understood it, too. Images of grief bring up images of grief.

In that moment, Raffi felt far from her mother. When they were on the same continent, there was always a chance Polly would walk through the door, run her finger along the windowsill, and say, "Raffaella. You call this clean?"

"Cremation is for the godless and political," said Donatella to Raffi. To both, she said: "I *will* usurp Rosalia Lombardo as the last mummy admitted to the Capuchin Catacombs." She lowered her head and grinned up at them. "Watch me."

"How will you do it?" said Isabel, fascinated.

Cousin Donatella smiled. "There are three things in the world that, if you have them, allow you to accomplish anything. Those things are money, power, and beauty. I, *cuscini*, have all three." She sighed. "But mostly it's the money and the fact I stick my nose in here every Tuesday."

Cousin Donatella directed them from the Chamber of Sorrows

to a hidden exit that opened into an alley behind the catacombs. They were in the heart of Palermo's Old City. The area was graffiti-ridden, soot-stained, and yet somehow beautiful. Donatella explained that, during World War II, artillery shells had devastated the city, its splendor extant in the few intact structures that survived: tiled Arab mosques, crenellated medieval palazzos, and Byzantine churches, most built on foundations of antiquity still visible below.

The palimpsest of Sicily, thought Raffi. So many layers.

As Donatella power-walked, she spoke of the many peoples who had called this place home. The city had as many names as it had conquerors. It was Ziz to the Phoenicians, Panormos to the Greeks, Balarm to the Arabs. With the sun descending behind remnants of Palermitan glory, the streets passed into shadow. Raffi looked up at an open window in an adjacent building, filmy white curtains twirling in the soft breeze. She thought she spied a figure behind the curtains looking out at them, but the sun came out again and no one was there. Perhaps only the ghosts of Palermo's past followed her now.

But she doubted it.

28

"*B asta*," said Cousin Donatella, whistling at a passing taxi. "Let's drink."

She directed the driver across town to a small back-street bar, the sidewalk outside lined with Vespas.

"*Tre Pare Brutti*!" she called to the waitress, ordering the local cocktail. After a few sips, and a bite of the complimentary *arancini* the manager brought over—"They know me here," said Donatella—the old woman's eyes took on a nuclear glow.

"Now, what fascinating sights have you seen on my island?" she said.

"Mount Etna," said Isabel.

"The Madonna della Rocca, La Sirenetta..." added Raffi.

"Colle Madore," they said together.

Out the corner of her eye, Raffi caught the girl looking at her. She knew how badly Isabel needed a strong woman in her life. Besides Raffi, Isabel had no one. The girl's desire for closeness, so plain to see, both warmed Raffi's heart and made her want to run. Raffi could not afford to trust the wrong people, nor to spread herself too thin. She had not decided whether there was room in her heart for Mary's niece.

"Colle Madore," hissed Cousin Donatella. "Shameful, how long it took them. They closed the mine thirty years before the first excavation."

"The mine?" Raffi searched her memory; Cousin Pasquale had spoken of a sulfur-mining era but not the mine itself. "What does the mine have to do with Colle Madore?"

Cousin Donatella rolled her eyes as if Raffi could not be more obtuse. "The mine *is* Colle Madore. Or, I should say, *was*."

Isabel registered the somber looks on their faces. "What's the big deal about a mine?"

Cousin Donatella spun toward her.

"The children, *ragazza mia*. In the poor times, the Lercarese families sold them to the mines. They were called *i carusi*—the dear little boys. But they were not dear. They suffered. In theory, their parents could have bought them back someday. In reality: no." She took another sip of her drink. "This is not something we are proud of."

Isabel put down her *arancino*. "There were cries coming from the ground," she said, remembering the wailing and whispers.

Cousin Donatella looked like the cries of the land did not surprise her at all.

"Why didn't they mention the mine on the signs at the site?" Raffi felt a mounting anger she did not understand. "The mine is part of Lercara's history, too." She thought of Cousin Pasquale's attempts to deter them from visiting it.

"*We* know the truth," said Cousin Donatella. Her expression hardened. "We don't tell our business to outsiders."

Ah, thought Raffi. Even the typically candid Donatella had a little *omertà* in her.

The waitress resurfaced to take final orders. All around them, the bar was turning into a nightclub. A red light hidden somewhere above illuminated the tangle of patrons with cocktails in hand, dancing close, laughing. The air was hot with abandon. The floor was a half-inch deep in *Pare Brutti.*

"We'll take three more cocktails and the check," Cousin Donatella said. She snapped her fingers and the waitress rushed off. "*Sometimes* it is wise," said Donatella, glancing at Raffi, "to look away from the past."

Raffi tried to catch Donatella's eye, but the old woman was too busy counting banknotes to look up. Raffi knew that comment was meant for her.

Leaving the bar, she felt a chill on the back of her neck. Turning, she saw an old man on a bench reading *Italia Oggi.* His shoes were battered, brown, and unremarkable. Peeking over the top of the paper was a tan fedora.

Cousin Donatella put a hand on Raffi's shoulder. "Look away," she said.

✦

"YOU HAVE A HEKATAION," said Raffi, spotting the familiar statue, still thinking about the man in the fedora, and Donatella's comments, and the mine.

They had retired, overstuffed, to the apartment, as Cousin Donatella commenced telling the story behind each work of art in her drawing room. In a shadow beneath yet another giant potted palm, Raffi had noticed the telltale triple-sided figure. In this rendering, the goddess held no weapons. Instead, the figures clasped hands.

"Yes," Donatella said triumphantly, "and I had to wait ten years for Dorothy Armbrust to die before I could get my hands on it." She extended her arms and wiggled her fingers as if willing the statue to appear in her hands. When neither Raffi nor Isabel took the hint, she screamed, "*Veru!*" and the dark-haired girl came running. "Bring me my Hekataion."

Veru lifted the statue and placed it on the marble table with great care. Donatella grabbed it with no more reverence than she would a *cannolo*.

"Second century, Imperial Period. From Agrigento. This beauty did not belong in London."

"Why are the Hecates holding hands?" asked Isabel.

"This is Hecate Triodia. *The Lady of the Crossroads*. All three forms of the goddess must join forces to protect her devotees."

Raffi thought of the trinity that had brought her to this island—the one she made with Isabel and Mary—and of joining hands with Sister Giuseppe Regina and Sister Agata atop Mount Tauro. Women in threes, the minimum needed for a coven. She remembered that from law school too.

Outside, a dog loosed a long, plaintive wail.

"Ah," Cousin Donatella whispered. "She is here."

Isabel sat up. "Who's here?"

Cousin Donatella closed her eyes. "*Her approach is heralded by the howl of a dog.*"

Isabel and Raffi looked at each other. Surely the girl remembered the same thing she did: the white dog at the crossroads in Ortygia.

Misreading their glances, Cousin Donatella laughed.

"Don't be scared. She protects us. Look—the way her eyes see in all directions. She has no blind spot." The light in the room seemed dimmer. "We live very close to the earth in Sicily. We grow in the shadow of the ancients. And she," Donatella pointed at the Hekataion, "has been here from the beginning."

A captivated Isabel tried to edge so close to Donatella that she fell off the couch, nearly slamming her chin into the marble tabletop. She was not an experienced drinker.

"You should go to bed, Little Girl," said Donatella.

"But this was just getting interesting," protested Isabel.

"To bed. My cousin wants to talk to me in private."

Raffi looked at Cousin Donatella. This time the old woman met her eyes.

"Fine," said Isabel, struggling to stand. "If you need me, I'll be watching *Las Brujas de Bal Harbour* on my phone." She paused. "Do you have wi-fi?"

Cousin Donatella nodded.

"*Lia!*" she shrieked. The redhead scurried in, and Cousin Donatella flapped her hands in irritation. "Sort it out, both of you," she said, as they ran in the direction of Isabel's bedroom.

"Now," said Donatella when they had gone. "What's on your mind?"

Raffi motioned for her cousin to speak quietly, but Donatella waved her hands again. "We can talk freely here. My servants are my family. They would never betray my trust."

Raffi took a deep breath. Tasked with voicing the question she'd had her whole life, she was suddenly shy. "I want to know the truth."

Cousin Donatella cocked her head. "Too vague. Try again."

"The truth about my family."

"Which side of your family?" Cousin Donatella said with eyes narrowed.

"Only one side matters. Not," Raffi added, "that I don't love my mother, or the Sampieris and Angelinis. But there's no mystery about my mother's family. They're all dead, anyway. Except you." She considered whether to say something about the woman in red, and was about to, when Cousin Donatella, her eyebrows almost through her hairline, spoke up.

"*'Angelini? Che Angelini?'*"

"I don't understand," said Raffi. Her heart was pounding. Something was off. "Angelini, my mother's maiden name."

"Not Angelini. *Andolini. Minch'*, you've been sold a bill of goods. I thought they'd tell you when you got older."

Raffi blinked. "Andolini. Like Michele Andolini?"

Cousin Donatella touched Raffi's arm with surprising gentleness. "*Ma non preoccuparti, picciotta*, not to worry. Apollonia never got mixed up in it. She left for America and never came back." Donatella cleared her throat. "Then she married your father and that was that."

Raffi went rigid, as if she had been strolling through the forest and encountered a wildcat. As if not moving would be enough to save her. "My mother left Sicily as a small child. A toddler."

Donatella gripped Raffi's arm and squeezed. "Bill of goods."

But this was impossible. Polly barely spoke Sicilian. She hated Sicily. Knew almost nothing about it. At least, this was what Raffi had been told. Rotate, click, rotate, click. "The Godmother mind" raced to recalibrate.

She had been lied to her whole life. Her blood was tainted after all. She was the last link in a chain of Mafiosi. Just not the ones she'd thought.

When she could manage to speak, she asked, "Who was Michele Andolini to my mother?"

Cousin Donatella shut her eyes to think. Raffi could hear Isabel and Lia chatting in the bedroom.

"Her...mother's brother?" She opened them. "*Allura.* Your great-uncle."

Raffi slid her fingers between the buttons of her shirt and gripped the Mary medallion until she thought it might break. The widow's "we" now made more sense. Serafina Andolini had known they were family. Everyone knew except Raffi.

"Raffaella, it is a mere accident of genetics. It means nothing to you. Why," Donatella said with a wink, "are you worried *he* will think your loyalties are divided?"

It took Raffi a moment to realize "*he*" was Sally T, and that Donatella was mocking her. Did this mean she wasn't kin to Sally T after all, and that Donatella knew "the Godmother" was an act? She could not catch up. Not in a decade had she felt this lost.

Lia came out of Isabel's bedroom and Raffi paused, waiting

for the maid to disappear into the kitchen. "How did you know?" Raffi said quietly, eyeing the kitchen door.

"I know everything. That's what happens when you're ninety-four."

This new reality set upon Raffi like an ill-fitting coat.

"Speak your question, Raffaella. You said it wasn't about the Andolinis, Angelinis, Sampieris, whoever." Cousin Donatella leaned in, cupping a hand around her ear. "What is it you *really* wanted to ask?"

"I just...always wondered if the Americans were right about me. If my name was bad, if my culture was, too. But it was the Truvarizzi name I was scared of—"

Donatella groaned.

"—and, just now, you spoke of *him*. He's the one who's been on my mind all these years. Since I was a child, I've wanted to know: is he...*u me sagnu?*"

"Your blood? Again, I say: what does it matter?"

"Wouldn't you want to know if you shared genes with a sociopathic criminal?" Raffi shuddered. "Michele Andolini may be cruel, but he's a playground bully compared to Sally T."

"No, I would not want to know, and that, *picciotta*, shows I have good sense." Donatella paused. "We have an expression in Sicily: *Cu pica parrau mai si pintiu.*"

"'Those who speak little have no regrets,'" Raffi translated. "Forgive me, *Cuscina*, but you don't exactly follow that maxim."

"The rule does not apply to Donatella Sampieri," she sniffed.

A crash came from the kitchen and drew their eyes to the door, now ajar. Raffi looked at her cousin, alarmed, but Cousin

Donatella shook her head, *no, trust me*, and shouted: "Which of you idiots did that?"

Anxious whispers drifted from inside. The two maids emerged.

"We were cleaning up," said Lia.

"I dropped a bowl," said Veru. "Nothing priceless," she hurried to say at Cousin Donatella's scowl. "I'm sorry."

"Fine, fine, *andare*," Cousin Donatella said, pushing air with her hand. "And close the door this time."

When the latch of the door clicked, Raffi leaned closer to her cousin. "Did they hear?"

"These girls have it made with me. They might be nosy, but they won't talk." Donatella patted her hair. "So, this is your big issue? You want to know if Sally T is your blood?"

Raffi held a finger to her lips. Donatella rolled her eyes.

"The question has followed me my whole life," whispered Raffi.

"You followed it right back," countered Donatella.

The words hit like bullets. Donatella had Polly's leveling candor. Raffi swallowed hard. "I still want to know," she said at last.

Donatella rolled her head in a circle, stretching, exasperated. "This is getting boring, Raffaella. You focus on the wrong things." She sighed at her cousin's earnest expression. "American girl. We don't push it here. That's how we survive."

Raffi sensed the proximity of the answers she had always wanted. She would not relent. Her eyes hardened and narrowed and turned up at the edges like the Andolini family to which she now knew she belonged.

Donatella sighed. "I think the answer is yes, but no one knows for certain. No one but Sally T and your mother."

Donatella let the implications of this sink in before she continued.

"You could go to the Municipio. They have all the records—unless they've been expunged, which is possible. But even an inquiry is very *public*. Discretion is prudence."

Sally T might be her *father*? Nino, Polly, Skaneateles, Sicily, the very Earth beneath Raffi shook. This was seismic.

"I suppose," Donatella continued, oblivious to Raffi's dismay, "I could ask one of the many important people I know. Everyone in Palermo is my friend, *picciota*." Donatella stretched her arms out wide as if hugging the entire city. "I am the mayor of this town."

"If you're so wise and influential," said Raffi, willing herself strong, "how do you not know already?"

Cousin Donatella wagged her finger, staring up at Raffi with a knowing smile.

"Never ask a question you don't need answered."

Omertà again—though it seemed to Raffi that adherence to this practice was as changeable as the Sicilians themselves.

"So," Raffi said. Omertà was no code of hers. "You'll help me?"

"Yes, *cuscina mia*. At my age, I have no fear. Though I will warn you: sometimes questions don't bring answers, but more questions."

"I will consider myself warned."

A worry surfaced.

"But Cousin," Raffi added, "I don't want to get you involved in anything dangerous. I thought you might *know*. I didn't expect you to investigate."

"I'll make some calls tomorrow," said Donatella in a breezy

voice, "after my regular date at the catacombs." Cousin Donatella would have made a great Godmother. She did not need to pretend to have no fear.

"You still think they'll let you in?" Raffi swiveled her head to the hooked side and appraised her cousin. "You'd be an elegant mummy."

"I haven't heard the word *no* in sixty years, *picciotta*. I'm not about to start now."

29

The next morning, Raffi and Isabel woke to the sound of Donatella screaming for her purse. Stumbling toward the sitting room from their side-by-side bedrooms, they lingered in the doorway as Raffi's cousin, notwithstanding her diminutive stature, stood *over* Lia, whose body shook from head to heel. Raffi stifled a laugh at Donatella's getup: a gold sweater, taffeta pants, and a black bowler hat. At 9:30 a.m.

Isabel was about to charge into the room when Raffi motioned for her to wait.

"Where is Veru?" Cousin Donatella roared.

"She said she was sick, *signura*. She left early this morning."

"I've been awake since early this morning."

Lia held up her arms as if to fend off a blow.

"I am waiting for you to tell me a time."

"I—I don't know, Signura Donatella."

"Were you not *here?*"

"I was, *signura*."

"Useless," Cousin Donatella said under her breath but loud enough to be heard. "Tell her to get better. *Fast.*"

"Yes, *signura*."

"And get me my handbag!"

"Yes, *signura*."

Lia raced from the room as Raffi and Isabel faltered in and made a show of stretching and yawning and pretending they had not witnessed Donatella's performance for the last five minutes. Before they could speak, Lia was back with the handbag dangling from her finger.

"Just the catacombs today, *signura*?" asked Lia.

Cousin Donatella's eyes contracted into coin slots. "Where else would I go?"

The girl flushed.

Cousin Donatella clicked her tongue with disgust, sending Lia sputtering from the room.

"Skip it today, Cousin," said Raffi, switching to English for Isabel's benefit. "The dead bodies can wait. Let's go see that Christ Pantocrator."

Cousin Donatella looked as if Raffi had proposed they not only visit the church but desecrate it.

"I will not skip the catacombs! What do you Americans say? *Slow and steady wins the race.*" The old woman brushed off her sweater and ambled to the entryway mirror to apply more burgundy lipstick. "I'll keep going every week until I get my way."

Isabel, sprawled across the couch in one of Donatella's fuzzy white bathrobes, sighed. "How long will you be gone? We need your help finding a very important bakery." She sat up. "Have you heard of a kind of cookie called *cuccidati?*"

"Have I heard of *cuccidati?*" Cousin Donatella huffed. "My mother made them every Christmas. Go to Pasticceria Luritu. He has the best. It's not far from the catacombs. But," she said, glancing at her watch, "you'll have to find it yourselves. I am always there by 10:30. I need to keep them honest."

"Can we meet you for lunch afterward?" asked Isabel.

"Call me." Donatella withdrew her phone from the outer pocket of her purse and brandished it; the case was studded with gold grommets and embossed with her name. "It's custom," she said, noticing their stares. "*Solo e meglio*—only the best!"

She dropped the phone back in her bag, threw open the heavy front door, and walked out.

Raffi cursed herself for the one question she'd omitted the night before. *The woman in red.* She had to know.

"Be right back," she said to Isabel, catching the door before it closed.

Out on the landing, Donatella was fumbling through her purse.

"Cousin," said Raffi.

"What now?" Donatella said, not looking up.

"I saw a woman in Lercara at Andolini's funeral. She looked like my mother."

Cousin Donatella raised her eyebrows, as if to say *"And?"*

"Is my mother in Sicily?"

Donatella heaved the great sigh of a teacher whose star student flubbed the exam. "What did this woman look like?"

"I already told you. She looked like Polly."

The old woman rifled through her purse again—a process

that seemed to take minutes. Raffi's temper rose; she thought her question ignored. At last, Donatella extracted the grommeted phone, tapped on the screen, and beckoned Raffi closer.

"Do you mean *this* woman?" said Donatella, holding out her phone.

Donatella had pulled up a social media profile. It was the woman from the Andolini funeral. Perhaps also the woman from Cefalù, though Raffi was not sure. Her stomach flipped. *Ma.* On the screen, the woman's widow's peak was concealed beneath a bright scarf, her upturned eyes hiding behind a pair of vintage black sunglasses.

"Yes," Raffi whispered. "That's her."

"This is your mother's sister."

Raffi felt a numbness sweep her body; too many shocking revelations at once.

Polly had no siblings, of which she had often complained.

Questions just bring more questions.

Maybe this sister was kept secret from her mother, too. This thought gave Raffi hope. Perhaps Polly had also been lied to. "There was a sister she never knew?"

Donatella snorted. "Tch. Never knew? They were thick as thieves!"

"No," said Raffi, the numbness spreading to her very core. "That's not right."

"Bill of goods, *picciotta.*" Cousin Donatella grabbed the phone from Raffi's hands and shoved it into her purse. She tapped her watch. "We will talk about this over lunch. Or when your *amica* goes to sleep tonight. Don't make me late."

Raffi grasped Donatella's arm. After more than four decades, the truth was so close.

"I haven't forgotten what I promised you, Raffaella," said Donatella, as if reading Raffi's thoughts. "I'll make some calls this afternoon. *Allura*. Sleeping Beauty is expecting me."

Raffi watched her cousin's back retreat down the stairs and felt a swell of love for this resurrected Cousin Dolly. Finally, one person who told it like it is; one person who respected Raffi enough to tell her something as fundamental as her lineage.

The numbness closed in further. Secrets were accumulating like snowdrifts. Soon they'd be so deep it would be like winter in Skaneateles; wait too long to call the plowman and you're snowed in.

Raffi had not, she realized now, truly believed she shared blood with *those* Truvarizzis: with *Il Erudito*, with Sally T. There was not a ruthless cell in Nino's brain. Deep down, she had doubted her meek father could be related to criminals. Now everything was up for grabs.

And then there was her mother. Polly's cold stare the night Nino spoke those eerie words: *You're no American. You can't deny what you are.* Her father had known about Polly, of course he had. Why they had concealed Polly's true family from Raffi and yet left her with the name Truvarizzi, though, made little sense. Perhaps it was a cover for the fact the Truvarizzis weren't the problem all along. Perhaps it was Andolini blood alone that condemned Raffi.

She shook her head and threw her shoulders back. Enough. This reality wasn't going anywhere. She had another four decades to process it. She would roust the girl from the couch and go in search of cookies.

With a deep breath, she pushed open the apartment door, and nearly hit Lia in the face.

"*Scusi*," Raffi said, a reflex.

From the way Lia reddened in response, Raffi knew the maid had been eavesdropping. Raffi's stomach flipped again. Donatella had revealed Andolini secrets, had even reiterated her promise to investigate Raffi's relationship to Sally T. This could be valuable information for someone. The Godmother brain took over. She would tell Donatella about Lia's behavior later. The girl was not trustworthy after all.

Raffi returned to the drawing room, and Isabel.

Forcing a light tone, she teased, "You're going to drag me around Palermo looking for these *cuccidati*, aren't you?"

Isabel smiled.

"Can we at least see the Christ Pantocrator?"

Isabel pretended to ponder the question.

"You're impossible. I'm going to get ready."

Back in her room, Raffi pulled a tailored white shirt over her head. Unwelcome emotions rose like wraiths, wrestling her out of her studied calm. She had always imagined it would be a relief to unearth these hidden things, the satisfaction of completing a puzzle with the pieces fitted snug together. This was nothing like a relief. She felt lost—and that was not a feeling she could afford.

Raffi retrieved her purse from where it sat on the bedside table and, from a zippered pocket inside, she removed the small, creased photo of Polly's bridal portrait. Tracing her mother's young face, she whispered, "Who are you?"

The air in the room changed.

You know who I am.

"All these years, you let me worry about *Dad's* family when your name was rotten."

Names are not everything, Raffaella. Neither are families.

"But you told me to find answers. You practically dared me."

That was you talking. I'm a ghost.

Raffi stuffed the photo back into her purse.

She finished dressing, subdued her wild hair into a loose bun, and went to find the girl. She was determined to enjoy the day and the pastries and the promise of Cousin Donatella handing her the final answer—the one she had sought for so long.

"It's this way!" Isabel shouted. In a reprise of the Ortygia debacle, she was leading them in circles.

Raffi seized the girl's phone, tapped a few buttons, and peered at the map on the screen.

"We're nowhere near this bakery, Isabel. You led us in the opposite direction. See?" She thrust the phone in the girl's face. "The little dot is going backwards."

"I don't like the map view. I prefer written directions," Isabel said with her nose in the air. "And this says *Girare a Sinistra*."

"Yes, but you're not turning left."

Isabel blinked. "Doesn't *sinistra* mean straight?"

"That's *dritto*."

"*Dritto* is left," Isabel protested.

Raffi raised her fist to mouth and bit it. "Isabel!" She laughed with affection. "Give me the phone. I'll get us there."

Isabel handed over the device like a dog relinquishing a slipper. She brought a hand to her temple.

"Too late for that now," Raffi said, looking up from the map. "I know where we're going."

Twenty minutes later, they were jostling for position in the crowded *pasticceria*. Raffi deduced the only way to place an order was to thrust elbows out and shove people aside.

"*Due cuccidati*," she shouted, using her arm to block a tenacious old lady who was trying to sneak past her to the counter.

"*Dodici cuccidati!*" Isabel yelled from behind.

Raffi turned. "A dozen! You don't know directions, but now you can count?"

The baker looked back and forth at them with irritation.

"Fine. A dozen," said Raffi.

She grabbed the cardboard box from the baker, avoiding the old woman's tentacles, and fought her way out the door.

"We're having lunch with Donatella in an hour," Raffi said as they reached the sidewalk. "Don't spoil your meal."

Isabel, in the process of tearing open the box and extracting a square pocket of fig-filled dough drenched in icing, ignored her. She bit into the *cuccidati* and made her Pastry Face.

"As good as the Archimedes Spirals?"

"Nothing is as good as the Archimedes Spirals."

Raffi removed a cookie from the box and nibbled an edge. It was childhood in a bite. Her *nonna* had made these same cookies,

Raffi realized, though Nonna had never called them by name. Raffi pushed the rest of the *cuccidati* in her mouth and reached for another.

"Uh-uh!" Isabel said, closing the box top. "You'll spoil your lunch."

Raffi was leaning over to swat at the girl when a muffled explosion sounded in the near distance. The air filled with smoke. Raffi met Isabel's eyes. Unspoken terror passed between them like static electricity.

Her first thought was *Etna*, but that could not be right. La Mamma was on the other side of the island. Raffi turned in what felt like slow motion, taking in the Palermitans all around them. When the first person screamed, Isabel dropped the pastry box.

Confusion, like an insurgent regime, installed itself, ousting its predecessor, Order, in an instant coup. People ran in all directions. Raffi grabbed Isabel's hand and hurried toward what she thought was sunlight but emerged as the bakery's illuminated sign. Brando and Trini flashed through her mind. Isabel shouted and pointed to a pair of fire trucks barreling up the wrong side of the street, headed straight toward them. They jumped out of the way and collided with a teenage boy who shouted at them to watch out.

Collective wisdom funneled the crowd away from the smoke. Cold hands clasped even tighter, Raffi and Isabel followed. The sun was blotted out.

They moved through a fragmented world of smells and sounds. The voice of a young man calling, "Cicilia!" A sharp whiff of griddled pork from a phantom food stand. The disembodied bell of a bicycle. The smoke was so thick, Raffi could not see her own arms pumping in front of her.

A woman and her son, probably standing mere inches apart, screamed for each other.

When Raffi felt she could run no farther, the sky cleared enough that she was able to read the street sign at the intersection. The opposing road was Corso Vittorio Emanuele: the way to Donatella's place. Raffi pointed in the direction of Quattro Canti. They turned onto the broad avenue. Raffi willed her legs to move.

"I can't keep going!" Isabel shouted. Her face was striped with tears and mascara.

"We have to!" Raffi screamed back. "We have to get inside! There could be another one!"

A bomb. There could be another bomb. Inside Cousin Donatella's house, they would be safe.

Donatella.

Raffi stopped running and grabbed Isabel's other hand, eliciting a stream of Sicilian curses from nearby runners, who forked and flowed around them like a line of ants.

"Donatella!"

Isabel's face crumpled. She looked over her shoulder at the smoke and back at Raffi.

"We'll get to her place and wait for her. She's probably in the catacombs. They're underground." Raffi swiped her forehead. "It's the safest place to be."

Isabel's eyes were unfocused. The girl was a witch, not a warrior. It was up to Raffi to save them. She released one of Isabel's arms and yanked at the other.

They retraced the same route they had taken with Cousin Donatella the day before. They were different people then. When this was over, they would either be among the dead or the ones that lived to eulogize.

She had to get home to Brando. She had to save the girl, whom she now loved like a daughter. She had to see Trini salsa around the living room with vengeance in her eyes. Raffi was determined: they would survive.

At last, the filigreed roof of the Quattro Canti loomed. Raffi had never run so hard in her life. She made it a point not to run at all.

They reached the Quattro Canti and turned right, passing beneath the serene gaze of Christina of Bolsena. Raffi tried the front door to Donatella's building. It was locked. With two fists, she pounded on the solid wood. The girl turned and slumped against the wall. Raffi knocked harder.

The door burst open. Lia rushed out.

"What's happening?" Raffi demanded in Sicilian, her own voice odd in her ears.

Lia took one look at them and bolted.

"Hey!" Raffi screamed after her, but the girl had disappeared.

They ran through the door and up the stairs to find the door to Donatella's apartment hanging open. Raffi held her finger to her lips and eased across the threshold. She had the offhand thought that she had seen all this before in a movie. The kind of movie where you watch, in comfort, things that will never happen to you.

The entryway was clear. Not so much as a fingerprint on the glass. Raffi walked around the corner to the sitting room. The porcelain lamps were all lit. Donatella smiled down from above the couch.

Raffi threaded her fingers through her hair, pulling the bun out so her frazzled waves hung around her face. Lia had run, and Veru, she remembered, was out sick. Isabel wandered into the room, crying without sound. Reassured no one else was there, Raffi darted around the penthouse calling "*Donatella! Donatella!*"

Raffi returned to the sitting room. She shook her head. No Donatella.

"Give me your phone," Raffi said. Hers was in the bedroom and she could not waste a minute more.

Hands shaking so much her bracelet sounded like a baby's rattle, Isabel managed to remove the phone from her purse. She tossed it to Raffi, then lifted a shaking hand to her temple. Raffi turned away so she did not have to see the girl's reaction to whatever her radio signal told her.

Raffi called Donatella's number. It went straight to voicemail. Typing with her thumbs, she searched *Palermo bomb,* and a list of hits appeared on the screen. The words could have been cuneiform. She threw the phone down onto Donatella's gold chair and sprinted to the bathroom with hand over mouth, arriving just in time to release undigested *cuccidati* into the marble toilet.

She had not read what she'd read. The media had released their reports too quickly. They would retract. They were mistaken.

The mirror over the sink showed a face she did not recognize. She splashed water on this new face and came back into the sitting room. Isabel was on the floor, staring at the Hekataion, hand limp at her side. Raffi sank down next to her. She picked up the phone and read again the words she could now register.

A bomb had gone off at the Capuchin Catacombs.

"We have to go there," Raffi said. "She might be in the streets."

Isabel shook her head. "There's no need," she whispered. "It's too late."

"Stay, then," Raffi said, refusing to acknowledge the girl's words. The girl was wrong too. "Better someone is here in case she returns."

Isabel curled into a ball, shaking her head, *no*.

Raffi shot back down the stairs, out the door, past Christina of Bolsena again, and onto the Corso. The crowds had thinned. Anyone still on the streets looked as dazed as she felt. A little girl limped by, blood streaming down her temple from a hidden wound, her hand held by a young woman with a baby in her other arm. A nurse pushed a wheelchair containing an old man who cried in loud, hacking sobs into a handkerchief. An old-fashioned pickup truck with at least thirty people crammed into every inch of space sputtered down the street. She met the eyes of each person as they passed: the little girl and her mother, the exhausted nurse and the old man, every soul on the truck. The survivors.

It took Raffi an hour to make the thirty-minute walk. When she reached the catacombs, she found the door—through which Donatella had sailed the day before—blown out, and the whole structure enclosed in yellow tape. A police officer stood talking to the handsome security guard who held a blood-soaked rag to each ear, tears coating his face. Raffi interrupted them in brusque

Sicilian. Pointing to the blackened hole that was the entrance, she asked: "Signura Donatella?"

The security guard's face crumpled. "She was just leaving." He removed one bloodied hand from his head to point beyond the charred entrance. "She said she was going to lunch with you."

Ignoring the policeman's orders to stay out, Raffi sprinted to the steps and strained to see through the haze. She made out a white sheet covering a lump that could not, she thought with relief, be a body. The angle was too awkward. She moved closer and saw that the sheet covered two lumps, not one. They looked like pillows strewn an armlength apart.

Her mind raced through a series of disjointed thoughts. Her conversation with Donatella the night before; Donatella's promise to investigate Raffi's connection to Sally T. The maid Veru leaving in the night, claiming illness. The other maid, Lia, lurking behind the front door that morning as Donatella spilled Andolini secrets. Lia running off without a word.

A foot away from the white sheet was a designer cell phone case covered in gold grommets.

30

Raffi sat in the front pew of the grandest Catholic church in Palermo: Chiesa di Santa Caterina. In the hundred-page document that prescribed the arrangements for the old woman's funeral, Donatella explained she had selected Santa Caterina for three reasons: its prestige, its Sicilian Baroque opulence, and, finally, its proximity to Donatella's beloved Pizzeria Pretoria. Also in the instructions was an open casket, but the elegant white vessel, resting beneath the most famous fresco, *The Soul in Glory Rises to Heaven*, was closed. Raffi was reminded of Mary Fortune.

The three rows behind Raffi were crammed with Lercarese cousins, among them Cousin Pasquale, who had broken his cardinal rule and entered Cousin Donatella's penthouse the day before to offer her a choice of Ginevra's best mourning-wear. Raffi had declined. She'd had dresses sent from Milan for her and Isabel. Cousin Donatella would be roiling in the afterlife had Raffi come to her funeral in one of Ginevra Randazzo's dresses.

A subdued Isabel sat behind Raffi with Pasquale and Ginevra. She and Raffi had not said much more than "Good morning" and "Would you like an espresso?" since the bombing. Raffi had been busy helping Donatella's son sort out his mother's affairs, and Isabel had been crying and watching *Las Brujas de Bal Harbour* in her guest room.

The three rows across the aisle were packed with Andolinis. The widow Andolini tried to catch her eye. Raffi ignored her. Polly's secret sister, who was, of course, nowhere to be seen.

It did not matter who was here, who wasn't. The entire island of Sicily might be comprised solely of Andolinis and Truvarizzis, but the Sicilians were wise. They shut their mouths and left things buried. Raffi had not learned this lesson. Donatella had paid the price.

The Mass was in Latin. Like Andolini, Cousin Donatella had pulled strings.

The homily was lengthy and pedantic, and were Cousin Donatella alive, she would have shouted at the priest to hurry up and get to the eulogies so she could hear about her favorite subject: not Christ's resurrection or the life beyond, but her own fabulous time on Earth. Her detailed instructions had included the first eulogy, written by a famed Sicilian journalist, which was to have been read by her son. But the poor man was unable to do anything save sneeze into his elbow and weep. Raffi went to the lectern in his place and set the church humming like an opened beehive. She settled herself, cleared her throat, and read without inflection.

"'Donatella Sampieri was a great scholar, a generous patron, and a devout Catholic whose interment at the Catacombe dei Cappuccini—" her lip twitched at Donatella's presumptive victory "—marks the first time this honor has been conferred in a century.'"

She continued, registering the crowd tittering at Donatella's humor—both intentional and inadvertent—and crying at the few sad parts, like Donatella's hope she would join in heaven a long-dead daughter about whom Raffi never knew. When Donatella's words ran out, Raffi cleared her throat.

If cell phone videos recorded her now, if media and government spies peered out from the crowd, she would give them words to quote and remember. For this reason, she had decided to give her own eulogy in English. This way the world would understand.

"My cousin Donatella knew how to live," Raffi began. "She did it without apology and in style. The best food, the most precious art, the highest fashion—Donatella savored it. After ninety-four years, her death should have been dignified." She swung her eyes across the Andolini pews like a boom. "But, as you all know, it was not. It was violent and unnatural. Donatella was robbed of her peaceful death. Perhaps even by some of the people in this room."

The crowd murmured and shifted, though, truth be told, accusations were common at Sicilian funerals. Blame was a favorite Sicilian pastime.

Raffi's eyes blurred. She wiped them and gazed down the nave. The bloodied face of a little girl stared out from the third row. Gold candelabra shining in the polished-stone floor glinted like a grommeted cell phone case. Behind her, the white cloth covering the altar concealed a broken body.

This is Cousin Donatella's funeral. You are speaking.

"My cousin did not deserve to die now." Raffi paused. "It should have been me."

A counterpoint of nods and protestations split the church. The old women pressed their lips together in grim approval.

Raffi glared at the Andolini pews. Beside the Andolini sons sat the old man from the breakfast room in Ortygia—the one who had also been reading *Italia Oggi* at the *aperitivo* bar; he had probably been the one checking in at the Hotel Francisca too. She was unimpressed with Andolini tactics, even emboldened by the knowledge she was one of them.

Turning her nose to the hook, she quoted the Bible straight at the most menacing Andolini son: the one who had watched her from the front of the room at his father's funeral with eyes like a shark. The one who had led his mother away before she could speak her mind.

With crisp diction, she said: "*Mediante la misericordia e la verità, l'inquità è purificata.*"

By mercy and truth, iniquity is purged.

"All we can give Donatella is justice. Justice comes from truth. *L'ultima verità*—the ultimate truth. If I were to find out any of you were even *near* the catacombs that day, then I am going to blame some people in this room."

She paused and thought of Colle Madore, of Polly-not-Polly, of the chasm of secrets and madness that had swallowed her mother. Staring up from the Andolini pew, the menacing son smiled. He was not afraid, and neither was she. The same blood ran in them both.

"But is the truth even possible in Sicily?" said Raffi. "I'm not sure it is. Even the ground beneath us is full of lies."

She glanced at Isabel for support. The girl was staring at her bracelet. Raffi wondered if Isabel agreed with her—that Raffi should have been the one to die.

There was a part of herself she *could* kill, though, if it had not died already.

The Godmother.

31

"Mama, she no let anyone in that room for a week," said Trini. "She say no one, *pero* no one, not even Brando."

Trini and Isabel sat opposite each other at the long wooden farmer's table in the Godmother's dining room, Brando pacing behind them. Isabel glanced toward the boy, whose striking teenage face, so like his mother's, revealed a touching naiveté. Even the unflappable Trini looked distraught, her hair and nails dyed black.

"Sometimes she's whispering, sometimes we hear her snoring,'" said Brando, his voice cracking. "She must be sleeping on the floor. I asked her through the door if she wanted breakfast yesterday. 'Donatella can't eat breakfast' was all she said."

"*Si*, Mami, I tell her Marina Ramón want to come thank her for *Las Brujas de Bal Harbour*, and she say, 'Donatella's gone.'"

"She thinks it's her fault Donatella died," said Isabel.

Trini looked at Isabel sharply. "You agree with her?"

In part, yes—Isabel did think so. The old woman would be alive today if the Godmother had enjoyed her *cuccidati* and gone home. But Isabel also knew Raffi Truvarizzi was unable to back down—both by constitution and genetics.

From the angry looks on their faces, Isabel suspected Brando and Trini could read her thoughts. Perhaps she should leave. She wasn't sure she belonged with these people. Her solar return was over. There was no more pretense for her and the Godmother's relationship. It could fall away, now, like a pending charge that never came due—erased from the record.

She found the answer in her instincts.

"Can I talk to her?" said Isabel.

Trini snorted. "Hah! I don't think so."

Brando touched Trini's arm. "Let her try. It could be only us she doesn't want to see."

Trini's head snapped back like she'd been slapped. She leapt up and performed an angry one-woman paso doble across the floor.

"Papi? No. Your mother never wanna see her," she jerked a thumb at Isabel, "before she wanna see her son."

Or see you, Isabel thought. She pushed back her chair.

"She's in the office?"

Trini's cheeks bloomed.

"Vamonos," she barked. "You gonna do it, you do it now. She want Piccolo anyway."

Trini whistled for the massive dog, who padded up and sat before her with ears pricked. Trini whistled again and the three of them trooped to Raffi's office, stopping at the closed door. Trini knocked a tango line by the doorknob and bent at the waist.

"Mama!" she shouted through the keyhole. "You want Piccolo?"

The door unlocked but did not open. They heard footsteps in retreat.

"Let him in and go away," said a low voice Isabel did not recognize.

Isabel nodded for Trini to leave. The Boricua stood and retreated toward the hallway, her expression furious and hopeful. Brando tiptoed after her like a lost puppy.

Isabel opened the door and the dog trotted through. Peering inside, she glimpsed the Godmother behind her desk in wrinkled white pajamas, her hair a dark Brillo pad. And she *smelled*. The Godmother raised her eyes, and Isabel wanted to run from the room. She looked as close to dead as a living person could be.

"I know I killed Donatella," said the Godmother. "Now get out."

Isabel said a silent prayer, calling on the spirits of her long chain of *bruja* ancestors to help her, starting with Mary Fortune. If there was any hope for the Godmother and for their friendship, Isabel would have to get tough. There was no one tougher than her aunt.

"Maybe you did, but you didn't mean to. You're not Sicilian, you're American. You didn't understand how it is."

The Godmother watched her with dead eyes. She forced herself to go on.

"But sitting in this room feeling bad for yourself doesn't help Donatella. What happened to all that stuff about truth at the funeral?"

"She said I'm not an Andolini," said the Godmother, glancing up at Polly's portrait. "She said I'm weak."

Isabel pressed the door open wider. "You're taking abuse from a picture?"

A flicker of anger passed over the Godmother's face, then dulled.

"Maybe this will cheer you up," said Isabel. She took a deep breath. "I need your help."

The Godmother snorted. "I'm done helping."

"*Please.*"

To Isabel's dismay, the Godmother drifted toward her. Even from a distance, the Godmother's breath smelled sour.

"I'm not the Godmother," she said in a strange echo of the long-ago article on Mary's wall. She thrust out her arm, pushed Isabel backward, and slammed the door. Isabel heard Piccolo whimper.

Trini and Brando appeared at the end of the hallway and motioned for Isabel to follow them back to the kitchen. They stood clustered around the island.

Glancing about as if someone might be watching from the shadows, Trini hissed, "You judge her, but you come ask her a favor? Hah!" She struck a flamenco pose. "You get it wrong, Mama."

"She draws strength from helping others," said Isabel. "If she feels needed, maybe she'll come back to us."

"You don't want nothing, then? You *pretend* you need her?" Trini spat.

Isabel twisted her lips and looked away. When she looked back, her eyes were filled with tears. "No, I do need help. Badly."

"You want her help, but you don't like how she give it, eh, Mamita?"

Isabel remembered her own words that night on Colle Madore. *The villagers got what they wanted from the witches and turned on them afterward.* Is this what she had done to the Godmother?

When Trini closed the gate on her, Isabel felt more lost than ever.

+

TRINI AND BRANDO LAUNCHED a campaign that started with Marina Ramón. The telenovela star had been asking to come thank the Godmother in person for getting Marina's children back and resurrecting her career. Fed up with the misery, and worried out of her head, Trini relented, thinking an outsider might perk Raffi up. Secretly, Trini also wanted to see Marina Ramón again in person. Marina was bigger than ever, her face on the side of every South Florida bus and plastered across every billboard. Trini hoped to catch another whiff of Marina's perfume and, maybe, if the chance presented itself, get Marina to autograph Trini's *Las Encantadoras* DVD collection.

On the prearranged day, Marina entered the house like a floral zephyr, an astonishing arrangement of sixty white roses in her hands and her children trailing behind, each clutching a piece of paper with scribbles and drawings in marker. Trini ushered her into the kitchen with a covetous expression. *Marina Ramón estuvo aqui!*

"*Hola!*" Marina sang, hugging Trini, exuding plumeria, and clucking over a blushing Brando. There was no trace of the dejected dishrag Trini had met at Brando's graduation party.

"Mami." Trini could not resist. She covered her mouth with her hand and stage-whispered: "Who got the nun *embarazada* with the baby? The mayor's son?" Marina smiled. "No—wait!" Trini snapped. "The guy who own the hotel and pretend to be cripple?"

Marina raised a finger to her lips and whispered, "*Shhhhhhhh.*"

Trini and Brando looked at each other with excitement.

Marina laughed and reached down to tuck a strand of her daughter's hair behind her ear. "Where is my Godmother?"

Trini dropped her elbows to the counter and looked up at Marina with a frank expression. "Mama? Her cousin die."

Marina's pretty face creased with pity.

"I heard. I know it's not much, but I hoped these flowers might cheer her up. And," she pulled her children close to her on either side, "Victor and Graciela brought her some cards they made all by themselves."

The children flushed.

"Well, we gonna go see the Godmother now and make her smile," Trini announced. She lifted the flower arrangement high over her head and led a merry procession to Raffi's office. "Mama!" called Trini, winking at the children. "You got visitors."

They all waited with expectant smiles for an answer.

"Marina Ramón is here to see you, Mami, with *sus niños*! They make special cards for you."

"Please," said the voice behind the door. "Go away."

Reflexively, Marina put her arms around her children. "Godmother?" she called. "It's Marina. I brought Victor and Graciela to see you. We wanted to thank you for bringing us back together." She squeezed the children and offered an uncertain smile to the closed door.

"Please," the voice repeated. "Go away."

Marina gestured for the children to approach the door and slip the cards underneath. From within the room, Piccolo emitted a low growl.

"Well," Trini said to Brando after Marina had left. "Give me a break."

✦

TRINI TRIED EVERYONE. THE Godmother's attorney, Moll Portage, came with documents to sign, but they were passed under the door like the children's cards. Dione Spinotti flew in with her sax to play her new song, "Dum Dat Desperation," in person; she ended up standing outside the office blowing her heart out to the door. Congressman Ramsburg came to say he wanted to present the Godmother with the key to the city of Miami for all her charity work. The only sound on the other side was the light snoring of either the Godmother or the dog.

When the Godmother slipped out of the room for a rare shower, Trini found the children's cards torn up in the trashcan and Moll's papers all over the floor. Piccolo had been using them for pee pads. The room would have to be torn apart and redone. When the Godmother recovered, she was going to be disgusted with herself.

Since her last visit, Isabel had been calling Trini's phone non-stop. Trini thought the girl sounded contrite, which she should, because anyone who blamed the Godmother for anything was both wrong and evil. At last, Trini allowed Isabel to return to the house—but she made the girl wait a few extra minutes outside the gate to remind her who was in charge.

Isabel entered with a box of cannoli from a local Sicilian bakery, and Trini plucked one from the box with a wary expression, as if tasting for poison.

"Not bad," she said, chewing. "You wanna try again?"

This time, Trini's march to the office was less spirited. She was an upbeat person, and all this gloom and suffering was messing with her *vibras*. Trini had excellent *vibras*. She had been blessed that way.

"Mama?" Trini rapped on the door. "Open the door, Mama. Isabel Ibarra is here." Even her mocking American accent was half-hearted.

"Godmother?" Isabel called in a clear voice. She held the box of cannoli up to the door. "I brought cannoli. They're not like the ones in Sicily, but they're—"

The door flung open. This time, the Godmother wore a different pair of wrinkled white pajamas, her temples bright with silver hair. She was fuming. Isabel raised the box to shield her face.

"Why are you here?" the Godmother demanded.

Isabel lowered the box of cannoli.

"To see if you're okay, and...to ask for your help again."

The Godmother seethed. "That's rich, Isabel. My cousin died, and you blame me, and you barely say a word to me while I'm at my lowest, and now *you* want help. You're a hypocrite. You've got some big *cugghiunes* on you. At least you get *that* from your aunt. The reason I even opened the door was so I could tell you to leave."

Isabel looked stricken, and Trini, despite herself, stepped forward to place a protective arm around the girl. She would never go so far as to take sides against the Godmother, but her demeanor beseeched the woman to return to herself—the self that helped other women at all costs, especially when the woman was a friend. Trini had never seen the Godmother like this, even when Polly disappeared, and she had blamed herself for Polly too.

The Godmother put her hands on her temples and squeezed,

her face contorting as if two warring sides of her were fighting for control.

"What is it you want?" she said, composure hovering around her like a hopeful specter.

Isabel took a big gulp of air and said: "I want to be a story consultant on *Las Brujas de Bal Harbour.*"

Trini pulled back from the girl and beamed with pride. "Mami!"

"I want to help the show present witches as we are," Isabel continued, chin lifted, "not as caricatures, not vindictive and scary, but as the dignified women we are."

"You're a witch?" said Trini with interest.

"I identify as one, yes," said Isabel.

"What a worthy goal," spat the Godmother. "In case you didn't notice, though, I'm not affiliated with *Las Brujas de Bal Harbour.*"

Isabel looked desperate. "But you know Marina Ramón. And—" she searched her mind for the guests at Brando's party, "—and Misa Riù. They'll do it if you ask them."

The Godmother shrugged. "The one with power is the Godmother, and I've given her up."

Trini's eyes widened. "Ho!" She crossed herself. "Mama, this is not you. You need a Cafecito and a massage and a reminder who you are."

"What I need is to be left alone." The Godmother pointed behind her to the portrait. "With my mother. She's the one that knows me."

"But—" said Isabel.

"*Pero—*" said Trini.

"Only the Godmother can help you. Go find her somewhere

else because she ain't me."

"Wrong!" Isabel shouted, poking a finger in the Godmother's chest. "You *are* her now. Your name is not your value. It's a crutch. You need to believe what everyone in this room already sees." She paused, waiting to see if her words hit. "You've been the hero we all needed. And you created yourself from scratch."

"Not from scratch. From two names: Truvarizzi and Godmother. Neither of which belongs to me."

Isabel reached into her pocket and took out a tarot card. The image on the card was of two naked people, a man and a woman, raising their arms to an angel blowing a celestial horn down from the clouds. "I pulled this last night." She held the card out. "It's Judgment. It's for you."

"Oh, Christ." The Godmother stepped forward and shoved the girl backward so hard that Isabel crashed into the opposite wall. The door slammed.

Isabel rose, shaking. She took account of her injuries, mostly to her pride.

"It means reflection," she said in a tiny voice to Trini and Brando. "Redemption. *Legacy.* It means she has to keep going."

Trini brushed a fist across her eyes and looked away. Brando slipped an arm across Isabel's back.

"Her work isn't done," said Isabel through her tears.

Together, they walked down the corridor, through the kitchen, and out the front door. At the gate, Trini patted the girl on the shoulder.

"You did good, Mamita," she said. "Now we pray."

32

Knocks came at predictable intervals. Raffi tuned them out. They were like church bells chiming in a village square: something to which you become so accustomed that you no longer notice it. The only company she cared to keep was Polly. Polly alone understood.

Each knock had its own character. Trini's were crisp and insistent beats punctuated by frustrated yells of "Mami!" Guests invited by Trini in hopes of luring Raffi from the room rapped several times at half-volume and gave up. Only the Brando knocks registered. They were loud and frantic and accompanied by his scratchy adolescent tenor saying, "Mom?"

Which is why the deep pounding that shook the torchiere caught her by surprise. It was a man's knock, with the side of the fist—the sides of both fists, by the sound of it. From outside the door, the voice that barked "Mom!" was a command, not a question. She rose from her desk and sat back down as quickly. He sounded like his father. She would not obey a teenager.

"*Mamma*," he said, his voice a warning. "*Ora!*" *Now.*

Raffi's surprise intensified. Brando never spoke Italian. He was a self-declared American. Whenever Raffi spoke Italian or Sicilian, he cringed. He said it was too put-on, too "full of itself." He could have been quoting his grandmother.

"*Va fa Napoli*," he swore through the keyhole. "*Mamma! Basta. Apri la porta, ora!*" He banged the door again. "I said, this is enough! Open it now!"

Curiosity triumphed. Weeks locked in her office and her son had a new personality? She approached the door, flipped the lock, and creaked it open. "*Ora sei Italiano?*" Now you are Italian?

"Let me in," he said, standing his full six feet and exuding a power redolent of his famous mother. "We need to talk."

Raffi swept her arm back, inviting him in without a word. Padding back to her desk chair, she sat, leaning back and regarding him with muted interest. He sat in the small wooden chair across from her, leaning forward, hands clasped.

His expression softened and, despite herself, her heart broke to see a glimmer of the little boy she'd once held in her arms in the ocean, clinging to his mother for life.

"I called Penn today. They'll let me defer my acceptance for a year. I said I'll let them know by Friday."

Raffi looked baffled. This, too, was not what she'd expected.

"I don't understand. Why would you defer?"

"I can't leave you this way, Mom."

Raffi rolled her eyes. "You're not serious. Go to college."

Brando lowered his head and looked up at her from under those thick, dark brows. She swallowed as her eyes trailed up to his widow's peak. The Andolini blood was in him too.

"Mom. I saw your eulogy for Donatella on YouTube. How

about some *verità?*" He tried to be playful. "Remember the Mouth of Truth?"

Raffi ignored his attempt to make her sentimental. The Mouth of Truth was a Roman monster described in Brando's childhood book. Legend said if you put your hand in the Mouth of Truth and told a lie, you'd lose the hand. It had been Brando's favorite story.

"I'm having a hard time," said Raffi stiffly. "I survived a bombing."

She felt sick doing it, but she turned cold eyes on her son. She wanted what she had never wanted before: to scare him away.

"I know what you went through, Mom—"

"No, you don't."

"I *know* what you went through, but this?" He pointed to Polly. "It has to stop."

Raffi followed his finger to the portrait, confused. Polly gazed downward as if to say, *I'm innocent.*

"What does Grandma have to do with this?" She shook her head to clear it. "Stop trying to distract me. You call that school right now and tell them you'll be there in September. You're not using me as an excuse to hang around the house watching telenovelas."

"Mom."

He was toggling back and forth before her eyes. *Boy. Man. Boy. Man.*

"I'm serious, Brando."

"I'm not staying home for fun."

In the brief pause that followed his words, he seemed to per-colate an angry energy, jumping up from the chair and rushing at the door. For a moment, Raffi thought that was the end of it, and she was relieved. They would discuss Penn tomorrow. The exertion of talking even to her son was too great.

But that was not the end of it. He pivoted. She was shocked to see his long eyelashes heavy with tears. Pointing a finger at Polly's portrait, he shouted, "*Fuck Grandma!*"

Raffi's mouth fell open.

"Fuck *Grandma?*"

In three steps, she was across the room, and, for the first time in her life, she slapped him hard across the face.

"You want to speak Italian?" she roared. "*Disgrazia!*"

"*You* want to speak Italian?" he countered. "*Fanculo la nonna!*"

Raffi stood there breathing hard until she steadied her breath, her anger thawing into bewilderment.

"Why?" she said.

Brando grabbed her hands and held them tight in his. Raffi was surprised at how large they were.

"Because she's dead, Mom. There are people right here, right now, who need you and love you, who can advise you, whom you can *trust*, and still you keep asking *her* for answers, Mom, and she's gone. Grandma's gone, and she's never coming back." He shook his head. "*Minchia.* All you're doing when you talk to her portrait is listening to yourself."

As he dropped her hands and stood back, Raffi regarded her son as if meeting him for the first time. Could this profundity be coming from the mouth of her baby? His judgments were mature and elegant. He was a man now; she saw it. The only thing boyish about him was his beautiful face. She reached out to touch his cheek.

"I can't decide which impresses me more: your words, or your command of Italian curses."

Brando did not smile. He was steel. He was *her*. He put his hand over Raffi's and brought it down from his cheek to cover his heart.

"There's a difference between being devastated and being destroyed, Mom. *She*," he jabbed his finger at the portrait, "was destroyed." His eyes sought hers. "And that's not her fault. She was sick. But you're not her, Mom. You're stronger than Grandma. Unlike *her*, you want to know who you are. She wanted to forget." His face crumpled and he started sobbing. "I'm so afraid I'll lose you!"

The crystalline structure that had formed inside Raffi when Donatella died began to break apart. This was her son. There was nothing more sacred. Abandoning herself to madness would sentence Brando to the same suffering she'd endured: the loss of a mother. She gazed up at Polly.

I'm sorry, Ma. If it's between you and Brando, I choose him.
Polly's smile looked sad.

Raffi backed up to her desk, eyes on her son. Opening the top drawer, she rummaged around and found her phone. She turned it on. As Brando watched, she dialed Polly and put the phone on speaker. The voicemail picked up. She drew in the deepest breath she could hold and exhaled until the beep sounded and it was time to speak.

"Ma? It's... Raffi. I'll always love you, Ma. I'll never forget you. I hope you're at peace."

She was crying so hard she could barely continue.

"I won't call again, Ma. Did I mention I will always love you?"

She wept into the phone until, at last, she pressed *End* and placed the phone on her desk.

Her hands shaking, still watching Brando, she bent to open the bottom drawer and withdrew another, older, phone. Her mother's. All these years, she had paid the fee to keep a line to Polly. Polly, who would never—*could* never—answer. Raffi came around the desk and stood before her son. She held the phone out to him in surrender.

"Take this," she said with all the strength she had left. The tears had reached all the way down to her pajamas, soaking the soft white collar. Her eyes were so red, they looked like they might bleed.

Brando held open his arms, and Raffi stepped away from the past and into the future.

33

"Look who's here!" Trini announced. "*Dios mio,* it's *La Madrina!*" She sambaed forward and threw her arms around Raffi with a relieved sigh. "Mami." She folded her arms. "You don't do that to us again."

Raffi smiled. Brando had led her to the kitchen still in her wrinkled, wet pajamas. She was disoriented. The overhead light was too bright; she shielded her eyes and Trini flipped the light switch off. It was late afternoon, the unlit room thrown into shadow. Trini busied herself lighting candles and whistling. "*Todo estará bien,* Mama," she said, more to herself than to Raffi. "All gonna be well."

Raffi looked around in a daze at Isabel, Brando, and Trini, the three of them gathered close around the kitchen island smiling. She was surprised they looked so happy. Isabel shone like a lamp. Raffi had not considered that anyone would miss her. For weeks, she had imagined herself the problem and her exile the solution.

The kitchen looked different. She had not seen it since her return from Sicily.

"Did you change something in here?" she said to Trini. "Something changed."

"Is the flowers," said Trini with a grin.

For the first time, Raffi saw that the room was filled with them. She was confused. Had someone *else* died? She approached the largest arrangement—sixty white roses—and read the card aloud. *Thank you from the bottom of our hearts, Godmother. You reunited us. We owe everything to you!* The card was signed Marina, Victor, and Graciela, the words in their own handwriting. The arrangement must have been delivered by hand.

"But they came here weeks ago," said Raffi. She pressed her nose into the nearest rose. "They're not fake. They lasted this long?"

Trini shook her head. "*Ho!* Marina bring new flowers each week. She say she keeping bringing them until the Godmother get well."

Raffi's throat was tight. Before she could speak, she felt Brando's hand on hers. He led her to the couch, Isabel and Trini following. They sat in a row, thighs pressed together, a warm strand of family.

Brando turned on the TV, revealing a paused clip from *Las Brujas de Bal Harbour*. Every pixel of the screen was filled with Marina Ramón. She wore a marigold cocktail dress, her bosom sheathed in concentric layers of diamonds (despite that it was midday), her scallop-shell lips blood red. Facing off with her were three attractive women Raffi presumed to be the *brujas* for which the telenovela was named. One wore purple, one green, the third black. These colors, Brando explained, were consistent for these characters.

The setting was a luxury boutique featuring a mirrored wall

of sunglasses and an array of headless mannequins dangling fur handbags. Brando pressed play and the clip began.

"*Pero—moriste hace años!*" cried the purple witch, pointing at Marina.

"*Tù... Còmo es esto posible?*" sobbed the one in green.

"Turn on the subtitles," said Raffi, intrigued.

Brando rewound and began again.

"But—you died years ago!"

"*You...*How is this possible?"

"I'm like a storm," said Marina, her fingers fanned around a cigarette holder that had appeared out of nowhere and turned out to be a wand. "I come and go as I please—and stay as long as I like."

"Just tell us this," said the one in purple. "How did you do it?"

"Do what?" Raffi asked.

"Shhh!" hissed Isabel.

Marina looked skyward—no more than a glance, but it was this sort of subtle insertion that won her awards.

"Which one are you? Blanca or Luz?" asked the one in black.

"I don't understand," Raffi stage-whispered. "Aren't those the characters from her other show? *Las Encanta—*"

"Shh!" shouted Brando and Trini together.

Marina smirked. "I am neither Blanca nor Luz."

The camera panned the three witches as it dawned on them.

The black-clad one understood first. "No," she said, backing away.

"It can't be," cried the one in purple from below, where she had fallen to the floor in shock.

"Why us? Why now?" wept the one in green.

This was the green witch's trademark lament, Trini explained. Trini herself had a tee shirt upstairs with that slogan printed on the front in emerald glitter. It was a merchandising phenomenon. In fact—

"*Shhhh!*" shouted Brando and Isabel.

Marina cackled, her eyes obsidian. "That's right, you fools. Blanca and Luz were not twins but triplets. *There were three of us all along!*"

She threw off her fur coat, shooting off a bright flash of electricity, the boutique obscured by a cloud of charcoal smoke. Raffi thought of Palermo and shuddered, but the thought passed quickly. There was no mistaking this telenovela for reality.

Marina cried: "I am the third sister, Minerva! The most powerful of all!"

Brando jumped up with his fist in the air as the credits ran. High-fiving Trini, he turned to his mother with a smile.

"Look what you did for her, Mom. You resurrected Marina Ramón."

"*Si*, Mami," said Trini, throwing an arm around Raffi's shoulders. "You change her life. She no Minerva on *Las Brujas* without *La Madrina*."

Isabel raised her hand.

"I *will* say, they need me on this show." She wrinkled her nose. "Those aren't witches, they're ..."

"Bitches?" volunteered Brando.

"I was going to say assholes," said Isabel.

Raffi chuckled but her face tightened as the girl's eyes pleaded in her direction.

"I wish I could help you, Isabel, but all I can do right now is put one foot in front of the other." She smiled at her son. "I need to get strong again."

Isabel nodded her assent, but Raffi was certain the girl was not done. Sure enough, Isabel jerked her head to the side, motioning for Raffi to join her in the kitchen, apart from the others. Raffi followed, resigned that the girl would not relent until Raffi heard her out.

"Yes?" Raffi said when they were relatively alone; Trini bustled into the kitchen and watched them from the vantage of the sink, where she was pretending to wash dishes.

"You won't *believe* what I found out," Isabel said with quiet excitement. "Thank God you're done with that depression thing, because we have to go to Arizona right away. It's *urgent*."

Raffi eyed her. "I thought you were going to ask me about *Las Brujas de Bal Harbour*—and I cannot help you."

Isabel looked down and nodded.

"And Isabel? I'm not taking another mysterious journey with no purpose."

"Sicily had a purpose," Isabel said defensively.

"It *ended up* having a purpose." Raffi frowned. "A failed purpose. I'm not convinced it had one at the outset."

"Godmother, you don't understand."

"Raffi. Call me Raffi."

"Fine. *Raffi*. Geez, first you get all weird when I *don't* call you Godmother, now you're all weird if I do." She exhaled. "Here's what happened. In Sicily, my signals were so attuned to you and your challenges—"

THE GODMOTHER | 321

Raffi's eyebrows went up.

"—that I didn't pick up on Mary."

"Wait," said Raffi, bemused. "Now you're a medium?"

Isabel puckered her lips as if considering this appellation. "I'm not sure it's that, though my gifts do seem to be getting stronger by the day. To be honest, I'm not sure what it is."

Raffi waited.

"Here's what happened," said Isabel. "I hired those Nerd Herd guys to help me trace the IP address on Mary's laptop—the one that went missing when she died. It bothered me that the laptop never turned up. It was like it disappeared." Isabel leaned so close Raffi could smell bubblegum. "But it didn't disappear. They *found* it, Raffi. Because—" She took on a vague expression, "—the IP address broadcasts its location through, like, electromagnetic waves that, like, bounce off the satellites—"

"You have no idea what you're talking about, do you?"

"You're missing the point. The point is the laptop is in Arizona."

Isabel's eyes popped wide with excitement. This statement was supposed to mean something to Raffi. It did not.

Isabel deflated. "Don't you get it?"

"Isabel, I'm trying to get over Donatella, and now you come at me with this—"

Isabel planted her hands on her hips. "It's been six weeks. Even Donatella would tell you to get on with it."

A familiar headache was forming.

"Remember the third horse blanket?" Isabel persisted.

Raffi thought back to the storage unit. The third blanket... Raffi had not thought of it since that day. A southwestern scene?

322 | LEIGH ESPOSITO

She looked at Isabel, who was watching her like a comedian waiting for the audience to get the joke.

Isabel sighed. "The first two horse blankets were meant for you and me—obviously. Cuba and Sicily. After the Nerds traced the laptop to Arizona, I went to the storage unit this morning to check the third one. It's got a big red rock, teepees, and a hawk circling in the sky. Irrelevant, right?"

Raffi did not like where this was going. "I would say so," she said with reluctance. But she was curious too. Everything Mary Fortune did had a point. The third horse blanket had to mean something.

Isabel's eyes glittered. "But what if it isn't irrelevant?"

A thought interfered. "Why did you need these Nerd people to find the laptop? Can't you just—" Raffi touched her temple.

Isabel shook her head. "It doesn't—"

"I know, I know," said Raffi. "It doesn't work that way."

"Raffi, listen to me," Isabel said, wresting them back to the subject. "I figured it out. *The third horse blanket is Mary.*"

Raffi wondered if her brain had become soft from weeks of solitude and poor hygiene. "Did you say the third horse blanket *is* Mary?"

Isabel nodded so hard, her curls bounced. "I did some research. I found this resort-commune place in Arizona called Red Rock State Park. They've got teepees and crystals and drum circles—New Age stuff. Godmother, it looks *just* like the third horse blanket. I think Mary left a message for us." The girl's fingers grazed her forehead. "This is the last stop in our journey."

"What kind of research did you do?" said Raffi suspiciously.

"I did an online search for teepee-desert-hawk-rock. It was the first image that came up."

Raffi almost laughed but restrained herself. She did not want to encourage the girl. Waving her hands in protest, she said, "I can't do it, Isabel. Some other time."

Isabel jutted her chin and drew up to her full, albeit diminutive, height. She looked identical to Mary.

"What could be more important than this?"

Mary. Raffi felt her resolve weakening. How could she turn her back on even a *possible* message from her late mentor?

"Talk to me in October," Raffi said, already knowing the girl had won.

"October is too late," said Isabel. "We need to go now."

"Why, are the teepees migrating?"

Isabel ignored her.

"The woman on the horse blanket sitting cross-legged in front of the mountain—I'm pretty sure she's the commune's founder. Get this—her name is Mother *Hawk*."

Raffi groaned.

"Hawk, like the hawk in the horse blanket!" said Isabel.

Raffi tried another tack. "What possessed you to search for Mary's laptop? You don't need it anymore. You're not an astrologer; you're a witch."

Isabel took Raffi's hand in hers, eliciting a sharp sidelong glance from Trini, who was still fuming at the kitchen sink.

"You, of all people, should understand why I need answers," the girl said. "I don't need the laptop. I need to *know*." Their eyes joined and Raffi understood. The girl was no longer a girl.

Fed up with what was transpiring in the corner, Trini threw down the dish towel and was advancing on them when Raffi relented.

"Alright, Isabel," she said as the girl leapt forward to embrace her. With a warmth she usually reserved for Brando alone, Raffi returned the hug.

34

There was no silver-haired woman meditating cross-legged in the foreground, but, otherwise, Red Rock Retreat was a 3D version of the third horse blanket, teepees and all: seven of them, scattered across combed russet gravel, each glowing with warm light from within. The flap-doors were closed, but the leather tethers that secured them hung untied and motionless in the cool desert evening. A lone hawk circled above.

Behind the teepees, the majestic rock ridge towered like a stern witness. As Raffi and Isabel drew closer, the sky blushed deep pink and faded. Slate and purple striations stretched out in both directions. Raffi felt like she had stepped into a video game—the kind in which, after a long quest, you reach a final screen and victory lies one challenge away.

An attractive, ageless woman with a shaved head had greeted them at the welcome center, which was nothing more than a small thatched-roof hut. Isabel had asked where they might find Mother Hawk, and the woman nodded as if unfazed by this request. Raffi got the sense Mother Hawk was sought often.

"Find the teepee with pale blue markings," the woman said.

"At this time of day, Mother Hawk is either inside napping or meditating in the circle."

"What circle?" Isabel asked.

"The circle beyond," the woman said in an enigmatic voice, then sighed at their confused expressions. "It'll be just past the teepees on the left."

They'd thanked her and set off across the grounds.

When Raffi and Isabel were close enough to see the colors on each teepee, they found that *all* the teepees had blue markings, in addition to other colors. Isabel was about to turn back to the welcome hut when Raffi motioned to the teepee in the center, which bore *only* blue marks. Raffi approached the teepee, Isabel close behind.

"Mother Hawk?" called Raffi, imagining what Polly would say if she saw her daughter creeping up on a teepee.

"Mother Hawk?" Isabel echoed, a little louder.

They exchanged a glance and, after a moment's hesitation, pushed through the flaps together. Inside was another world.

Ten-foot beams of smooth, pale mariposa held up the canvas, filling the air with a fresh forest scent, and the floor, made from this same wood, was strewn with patterned throw rugs held down by four vintage copper lanterns. A cascade of colorful quilts made a cheery headboard for the bed, which was flanked by a leather couch with shaggy white cushions on one side and a chair covered by a cow-print blanket on the other. Two standing lamps, their iron stands forged in the shape of interlocking horseshoes tipped to look like crescent moons, gave soft light. Otherwise, the teepee was empty.

"Huh," said Isabel.

Raffi stepped back out through the canvas flaps and came around behind the teepees to look for the meditation circle. Next to her, Isabel drew in a sharp breath. Ahead, where a small juniper forest grew at the base of the rock, a powwow of women sat in the uncombed red dirt. *Something is here.* Even Raffi felt it. Fortune's wheel turned.

Isabel strode toward the women. It was Raffi's turn to follow.

As she got closer and the figures emerged from the dusk, Raffi's eyes went to a woman with dark skin and a giant mass of braids streaming down her back. The woman's hand entwined with that of a lithe woman next to her, who leaned in her direction like a palm tree toward the sea.

The hawk flew lower, tracing a parabola through the sky. A shiver swept Raffi's spine. *Something is here.* This was Isabel's world, now, far from Andolinis and buried histories.

The hawk was startled off course by a loud yelp from Isabel's direction. The girl was running. Raffi looked around for danger but saw nothing out of the ordinary, other than her distinct feeling there was nothing ordinary here.

Isabel had thrown herself at one of the women in the circle, and Raffi concluded the girl had gone mad. She ran toward Isabel but stopped halfway. The woman in whose arms Isabel was enveloped had silver hair and a giant feathered headdress. Head bent down to Isabel's, her face was concealed. *This must be Mother Hawk,* Raffi thought.

Isabel pulled away from the silver-haired woman, her cheeks wet with tears. She and the woman were laughing. At last, Raffi saw the woman's face.

It was none other than Mary Fortune.

+

RAFFI DID THE ONLY thing that made sense: she sat in the dirt. A stream of animated Spanish issued from Isabel's mouth, so fast it sounded like she was speaking in tongues. Raffi considered whether she and the girl were sharing a lucid dream. Either that, or Raffi was delusional like Polly.

Isabel and Mary were volleying back and forth now like expert tennis players, chattering like it was no more than a delightful surprise to find your dead aunt sitting in Red Rock National Park wearing a feathered headdress.

Mary turned from the girl to Raffi and winked, then went around the circle introducing the others.

"This is Telluride Amy. She's a Wiccan priestess from Pittsburgh." Mary paused to allow a wave from the pretty woman to her left, who wore a celestite circlet over long pink hair. "That's Clara Estevez-Pince, *psicóloga* and *cantadora*." Next to Telluride Amy, a woman with a head of salt-and-pepper fusilli nodded. Mary pointed to the women holding hands. "Freedom Power, Professor of Women's Studies at Arizona State, and her partner Gabi." They raised their outside arms in greeting, clasped hands unbroken.

"I breed cacti," Gabi offered.

"And this," Mary said, coming at last to a white-haired nonagenarian with an age-battered Hopi *kopatsoki* in her lap, "is Mother Hawk, our spiritual guide and ritualist."

Mother Hawk's smile awakened a network of wrinkles around her warm brown eyes. She looked like a mass-card saint.

"You just missed the Butterfly Dance," Mother Hawk said in a high, sweet voice. "If I get up the energy, I'll lead another one tomorrow."

Mary clapped her hands with delight. "This is our group, Little Girls!" She wrinkled her nose. "It took you long enough to find me."

Raffi had not moved from the ground. "But, you died," she said. Someone, at least, should state the obvious.

Isabel and Mary exchanged a look and fell into hysterics, the other women chuckling along. Raffi surveyed them all, dumbstruck. At last, Isabel wiped the mirth from her eyes.

"She sent us on a fool's errand. She ran us around so she could disappear without me picking up on it. But," Isabel said, turning to her aunt and grazing a hand against her temple, "I don't understand why."

"Why?" Mary thundered. "Isn't it obvious? I'm dying!"

Isabel's face fell, and Raffi felt a surge of pity. The girl had weathered so many disappointments; if Mary Fortune was alive, she should at least have the courtesy to stay that way.

"I have cancer," Mary admitted, rolling her eyes as if the malignant progression of abnormal cells were no more than a tiresome nuisance. "The doctors wanted to give me *la quimioterapia*, all those poisons and tubes, but I said no. They'd have me bald by now." She brushed her hands against each other, releasing a small cloud of red dirt. "That kind of medicine is not for me. These women will let me die in their company with all my hair."

"You're living in a teepee?" Isabel said. "I know how you are about bathrooms."

"Oh, we rotate lodgings," said Mother Hawk. "Next season, we're doing adobe hogans. If we can get the seed money, I'd like to build a solar-powered pueblo village."

Raffi had a feeling that comment was meant for her.

"You never told me you wanted to die in the desert," said Isabel.

"I didn't always know it, Little Girl," said Mary. "It came to me in a dream."

Isabel seemed to accept this. To the Ibarra women, dreams were as binding as law.

"I found this place, and I fell in love with it. And I do have the blood of the *indígena* in me. I am part Taíno," Mary said, tossing her feathers.

Isabel laughed. "Aunt Mary. We did the genetic testing. You were, like, one percent."

Mary scowled. "It counts!"

"I still don't understand why you're here," said Raffi.

"Because she wanted to choose her own death," Freedom Power interjected, in a voice that could command armies.

Mary nodded.

"I was delivered into this world in my Abuela Isabel's bedroom in Camagüey, Cuba, where Venus herself kissed the sand. I would have loved to pass the rest of my life in that little house on Varadero Beach. The house on the horse blanket I gave you," she said, turning to Isabel. Her face grew weary. "But the Communists took that house; now it's a bed-and-breakfast. So, my dream led me here, where I can end my life the way I want to. This is my final journey."

"You didn't want to spend the end of your life with me?" Isabel asked, tears at the ready.

"Little Girl." Mary pulled Isabel in for another embrace. Over the top of her niece's blond head, she addressed the group. "I want to spend the end of my life taking care of *me*. Not anyone else, for once. Just me."

This sentiment was met with a chorus of agreement.

Raffi thought of Polly. What if her mother was somewhere in a circle like this? What if she had chosen to disappear so she could stop being a wife and mother (and crazy person) and be Apollonia for the first time in her adult life? It was a happy fantasy.

Mary pulled Isabel up by the chin to look into her eyes.

"If you ever need me, this is where I'll be. And when I'm dead? Then I'll be everywhere."

The tears won out. Mary patted her niece's back.

"You will never be alone."

"And please come back any time," piped up Mother Hawk. "You'll have to rent a teepee," she added apologetically. "It's how we make our money."

"Also," Mary continued, "take my laptop. It's what brought you here."

Isabel fidgeted. "I don't need it, Aunt Mary. I'm not—" She paused. "Wait. How will you follow the stars?"

"I don't need them to tell me where I'm going."

The hawk swooped down and sat outside the circle, blinking.

"I'll be a wolf in my next life," said Mary. "A white wolf."

Raffi and Isabel shared a glance. *A white wolf.* They were at a crossroads now too.

"I came out to the desert to die like a wolf, to accelerate my karma. When I'm ready, I'll go up on the mountain and howl."

The women made room in the circle for Raffi and Isabel. As they sat, Raffi took Isabel's hand in both of hers.

Mary smiled. "You see?" she said, pointing at their hands. "You don't need me anymore. Haven't I taught you girls everything I know? What have I said? What does any good mother tell her daughter? That you can do anything if you have good women at your side. That there is nothing out of reach. Except math," she said to Isabel. "That's not for you."

Isabel opened her mouth to protest.

"As big as you can dream, Little Girls, dream bigger. And you," she said to Raffi. "I don't know what you think you're doing, but you can stop it. You took care to *create* the Godmother, and you did it for a very good reason. To help!" She shook her head. "I know about your cousin. It's terrible." She crossed herself. "I know you blame yourself."

Raffi looked away.

"*Don't*," said Mary.

"What do you know of it?" Raffi said.

"I saw the eulogy on YouTube," Mary admitted. Her face went hard. "I don't care what you call yourself. You've pledged to help women, and you owe them that, Godmother or not." She pretended to examine her nails. "You can start by helping my niece get that job on *Las Brujas de Bal Harbour*."

Isabel grabbed her aunt's arm. "How did you know?"

Mary smiled.

Isabel said, her voice a toe in the water: "You know what I am?"

"I've known what you were from the moment you were born, my little *bruja*. You had to find it out on your own. Now you have."

Mary turned to Raffi.

"And you do not need a mother or an answer or a name. Yes, there is power in your blood. You've done something good with it." Mary paused. "I always told you I made you; I lied. *You* made you. I just had the idea."

Raffi caught Isabel's eye. She found adoration there, and trust.

"There!" Mary exclaimed. "That's what it's all about: you two motherless girls together."

It was not weak to need the girl. Looking around, she realized that behind every powerful woman was sometimes a man but *always* a circle of women.

"What do you need from us, Mary?" said Raffi. "How can we help?"

Mary shot her a look. "You can start by sending me my horse blankets. They're in the other storage unit in Miami, on the top floor." Mary turned to Mother Hawk. "I needed to be very clear about my intentions for their fool's errand; I couldn't risk being subtle, you understand? The horse blankets had to be separated." She turned back to Raffi and Isabel. "But now I want them. It will be cold here soon." Mother Hawk put an arm around Mary's shoulder and squeezed.

Raffi was touched. Mary had found her final family on Earth. The one she'd not been born to but had chosen.

"So that's all, Little Girls. You," she said to Raffi, "have your calling, and you," she said to Isabel, "have yours, and I," she said to the group, "have business with *El Señor*."

"I still want answers," said Raffi in a quiet voice. "I'm not done."

"I know, Little Girl. You have a right to them. But remember that questions don't always bring answers. Sometimes they bring more questions."

Raffi looked at Isabel, who shrugged and smiled.

"Now take the laptop, send me my horse blankets, and close those storage units when you're done. They're costing me a fortune." She heaved a great sigh, sending headdress feathers aflutter. "This whole faking-your-death thing—I mean, it's expensive, let's face it."

35

One week after Arizona, Raffi visited Marina Ramón on the set of *Las Brujas de Bal Harbour.* The show was typically filmed at a sound stage in Davie, but today they were on location in Miami Beach, where Marina's character would use telekinesis to rescue the secretly-not-crippled hotelier from a dangerous rip current sent by the witch in purple.

Raffi had allowed Trini to come along if she promised to behave. "I don't promise nothing, Mama," was Trini's response. "I get on the set of a telenovela, and I get crazy." True to her prediction, Trini, duded up in her glittery *Why Us? Why Now?* tee shirt, stood next to a cameraman, pointing in various directions and chattering away as if telling him how to shoot. He did not look pleased.

"Godmother!" Marina called, sidestepping a portable fog machine to hug Raffi. Marina wore a yellow bikini top and a banana-print sarong, the scant ensemble a glorious display of her question-mark curves. No one would forget Marina Ramón again. "I'm so happy to see you." She pulled back from the embrace with tears in her eyes. "My children and I can never repay your kindness."

Raffi inclined her head with a sphinxlike smile.

A sound technician approached and began to insert a wire into the cup of Marina's bikini top. She slapped his hand away.

"Please," she said to Raffi, motioning toward her nearby trailer. "The children are inside with their tutor. They want to thank you too. Also," she eyed the sound technician, "we will have privacy."

Raffi waved to Trini, who waved back and returned her focus to the cameraman, with whom she was now engaged in a heated debate.

"Come," said Marina, pushing open the trailer door to reveal a young woman with a pencil sticking out of her mouth. It was clear she recognized Raffi. "Godmother, this is Manuela, the children's tutor. Manuela, this is my Godmother."

Manuela reddened as she plucked the pencil from her mouth. "Godmother. It's an honor."

Reaching into the pocket of her white pants, Raffi withdrew a white card containing the words 2020 Northwest Fourth Street and handed it over. "If you ever need me."

"That's how it begins," said Marina, her dark eyes sparkling.

The children ran forth from the recesses of the trailer and flung themselves at their mother.

"Children," said Marina, "this is our Godmother."

Graciela separated from Marina, her small face screwed up in concentration, and approached Raffi, holding out her arms. The child could not have been older than eight years old, an age at which Raffi had vivid memories of Brando. For her son, it was a time of matchbox cars, slime, booby traps, and chicken nuggets. She crouched and hugged the little girl.

"I'm so happy you're with your mother again," she said, her tenderness toward children warming her studied marble façade. She lived for these moments. She could never give this up.

Marina flicked her eyes at the door and Manuela clapped her hands.

"Alright, children, let's have a break. What do you say?"

"I want craft services," said Victor, with all the command of a ten-year-old.

As Manuela wrenched the door closed behind her, the children were still bickering about whether to kick the soccer ball or get a snack. When they were gone, Marina sighed. "It never ends."

They sat on two small leather couches facing each other across a Formica coffee table covered with schoolwork.

"It never will," said Raffi. "God willing." She fingered the Mary medallion on her chest. "Incidentally...Were they ever able to fix your ex-husband's car?"

Marina smiled. "It was a total loss."

Raffi clicked her tongue. "Is he well, I hope?"

Marina shook her head, clicking her tongue as well. "No, Godmother. His *amante* left him. My director saw him hitting on a bartender in Brickell the other day. Unsuccessfully." She shrugged, a slight smile curling her lips. "He's lost his appeal."

"Some men have such short expiration dates," said Raffi.

"They really do."

Raffi reached out her hand, and Marina took it between hers.

"God bless you," Marina whispered.

Raffi knew Marina's gratitude was sincere and that it extended to everything she now enjoyed: the trailer, the yellow bikini top, the children's schoolwork, the mansion in Coconut Grove she'd recently purchased from Raffi's realtor with cash.

Raffi put her other hand over Marina's.

"Remember when we first met, I told you there would come a time that I would call upon you for a favor?"

A knock rattled the trailer door. "Five minutes, Marina!" shouted a male voice.

"Yes!" Marina shouted back to the man outside. "Yes," she said, quietly, to Raffi. "I do. Anything you need, Godmother."

"This is that time."

Marina held her arms open wide. "Anything," she repeated, with less enthusiasm.

Raffi sensed Marina's unease at being called on her debt. No one liked to pay. This did not bother Raffi at all. When she wanted to collect, collect she would.

"I have a very talented friend. She's a *big* fan of your show. I want you to hire her as a story consultant. *Lead* story consultant. I want you to pay her well."

Marina blinked. "Forgive me, Godmother. Is this not a request for Misa? I'm an actor, not a producer. And I can't determine anyone's *pay*—"

"No, Marina. The request is for you. I just asked Misa for a favor. That's how you got this job."

Marina flushed. "Of course."

"As for how you make it happen, I'll leave that to you. Here's a tip: you're the star of a hit show." Raffi cupped her hands around her mouth and whispered, "You can have whatever you want."

Raffi winked and stood. "They need you on set, now. I'll find my way out." She placed a hand on the door handle. "I'll be watching," she said, the ambiguity unintentional.

"Wait!" Marina fiddled with the yellow bow on her bikini top. "How can I sell this to the network?" At Raffi's quizzical expression, she added, "What I mean is, your friend—what are her qualifications?"

Raffi paused, remembering a warm Sicilian night on an ungainly hill.

"She's a witch."

36

Two months later, on a crisp October Sunday, the scent of chestnuts in the Manhattan air, Raffi and Brando had dinner at a small Italian restaurant on the Lower East Side called Il Ritrovo. Brando had taken the train up from Philly, complaining all the way from Penn Station to the LES about lacrosse practice and the seventeenth-century British poetry teacher who had given him his first-ever C.

The restaurant was rustic and elegant. Raffi had chosen it for Polly's birthday dinner because this was where they had eaten together the night before Raffi started at Columbia. Polly had loved the look of it, despite its 'pretension'. And, although it was famous for its *osso buco*, Polly, Raffi recalled, had ordered the lasagna. *Osso buco*, quoth Polly, was too full of itself.

"Will anyone be joining you tonight?" asked the maître d', practically genuflecting as he led them to a table by the window with three place settings. Removing the *Reserved* sign, he pulled out Raffi's chair.

"No, but please leave the third setting." She smiled up at him. "We're remembering someone tonight."

"Ah, *signora*," said the maître d'. "I am from Naples," he said, meaning *I understand.*

The dinner was perfect. They had the lasagna and two bottles of wine poured by a waiter who winked at Brando and did not ask for ID. They talked about Polly, they laughed about Polly, they lit a candle stuck in the middle of Polly's favorite *tartufo* and sang "Happy Birthday," the entire restaurant joining in. Raffi tried to feel happy in that bittersweet, post-ordeal, post-epiphany way, and she almost succeeded. Whenever her mind went to the portrait-bride, and it still did, she thought of Brando. Tonight, she had the pleasure of looking at him too.

After dinner, Raffi kissed her son goodbye and put him in a cab to NYU, where he would spend the night with a high school lacrosse friend before taking the train back to Philly in the morning. Then she called Karintha Kesi. Karintha was expecting her call.

"Would you join me for dessert?" Raffi asked at Karintha's smoky greeting.

"I'm in my pajamas," said a voice like molasses. "You come to me."

"I CAN'T BELIEVE THIS view," said Raffi.

"I've been on Harlem rooftops my whole life. I don't have to believe it—I live it."

They were lying on Karintha's roof on a mattress, the sky above the brownstone spangled velvet. Karintha had covered their bodies in wool blankets, their cheeks pinked by the autumn air. Overhead, Raffi made out Venus, implausibly bright, and the first luminous threads of Great Comet Sadik-Weisman making its final journey below.

"I saw it in Sicily," said Raffi. "The night it appeared."

Karintha shook her thick braids and smiled. "Oh, they love me in Sicily," she said. "They call me *La Maestra Negra*: The Black Master."

Karintha and Raffi watched the comet burn through the sky.

"You know what I love about Sicily?" Karintha asked a few minutes later.

Raffi didn't hesitate. "The food." She paused. "Have you been to Gelsomina's?"

"Nah—not the food. The *pain*. Sicily is one big bowl of it. Pain of being conquered, being chained, being changed. Lotta people stuck their flag in Sicily. I felt it when I sang there. Such extraordinary pain."

Karintha spoke as if pain were a wine and she the sommelier.

"Lot of mama-pain in Sicily," continued Karintha, watching Raffi with eyes deep as a well. "No one loves us like mama, and no one can hurt us like mama, either."

"Hmm," said Raffi. "Like the volcano."

Karintha nodded. She gathered the general meaning. "Know what I love most about America?"

The question was rhetorical. Raffi waited.

"We've got every flavor of pain here: Sicilian pain and West African pain, Haitian pain and Irish pain, Cuban pain and Vietnamese pain. Muslim pain, Buddhist pain. One, three, four hundred years ago all these folks were in their villages with their village pain, not knowing someone down the line was going to take that whole long root, bring it to America, plant it in the soil, and watch it multiply."

Raffi's eyes were getting heavy, not only from the wine and dinner, but from the massive spliff Karintha had rolled with intense concentration and insisted Raffi try. She had not smoked weed since Columbia, and, if she hadn't handled it well in college, she was leveled now.

"What do you think of names?" Raffi asked, remembering that Karintha, like "the Godmother," had named herself.

Karintha did not hesitate.

"Overrated," she said.

Raffi stared up at the stars, the real world a construct that merged into a dream that Polly had sat with her and Brando at Il Ritrovo that night, complaining about the service and devouring *tartufo*.

"We'll get down to it in the morning," Karintha whispered. "You'll feel better from some star-sleep. I always do."

ALBERT SHAWN MARBLES, KNOWN as Witch Daddy, had released six albums on a six-album contract with HRH and its hip-hop label, Old Guard. He'd had a lot of offers before the Old Guard deal; some label or another had been wanting to sign him since his college *a cappella* days. Those early deals would have sentenced him, however, to a form of musical indentured servitude, and he was smart enough to know it.

Instead of letting a label develop him and take all the profits, he had developed himself. The ink that eventually dried on HRH paper was unprecedented: he owned the note on his tour group,

344 | LEIGH ESPOSITO

and all his own masters, before he released a single hit. The ghosts of musicians past were doing soul claps.

But not everyone with genius for music has genius for business. Witch had been wanting to liberate his fellow artists for a long time. When Jimmy Algiers's daughter, Karintha Kesi, called him, her proposal hit every note: a sound and final chord, the one he'd been listening for. He trusted Karintha—his biggest song was based on a tune by her father—and if Karintha trusted this Godmother woman, then he would too.

Dressed in a white tee shirt and jeans, he welcomed Karintha and the Godmother into his Soho office. Unlike Juju Taylor, Witch's décor held actual significance for him. A bottle tree stood in the corner, "just like my mother had." A knotty wood walking stick leaning against the sleek marble desk had been carved by his great-grandfather in Ohio. The walls were lined with framed platinum records.

Witch's usually close-cropped curls were grown out in all directions like a wiry virus. Lately, he liked to run his fingers through his hair and imagine all the ideas captured in those strands. His oeuvre enclosed in keratin.

The Godmother offered her hand. He took it and smiled off at the bottle tree. Like many prodigies, he disliked interactions up close; he probably had Asperger's, though he hated when people said so-and-so "suffered" from the condition. Assuming he had it, he'd say he benefited.

"Karintha tells me y'all have a pitch for me."

He had started the process already: creating his own label.

He had a fifty-person management team; an arsenal of projects in film, music, and television; and scores of artists in development. There were reasons he might want to do this with these women and reasons he mightn't. In the no column: he didn't need the deal, and he reserved his energy for the necessary. But, for some time, the yes column had glowed red in his mind—and now, standing here with Raffi Truvarizzi and Karintha Kesi, scarlet ribbons, the color of Karintha's silk caftan, snaked through the air.

Witch was the opposite of color blind. His mind operated chromatically. He looked at the Godmother, all in white like a Zionist priestess, the vermilion ripples spreading over her, now, too. She seemed like his kind of person, though he couldn't say why or what that meant. He played by feel, not by sheet.

The red would dance with him until he decided. It had happened with "Ring Shawt," "Ya Tune Day," and even, all the way back when he was a boy, with the hymns he arranged for the church choir, of which he was musical director by age ten. The colors always guided him. They had not failed him yet. Like a cellophane screen dropped over a lens, the whole room turned red—not only the Godmother and Karintha, but him, too, his skin, his hair, he could even feel red in his eyes.

In the unique world of Witch Daddy's creation, red meant go.

THE EXODUS OF WITCH Daddy and the entirety of HRH's jazz catalogue, including Dione Spinotti, synth-rock violinist Vanessa Liao, and Karintha Kesi, hit big in the trades. Under the egis of Witch Daddy's newly launched Hoodoo Records, Dione Spinotti, Raffi

Truvarizzi, and Karintha Kesi had created a jazz label: Hekataion Records. Raffi stayed in New York for a month getting the venture off the ground.

Each night, she and Karintha slept out on the roof. On Halloween, they threw candy down at the trick-or-treaters, cackling and reminding Raffi of Isabel. By the time Raffi was ready to leave, Comet Sadik-Weisman had gone, not to return for a hundred years.

Raffi called Dione the night before she left for Miami. "Come to Harlem and bring your sax," she said. Raffi knew Dione had never collaborated with someone of her own caliber. She'd had the Spinettes, the trio, but she'd always run the show. In Karintha, whom Dione remembered from childhood, she met her match.

"You know you're part of history now, for real," Witch told Raffi, watching Dione and Karintha come together on the Harlem roof. "You created something that matters—to the world, yes, but also to *you*."

Raffi had told him of her jazz aspirations, and his response had been to smile. She suspected that, were his temperament bold enough, he wouldn't mind a crack at her job, either. It was a seductive thought, imagining yourself in someone else's shoes, and it was the root of both envy and empathy. Raffi chose the latter, and she could tell Witch did too.

When their initial work was done, he offered to send Raffi back to Miami on his private jet. She accepted. She wanted privacy; she was formulating her next move. In the town car to Teterboro, she decided she did not belong in Miami anymore. Brando was leaving.

Mary Fortune was, if not quite dead, gone. The girl would be able to handle herself. Raffi was free to go anywhere.

The afternoon sun was blinding on the tarmac. It bounced off the gold wings of Witch's jet, flaring off the pilot's mirrored lenses as she greeted Raffi atop the steps. By size, the jet rivaled Air Force One; Witch Daddy had invested with the Baldessaris and amassed oligarch wealth.

Inside, Raffi found the jet outfitted with six seats. She let the attractive flight attendant lead her to a creamy leather armchair and bring her a glass of champagne. Outside her window, the sun descended through the Manhattan skyline, shooting fire between skyscrapers and intermittently vanishing. Stellar hide-and-seek. Although Raffi knew this was the same blood-orange sun that hung over Ortygia, it felt different. Outside of Sicily, the sun was just the sun.

She knew where she would go.

On the polished teak table beside her chair was fanned a selection of that day's newspapers from around the world. Witch must have called ahead to request *Oggi Italia* for her, along with papers out of London, New York, and Tokyo. She picked up *Oggi*, not because it interested her most, but so the flight attendant would report back to Witch that his gesture had been appreciated. It was.

She took a sip from her champagne and nearly spat it out.

Across the front page was plastered the blown-up photograph of a man's face and the headline: "*Sally Truvarizzi: Vivo in Sicilia.*"

Sally Truvarizzi: Alive in Sicily.

According to the article, the mobster had been spotted that day near the Catacombe dei Cappucini. The photograph memorializing the sighting was poor, but witnesses vouched it was him. Although Truvarizzi had undergone extensive plastic surgery since he was last seen, the condition known as Dupuytren's syndrome—a twisting and contracture of the hands—gave him away.

As the plane took off and banked northward over the city, the sun's final encore blinded Raffi, touching off the first pulse of a headache. She pulled down the shade and flipped on the reading light. The photo was, indeed, grainy, but, having seen him so recently, Raffi had no doubt. The man in the photograph and the old man from the café in Taormina were one and the same.

37

Two months into her tenure with *Las Brujas de Bal Harbour*, Isabel Ibarra was already an icon. Now the chief story consultant thanks to a string-pull by Marina Ramón, Isabel's plot points had driven ratings higher than ever, not only for how they elevated the show's arc and legitimized its portrayal of witches, but, moreover, for their real-life significance. In short: anyone who refused to watch *Las Brujas de Bal Harbour* did so at their own peril.

It began with the eyelash incident.

In an episode entitled *"Cierra tus Ojos,"* Marina Ramón's Minerva cast a spell to glue a rival *bruja's* eyelids shut, a karmic punishment for seducing Minerva's evil perfume-magnate boyfriend. The eyelid-gluing scene was so graphic that many viewers canceled their routine eyelash extensions afterward, unable to exorcise the image of pus-oozing eyelids from their minds. As chance or magic would have it— "It wasn't chance!" protested Isabel—the eyelash-glue manufacturer issued a sweeping recall. Something had gone terribly wrong with the nation's supply of eyelash glue.

Miami went into a tailspin. God help them, a few unlucky

glamoristas who'd failed to heed what was now believed to be the show's hidden warning suffered permanent damage from the virulent batch of adhesive. One poor woman had gone blind.

Now viewers were studying *Las Brujas de Bal Harbour* for hints of the next catastrophe, and the makers of everything from hair dye to nail gel were sending free products to the new chief story consultant in the hope there would be no melting cuticles or exploding highlights in upcoming episodes. Isabel would accept none of these gifts. She followed the narrative where it led her.

Unfortunately for the municipal water company, but fortunately for the makers of bottled water, the story led Isabel to the poisoning of Miami's drinking water by the evil perfume magnate, who, armed with heliotrope, was sending the whole town mad.

In an interview with Rhona Corrado of the *Miami Times*, Isabel attributed her meteoric rise to three key factors: hard work, generations of *bruja* ancestors, and the Godmother.

IT WAS A SHORT walk from 2020 Northwest Fourth Street to the house numbered 2002, the former residence of Mary Fortune, where Isabel now lived. Isabel had bought the house from her cousins two months ago, just before Christmas. It had only idled so long on the market because of the false belief that Mary Fortune died there. If anyone could haunt a house, it was Mary.

Although they'd had no other offers, Mary's daughters would not sell it to Isabel out of spite. They were angry at Isabel's lightning ascent and eager to douse her triumph. The whole matter was laid to rest, however, when Raffi intervened and made them an offer they could not refuse.

Raffi chuckled to herself, remembering the looks on the daughters' faces when they signed over the house for a dollar, having also agreed to cover the real estate taxes and closing fees on Isabel's behalf. All Raffi had done was place the documents in front of these petty women, so unlike their mother and cousin, and watch as they trembled. The key was to make a demand so enormous that the target assumed the threat behind it was even bigger.

Raffi approached the familiar doorstep on which she had stood so long ago, when she was nothing more than a pretty divorcée—and suspected Mafiosa—who was too used to taking everybody's shit. The late owner of this house had changed everything for her, and she knuckled away a tear at the thought of Mary, who had died in Arizona —for real this time—at the stroke of midnight on New Year's Day. One week later, at the outdoor memorial service, a white wolf had come halfway down from the rock ridge to watch with yellow eyes as they buried Mary's body beneath the juniper trees. Isabel had sworn she saw the wolf wink, but they had all taken peyote, so no one could be certain there was a white wolf at all.

Raffi knocked on the door, above which was carved a Latin motto she had helped the girl choose: *Astra Inclinant, Sed Non Obligant.* The stars incline us, they do not bind us.

Isabel opened the door so quickly Raffi suspected the girl had been watching from the window like a teen waiting for her date. She wore a beige cashmere sweater dress, unruly blond hair piled on her head, gold reading glasses plunged into the curls like a diadem. Raffi had interrupted her working.

"You're going back," Isabel said.

"I'm going back," said Raffi, pulling the girl in for a hug.

Isabel pulled back and pouted. "You didn't ask me to come."

"Do you even have *time* to come?"

The girl thought for a moment. "No," she said.

Isabel had opened a small private practice in addition to her work on *Las Brujas*. Her client list included heads of state and entertainers; the wait list for coveted sessions was so long, she'd had to close it to new clients after one month.

"Can you come in for coffee?" asked Isabel. She might be a big, successful showrunner now, but Isabel was still a girl sometimes. Maybe, on some level, every woman was.

"I thought you didn't have time," teased Raffi.

"I always have time for my Godmother."

Isabel ushered Raffi inside, pointing out newly added flourishes in the family room: an antique Venetian étagère displaying mementos from her grandmother in Cuba, a crystal scrying ball on a walnut pedestal— "walnut for the witches of Benevento"—and, in the corner, a freeform citrine the size of a toddler.

On their way into the kitchen, Isabel beckoned Raffi toward the door to Mary's former office. The girl pushed the door open, and they entered, both becoming subdued as they scanned the walls. Isabel had preserved the room exactly as it had been when Mary was alive. Emotion welled up and threatened to manifest. Raffi turned to Isabel.

"I thought you would have modernized it." She paced past the portraits of saints and arrived at the newspaper clipping of her first interview as The Godmother.

"*Raffi Truvarizzi: 'I'm Not the Godmother,'*" read Raffi. She shook her head. "We pulled it off."

"I know why you said it, and it was ingenious," said Isabel. "The statement was true back then. You were *not* the Godmother ten years ago." She grinned. "And now you are."

Raffi smiled back. Until she'd been able to stand on her own, she had been held up by a scaffold of women. She had not done this alone.

Isabel led her out of the office and into the kitchen. She had become an ardent amateur barista and Italian baker since their return from Sicily. The girl made two *espressos granita* and set out a plate of attempted Archimedes Spirals; she hadn't quite mastered the recipe, Raffi thought, feigning enjoyment.

Isabel joined Raffi at the blue-tiled island. They ate the granitas first in a companionable silence.

"Your reasons have changed," Isabel said when she had placed the empty glass bowl on the counter, one finger tapping her temple. "You know, now, who you are. Your curiosity comes not from fear but from the desire to uncover your origins." She added, "There is also the matter of Donatella." She dropped her finger. "All these motivations can be combined under one heading. *Verità.* Truth."

Raffi looked at the girl with a fondness that still surprised her. "More *bruja* every day. Have you already seen how it all ends?"

Isabel regarded Raffi with eyes as deep as the ocean between Miami and Cuba. In that moment, the girl was fathomless. "I don't try to know the future. Knowing the future is a paradox. The forecast fulfills itself. I find it best to stay in the present."

Raffi raised an eyebrow, thinking of the predictions for which *Las Brujas de Bal Harbour* had become famous.

"Or as close to the present as possible," Isabel said with a

wink. "And sometimes the future comes to me without my encouragement, or without my understanding what it is. I didn't know
the eyelash glue was contaminated; the story line appeared in my
mind. I went with it."

Raffi wondered if any ideas had come to Isabel about what
lay ahead for Raffi, but she did not press further. The future was
hers to unearth.

"Are you scared at all?" asked Isabel, watching Raffi.

"A little," Raffi admitted. "But I don't mind that anymore. A
friend told me I don't have to act strong. I *am* strong."

"Your friend sounds wise," said Isabel.

"Very," said Raffi. "And strong herself."

The girl's cheeks dimpled and flushed. She brought both fists
to her chin and made a puppy-dog face.

"And how long will you be gone?"

Raffi gave her a pointed look. "I appreciate you even go through
the charade of asking."

The girl touched her temple again and met Raffi's eye.
"That long?"

"As long as it takes."

+

IN THE CAR TO the airport, the driver tuned in to jazz, and "Dum
Dat Desperation" shot out from the speakers like a firecracker.

The song had gone triple platinum to unseat Jimmy Algiers's
'Killing Time' as the best-selling jazz single ever. Dione Spinotti
and Karintha Kesi were the new First Ladies of jazz. Raffi was
prouder of this outcome than almost any fix she'd made since
assuming her mantle. She might not have had the brass chops

herself, but she'd contributed to the idiom—and helped an old friend ascend.

Her thoughts turned to Trini, who had been less than supportive about Raffi's move to Sicily. Her salty old protector had seemed almost panicked when Raffi announced her decision. But Trini, Raffi knew, would come around. She always did. Raffi needed Trini to hold down the fort in Miami while Raffi was gone, and Trini could be counted on for that. Trini could always be counted on.

The car pulled up to the curb, and the driver transferred her trunks and baggage onto a porter's cart. The fuss with the luggage and curbside check-in took longer than usual given the size and number of bags. It was a good ten minutes before Raffi turned toward the entrance, ticket in hand—and found Tex.

He was outfitted in frayed jeans, buckled belt, and red-and-black-checked button-down: a better look for him than the knockoff suit and fishing shirt, though he could not seem to relinquish that abysmal Julius Caesar haircut. The same doltish expression was plastered across his face, but he also looked cocky, like his hand had gone from a bluff to the nuts.

Tex was not alone.

Behind him, wearing mirrored sunglasses, her tanned face expressionless, stood a compact, slender woman with straight blond hair. From the sudden heat that swept her body, Raffi knew this was the woman from Arethusa and Colle Madore. As Raffi watched, entranced, the mirrored sunglasses came off to reveal narrow eyes so vivid, Raffi could see them from a distance: they were the exact color of Sicilian olives.

Raffi had the answer to her question. An impossible shade of green. She had an urge to run for the ladies' room and vomit the way she had before her fourth-grade trumpet recital.

The woman stepped around Tex. "*Allora, vai in Sicilia.*"

She was Italian-Italian, not Italian-American. Her voice was pitched deep and her pronunciation immaculate. Raffi felt the voice reverberate within her.

"You're as perceptive as your partner," said Raffi. She willed her breath to even. "Was it the ticket to Sicily that clued you in?"

"One-way ticket this time," observed the woman. "Planning to repatriate?"

"*Rematriate.* And yes—at least, for a while." She paused. "Why? Is my presence required in the States?"

"Not yet," said the blonde.

Adjusting the leather duffel over her shoulder, Raffi shifted to Sicilian. "*Allura.* Do you answer to this idiot," she nodded to Tex, "or is it the other way around?"

"What do you think?" the woman said in Sicilian so pristine that Raffi must have looked surprised, because the woman added: "I come from Milano, but I've also studied the Southern Italian languages. This is prudent, considering most of our criminals come from the south."

Raffi flipped her nose to the hook. "Milanese. Can't get over the Risorgimento, can you?"

The woman shrugged. "The Italian government was too inclusive. We should have stopped at Rome."

"I assume you're not here to discuss intra-Italian rivalries."

"I'm here to let you know *come se chiam'* over here," she jerked her head at Tex, "is off your file. I'm taking over."

Raffi felt a thrill—of anticipation, of dread, of things she could not yet name.

"Welcome to the team," she said, extending her hand. The woman slipped her fingers into Raffi's palm, and Raffi felt another jolt at the smooth, cool skin. The grip was hard. She did not let go.

It was not the first time the thought flitted across Raffi's mind that perhaps Cousin Pasquale had been right about her after all.

"Raffaella," said Raffi, fixing amber on olive.

"Ornella."

Ornella. Raffi's breath caught. It was a rare name; Raffi had considered it for a future daughter that never was. Mary would call this a sign. The mysterious plans of the Universe at work again.

"I'll try to keep it interesting, Ornella."

The olive eyes glinted. "*Di certo.*"

Ornella turned to leave, and Raffi noticed the woman's nose had a sharp side too. In profile, she resembled a tawny eagle.

An unmarked car pulled up and Ornella slid inside, Tex climbing in after her. Raffi pretended to look for the plane ticket in her bag, but from the corner of her eye, she watched the car pull away with a sinking feeling, her heart pounding, snippets of their encounter flashing in her mind like peripheral lightning strikes. She did not want the woman to go.

Even through the tinted windows, she felt Ornella's eyes on her, too.

✛

RAFFI WAS GREETED AT the Catania airport by Renata Trapani, a local realtor who specialized in the most opulent Sicilian real estate. Cousin Pasquale had made the introduction. A courier would bring Raffi's luggage to her suite at the Hotel Francisa so they could begin house-hunting at once.

"I've selected some of the finest properties on the island, *signura*, and only those available now, as you ask. I am certain at least one will be to your liking."

They drove north in Renata's custom yellow Maserati, headed for picturesque Bronte, "the town of pistachios," where Renata had arranged lunch. Raffi rolled the windows down, the April air cool against her face—a welcome change from Miami, where it was already summer. Ahead stood La Mamma: the volcano that gave and took away, spectacularly in both regards. Today, She was glazed with a thin white film. Most of her winter cloak would soon melt.

"Tell me what you've found," said Raffi.

"Well." Renata swelled with excitement, talking with her hands, steering with one knee. "I have one in Noto for which you will die. *Gigantic* villa, 19th century, but modern plumbing and wiring, all the conveniences. *Fantastica*. It comes with thirty acres, perfect for growing the sweet grapes, like Moscato. You like Moscato?" she asked, her voice hopeful.

"No," said Raffi.

Renata frowned. "Maybe not the one in Noto, then."

"What else?"

She brightened. "I have another in Faro, which is here on the eastern coast, where you say you prefer to be. This one comes with a working vineyard for the red-wine grapes. The villa is also spectacular."

She eyed Raffi.

"That sounds interesting," said Raffi without interest.

Renata nodded. "We have a property outside Siracusa near the water. This, I *love* for you. Two-hundred-degree sea views. New construction—very rare—done in the Mediterranean style. You can smell the salt from your wraparound veranda. Of course, this is the most expensive—although," she added shrewdly, "I understand price is not a consideration."

"You understand correctly."

Raffi felt for the wrinkled photo in her pocket. Once she'd settled on a place, she would visit the sisters atop Mount Tauro. She had the idea to leave the bride's photo up there, with them, in the sight of two sacred figures: La Mamma and the Virgin.

Renata paused, cocking her head, searching her brain for more options. "Ah, yes! There is one not far from here, very near to Etna, *molto buono*. No vineyard and no sea, though, so I put it at the bottom of the list. The villa is pretty, not as big as the others, but grand. And it does have a lovely olive grove, thirty acres, you could even produce. Then there is a *gorgeous* property on the Trapanese coast. I know it's to the west, but, as a Trapanese myself, I am partial—"

"Wait," Raffi interrupted. "The one near here. With the olive grove. Are they green olives?"

Renata had not expected this question. "All olives are green if picked early enough," she said. "But, yes, I believe they are."

Raffi closed her eyes.

She saw a crumbling fountain in the folds below Etna. The mountain fuming behind her as she walked south through acres of ancient trees stretching out in all directions. The slick green flesh of fruit blessed by a light rain. In September, the harvest, she imagined she would pluck and eat straight from the branches. How would the olives taste? Bitter and premature, or succulent and ripe? Crisp between her teeth, or slower to surrender? How long would their salt linger on her tongue? She would place more olives in wicker baskets, confer with the groundskeeper about how much sun, how much rain, when to press, how to bottle.

Strolling the grove alone at dusk, La Mamma at her back, the stillness of 500-year-old trees with roots stretching beneath her like clasped arms, the sky seashell pale, and all around her, the olives—so many that two eyes could blend in among them, an impossible shade of green, just two among a thousand, silent, patient, narrowing as they watched her pass.

"Take me to the one with the olive grove," said Raffi.

ACKNOWLEDGEMENTS

THE BIRTH OF A book is not unlike the birth of a human. There is conception and gestation; there are midwives; a village helps to raise it, until the novel stands on its own. I have been privileged in this regard.

Thank you, first, to my son Declan Brando, who sat by Mommy's side eight hours a day for two straight months while she wrote the first draft. Yes, my angel, the good news is the book is finally done. The "other news" is Mommy's writing her second book—but I'll try to be quick about it. Thank you for sharing me with the world of make believe.

There is a special place in heaven for the early readers of a book. Lee Syben, Elizabeth Weisman, Robert Esposito, and Abigail Gamble Rogers-Berner—you were there from the beginning. Thank you for seeing through the morass to what this novel could become.

My business partner, fellow debut novelist, and beloved friend, Sarah Arcuri. This would not mean nearly as much without you. We have been brought together by forces larger than ourselves, and I see many years of health, happiness, and close friendship in our future. I can't wait to welcome other authors into our special famiglia of female, Italian American storytellers.

To Professor Rossella Di Rosa of my alma mater, the University of Pennsylvania, and her husband Tony Leyh for their invaluable insights into the Sicilian language, especially the dialects of eastern Sicilia. Grazi, amici.

Grazie tante to the community of Italian American women who have rallied around me as I explore and reclaim the culture of my ancestors: Marybeth Bonfiglio, Dolores Alfieri-Taranto, Denise Sandole, Danielle Caminiti, Marianna Gatto, and Oriana LaMarca. Siete bravissime.

Ashleigh Renard, you have been my coach and champion since the moment we met. Thank you for teaching me that my authentic self is the only brand I ever need.

Jacki Crawford, thank you for helping me navigate the Nation of Images. I could not do Earth School without you.

My real-life godparents: Aunt Lorraine Esposito Stanton and Uncle Tony Blue Eyes. Your love is a gift.

To my dear Instagram family: I am thrilled and grateful to be on this crazy ride with you. Thank you for listening to what I have to say—and, more importantly, sharing your truth in turn.

To Isabel Dapena, my real-life Trini. Thank you for always having my back. You are my rock.

To Graham Schofield, my fearless editor, who took one look at this manuscript and said, with trademark British candor, "This book *could* be great." I've loved every minute of our collaboration.

For Layla Summers, Noraan Sadik, Shannon Curry, Colleen Smeryage, Andrew Trapani, and Dani DeCespedes, my dear friends. I adore you all.

I am grateful to my cousins in Sicily for welcoming their prodigal cousin back home. Biagio Favarò and Franco Vitrano, in particular, have been so loving and generous with their time. Ancora grazie, cugini!

To Lercara Friddi, the town of my Sicilian ancestors. Thank

you for letting me share your secrets—not that I asked permission, but what Sicilian ever would?

Lou Mendola, my good friend and expert on all things Sicilian: it's been a pleasure to see Palermo through your eyes.

To the wonderful people I've met through Instagram: thank you for all your messages of support and love. I'm thrilled to share this with you.

For my mother, Deborah Esposito. You made me the woman and writer I am. My life changed the moment you placed *Little Women* atop my stack of Sweet Valley Twins books and said, "Now read this." So much of this book was inspired by you.

For my father, Jerry Esposito: il Siciliano verò, and my biggest cheerleader. I'm fortunate to have a father whose belief in my abilities is so wholehearted as to, at times, appear delusional. You have empowered me in so many ways. Te amo.

For my ancestors: you boarded ships and sailed for America— poor in money, but rich in determination. I stand on your shoulders with unending gratitude. I hope I make you proud.

My paternal grandparents, Vincent and Lillian Esposito. Grandpa Vin, you taught me how to dream. Grandma Lil, my Sicilian queen: even in heaven, you're my consigliere.

And finally, for my maternal grandparents Patrick and Delores Vassallo. Throughout my life, you *always* held my hands and showed me God's love. While I wish you could have been here (in physical form) to see this day, I know you're with me. This book is, and has always been, for you.

AUTHOR BIO

LEIGH ESPOSITO HAS A B.A. in English from the University of Pennsylvania and a J.D. from Columbia Law. A recovering attorney, she is now a sought-after strategist, speaker, and author. Leigh is a dual Italian-American citizen with roots in Sicily, Naples, Salerno, and Molise, and her burgeoning Instagram account celebrates the culture and lore of her ancestral homeland. Together with her precocious son and his canine sidekick, Leigh lives in Miami, Florida—when she's not in Italy. *The Godmother* is her first novel.

 @msleighesposito

CPSIA information can be obtained
at www.ICGtesting.com
Printed in the USA
BVHW040408190423
662580BV00001B/3